TALES FROM THE EDGE
Volume Three

Rough Around the Edges

Scorched Edges

L.M. SOMERTON

Tales from The Edge Volume Three
ISBN # 978-1-78430-779-0
©Copyright L.M. Somerton 2015
Cover Art by Posh Gosh ©Copyright September 2015
Interior text design by Claire Siemaszkiewicz
Pride Publishing

Published in 2015 by Pride Publishing, Newland House, The Point, Weaver Road, Lincoln, LN6 3QN, United Kingdom.

Pride Publishing is a subsidiary of Totally Entwined Group Limited.

Pride Publishing books by L.M. Somerton:

The Portrait
Black Dog
Stroke Rate
Mountain Rescue

Tales from The Edge Volume One
Reaching the Edge
Living on the Edge

Tales from The Edge Volume Two
Dancing on the Edge
A Double-Edged Sword

Tales from The Edge Volume Three
Rough Around the Edges
Scorched Edges

Investigating Love
Rasputin's Kiss
Evil's Embrace
Tarot's Touch

The Wyverns
Mantrap
Deathtrap

What's his Passion?
Picturing Lysander
Testing Lysander

ROUGH AROUND THE EDGES

Dedication

For all those folks who don't want their rough edges
smoothed down.

Chapter One

The moment Kai walked into The Underground clutching Olly's hand, he knew he'd found his place in the world. The club smelled of leather and polish and men. The low light soothed his eyes and made him feel less visible, which suited him just fine. He liked to disappear into the background — it was safer that way. Joe steered them toward a table ringed by comfortable low chairs but they couldn't sit down straight away as there were so many people milling around them that it took a while to get through the throng. Kai lost his grip on Olly and grabbed hold of Joe's sleeve instead while Olly held onto Joe's other arm — it was the only way to avoid being swept away.

"Cut the crowding, people!"

Kai turned around. Someone was standing on the bar, yelling.

"Give them some space. You'll hear all about it soon enough."

The crowd thinned as people went back to their tables and settled down, though the level of chatter and sense of excitement remained high. The man from the bar hopped down and came across to speak to Joe. Kai earwigged shamelessly and caught a little of their conversation.

"Why don't we let Carey and Alistair get reacquainted and I'll get the three of you some drinks?" Though he was talking to Joe, the man—who Kai figured had to be one of the bar staff—kept his gaze firmly fixed on Kai.

Kai examined the floor, afraid that if he looked back, those stormy gray eyes would mesmerize him.

"Sounds good," Joe answered. "It was a long drive. Fresh orange juice for all of us please, Harry."

Now Kai knew the man's name. Harry. He liked it. It sounded strong and confident, just like the way the man appeared. Joe took a seat at the table and Olly immediately clambered onto his lap. Kai didn't sit down straight away—he stood and took in the view. Everywhere he looked there were gorgeous men—all shapes and sizes, all colors and ages. Men who seemed comfortable in their skins.

His eyes widened as he realized just how little some of the club's members were wearing. He spotted latex and leather in a variety of colors, though black was in the majority. Most of the chairs were occupied, but there were also men sitting on cushions on the floor or kneeling, with their heads bowed. It was a feast for Kai's eyes. Belatedly, he realized that he was staring and that his mouth was open. He snapped his lips together and cast around anxiously to see if he'd offended anyone. If the winks he got when he made eye contact were anything to go by, apparently he hadn't.

Kai checked the whereabouts of his new friends, needing the security of knowing where they were and that he wasn't alone. Alistair stood a few feet away, wrapped in the arms of a handsome older man who acted like he'd just won the lottery. Kai assumed that must be Carey, Alistair's Dom. Just behind where Kai loitered, Olly sat in Joe's lap, chattering away while Joe listened, looking cool and serene. Kai felt a little pang of envy at how happy they all seemed. Still, he should be grateful. He'd just been rescued from a terrifying ordeal. Alistair had said he could stay with him and Carey for as long as he needed. He was safe. He had somewhere to go, people who cared about what happened to him. He had much to be grateful for.

"I've never seen so much leather in one place before," Kai whispered. He hadn't addressed the comment to anyone in particular. It was just an observation but Olly grabbed his hand and tugged him to a chair.

"You should be here in the evenings. There's considerably more bare flesh to ogle then. Though it's hard to beat hot men in tight leather at any time of the day. I don't think there should be time limits on visual stimulation, do you?"

Kai shook his head hard. Olly made a good deal of sense.

"You shouldn't be eyeing up other men," Joe snapped at Olly. "And they shouldn't even be glancing in your direction. You're mine."

Kai stared. It was the first time he'd seen Joe's icy-cool demeanor slip into something more emotional.

Olly chewed his lower lip and gazed back at him adoringly. "You'll just have to punish me, Sir."

Kai giggled. Olly was so naughty. He liked him enormously. They could have loads of fun together. He perched on the edge of his chair and people-watched for a couple of minutes. There was so much eye candy to enjoy. *Not that I'd have the first clue what to do if one of these men approached me. Olly and Alistair seem to think that I'm a sub, but what does that mean? I'm not sure I want to be spanked!*

Kai squirmed in his seat, surprised that the thought of having his arse smacked was making him hard. A looming figure blocked out the light and Kai looked up nervously. A tray laden with drinks landed on the table in front of him before the tray's bearer straightened up and Kai got his first prolonged chance to inspect Harry, the barman.

Oh! Oh wow! Kai's brain short-circuited as he took in well over six feet of male gorgeousness. Leather trousers too tight to be legal encased long, long legs. Heavy, buckled boots added an extra inch of height that the man really didn't need. A black T-shirt hugged his lean, tapered torso that Kai badly wanted to touch, ideally without the annoying garment in the way. Defined abs were not in question—Kai just wanted to know if there was a six-pack or the full eight hidden beneath the clingy cotton.

To Kai's delight, Harry sat down with them and handed out their drinks.

"It's great to have Alistair back. I don't think Carey could have lasted without him much longer."

Harry addressed them all, but Kai wasn't interested in conversation, he just knew that the beautiful man's eyes were on him.

"Hi! I'm Kai. You're gorgeous," he blurted out.

Olly dissolved into laughter.

"Don't think Kai's as shy as we thought, Sir!"

Kai's face burned. *Oh my God! I didn't just say that out loud, did I? I did. Fuck.*

"Harry Croft. I'm the bar manager here."

"Harry, let me introduce Kai Smithson. We met him at the clinic and he didn't really want to be there, so he'll be staying with Carey and Alistair for a while." Joe rescued Kai from his embarrassment.

Kai decided that as he'd already made a complete idiot of himself, he might as well keep going. "Are you a Dom?"

Harry smiled. "Would that scare you?"

He shuffled his chair a little closer to Kai, who reached out his hand and stroked the leather that was stretched taut over Harry's knees.

"That feels nice," Kai purred, then snatched his hand back. "Oh! I'm so sorry! I don't know why I did that."

To Kai's shock, Harry took a gentle hold of his hand and laid it back on his knee.

"You can keep that right there. Joe, I wonder if I might take Kai back to my place, get him cleaned up and out of those clothes. I mean into some clean clothes. I mean…"

"Oh, I think I know exactly what you mean, Harry. If Kai wants to, then of course that will be fine. He's supposed to be staying with Carey, but I imagine your boss has his mind on other things at the moment. I need to get Olly home too."

Kai stood up and tugged on Harry's hand. "Let's go. I'm really dirty and I love having my back scrubbed. Do you have a loofah?"

Harry stood, and Kai looked up and up into a deliciously stern expression.

"Behave. I'm pretty sure you're running on adrenaline right now and don't really know what you're saying, so I can cut you a little slack, but you need to understand from the get go that I have little patience for brats."

Beneath his soft white trousers, Kai's dick hardened. He didn't really understand what it meant to be with a Dom, but he suspected that he was getting a little taste. Harry dropped his hand but before Kai could worry about it, he grasped his wrist instead and towed him toward the exit.

They stopped by the staff changing room where Harry pulled a beaten-up leather jacket from his locker. He turned and gave Kai an appraising examination then thrust the jacket toward him.

"Here, put this on. You need it more than I do."

Kai stuck his arms in the sleeves and pulled the garment on, taking a deep sniff. The scent of leather and aftershave was enhanced by a hint of oil and he knew that the smell would always remind him of this moment. The jacket swamped him. The sleeves covered his hands completely and the collar came up to his ears.

"I must look ridiculous." He flapped his arms.

"Better that than road rash," Harry replied. "I wish I had some extra trousers for you—those things you're wearing wouldn't protect shit."

Kai stared down at the cheap, nasty bottoms that the clinic had provided, along with the white plimsolls on his feet.

"They're all I have. We left the clinic so quickly there was no time to collect anything, and, regardless, they took my clothes away when I got there and gave me these instead." His breath hitched. He really had nothing but the clothes he stood up in and the thought was terrifying.

A gentle touch on his chin tilted his head back. "Hey. Don't worry about it. Clothes can be replaced. The only thing that matters is that you are out of that hellhole and safe."

Kai folded his arms around his body. "I know. It's just a bit overwhelming. I went with the flow and grabbed the opportunity to get away. I didn't think any further than that."

Harry pulled him into a hug, and he sagged against the bigger man. Wrapped in Harry's arms, he felt safe.

"I don't live far away and there's a spare helmet with the bike. I'll ride real slow."

Harry's deep tones rumbled through Kai's body in a reassuring wave.

"Come on. Let's get out of here."

Kai followed Harry to the lift, then out onto the street. It was late afternoon and the noise of traffic rumbled in the distance. The world was going about its business as usual but Kai felt different. Like a butterfly breaking out of its cocoon, he could finally unfurl his wings. The sense of freedom made him lightheaded and he staggered, only to be steadied by Harry's firm grip.

"You're exhausted, aren't you? Maybe riding the bike isn't such a great idea."

"No, please. I'm fine—I'd really like to try it. I've never been on a motorbike before."

Harry frowned. "Okay, but you have to promise to hold on tight. No falling asleep until we get home."

"Promise."

Kai followed Harry to a nearby parking garage and down the access ramp. There were several vehicles lined up against a wall, but only one bike. The gleaming red and black beast had Kawasaki emblazoned across the tank, and even with his limited knowledge, Kai could see that it was a powerful machine. There was a set of metal lockers in a corner. Harry plugged in a code and opened one of them. Inside were two helmets and a pair of leather gauntlets.

"Carey keeps this place for employees to park. Not many of the staff have cars, but quite a few of the servers cycle in and this is a safe place to leave their bikes. There are concealed security cameras down here and the club bouncers do regular checks during the night." He handed a helmet to Kai before putting on his own.

"I keep a spare helmet here in case anyone ever needs a lift, but they don't have mics in them so I won't be able to hear you once we're on the road. Just hold on tight, lean with me and you'll be fine."

Kai nodded and pushed the helmet on. He was surprised at how snug it felt, the inner pads hugging his cheeks closely. Harry swung a leg over the bike and got comfortable. He walked the machine backward out of the space and gestured Kai to get on. Kai clambered on with a lot less grace than Harry had managed. Tentatively, he leaned against Harry's back and reached forward until his hands met in front of Harry's waist. Harry pulled him closer then pushed the ignition. Immediately the thrum of the engine reverberated through Kai's arse and up his spine. He let out a little gasp. Even through the padded seat, it was like sitting on a giant vibrator.

Holy crap, I'm not going to last ten minutes on this thing. I'm gonna come and embarrass myself. I just know I am. Being pressed so close to Harry's body didn't help at all, and when Harry revved the throttle, Kai whimpered. His senses were in overload but he still had time to process that he had practically thrown himself at a complete stranger and was now going home with him. For all he knew, Harry could be a psychopathic ax murderer.

"No, he can't be. He's far too good-looking to be a nut job and, besides, I don't think Joe would have let him take me away if he wasn't a good guy." Kai was talking to himself and that wasn't a good sign. At least Harry couldn't hear him through the roar of the bike and his helmet.

They ascended the ramp and roared off down the street. Logically, Kai knew that Harry wasn't going very fast, but he'd never ridden on a motorbike before and it felt really, really quick. He shut his eyes and held on as tightly as he could. After a few minutes they hadn't crashed and he eased his grip. It wouldn't do to stop Harry breathing – then they really would crash and Harry didn't have a jacket on. Kai didn't want to see cuts and grazes marring Harry's smooth, lightly tanned arms because they were really beautiful. He could see muscles flexing beneath the skin and there was a dusting of dark hair there that looked so soft Kai wanted to touch.

As buildings blurred past, Kai let his fantasies take him away.

"You can let go now, Kai. We've stopped."

He was still drifting happily when Harry's amused voice disturbed him.

"Oh! Oh... Sorry." Kai unpeeled himself from Harry's back and climbed off the bike. He reached the pavement and stood on slightly wobbly legs, trying to get his balance. He got the helmet off with some difficulty and looked around. The street where Harry had pulled into was clean and quiet, one side edged with expensive cars. The buildings formed a terrace, some four stories high if he included the attic level. From the doors Kai could see, there were several bells, so he guessed that the houses must be divided into separate flats. They were still in central London and, even with his inexperienced eyes, Kai could tell that the area was upscale and expensive. Perhaps Harry shared with some flatmates. Surely a barman couldn't afford to live in a place like this all by himself.

"There's a garage around the back, but I'll get you settled before I put the bike away." Harry strolled up a short flight of steps to a black front door and slipped a key into the lock. This door didn't have a set of bells, just one round brass button set into the stone. Kai hefted his helmet in one hand and followed Harry into a light, airy hall. Harry took the helmet from him and put it on the tiled floor beneath a small side table, next to his own. He dumped his keys into a silver dish on the table.

"Let me take your jacket."

Kai gave himself a little shake and drew down the zip. He was reluctant to relinquish the soft, warm leather that smelled of Harry but he shrugged it off his shoulders and handed it over. He shivered, even though it wasn't cold in the hall.

"You're cold?" Harry didn't miss anything with those keen eyes.

"No... Just a little shaky. I... It's been a rough few days."

"I'm sure it has. And you're going to tell me all about it, but not now. First things first. Are you hungry?"

Kai shook his head. "No. Joe had snacks in the car. I ate a little on the way back."

"Well, how about a bath then? A nice long soak and then sleep — for as long as you need."

"That sounds..." Kai fought back tears. "It sounds wonderful. Thank you."

He met Harry's eyes, expecting to see scorn for his weakness, but all he saw was understanding and sympathy. Then the tears fell and he couldn't stop them. He dropped to his knees and sobbed, not really knowing why. It barely registered when Harry scooped him up and carried him upstairs. He pushed open the door to a palatial bathroom dominated by a huge claw-foot tub, then settled Kai onto a wicker chair in the corner. Kai watched through blurry eyes as Harry filled the tub and added scented oil that foamed and smelled of juniper. He placed a pile of fluffy towels on the floor, then came to stand in front of Kai.

"I'm going to undress you now. Don't be scared, okay? I'm not going to do anything else."

Kai nodded. He toed off his plimsolls and lifted his arms so that Harry could remove his T-shirt. Then he stood and tried not to shake as Harry released the drawstring on his trousers. When they dropped to the floor, Kai stepped out of them. His face heated as Harry eyed the hideous white Y-fronts that the clinic had provided.

"They're not mine." Kai felt the need to defend himself.

"Thank Christ for that." Harry pulled them down decisively, and Kai kicked the offending garment away. Harry scooped him up and deposited him in the warm, bubbly water.

Kai fancied that the bits of skin that had been in contact with Harry's hands were warmer than the rest of him. He sank beneath the water, thankful that the bubbles covered him. The heat soaked through to his bones and he sighed happily.

"If I leave you alone, can I trust you not to drown?" Harry asked, arms folded across his chest.

Kai nodded. "I'll be fine. I just want to wash the stench of that hideous place away."

"I'm going to put the bike to bed and then ring the club to let Carey know that you're here, safe and sound. I'm going to tell him that we won't be back for dinner either. You need peace and rest, not a night at The Underground."

It wasn't a question. Kai was thankful that Harry had taken control, relieving him of any need to make decisions. All he could think about was getting clean. Everything else could wait.

When Harry left the room, Kai immediately missed his presence. Even though he found it difficult to be naked and vulnerable with another man, Harry made him feel safe and he hadn't felt that way for a long time. He giggled as he spotted the loofah resting on the end of the bath and grabbed it. He might have to wash his own back, but it felt great. He scrubbed until he was pink and glowing then shampooed his hair before rinsing the suds away with a shower attachment linked to the taps.

He'd just finished when there was a light knock at the door and Harry walked in. He'd changed out of his leather trousers and wore a pair of soft jeans and a loose white shirt. His feet were bare and he looked relaxed. He picked up a towel and shook it out, then held it up for Kai to step into. Trying not to feel bashful, Kai climbed out of the bath and Harry wrapped him up in soft warmth.

"Feeling better?"

"You mean have I stopped crying like a girl?"

Harry's lips twitched. "You're allowed to be a bit emotional. That doesn't make you a girl."

Kai shivered as Harry raked him with a smoldering look.

"You certainly don't look like a girl."

"I do feel a lot better. Thank you." Kai scuffed at the bath mat with his toes.

"I'll leave you to get dry. I don't think any of my clothes will fit you, but you can use the robe on the back of the door for now. Come downstairs to the kitchen when you're done."

Kai dried off quickly and puttered around the bathroom naked. He cleaned the bath and hung up the towels, making everything neat. Under the sink he found a wrapped toothbrush and a sample tube of paste, so he used those then gave himself a critical look in the mirror. He didn't need to shave often so his chin was still smooth but he was too pale and there were dark rings beneath his eyes.

"What a state." He sighed heavily. He turned away and grabbed the robe that Harry had pointed out to him. He had to roll the sleeves up a couple of times and it reached to his ankles, but it was soft and cozy. He padded down the stairs and followed the faint sounds of music, playing at low volume, to the kitchen. For a moment he hovered in the doorway, watching Harry as he worked at the stove. Delicious smells floated past Kai's nose and his stomach growled.

"Sounds like you are hungry after all." Harry didn't turn around. He waved a spatula. "Take a seat. I'm making omelets. Won't be a minute."

The kitchen was vast, with a marble topped island in the center and an array of shiny cabinets. The appliances were stainless steel and everything was spotless. Surprisingly it wasn't too clinical. Splashes of color from prints on the walls, bright blue pots and a rainbow of pans made it homey. Jars of spices and bottles of oil stood next to a set of gleaming copper scales. Kai loved it. He clambered onto one of the stools set next to the island and waited. Harry turned off the heat and brought a couple of plates across, setting one in front of Kai. He laid out a couple of forks and fetched a bowl of salad from the fridge, then brought the pan across and divided the omelet, sliding a generous portion onto Kai's plate. He put the rest on his own plate then pulled up a second stool. He spooned some salad out and handed the bowl across to Kai.

"Eat. You're as white as a ghost. You need something in your stomach."

Obediently, Kai served himself some salad. When the first forkful of omelet hit his taste buds, he moaned.

"Oh… This is delicious." There were little pieces of ham and yellow peppers, chopped herbs and tomatoes all mixed in with light, fluffy egg. Kai ate steadily and before he knew it, his plate was clean. He patted his stomach. "I haven't had much appetite for ages, but that was amazing!"

"The chef welcomes compliments." Harry grinned. He poured himself a coffee from a large pot but gave Kai a glass of milk. "I don't think you need caffeine right now."

"I don't like coffee." Kai sipped the milk.

Harry gaped. "That's a first. Most of my friends survive on the stuff, though Joe doesn't let Olly drink it."

"What do you mean, he doesn't let him? Can't Olly choose what he drinks?"

"Joe's a Dom, Kai. He takes care of Olly and decides what's best for him. It's Olly's choice to submit to him."

"That sounds a bit one-sided."

"Not at all. Most good Doms are very protective. True submissives want to make their Masters happy. For the right couples, it's a way of life that has equal benefits to both partners."

Kai shuffled on his stool. "You said it's a way of life. Does that mean it's not just something you do at the club?"

"Some people just like to play occasionally, but for me it's a lifestyle choice, as it is for Olly and Joe, and Alistair and Carey."

"But you don't have a…submissive?" Kai looked at Harry from beneath his lashes.

"I haven't found the right person yet."

Kai's stomach did a little flip-flop. Harry stared at him intently, and he squirmed under the scrutiny. He gave silent thanks for the voluminous robe as his cock twitched into life. He desperately wanted Harry to tell him what to do.

"It's time you got some sleep. I'll show you the guest room."

Oh my God, he can read my mind! Kai swallowed. When Harry offered him a hand, he took it. The guest bedroom was two floors up and by the time they got there, Kai's legs were trembling with fatigue. He sat on the edge of the bed, feeling lost.

"Take off the robe, Kai."

He unbelted the garment and handed it over. Harry pulled back the covers and Kai snuggled into a world of softness.

"Stay with me?" Kai asked.

"Not right now, sweetheart. You're far too tempting. You and your cute little butt need to get some rest."

He thinks my butt's cute was Kai's final thought before he drifted into sleep.

Harry pulled the door to but didn't close it completely. He had a feeling he'd be checking on the sweet young man in his guest bed fairly frequently. He took a last look and shook his head wryly before padding down the corridor. "He's too young, too pretty and too innocent to be within a hundred miles of me. What the hell am I doing?" He wandered back to the kitchen, poured himself another cup of coffee then picked up the phone. He dialed a number and listened to the ring tone. It went on so long that he almost gave up, expecting voicemail to click in at any moment, but then the line connected.

"Hello?"

"Joe, it's Harry. Sorry to interrupt your evening."

"No problem. I guess you need to talk."

"That obvious, huh?"

"Give me one minute. I just have to deal with something and then I'm all yours. Just hold the line."

Harry put the phone on loudspeaker and made himself comfortable. In the background he heard some interesting squealing, then silence.

"Apologies, I just needed to make sure we wouldn't have any commentary while we talk." Joe came back on the line.

"Olly?"

"Olly. Don't worry—I have him in the sling with a remote control vibrator keeping him entertained. I just added a ball gag—things were getting a bit noisy."

Harry snorted. "I'll bet."

"So, how are things with Kai? He's a sweet little thing, isn't he?"

"He is. I've put him to bed. I don't know what he's been through, Joe, but I think he needs careful handling." He paused. "I'm not sure I'm the right man for the job."

"Why ever not?" Joe replied. "I saw the way you dragged him out of The Underground."

"I don't know what happened. Instant attraction isn't usually my thing, but I took one look at him and the idea of any other man getting near him made me see red."

Joe chuckled. "It sounds to me like you are the perfect choice for him."

"He's completely inexperienced, Joe. He may have done a bit of net surfing, but that's it."

"And you don't do vanilla. Is that it? I wouldn't worry on that score. Kai has submissive stamped all over him."

"He does. He craves direction and every protective bone in my body screams at me to take care of him...

But he's so young. He should be trying things out... Shouldn't he?"

"Harry, not every young submissive needs to play the field. Kai is safe in your hands. You're not going to make him do anything he doesn't want to."

"But what if he doesn't know what he wants?"

"I'm sure he'll work it out. Look, give him some time. Bring him to the club with you and let him observe. I'm afraid Olly and I are leaving for Yorkshire tomorrow, but to be honest, Kai would be better spending some time with Alistair. He's a bit more...grounded."

Harry chuckled. "Well, thanks, Joe...for the reassurance. I'd better let you get back to the brat. Enjoy the celebration supper tonight and give my apologies to Carey. Kai needs sleep more than anything at the moment."

"No problem. Call me any time, or Heath for that matter."

"Thanks. Oh—would you have time to drop off some clothes for Kai in the morning? He's only a little smaller than Olly and all he has are those clothes from the clinic, which I fully intend to incinerate."

"Of course. Olly has enough clothes to stock an entire store. I'm sure he'll be happy to dig a few things out."

After a few more pleasantries, Harry rang off. He took his coffee through to the lounge and turned on the television. He flicked idly through the channels but there was nothing that caught his interest. The only thing on his mind was Kai.

"I should be there in case he wakes up. He might be scared," Harry muttered. He abandoned his drink, grabbed a random paperback thriller from the bookshelf then went back to the guest bedroom. It wasn't quite dark outside and a crack in the curtains let a little light fall across Kai's face. He was sleeping peacefully, one arm flung across the bed, the covers pushed down to his waist. Harry wondered at how thick his eyelashes were, resting against his pale cheeks. His lips were plump, ripe to be kissed, if a little bleached of color. His glossy, freshly washed hair reminded Harry of the color of conkers just released from their spiky cases. He settled in the armchair in the corner of the room and opened his book, but watching Kai sleep was more entertaining, so in the end he discarded the novel and just observed. When his eyelids started to droop, he debated climbing into bed next to Kai, but decided that would be a bad move. If anything was to happen between them, then Kai had to know that he could trust Harry implicitly. He stole from the room and went to the master suite across the corridor. He left both doors open, stripped off his clothes then slipped beneath the covers. He had no doubt at all that his dreams would be of Kai.

Chapter Two

Harry woke earlier than usual. His job managing the bar at The Underground meant that he normally worked very late, then slept in. Having taken the previous evening off to watch over Kai, he'd woken with the dawn chorus. Not that he'd slept a whole lot. He'd been restless, waking every hour, listening for any sounds of distress from the room across the hall. He'd managed to resist taking a look at his sleeping guest, but it had been a close thing. So now he puttered in the kitchen, brewing a fresh pot of coffee and pulling out the makings of a decent breakfast. It wasn't a meal he usually bothered with, but his bad habits would have to change if he wanted to set a good example for Kai.

A few rashers of bacon went on the grill, alongside some tomatoes and mushrooms.

"He could be vegetarian for all I know," Harry muttered to himself.

"I'm not."

Harry whirled around to see Kai leaning on the doorframe, chewing on a thumbnail. He wore Harry's robe again, looking ridiculously swamped and utterly adorable.

"You move quietly," Harry said with a smile. "Come in and sit down. Breakfast is almost ready." He poured a tall glass of cold milk and set it in front of Kai.

"My uncle didn't like me to make too much noise around the house."

Harry raised an eyebrow. "Oh really? You lived with him, did you?"

"I did. Past tense. I'm never going back there. You won't make me, will you?" Kai's voice fractured.

"You're a grown man, Kai. You make your own decisions. You can stay here as long as you want to. I have plenty of space."

"Don't you have roommates?"

"No. I live alone. It will be nice to have company."

"This whole house…is yours?"

Harry nodded and dished up the food. "And you want to know how a bar manager can afford to live in a house like this?"

Kai shoveled food into his mouth as if he hadn't eaten in weeks. "'S'none of my business."

Harry hid a smile and ate his food at a more sedate pace, waiting for the inevitable question.

"You're not a drug dealer, are you?"

Harry almost choked on a piece of bacon. That wasn't quite the question he'd been expecting.

"No, Kai. I'm not a drug dealer—or anything else criminal… Well, depending on your point of view." He took in Kai's wide eyes and laughed. "I am—or should say was—a stockbroker. I went into a career in the city out of university and spent ten years making obscene amounts of money. Some people might brand me a thief because of that career choice."

Kai gaped.

"Close your mouth, Kai."

" Sorry. So you're thirty...one?"

"Thirty-three. I retired from the city two years ago."

"I'm twenty. Nearly twenty-one." Kai cast his eyes down and didn't speak again until he'd cleared his plate.

Comfortable with the silence, Harry waited for Kai to ask another question.

"So why do you work at The Underground?"

"I've been a member there since my early twenties. I know Carey Hoffman well. He's a good friend."

"That's Alistair's...Dom?"

"Yes. Carey is Alistair's Master. He also owns The Underground. When he heard about my retirement plans, he offered me a job as bar manager. It keeps me busy, though I also handle the personal investment portfolios of several club members. Carey finds it useful to have someone with a good head for figures around the place."

Kai twirled the end of his dressing gown cord. "Do you have to work today?"

"Yes. I need to go in by twelve. You'll come with me." Harry had no intention of letting Kai out of his sight.

"Okay." Kai's smile lit up his face and his eyes sparkled. "But I don't have anything to wear."

Harry was just about to reply when the front door bell chimed. "That should be the answer to your wardrobe problems. Wait here while I let Joe and Olly in."

He padded along the hall and opened the door. Olly, dragging a large holdall, fell past him.

"Kai's in the kitchen, Olly."

"'Kay. Morning, Harry." Olly and his baggage disappeared toward the kitchen, and Harry turned to greet Joe who stood on his doorstep shaking his head.

"I apologize, Harry. Olly has been bouncing off the walls this morning. He's cleared out half his closet for Kai."

"Joe, Olly bounces off the walls every morning, noon and night unless you have him strapped down. It's fine. Thanks so much for coming round. I know you must want to be getting back north."

"I have time for coffee." Joe smiled gently and stepped into the hall. "We should probably get to the kitchen before too much damage is done."

Chaos had descended on the kitchen when Harry and Joe arrived there, with Olly and Kai engaged in a tangled hug, straddling the enormous holdall, which had started to eject its contents.

"Why don't you take Olly upstairs to your room, Kai, and have a look through the clothes he's brought to lend you? I'll give you a call when Joe's ready to leave."

Kai nodded and grabbed one handle of Olly's bag after stuffing a couple of items back inside. Between them, they lugged it from the room toward the stairs. Harry just caught the start of an excited conversation.

"I've never seen Harry naked, Kai. Is he as completely gorgeous as I think he is? Does he have a huge…?"

"Oh my God!" Harry leaned against the kitchen counter. "Is this what it's going to be like from now on? Are they going to be comparing our assets every chance they get?"

Joe chuckled and poured himself a coffee. "Get used to it. Nothing—and I mean nothing—is sacred. If you do decide to take things further with Kai, he'll bring with him a ready-made support network of subs, all of whom are very open with their opinions."

"Terrifying. How do you deal with it?"

"Heath and I have regular therapy sessions, believe me. Olly is… Well, he's Olly, and Aiden breaks the entire D/s rulebook every chance he gets. They keep life interesting."

Harry pushed down a twinge of jealousy. Joe looked completely self-assured and at ease. Thinking about it, Harry had never seen the man look ruffled or with a single hair out of place. Joe had poise, elegance and model good looks in spades. He also exuded an aura of absolute control. Harry felt like an inexperienced beginner in comparison.

"I've never had a full-time sub, let alone taken one on with as little experience as Kai. I don't even know if it's what he wants."

Joe looked contemplative. "It's what he needs. I'm fairly certain of that, and there's no doubt that there's attraction between you. He looks at you like a love-struck puppy."

"I want him. He's beautiful, responsive and desperately in need of guidance, but I won't force this. It has to be his decision. I'm going to take him to work with me so that he can observe at The Underground. He needs to understand what it means to be part of the lifestyle before we even consider a relationship."

"And that's exactly why Carey and I know he'll be safe in your hands, Harry. Stop worrying. Things will work out and I'm sure Carey will be very happy to help. Perhaps he and Alistair can give you some demonstrations." Joe put his mug down. "Better call the brat. He'll be getting into all kinds of mischief by now and we've a long drive ahead."

Harry grinned. "Let's go and surprise them, shall we?"

The two of them headed upstairs and followed the noise. Kai's door was ajar and hysterical laughter punctuated the chatter. He knocked softly and pushed the door wide. The room looked like an explosion in a clothing factory, with garments strewn everywhere. Olly lay stomach down on the bed, chin propped in his hands while Kai modeled for him.

"Do these shorts make my arse look...? Oh! Harry..." Kai's voice trailed off and he went bright pink.

Olly buried his head in his arms and his whole body shook with silent laughter.

Harry gaped. Kai wore white leather shorts that could just as well have been described as a belt, they were so small. His white top seemed to consist of a loosely joined collection of fabric strips that accentuated his narrow waist and left his nipples exposed.

"Fuck, Joe, he's going to kill me." Harry took a couple of deep breaths and made a brave attempt to ignore the raging erection challenging the buttons at his fly.

"Olly." The quiet command in Joe's voice had Olly kneeling at his feet in three seconds flat. "If you've done spreading chaos, we need to get going."

Olly nuzzled his thigh and gazed up at him. "My work here is done, Sir. I've left Kai with enough options that there should be something that Harry likes." He gave a mischievous glance at Harry's crotch. "Though I think he may have discovered that already."

"We'll see ourselves out, Harry." Joe tugged on Olly's unruly blond curls and brought him to his feet. "Good luck. I think you'll need it."

"Thanks for all the clothes, Olly," Kai whispered. "I'll look after them. Promise."

Olly gave him a hug and kiss. "They're yours as long as you need them. Call me, 'kay?"

"I will." Kai replied.

Harry thought he looked a little wistful as Olly and Joe left them alone. "You can call him any time, Kai. The number is programmed into the phone."

Kai nodded but looked anxious. "Sorry about the mess. I'll clear it up."

"I'm not cross with you, Kai. It's a few clothes, that's all, and you were having fun with Olly. That's not a crime."

"I'm supposed to be tidy…"

"Your uncle?" Harry wondered exactly what kind of man Kai's relative could be to have had such a negative impact on a vibrant young man.

Kai just bowed his head and twisted his fingers together.

"Well, this is *your* room now and in here you can do as you please. I won't come in here uninvited."

"Really?"

"Really." Harry wanted Kai to have his own space, a place he could feel safe. "Now, I want you to pick out something to wear to the club because you're coming to work with me. Much as I…appreciate that outfit, I'd prefer you to look a little more conservative." *Or I'll be fighting off every fucking Dom in the place.*

"I'm not sure Olly owns anything that could be called conservative." Kai glanced around. "Help me choose?"

Harry almost melted at the plea in Kai's tone. "Of course. It's lucky you and he are such a similar size."

"He's a whole inch taller than me. We measured."

Harry wondered what else the pair of them had measured. "Well, let's see. You need to fit in, so we should probably start with black."

Kai crawled onto the bed and began rummaging through the pile. His arse, encased in tight white leather, wiggled enticingly.

God help me. Harry fixed his eyes on a colorful abstract print on the wall. His erection was painful but freeing his cock was out of the question. He tried to think of the most boring trades he'd ever completed on the stock market but it didn't help.

"How about these?" Kai held up a pair of black jeans. "These look harmless."

"Try them on." Harry counted backwards from a hundred and studied the ceiling as Kai stripped off his shorts and pulled on the jeans.

"Oh!"

At Kai's exclamation, Harry looked at him.

"No. Absolutely not." Harry snapped. The entire front panel of the jeans was made from mesh and it was all too apparent that Kai had not bothered with underwear.

He's going to give me a coronary!

"No?"

"No. How about those leather ones?"

This time, Harry turned away as Kai changed. "Are you decent?"

Kai giggled. "You've already seen me naked, Harry. I don't mind."

"That was different. You were exhausted and I just helped you with a bath."

"Well, I've got them on. What do you think?"

"Bloody hell!" Harry couldn't stop the exclamation. The trousers were sinfully tight, clinging to every curve of Kai's slender legs. The waistband defied the Trades Description Act because it sat nowhere near Kai's waist but rested precariously on his hip bones.

"You don't like them?"

Is that a hint of a pout? Harry grinned. It seemed that with suitable distraction Kai forgot his worries about how to act and did what came naturally.

"I love them. I'm pretty sure everyone at the club will love them too." He swallowed hard as Kai stuck his hand down the front of the trousers and adjusted his cock. The plump ridge was clearly outlined beneath the soft leather. Harry sifted through the pile of clothes on the bed until he found a soft white shirt with a granddad collar.

"Try this."

Kai pulled on the shirt and smoothed it out. It was baggy and reached almost to his thighs.

"It's a bit big." Kai twirled, and the floaty fabric ballooned around him.

"It's perfect," Harry said firmly, relieved that Kai was more covered. "We need to go in about half an hour so I'll leave you to finish getting ready. Come down to the kitchen when you're done."

Harry tidied up the kitchen then found a spare leather jacket that Kai could use. It would be far too big, but it would do the job until he could find something more suitable. He kept his work clothes at The Underground, so Harry killed time on his laptop, reviewing the news and browsing through his email while he waited for Kai.

"What do you think?"

Harry peered over the top of his screen and examined the young man standing in his kitchen doorway. Kai looked stunning. He'd added chunky work boots to his ensemble, partly lacing them so that the tongues stuck out a little. Thick charcoal liner accentuated his eyes and a slick of clear gloss made his lips shine. Harry badly wanted to kiss them, to nip at the soft flesh and make them swell. He quirked an eyebrow. "You'll do."

Kai beamed as if he'd just been given the biggest compliment in the world. Harry handed him the jacket, and Kai shrugged it on his slim shoulders before zipping it up.

"Are you going to be okay on the back of the bike again?" Harry asked.

"I don't remember much about the ride back here last night, but I just have to hold on tight, don't I?" Kai glanced up coyly from beneath his lashes, and Harry caught a hint of mischief in his expression.

He grunted his agreement, slammed the lid of his computer down a little too hard and headed for the door.

* * * *

Kai loved every second of the short ride to The Underground — not because he appreciated the powerful bike but because it allowed him to cling to Harry's lean body. The man had serious muscle tone, which Kai could feel flexing even beneath the layer of thick leather he wore. He allowed himself a little daydream where he got to peel the clothing from Harry's body and stroke every inch while Harry just stood there and let him…until he reached the hard cock jutting from his groin. Then Harry grabbed him, flung him across his bike and fucked him hard, right there on the saddle. Kai shivered and wished he'd chosen looser trousers — not that Olly seemed to own anything baggy. Kai wondered if that was a rule of a D/s relationship — subs were not allowed to wear clothing unless it fit like a second skin or was revealing enough that it didn't matter.

He was still daydreaming when Harry rode the bike down the steep ramp to the parking garage near the club and turned off the engine. It took Kai a few seconds to realize that they'd come to a halt. Embarrassed, he slid from the bike and yanked off his helmet. Harry remained astride the powerful machine as he pulled off his own helmet and gave Kai an amused glance.

"Enjoying yourself back there, were you?"

"Maybe." Kai scuffed a booted toe against the concrete, feeling shy. He wasn't sure how much he could admit to Harry about the way he was feeling. Harry had been kind and considerate. He'd also been very careful not to step beyond the boundaries of friendship. Perhaps Harry only saw him as young, inexperienced and in need of protection. Kai would prefer that the handsome bar manager saw him as a prospective sub. Perhaps if Kai knew more about what that meant, he could behave in a way that was more enticing. He loved the idea of belonging to Harry, being cherished and cared for in the way Joe cared for Olly. There was so much love between those two that it hurt to watch them. Kai had never felt love like that and he wanted it, more than anything.

Harry stored the helmets in his locker, and the two of them walked around to the club's entrance. There was no one on the door. Harry punched in a code and they walked straight to the lift.

"Christian mans the reception desk from twelve o'clock. You'll like him. I'll introduce you when the initial rush dies down."

"Is he another Dom?" Kai asked, feeling a bit nervous.

Harry chuckled. "No. He's not. And you have nothing to worry about, Kai. I won't leave you alone with another Dom unless you specifically ask me to."

"Good. That's good."

The lift opened into the empty club. It was strange to walk through the quiet space having seen it full to bursting the previous afternoon. Chairs were neatly pushed under tables, surfaces shone and there was a scent of furniture polish in the air.

Harry went straight to the bar and lifted a hinged hatch to get behind it.

"Take a seat. I need to do a quick inventory before we open."

"Okay." Kai took the stool at the end of the bar and pushed himself up onto the padded leather. The height gave him a great view and he scanned the room, taking in all the details.

Wow, I didn't realize just how high-end this place is. Everything's the best quality – all wood, leather and marble. No corners had been cut in the club's décor and the place was immaculate. Kai relaxed a little. People who cared about their surroundings this much couldn't be too scary.

"Oh fuck!" The level of scariness changed instantly as Kai turned around to find his nose only a few inches from a mountain of a man. His gaze was drawn up and up until he found a handsome face, broad grin and hair cropped so short it was barely fuzz.

Kai peered around the huge, muscular body seeking the security that Harry offered. He panicked a little when he couldn't see him but then, to his relief, Harry appeared from beneath the bar where he'd been bending down. The little lines around Harry's eyes crinkled as he grinned. "It's all right, Kai. He's not an escaped convict. This is Goran, my assistant bar manager."

Kai let out breath he hadn't even realized he'd been holding and shook Goran's hand. His small, delicate fingers disappeared inside the huge paw, but Goran was gentle and didn't squeeze too hard.

"Hi, Goran. Nice to meet you." Kai gave what he hoped was an endearing smile.

Harry chuckled. "Goran, this is Kai. Joe and Olly rescued him from the clinic where Alistair was being held. He's going to be staying with me for a while."

Goran nodded and patted Kai on the head. "Sweet."

Harry rolled his eyes and handed Goran a piece of paper. "Just a short list of under stock needed today. Check with the kitchen in case they need anything as well."

Goran took the list and headed toward the kitchen door.

"He doesn't say much, does he?" Kai watched the huge man move smoothly across the room.

"He's a bit shy," Harry commented.

"You have got to be kidding me."

"No, it's true. If you get a full sentence out of him then you'll know he likes you. You're with me, so he'll keep an eye out for you when I'm not around."

Kai wasn't sure how he felt about that. Goran was one intimidating giant.

"The subs love him. I think they have a book running on who might eventually snag him as their Dom."

"I believe the right person is out there for everyone," Kai said emphatically. "You just have to be in the right place to find 'the one'." He gave Harry a coy glance. "I think I'm in the right place now."

Kai thought he detected the slightest flush of pink on Harry's well-defined cheekbones. He wanted to give himself a high five at what felt like a significant success. Harry cleared his throat. "Well, I need to go and change before we open. Will you be okay here for a few minutes?"

"Sure. You don't have to worry about me."

"Maybe I can't help myself," Harry muttered as he strolled away.

As soon as Harry disappeared through a door at the back of the club, Kai's nerves returned. Harry was his anchor in a sea of uncertainty and, at that moment, his stool felt like an island surrounded by sharks. Kai hadn't had time to worry about his situation, but now there was little he could do *except* think about it. He chewed on the corner of a nail, his anxiety manifesting in a need to distract himself. "What the hell am I doing?" He asked the question but already knew the answer. "Breaking free. That's what." There would be no going back. Kai would rather be homeless than return to the cold, controlling world of his uncle. "I won't pretend to be something I'm not anymore." He jumped as the door leading to the staff room swung open. He didn't want Harry to catch him having a conversation with himself — that would be too embarrassing! But it wasn't Harry who emerged. It was Alistair.

Alistair appeared completely different now that he was away from the clinic. There were still dark circles beneath his eyes, but those eyes now glittered, all trace of dullness wiped away. He wore a black military-style jacket over jeans and looked hot as hell. Around his neck sat a slim leather collar. Kai stared, transfixed by the thin strip of supple fabric. He touched his own neck with his fingertips, wondering what it would feel like to have something wrapped around it that he couldn't take off. His cock twitched.

"Kai! You scrub up well. Are those Olly's clothes?" Alistair's voice was soft and melodic.

Kai hopped off his stool. He nodded. "Yes, they are. He and Joe came by Harry's place this morning and Olly left me a whole load of things that I can use until I have some of my own. Do I look okay?"

"We're going to have to put an electric fence up around you to keep the Doms away." Alistair held out his arms, and Kai walked into a big hug.

It felt good to be held, and Kai reluctantly moved away. Alistair climbed onto the stool next to Kai's and swung his legs. "Where's Harry?"

"Gone to change. Goran's fetching fresh stock." Kai reclaimed the end stool.

"Ah, so you've met Goran." Alistair laughed. "Big, isn't he?"

"He's enormous!"

"Well, I've come to ask Harry if he'll let me introduce you around. He'll be working and you don't want to be stuck on a bar stool all day."

It didn't even cross Kai's mind to dispute that Alistair needed permission from Harry.

"That sounds great. Only if you don't mind, though." Kai worried that Alistair might have better things to do than look after him.

"Of course I don't mind! We are going to be good friends, I just know we are." Alistair's voice was full of warmth.

Kai immediately relaxed. Alistair seemed so calm and steady.

"I want to see everything. Learn everything. There's so much I don't know about...Dominance and submission." There, he'd managed to say it without stuttering over the words.

"You're certainly in the best place to get the broadest introduction. Just remember— No matter what you've read on the Internet, there is no set rulebook. Safe, sane and consensual are words to live by but every relationship is different. I can show you all kinds of things, but only you can make up your mind about what you like or don't like."

Kai's response dried up, along with his mouth, as he spotted Harry walking toward them. The club's bar staff uniform of black leather trousers and fitted black T-shirt looked as if it had been designed for Harry's tall, slim frame. As he approached, Kai fought the urge to slide to his knees and nuzzle a leather-wrapped thigh. *Fuck, the man is sex on legs. I'm gonna come in my pants...*

"Hiya, Harry."

"Morning, Alistair. It's good to see you back where you belong." There were a lot of words unspoken in Harry's reply, but Kai heard the subtext.

"Thanks." Alistair's wide smile said it all. "It's good to *be* back. I've come to ask if I can steal Kai away from you for a while, to show him around."

"That sounds like a good idea. I'm going to be busy for a while." Harry pulled something from his pocket.

Kai's eyes widened as he recognized it as a collar.

"This is a club collar, Kai. It's the same as the ones the servers wear. It tells the members you are off limits. I want you to wear it."

"Oh! I... Oh!" Kai looked from the strip of leather to Harry's implacable expression and back again.

Alistair took his hand and squeezed. He gave Kai a reassuring smile. Harry slid the collar around Kai's neck and buckled it. He ran a finger beneath it and Kai shivered at the contact with his skin.

"How does that feel? Not too tight?" Harry asked.

"No... It... It feels perfect." It felt amazing. Kai barely resisted touching it. He folded his hands in his lap, attempting to conceal his erection. He didn't have time to analyze his feelings because the bar area was getting crowded as the serving staff arrived for their daily briefing. Kai couldn't help but stare at their skimpy attire. He didn't think he'd look so composed if he were clad in a short leather kilt and not much else, but the servers chattered away with each other until Harry rapped on the bar to get their attention. As Harry began to talk about the day's lunch specials, Alistair pulled Kai away. "Let's go and steal coffee from Carey's office. It always gets really busy for the first hour or so. Once

things have settled down, I'll give you the tour. Oh...
And I find that thinking about naked politicians helps."

"Helps with what...? Oh!" Kai saw that Alistair was
looking pointedly in the direction of his groin. He
grinned sheepishly. "Harry in leather. Sorry. I thought
this shirt was long enough to hide anything going on
down there."

"Oh don't apologize. Harry's smoking hot. I may be
in love with Carey, but I'm not blind. The shirt almost
works..."

Kai chuckled. "A hot drink sounds good, but I don't
like coffee."

"Carey keeps packets of expensive instant hot
chocolate in his desk. He thinks I don't know about
them. We can use the coffee machine to heat water."

"Yum. As long as it won't get you into trouble."

The two of them made their way to Carey's cramped
little office. The coffee pot was already full and a
delicious aroma filled the tiny space.

"We have a state-of-the-art machine at home. Carey
can't even work it. He says you need an engineering
degree just to understand out how to turn it on."
Alistair poured himself a mug and took the seat behind
the desk. He rummaged in a drawer and pulled out a
sachet of chocolate.

"Here. As Carey's already made coffee, you'll have to
use the kettle. Just swap the plugs over. It should be
full."

Kai made his drink then took the smaller chair facing
Alistair.

"Where is Carey? Are we going to be in his way?"

"He always does the rounds of the staff before he
comes in here. We're safe for a while. He's probably in
the kitchen annoying the hell out of the chef. Then he'll
go and talk to each of the servers and finish up at the

bar to gossip with Harry. Doms always say that it's the subs who gossip all the time but believe me, they are just as bad."

Kai sipped his drink. "This is great. People really care about this place, don't they?"

Alistair nodded. "The Underground is special. In the BDSM community, membership here is highly sought after. Acceptance is seen as confirmation that you are a genuine, respected part of the lifestyle. There's a stringent vetting process for Doms. They have to have a minimum of two references before they'll be considered and even then, Carey or one of the dungeon masters will observe a scene with them. Then they're supervised for a probationary period as well."

"Wow, it sounds really strict."

"It needs to be. Subs come here knowing that they can trust the Doms they play with. Limits are always respected." Alistair looked as serious as he sounded.

Kai gripped his mug a little tighter than necessary. "I know so little about all this, but I know it feels right. I just don't understand why."

Alistair grinned. "Finding out is going to be so much fun."

Chapter Three

Harry polished the bar for the umpteenth time, the movements automatic as he tried to make it seem that he wasn't looking for Kai in every corner of the club. Goran grabbed the cloth from him and tossed it on the shelf below the bar.

"Chill. He's fine."

"Am I that transparent?" Harry asked, as Goran poured a couple of sodas for two giggling subs.

"Like glass." Goran switched his attention to his customers. "Hey, pretties, you free later?"

"Which one of us?" the blond said, as he and his friend bounced up and down.

Harry half expected them to be yelling, 'Pick me, pick me!'

Goran grinned. "Both."

"Yay!"

"I'll come and find you when my shift finishes." Goran went back to serving.

"Greedy sod. Two of them? When are you going to hook up with someone more permanent?" Harry scanned the tables around the dance floor.

"Nothing wrong with double the satisfaction. One sub on his own always wears out too quickly."

Harry rolled his eyes. The big, quiet man was a solid, loyal friend. It would be good to see him settled. Harry sighed—maybe he was just transferring his own desires onto Goran. He spotted Kai across the room. Alistair was holding his hand and towing him toward the door leading to the private playrooms.

"No fucking way…" He went to lift the bar hatch but someone leaned their weight on it, holding it down.

Carey's eyes twinkled as he met Harry's annoyed stare. "None of the playrooms are in use at the moment. Alistair is giving Kai a tour. It will give him a chance to ask questions he might not be so comfortable asking you."

"I wasn't bothered," Harry lied.

"Of course you weren't." Carey smirked. "I'll have a sparkling mineral water with ice and a slice of lime."

Harry made the drink and one for himself. He slid Carey's glass across the bar to him. Carey waved to Goran. "Are you okay on your own for a bit? I think Harry needs a break."

Goran grinned. "Sure, boss. He's as good as useless today anyway."

Harry scowled. "Are you two ganging up on me?"

A simultaneous "Yes" came from the men. Harry had the sense to know when he was beaten. He lifted the hatch and joined Carey on the other side of the bar.

"Let's go and sit somewhere a bit more comfortable," Carey said and led the way to a couple of armchairs grouped around a small table. Harry sank into the soft upholstery and sighed. He hadn't realized just how tense he'd been until he let his shoulders drop. Carey sipped his drink and looked at him with an enigmatic smile, not saying anything. Harry groaned inside. This was one of Carey's well-known tactics to get people to spill their guts. He used it very effectively at staff interviews. Not many people could withstand the silence for very long. Harry didn't have the energy to be stubborn. His boss could outdo him in the passive resistance game any day of the week and he knew it.

"What do you want me to say, Carey?"

Carey tapped his elegant fingers on the arm of the chair. "How about we start with how you've been getting along with Kai. There is still an open invitation for him to come and stay with Alistair and me if you want him out of your hair."

"No! I mean... No, thank you. That won't be necessary. We're getting along just fine. Of course, if Kai would prefer to be with you guys then that's okay with me too."

"Really? Would it be okay with you, Harry?"

Harry examined the water droplets on the outside of his glass. "Fuck it. No, it wouldn't be."

Carey chuckled. "It's tough isn't it? Falling for someone so hard? It gets so you can't think about anything or anyone else."

Harry rolled his head from side to side, getting some of the kinks out of his neck. "I've never believed in love at first sight. Insta-lust maybe, but not something deeper." He sighed. "But I don't think that's what I'm feeling."

Carey stretched out his legs and crossed them at the ankles. "So how *are* you feeling?"

"Shit, I don't know! Confused. Possessive. Protective. I've had a hard-on for about twenty-three of the last twenty-four hours."

Carey arched an eyebrow. "Sounds uncomfortable."

"What am I going to do, Carey? I don't want to let him out of my sight and we've only known each other just over a day. I put that club collar on him and I wanted it to be mine. Fuck, what an idiot." He closed his eyes and leaned back in the chair.

Carey steepled his fingers. "You're not an idiot. I knew I wanted Alistair to be mine about ten minutes after I first set eyes on him. The idea of any other man laying a finger on him had me climbing the walls."

"But at least Alistair knew all about the scene when you met. He came here for a job interview, after all. Kai knows next to nothing. He may not even be a sub..."

Harry was interrupted by Carey's undignified snort.

"You're joking, aren't you? That young man has submission tattooed on his cute little arse. Alistair and Olly both instantly recognized it in him. Alistair is terrified he'll fall into the wrong hands. He's probably doing a full-scale sales pitch on your behalf as we speak."

"How come you noticed his arse, Carey?" Harry felt like growling. Not a great plan, considering that the man seated next to him was his boss.

"Because I'm not blind, Harry. I'm pretty certain that every Dom in here has noticed that divine little butt, along with the puppy dog eyes, dimples and aura of utter virginal innocence. You're absolutely right to takes things slowly, but you need to take them *somewhere*... If not, he'll be snapped up like a guppy in a shark tank."

"So what should I do? I can hardly offer him a contract. I doubt he'd even know what one is."

"So tell him. Offer to teach him. Take him on as a trainee sub... No sex, just training. You can contract on the basis of a rolling week's commitment. I'd be happy to witness it for you, and Alistair can mentor Kai from a sub's point of view."

It all sounded sensible and a bit too good to be true. Apart from the no sex part. That sucked, but Harry knew it was the responsible way forward.

"Sounds…workable. But how the hell am I going to raise the subject of a D/s contract? It's hardly a usual topic of conversation."

"Oh, I don't think you'll have to worry about that." Carey grinned.

Harry's stomach did an uncomfortable flip-flop as he noticed Alistair and Kai walking in their direction. Alistair gave Carey a kiss then sank gracefully to his knees next to his Master. Kai watched him carefully then moved to Harry's side and mirrored the action. His movement wasn't as smooth and as well-practiced as Alistair's, but for a first effort it was fantastic. Harry slammed his gaping mouth shut and automatically ruffled Kai's hair. Kai beamed, revealing his dimples.

"Alistair said I should call you Sir. Is that okay, Harry? I'd like to. If you want me to?"

Harry nodded, not trusting himself to speak.

"And he explained all about contracts and that you might be prepared to teach me. Will you? I know I'm new and I don't know anything and you probably want someone more experienced, but I'd love it if you'd consider helping me. I want to learn…everything!"

Harry gave Carey a helpless look. "I…"

"I have a suitable contract in my office that you can use, Harry." Carey saved him from making a complete idiot of himself.

Alistair nuzzled Carey's thigh. Carey cupped the back of Alistair's neck and squeezed. Harry could see Kai casting sideways glances at him. He stroked his hair in what he hoped was in a reassuring way.

"Thank you, Carey. I'd appreciate that."

"Good. That's settled. You should get back to work, and if it's okay with you, Harry, perhaps Kai would like to go upstairs to the flat with Alistair? I imagine he has a lot of questions."

"Please, Sir. Can I?" Kai looked at him with big, pleading eyes, and Harry knew he was in trouble. How was he ever going to be able to deny Kai anything, let alone punish him?

I am so fucked. "Of course you can."

Kai looked as if he'd just been given the moon. Carey chuckled. "Alistair can give Kai some lunch and then perhaps you would care to be my guest for dinner, Harry. We can eat in the restaurant before your evening shift starts. Kai and Alistair can join us, as this is a celebration of sorts, isn't it?"

Harry nodded. His head was so full of all the things he would teach Kai that he barely registered the conversation. He was stupidly pleased that Kai wouldn't be in the club for the rest of the afternoon. That would have to be one of the first rules... No unaccompanied visits to The Underground. He switched back to reality as Kai got awkwardly to his feet. Tight leather flexed around his thighs and Harry swallowed. *No sex, no sex, no sex... Think pure thoughts.*

"I'll see you later then, Sir."

Kai's soft voice and anxious eyes sent a shiver down Harry's spine. Acting on instinct, he pulled Kai into his lap and gave him a hug. "I'll be waiting. Be good."

The instant Kai left Harry behind, his nerves returned but Alistair held his hand and provided the comfort he needed.

"We have a flat two floors up in this building. It's not home... More like a crash pad... But we spend so much time here that it's great to have a place to escape to.

When I used to work here, I'd come and wind down after my shift. Just hang out and watch films, you know?"

"Not really. My uncle didn't like me watching too much television. He said it was a corrupting influence." Kai shuddered. If he never saw his uncle again, he would have no regrets.

"He sounds like a real piece of work. Did your aunt not stick up for you?"

"Oh, he isn't married. Uncle Francis said he never found the right woman. After I lost my parents, he was my closest surviving relative. He said it was his duty to take me." Kai felt no emotion, He'd long come to terms with his uncle's lack of compassion.

"Can I ask what happened to your parents?" Alistair asked, then patted Kai's arm. "Sorry. It's really none of my business...."

"They were both doctors. They decided to volunteer for an overseas posting in Uganda but they had the worst timing. There was an outbreak of Ebola and they insisted on looking after the people who got sick. The disease killed both of them within days of each other. I was six, being looked after by a nanny hundreds of miles away."

"Oh my goodness! I'm so sorry, Kai."

"It's okay. It was a long time ago and they were always so busy... They were practically strangers."

"I sometimes wish *my* father was a stranger. Enough with the depressing stuff. We're here."

They stepped out of the lift, and Alistair used his key to open the only door on the small landing. "Make yourself at home, Kai. How about we get snacks, then Skype Olly? He should be home by now. With any luck, Aiden might be around as well. Between us, we should be able to answer all your questions."

"Sure. Uh... Who's Aiden?"

"He's Heath's sub. Heath is Joe's best friend and business partner. They run The Edge together."

Kai followed Alistair into the small kitchen where he began pulling food from cupboards.

"Olly told me a bit about The Edge."

"The island is amazing. Maybe Harry will take you to visit. Are you good with junk food? I think we need as many different E numbers as possible. I have Wotsits, rocky road bites, cocktail sausages, chocolate raisins... They're healthy, and they count as one of our five a day."

Kai giggled, and let Alistair pile his arms with goodies.

"What would you like to drink?" Alistair asked. "There might be wine..."

Kai's face heated. "I know it's really lame, but could I have milk?"

Alistair beamed. "Two glasses of cow juice coming up. Go through to the lounge and I'll bring them in."

Kai wandered through to the cozy sitting room and dumped his booty on the low coffee table. Alistair wasn't far behind him. He put two glasses onto a side table and collected a laptop from the top of a bookcase.

"Let me just set this up."

Alistair fiddled with cables, fired up the computer and connected to Skype. "Fantastic, Olly and Aiden are both online. Of course that doesn't mean either of them are actually anywhere near a computer, but I'll try to conference them in."

The dial tone was a strange burbling sound that made Kai laugh, then Olly's face appeared on the screen.

"Ooh, exciting! An online party and I've only been home an hour." Olly's head disappeared.

"Olly, stop bouncing! We can't see you," Alistair yelled.

He and Kai cuddled up so that they were close together and both their faces appeared on the little screen within a screen.

"Sorry," Olly sang at them. "Have you called Aiden? He'll get all snarky if you leave him out. Well, snarkier than usual. He's working down in his cave, but he's got three screens down there. He can spare one and his brain's big enough to multitask."

"Just give me a minute." Alistair dialed again and another face appeared.

Kai's eyes widened.

"Pretty, isn't he?" Olly said. "Don't mention it, though, Kai. Aiden's head's big enough already."

Aiden raised his middle finger and scowled. "Shut it, Olly. Have you been on the coffee? Hi, Alistair, and you must be Kai. Nice to meet you." He smiled.

"Hello." Kai gave a shy smile back. He'd never seen a man quite as pretty as Aiden before, but what had really grabbed his attention was the thick leather collar around Aiden's slender throat. It didn't look comfortable. He touched the narrow, supple strip around his own neck.

"Don't worry, Kai, Aiden's Master likes to make sure he can't forget he's a submissive, hence the brutal neckwear. I'm a good boy. Look at mine!" Olly lifted a slender chain from beneath his shirt and held the little padlock up toward the camera. "See?"

Aiden looked like he was having some kind of fit.

"Is he okay?" Kai asked.

Alistair nodded sagely. "He's fine. It's just a reaction to Olly declaring himself a good boy. Olly gets into more trouble than the rest of us put together. Look, you two, Kai and I have snacks and he's got lots of questions, so behave! Guess what? Harry's agreed to a rolling one week contract!"

The exclamations were almost simultaneous. "Wow! You really made an impression, Kai. Harry's never contracted with anyone and he's soooo gorgeous."

Olly's delight was overlaid by a more staid, "Congratulations, Kai, Harry's a lovely guy," from Aiden.

"He is. I know. But I need your advice... I'm kind of working out that I'm a sub and I really, really like the idea of bondage and spanking and plugs and, and...everything! But I have no idea what I'm doing. What if I fuck up?"

"You can't fuck up when you're learning, Kai. Harry will explain what he wants from you and he'll correct you if you get it wrong. If you listen and pay attention, he'll be happy," Aiden said.

Olly's curls bounced as he nodded. "Doms are all different, but the good ones have a few common traits... They like to think they're in charge, they are more overprotective than mama bears and they always, *always* respect your safe word."

"What do you mean they like to *think* they're in charge? Aren't they? I don't want to be in charge."

Alistair handed Kai a bowl of chocolate raisins. "Eat these...You need a sugar rush right now."

Kai scooped up a handful and stuffed them in his mouth, then chased the sweetness down with a long swallow of milk.

"In a D/s relationship, the sub holds all the power, Kai. That doesn't mean you have to make decisions... Harry will be in control but he won't do anything that you don't consent to. You set the limits on what you will and won't do," Aiden said solemnly.

"Oh... Oh that's okay then, but what if I don't know what my limits are?" Kai fought back his rising panic.

Olly's expression was full of sympathy. "You can have hard and soft limits. Hard limits are for things you know you absolutely, definitely don't want to do. Soft limits are for things you think you might like to try but aren't sure about. Those, you would discuss with Harry beforehand."

"Do you all have hard limits? Sorry... Is that too personal?"

Olly fell about laughing. "Nothing's too personal between us, Kai. You can ask anything you want! I have hard limits... Some things belong in the bathroom." He shuddered. "I don't do tickling either. Hate it!"

"Water sports goes without saying. Yuck. I don't do full sensory deprivation," Aiden tapped on his keyboard. "I am listening... Have to work at the same time or Becket will rip me a new one."

"And I draw the line at bull whips. They bloody hurt and I'm not that much of a masochist," Alistair made his contribution as he ripped open a catering pack of Wotsits.

"You guys are making me hungry!" Olly complained.

Aiden peeled the wrapper from a chocolate bar, took a bite and made orgasmic noises.

"Aiden! I hate you..."

Aiden grinned. Alistair giggled, and all the tension Kai had been feeling drained away. He had friends. They might be people he hardly knew, but these three men made him feel wanted and safe. He felt brave enough to ask another question.

"You all have jobs. How does that work out...? Don't your Doms want you around all the time?"

"Being a sub doesn't mean you have to give up your independence, Kai. If you want to work or study, then

Harry will support you — and I don't just mean financially. None of us are into the whole slavery thing, but some guys love it, I know," Alistair said. "What did you study at college?"

"Industrial design. I wanted to do interior design but my uncle wouldn't allow it, and he controlled access to funds my parents had set aside for my education."

"Wow, you're all artsy like Alistair. I can only draw kinky stick men," Olly pouted.

"Don't you mean dick men?" Aiden snorted. "I've seen your doodles and I can tell you those things are not anatomically possible."

Olly poked his tongue out. "Look spy-geek boy, you need to be more imaginative."

"Spy? Aiden's a spy?" Kai stared at the screen with his mouth open.

"Oops." Olly looked everywhere but at the camera.

"You better have your running shoes on, Olly..." Aiden's camera shut off abruptly.

"Gotta go, guys. Have a fun day. Call me later 'kay?" Then Olly disappeared too.

Kai looked at Alistair, and the two of them dissolved into a giggling pile.

Once he'd managed to stop laughing, Kai asked, "Is Aiden really a spy?"

Alistair nodded. "Olly's going to be in so much trouble! Aiden works for British Intelligence. His boss, Dave Becket, is a member at The Underground. Aiden's a bit of a genius — he does secret computer stuff."

"And he's a sub?"

"Did you see that collar? Aiden's Dom is really scary, but they are great together."

"He seems really cool."

Alistair broke open a tub of rocky road bites. "He is, and, despite appearances, he and Olly are best friends."

For a while the two of them munched snacks, drank their milk and gossiped about club members. Alistair picked out a couple of films and they settled down for an afternoon of mindless entertainment. Kai had never felt happier. At ten to six Alistair decreed that they needed to go down to the restaurant and join Carey and Harry for dinner.

"Harry will be back on shift at seven."

"He works long hours, doesn't he?" Kai followed Alistair back to the lift.

"Split shifts take some getting used to, but Harry only works four days a week, Thursday to Sunday. Those are the busiest days here. Carey doesn't like to close, but Mondays are really quiet. There's just a skeleton staff on and the kitchen does light snacks rather than a full restaurant service."

"Perhaps I could help out somewhere?" Kai asked. "I don't want to be sitting around all the time. I can wash up or wait tables."

"I doubt Harry will want you on the serving staff… Have you seen the uniforms?" Alistair chuckled. "That's how I started here and I can tell you, those kilts are really drafty."

Kai remembered how Harry had wanted him covered up when he'd chosen his outfit. "You could be right. But I could do stuff in the kitchen."

"We can ask. Chef's always looking for prep assistants."

Kai fell silent as they crossed the busy restaurant. It didn't escape his notice that lots of people were looking at him, but his attention was focused on Harry, who sat at a private table in a corner, chatting with Carey. As he and Alistair approached, the two Doms stood. Harry pulled out a chair for Kai, and Carey did the same for Alistair, who stole a kiss before he sat down. A pretty blond server approached and handed menus to Carey and Harry.

"Can I get you some drinks, Sirs?" he asked in a very soft voice.

"Just a jug of iced water for now. Thank you, Saul," Carey said.

The server scurried off in the direction of the kitchen, and Kai took the opportunity to peep at Harry, only to find Harry's gaze firmly fixed on him.

"Oh...!"

"Did you and Alistair enjoy your afternoon, Kai?"

Kai twitched as Harry placed a hand on his thigh beneath the table. It was hard to concentrate when Harry touched him.

"Yes... Yes, Sir."

Alistair stepped in. "We Skyped with Olly and Aiden, Sir. I think Olly may be dead now... Or at least dismembered. He let slip something he shouldn't have."

"Why doesn't that surprise me?" Carey shrugged. "I'm sure Joe will save the brat from Aiden and dole out an appropriate punishment. I hope you two behaved with some decorum?"

"Of course, Sir," Alistair protested. "We were good. We ate snacks and watched films."

Kai nodded in support.

"Saul will be back in a minute to take our order. What would you like to eat, love?" Carey covered Alistair's smaller hand with his own and squeezed.

"Will we be playing later, Sir?" Alistair asked.

"Oh yes. I have some very interesting plans for you this evening." Carey smirked, and Alistair blushed.

"Then I'll just have the Caesar salad. Thank you, Sir."

"What about you, Kai?" Harry asked. "Would you like me to order for you?"

Kai gave a sigh of relief. The menu was extensive and there were so many choices. "Yes please, Sir. I'd like that."

Saul glided up to the table and stood at Carey's elbow, head bowed.

"One Caesar salad please, Saul, and I'll have the poached trout," Carey said.

Harry didn't even glance at the menu. "And two portions of the salmon and dill pasta please, Saul. It's absolutely delicious, Kai. I'm sure you'll like it."

Kai wanted to lean against Harry's arm. The tanned skin and light dusting of dark hair looked warm… He caught himself before he made contact, but only just. He probably needed permission to touch and he didn't want to make Harry ashamed of him. Harry had some kind of mind reading ability because he encircled Kai's shoulders with a strong arm and pulled him close.

"Don't look so worried, Kai. You aren't going to do anything wrong."

Kai sighed and snuggled happily into Harry's side. He was just as warm as he looked.

"Harry and I have been discussing your situation, Kai. We think it would be wise for you to make contact with your uncle and make arrangements to fetch your belongings." Carey's tone was kind but firm.

"And there's no need to worry, Kai." Harry gave him a squeeze. "I'll go with you. You won't be alone."

"I don't know… I don't really want to see him ever again. He sent me to that clinic." He shivered.

"You need to make a clean break and I'm sure there must be some things you'd like to have from home? And what about finances? There must be papers and documents you need to have with you?" Carey asked.

"I suppose," Kai mumbled. "My parents left money for me in an education trust, but my uncle managed it.

I don't know anything about it. I do have a few things — clothes and books and some drawing equipment. My phone and wallet are still at the clinic."

Harry frowned. "Sounds like we should get a lawyer involved. You're an adult and should have control of your finances, unless your parents stipulated in their will that you had to be older than twenty-one. We can get your things back from the clinic too... I doubt that place will be open much longer. You may also have to testify about what you saw there. Alistair too and Olly, God help us."

That made Kai smile. He could just imagine Olly entertaining a courtroom. "I can do anything if you're there with me, Sir. I want a new life and I'm prepared to fight for it." He spoke with quiet determination, even though his stomach was churning.

"We'll be with you all the way, sweetheart." Harry put a finger beneath Kai's chin and tilted his head. Then he kissed him and nothing else mattered.

Chapter Four

Three weeks later…

Kai looked down at his bound hands. A dark red ribbon held his wrists together, tied off with a small bow. All he needed to do was lift his arms and use his teeth to pull one end of the ribbon then he would be free. But Harry had put the ribbon there. He had wrapped the silky strip of fabric round and round until Kai's wrists were snug and secure. Now Kai's hands rested on his bare thighs and he couldn't seem to pull his gaze away from them. The red contrasted dramatically with his pale skin. It reminded him of ripe cherries. He could almost smell the fruit.

"You're drifting, Kai. Is this all it takes to get you into subspace?" Harry's voice broke into Kai's daydream.

"Oh! Sorry, Sir. I was thinking about cherries."

"I shouldn't even ask, but what the hell. How did you get to cherries?"

"The color of the ribbon, Sir." Kai gave himself a little shake. He needed to concentrate better. He was too easily distracted.

He knelt on a soft cushion, facing the armchair where Harry sat with one ankle resting on the opposite knee. Kai wore only his trunks. The thin layer of bright blue cotton did little to hide his erection. He shivered, not from the cold because the living flame fire in the hearth next to him kept him toasty warm, but rather from reaction to the confusing mix of emotions he was feeling.

"Talk to me, Kai. I want you to describe how you're feeling in as much detail as you can manage." Harry leaned toward him slightly, giving Kai his full attention.

Kai tried to separate out in his head all the sensations affecting his body.

"I… Well, I ache, Sir. I'm hard and I want to come," he whispered.

"What's making you hard?"

"Being almost naked when you're fully dressed. Kneeling for you. Being bound. I can't say it's just one thing, Sir."

"Okay, that's good. What else?"

Kai blinked and looked up at Harry, unsure what to say.

"There's no wrong answer, Kai. Just say how you feel." Harry's smile reassured Kai.

"Well, I feel safe. I know you'll take care of me. I feel calm and peaceful… Like I don't have to worry about anything."

"That's right. You are completely safe. What about the bondage? Do you like it? Does it scare you?"

Kai looked down at his hands. "Oh… I'd forgotten. I like it…a lot. It's not scary at all."

Harry uncrossed his legs and stood up. He walked in a slow circle around Kai then stopped in front of him.

"I want you to stand up. Just like we've practiced."

Kai focused on his body, his limbs. It was much harder than it looked. Not the act of rising and dropping, but making it smooth and graceful. He tensed his muscles and rose in one fluid motion.

"Excellent! That's perfect, Kai. Well done."

Kai preened at the praise. Pleasing Harry made his world a wonderful place to be.

"I think it's time we took things forward a step. How do you feel about that, Kai?"

"If you think I'm ready, Sir?" Inside, Kai jumped for joy. He couldn't wait.

"How would you feel about extending your contract to a rolling four week arrangement?" Harry stroked Kai's arm and waited for a response.

"Oh! Yes... Yes please, Sir!" Kai bounced on his toes, forgetting to keep still until Harry squeezed his shoulder lightly, reminding him.

"Very well. I'll ask Carey to amend the paperwork. In the meantime..." Harry released the bonds around Kai's wrists.

Kai frowned. Had he done something wrong? He liked being tied. But then Harry pulled his arms behind him and bound his wrists again. Kai's cock jerked. Now he was more vulnerable, more helpless. He couldn't untie his hands without Harry's help and it felt amazing. He pulled at the ribbon experimentally, but there was no stretch.

"Giving your body into my hands is a big part of submission," Harry said calmly. "Every part of you is mine, to do with as I see fit. I will take my pleasure from you, Kai. Dominating you, playing with you... These things give me enormous gratification."

Kai gasped as Harry took hold of the waistband of his trunks and pulled them down to his ankles. Every instinct he possessed told him to cover his genitalia, but he couldn't. With his hands bound behind his back, he could only stand there and submit to Harry's scrutiny.

"You may step out of your underwear."

Kai's legs shook as he took the small step required. His balance was shot to pieces, but Harry steadied him.

"You have a beautiful body, Kai."

Kai's mouth was so dry he couldn't have answered if he had wanted to. He cast his eyes down, shyness overcoming him.

"You are mine to touch, mine to torment. Do you understand?"

Harry fondled his arse, and Kai's response was little more than a squeak. "Yes, Sir!"

"From this moment on, you don't come without my permission. Lose control and you will be punished."

Kai moaned. He was so close to coming already. It wasn't fair!

"Look at me, Kai. Do you know what this is?" Harry held something in his hand. Small and round, it looked a bit like a black elastic band. Kai might be innocent, but he knew what it was.

"It's a cock ring, Sir."

"It is. I'm going to put it on you now. This is a very simple neoprene ring. It's nice and stretchy, so it's easy to get it on, even when you're erect. In time, you'll progress to leather and metal versions." Harry stretched the ring and passed it down the length of Kai's cock. "Do you remember those fairground games where you have to pass a metal loop along a wire without touching it?"

Kai nodded, his teeth clenched. "Yes, Sir. Touch the wire and a buzzer goes off."

"This is similar, isn't it? If I touch you, will you go off, Kai?"

"Oh God." Kai squeezed his eyes shut and prayed that Harry had a steady hand. When the rubber finally constricted around the base of his cock and balls, Kai almost sobbed in relief. The pressure was strange but it didn't hurt. He let his breath out very slowly.

"Does it pinch at all?" Harry asked.

"No, Sir... It's very comfortable. Thank you." Kai was fascinated by the way the ring made his cock jut higher from his body.

"Very well. I want you to kneel and present yourself as I've taught you. Take it nice and slow. It will be harder with your hands tied behind you."

Kai made it to his knees without falling on his face and counted it a huge success. He shuffled his legs farther apart and pushed his chest out, keeping his eyes fixed on the floor at Harry's feet. The position made a lewd display of his erection — a realization that heated Kai's skin into a full-body blush. Until then, Harry had never trained him naked. They had started with Kai fully dressed, progressed to no shirt then to underwear but this was the first time that Kai had been bared to Harry's critical gaze. It was a significant step and Kai couldn't help but feel proud of himself.

"Not bad at all for the first attempt. It takes practice to do that with grace. You can practice without me — just hold your hands behind your back and do it a few times before bed. Your muscles will soon adjust."

"Yes, Sir."

"Very well. On your feet again."

Kai stood smoothly. His cock bobbed as he rose, reminding him of just how badly he needed to come. His breath hitched as Harry moved to stand behind him. Kai only had to lean back a fraction and he would be pressed against Harry's body. He froze, hardly daring to breathe. Denim brushed against his arse, cashmere tickled his back. If Kai wiggled his fingers, he'd feel the metal studs of Harry's fly. Kai whimpered as Harry encircled his chest with a strong arm and laid the palm of his hand flat across Kai's nipple. He brushed Kai's stomach with his other hand and splayed his fingers across Kai's lower belly. Kai let his weight rest against Harry. He had no choice. It was that or fall over. Harry didn't object. He pushed Kai's legs a little farther apart with his knee.

"Good. Now relax, love."

Love! He called me love! Kai's mind couldn't process the words. It was too busy analyzing sensation. Harry rubbed little circles into his belly with one hand and pinched a tender nipple with the other. Kai tilted his head and nestled into the curve of Harry's neck.

"Oh! Oh… Please…"

Harry shifted his hand a fraction lower, grazing the cropped hair at the top of Kai's groin.

"We'll need to shave this very soon, Kai. I want you smooth and sensitive for me."

At that moment, Kai would have dipped himself in a vat of depilatory cream if Harry would only move his hand lower!

Kai attempted to manipulate his position to get what he wanted, but Harry just held him tighter and twisted a nipple hard enough to hurt. The twinge of pain shot a lightning bolt of pleasure straight to Kai's balls. He fluttered his fingers helplessly, fighting the gentle bondage. His vision blurred at the edges as Harry took the weight of Kai's cock in his hand and held it. That was all he did. He just supported its weight and continued to play with Kai's nipples, driving him into a frenzy of need.

"Sir, please! Harry… I need… It hurts!"

Deftly, Harry removed the cock ring and rubbed his thumb over the leaking head of Kai's cock.

"Come!"

The order snapped into Kai's consciousness and his cock responded. Kai screamed and shot hard into Harry's hand. The intensity of his orgasm overwhelmed him. Spasms racked his body as Harry tenderly milked him dry. When his cock finally lay flaccid in Harry's grip, Kai sighed and settled back against him. He'd happily stay there forever, held snug and safe in Harry's arms. He drifted as Harry stroked his belly then belatedly realized that Harry must have been aching too.

"Oh, Sir! I'm sorry... Can I...? I mean should I...? Do you want me to...?" He couldn't quite find the right words. 'Shall I suck you?' just didn't seem right.

"Shh." Harry hushed him into silence. "If I needed anything from you, Kai, I would tell you. Just relax and stop worrying." He untied the ribbon, releasing Kai's wrists, and gave Kai's arms a soothing rub then scooped him up and carried him across to the sofa. "I want you to rest here and take a nap. It's been an intense morning and we're visiting your uncle later. I thought we'd stop for a pub lunch somewhere on the way. It will break the journey a bit."

Even the thought of being in the same room with his uncle couldn't upset Kai's calm. Harry would be right there with him and he really wanted that chapter of his life over and done with. His past was an aching tooth in need of extraction. Harry covered him with a soft blanket and tucked him in.

"I'll be next door in the study." He stroked Kai's hair. "You've done exceptionally well today. I'm proud of you."

Kai wasn't used to praise but it gave him a wonderful warm feeling in his belly.

"Thank you, Sir," he murmured and snuggled into his blanket.

Harry paused at the door and looked back at the form huddled on his sofa. He could just see the top of Kai's head, his hair all tousled and spiked. A soft snore told him that Kai was already sleeping peacefully. He smiled. He understood how exhausting training could be and he was pushing Kai hard. The young man responded so beautifully to every new challenge. He was a pleasure to work with. Harry pulled the door until it was open a crack, visited the bathroom to wash his hands then went to his study. He settled behind his desk and pulled out the diary he kept about Kai's progress. It wasn't Pulitzer prize-winning material but he liked to write a few lines each day on his observations and thoughts regarding where he and Kai should venture next. He picked up the fountain pen he preferred to write with and jotted down a few lines before reading them back.

K has perfected kneeling and rising. He presents himself well and is able to be still for longer periods. Responded beautifully to light bondage today. A little shy concerning full nudity, but no hesitation. Came on command. Stunning.

Moving to four-week arrangement. Intend to discuss penetration.

"God yes!" he said aloud. "The whole no sex thing is driving me insane." He tapped the end of his pen against his lip. "I need to start stretching him. Hmm." He flipped up the cover on his laptop and clicked onto his favorite toyshop. There were several training kits available with sets of plugs in varying sizes. He chose a set of three in soft silicone and added them to the shopping cart. On a whim he added a locking leather plug harness with an integral cock ring. "Perfect. He's going to hate it!" Harry chuckled. He could visualize Kai squirming and wriggling as Harry locked him into the belt, nicely stuffed with a fat plug. He went to the checkout and paid for his purchases, then leaned back in his chair, tilting it slightly. He undid the studs on his jeans and released his cock with a sigh of relief.

"Anyone would think this is all about my denial, not his. Fuck, that's good!" He moved his hand in leisurely strokes. His skin was too sensitized and within seconds, his balls drew up tight against his body. Harry paused, tormenting himself a little, enjoying the exquisite agony of forcing himself to wait. He closed his eyes and pictured Kai wrapping his lush lips around the head of his dick. One squeeze and he shot hard, grunting through the orgasm that left him panting. He grabbed some tissues from the box on his desk and did a cursory clean-up before tucking his cock away.

After a few minutes spent gathering his thoughts, he picked up the phone and dialed Carey's home number.

"Hello?" Alistair's soft tones answered.

"Hi, Alistair, it's Harry. Is Carey around?"

"Hi, Harry! Let me call him for you... He's supposed to be making me a sandwich in the kitchen."

Alistair sounded dubious. Harry heard him calling for his Master.

"He'll just be a minute. I think he's wiping something up off the kitchen floor..."

Harry chuckled. "Carey's not the most domesticated creature, is he?"

"You could say that," Alistair giggled. "He can't slice the bread straight. I'll probably end up with a jammy doorstop. Oh… Here he is."

There was some shuffling as Alistair transferred the handset to Carey.

"Harry?"

"Hi, Carey."

"Oh thank God! You've saved me from death by strawberry jam. Fuck, that stuff is sticky."

"So Alistair is making his own sandwich then?"

"He is now. I should have let him do it from the start, but feeding a sub after a scene is the Dom's responsibility."

Harry snorted. "I don't think Alistair will think any the less of you if you stay out of the kitchen. In fact, he'll probably kiss your boots in gratitude."

Carey sighed. "You're probably right. Enough about me and my culinary issues — how's Kai?"

It was Harry's turn to sigh. "Stunning. He's hooked me, Carey, good and proper. He's like an eager puppy and just as endearing. We are making great progress. We've agreed to move to four-week contracts."

"That's fantastic. You two are great together. Alistair and I hope that this will be a long-term thing for you."

"That's what I want too, but he's very young, Carey. I don't want to trap him into a serious relationship if he wants to be out there experimenting and having fun."

"Kai needs stability and a firm hand. He's a sub through and through. The last thing he needs is to be left to drift on his own and you know it, so put that guilt away."

Harry rolled his shoulders and glared at the phone. "I hate it when you're right, Carey. I want to remove the 'no sex' clause from the contract."

Carey laughed. "To be honest, I'm amazed you've lasted this long. Have you discussed this with Kai yet?"

"No. This afternoon we have a long drive to his uncle's place. It'll be a great chance to talk."

"Good." The sound of papers shuffling told Harry that Carey was leafing through some documents. "As we discussed, I've arranged for a solicitor to meet you there. His name is... Hold on a minute... Ah, here we are... His name's Blair Anderson. He works for a regional branch of the firm I use. You've met Richard Muir at the club. He's my solicitor and he recommended Blair personally. He's been briefed on the situation and will know the right questions to ask. I'll text you his number, in case you need to get hold of him."

"Thanks, Carey. I really appreciate your help on this. I'm convinced that there's something not quite right about Uncle Francis. I can't imagine that Kai's parents would have knowingly left him in such a difficult financial situation. Kai's completely in the dark and he was so young when his parents died that he's never known anything different." Harry frowned. As if being orphaned hadn't been enough for Kai to deal with, he'd grown up with a man who was at the very least cold and manipulative — at worst an abusive liar. Harry's money was on the latter option.

"Well, let me know how you get on," Carey said. "Are you intending to drive back tonight?"

"Yes. Neither of us has to be up tomorrow and the roads will be quiet later on. We'll probably stop for something to eat on the way but I want Kai safely back here, in his own bed." Harry would much rather that Kai shared *his* bed and he intended that it would be the case sooner rather than later.

"Drive safe. We'll see you at work as usual on Thursday. I think Alistair has plans for a film night with Kai and Christian once they've finished work."

Harry chuckled. "Kai will love that. He's very grateful for his kitchen job but I think prepping veggies gets old pretty fast. See you Thursday." He ended the call and pulled up Google Maps on the computer. He wanted to plan the route for the journey to Kai's uncle's place. From central London, Harry judged that the drive would take about three hours, if they didn't hit traffic. The weather forecast wasn't great, with heavy showers due to arrive by mid-afternoon. Harry was glad he'd opted to take the car rather than the bike. It would be a long trip for an inexperienced biker like Kai and too difficult to talk, even with the helmet mics he'd had installed.

Wells-next-the-Sea sat about a mile inland from the north Norfolk coast, with Cromer to the east and Hunstanton to the west. Kai's uncle didn't live in the small town but in a tiny hamlet about half a mile away. It looked quite isolated and Harry wondered what it must have been like for Kai growing up there. Kai didn't volunteer much information about his childhood, and Harry didn't like to interrogate him. Kai would talk when he was ready, and Harry was happy to wait. He did a bit of research on good pubs in the area and noted the postcodes of a couple of possibilities. He checked his watch. Kai had been napping for half an hour.

"Time to wake the sleeping beauty." Harry pushed back his chair and walked through to the lounge. He bent over Kai and brushed a stray strand of hair away from his eyes. "Time to wake up, sweetness."

Kai snuffled and clutched his blanket close. Harry chuckled. "Wake up, sleepyhead."

Kai opened his eyes and blinked. "Hello, Sir. Is it time to go? I was having a lovely dream about you."

"Were you now?" Harry liked the idea that he remained in Kai's head even when he was asleep. "You can tell me about it in the car, if you can still remember. Go and have a quick shower. We need to leave in about half an hour. I'm going to get the car from the garage and bring it round to the front of the house."

Kai yawned. "'Kay. A shower will wake me up." He stood and let the blanket fall to the floor.

Harry licked his lips before he even noticed what he was doing. Kai's lithe, naked body begged to be tasted and kissed. Harry wanted to raise a few marks on the pristine skin. Everyone needed to know that Kai was his.

"Oh!" Kai realized that he was bare. He bent to grab the discarded blanket.

"No." Harry stopped him with the brief command. "You'll be naked in the house from now on, so you might as well get used to it."

"I will?" Kai's pretty eyes widened.

"You will." Harry paused, giving Kai the chance to protest, but he didn't. His cheeks pinked and he lowered his eyes.

"Yes, Sir."

Harry pulled his sweet sub into a hug, soothing away the worry. "You have a beautiful body, Kai. I want it on display for me."

Kai trembled in Harry's arms. Harry kissed the top of his head. "Hey now, there's no need to be scared."

"I'm not scared, Sir," Kai mumbled against Harry's chest. "You're making me hard and you said I can't come without permission. How am I going to stand being in a car all afternoon with you?"

Harry laughed. "You have my permission to jack off in the shower. I'd help you out myself, but if I do that, we'll never get on the road. This is a one-off thing, though, Kai, for exceptional circumstances."

"I understand, Sir." He sounded resigned. Harry gave Kai's arse a little pat and sent him off to the bathroom.

Chapter Five

Kai had never been anywhere near a Porsche before. He let his fingers drift across the soft leather of his seat. It was so supple and a gorgeous shade of honey-tinged cream. He wondered what a collar in the same color would look like against his skin. *Too pale. It wouldn't show up enough.* He touched his bare throat. *I think I'd like leather rather than a chain. Something obvious. Something that makes it clear that I belong to Harry.* He sighed. He'd never be a good enough sub to merit a collar. His friends were all so confident. Nothing phased them. *And I worry about everything! Kneeling, standing, touching, coming, kissing...* He glanced sideways to where Harry sat behind the wheel.

"What are you thinking about that's got you so agitated? Your knee hasn't stopped bouncing up and down since we got on the road."

Harry didn't look at him but Kai didn't have to see his expression to know that staying silent was not an option.

"I... I just..."

"You can tell me anything, Kai. Anything at all. I will never be mad at you for speaking your mind. I *will* get angry if you keep things from me."

"I don't think I'll ever be good enough for you." There. It was out in the open.

"And whatever makes you think that?" Harry's tone was mild and curious. There was no hint of annoyance.

Kai played with a loose thread sticking from the in-seam of his jeans. "I don't know anything... I'm confused... Everything we do together makes we want more. I don't know my limits. I don't know if I like pain. What if we're not compatible? What if I get scared...?"

Harry shook his head. "How have you got from snoozing on the couch dreaming about me to this?"

"Sorry," Kai whispered.

"Don't be. You're young, inexperienced and very new to everything. You are going to be uncertain, but, Kai... Never doubt that you have the potential to be a stunning submissive. I've never come across anyone so responsive or willing to learn."

Kai fidgeted in his seat. "Really?"

Harry gave a low chuckle. "It would be in your interest not to question me, Kai. That could lead to consequences you might not enjoy."

Kai's cock jerked within the confines of his jeans. He shifted his hands to cover the obvious bulge, attempting to move at a pace that Harry wouldn't notice.

"The thought of punishment turns you on. Interesting."

A low whimper escaped Kai's lips before he could prevent it. All sorts of delicious images flashed through his mind. Being turned over Harry's lap, bare-arsed naked, featured high on his list of daydreams. He could almost feel the heat warming his buttocks. He squirmed in his seat.

"Could we have the air conditioning on for a while? It's feeling a little warm in here."

Harry didn't look directly at him but Kai could see his smile as he adjusted the temperature dial.

"Are you wearing underwear, Kai?" Harry's tone was low and seductive.

"I… No, Sir. I may have forgotten to put any on after my shower."

"Is that so? Well, we'll discuss your standards of dress another time. For now, I think you should unzip and give your cock some air."

"I should… You want me to *what*?" Kai thought he might hyperventilate.

"Were my instructions unclear?" Harry growled.

"Nnnno, Sir." The ability to speak properly seemed to have deserted Kai. Undoing his trousers had never presented a challenge before, but now, the metal stud fastening and zip could have been fused shut, they were that difficult to deal with. After a prolonged period of fumbling and muttered curses, Kai managed to free his dick.

"Finally!" he whispered, feeling more than a little hot and bothered. The combination of excitement and embarrassment he felt had not deflated his rigid erection at all. He parted his thighs a little farther in an attempt to get comfortable, but within the confines of the car's bucket seat, there wasn't a lot of room to maneuver.

"Sit on your hands."

Kai detected a hint of amusement in Harry's voice. He turned and stared at him.

"I… What do you mean?"

"You heard me. I swear, Kai, every time you hesitate before obeying me, it's going to add another stroke to the caning you're going to get this evening."

Kai lifted his arse a fraction and slid his hands beneath his thighs. He ducked his head but it didn't help because the position gave him a perfect view of his aching dick, standing proud from his open fly, in full view of anyone who cared to look through the car window. His arse clenched. He couldn't think clearly. His head said to cover himself up before he got arrested for indecent exposure in a moving vehicle. His heart would not allow him to disobey. His entire body tingled with excitement.

"Five minutes." Harry's voice broke into his scattered thoughts and pulled them back together. "You'll sit like that for five minutes."

Kai observed his Dom. Harry drove with a relaxed posture, one hand gripping the steering wheel lightly, the other resting on the polished gear knob. As Kai watched, Harry began to caress the gear stick. He massaged the walnut top with his palm then stroked the shaft with his fingers. His eyes were firmly fixed on the road.

Oh my God! I wish he were doing that to my cock. Kai wriggled on his hands. *He knows exactly what he's doing. He knows I'm watching. At this rate I'm going to come without anything touching me! Oh! Then he'll cane me even more...* That thought made him even harder and the gleam of pre-cum glistened in and around his slit. *No, no, no, no, no... Think of something boring. Library... Books... Kama sutra... Fuck... Slicing vegetables in the kitchen... Shit, why are so many vegetables phallic?... Cabbage, that's safe... Slicing... Shredding... Shred rhymes with bed. Fuck.* Kai turned and stared out of the window. The suburbs thinned as he watched — houses were replaced by fields inhabited by grazing cows and munching sheep.

"I hope you're keeping track of the time, Kai."

"What? I… No, I thought you would… Oh fuck." Despondent, Kai stared at the digital clock on the dashboard — the glowing blue numbers mocked him.

"Better start again then. Five minutes from now — you keep time for me."

Harry spoke as if he'd given Kai a gift. Kai didn't consider the responsibility of monitoring his own torment a positive thing. He sighed heavily. Five more minutes. He couldn't remember ever wanting to touch his cock more than he did right at that moment.

Harry turned on the radio, which was tuned into a station playing rock music. He began to hum and tap his fingers on the wheel.

"It's a beautiful day, isn't it? Perfect for a nice relaxing drive."

Kai didn't dare open his mouth to respond. It was an absolute certainty that any words he might manage to utter at that moment would get him into even more trouble. He decided that all Doms, even Harry, were intrinsically evil. They lived to torture innocent, unsuspecting submissives. Of course he could just rebel, free his hands, grab his cock and get some well-deserved relief. Couldn't he? Kai fought back a sob of frustration. He could no more disobey Harry than leap from the moving vehicle. He blinked as the numbers on the clock finally told him that five minutes were up.

"That's five minutes, Sir." The note of pleading in his voice was impossible to prevent.

"Very well. I want you to hold your dick with one hand. Tuck the other behind your back."

Kai shook the pins and needles from his hands. He got into the correct position and wrapped his fingers around his stiff member. It was worse than not touching at all. The temptation to jack off increased a thousand fold.

"Ten minutes this time, I think. Keep your hand absolutely still."

How could Harry be so calm? It wasn't fair! Kai tensed his thighs and willed his hand to freeze in place. Beneath his fingers, his cock felt hot and Kai wondered how that could be considering Harry had obliged him and turned the air conditioning on. The air in the car was frigid but Kai's skin refused to cool. Just like his stubborn dick refused to soften. Nothing was going to have any effect until he was allowed to come. Kai had a horrific thought. What if Harry didn't let him come at all?

He wouldn't be that cruel. He got me into this state – it's his responsibility to get me out of it. But he's a Dom – he probably gets off on watching me suffer. My balls will turn a pretty shade of cerulean and Harry's day will be complete. Oh God, I'll bet he's into chastity play too. I think I'm going to cry. I'm twenty, for Christ's sake. Chastity is against my religion.

During his recent online explorations Kai had seen the range of devices that could be used to imprison a man's cock. Most of them looked scary as hell. He'd still been aroused at the thought of someone else literally holding the key to his pleasure. He'd have to ask Alistair if it was common practice in a D/s relationship.

He'd been lost in his thoughts and hadn't been watching the clock. Ten minutes had passed.

"Time's up, Sir," he pointed out, still not daring to move a millimeter.

"So it is. How are you feeling?" Harry asked.

"Frustrated, Sir," Kai said, jaw clenched.

"Excellent. I want you to start stroking yourself. Slowly. You are not to come."

"For how long, Sir?" Kai asked desperately.

"Until I tell you to stop."

A little tick started just below Kai's left eye. At least with a defined target to work toward, he knew the torment would end. Trust Harry to come up with a way to make things even harder. Kai snorted at the thought. He didn't think it was possible for his dick to get any harder. He closed his eyes and stroked his shaft as slowly as he could. He gasped, teetering on the brink of orgasm.

"Please, Sir, I can't... I have to come!"

"You don't have my permission, though, do you?"

Bastard! Kai thought uncharitable thoughts about his Dom. This was a side of Harry he hadn't seen before. Unbending. Strict. It should have been a turn-off but wasn't. Kai loved the agonizing frustration as much as he hated it. *He's driven me mad. I've lost it. I cannot be enjoying this!*

"Stop."

Kai squeezed the base of his cock hard. The command in Harry's voice was almost enough to make him spill.

"Open the glove compartment. You'll find a packet of wipes. Takes them out."

Kai abandoned his dick and fumbled with the catch. With one hand still trapped behind him, his dexterity was shot to pieces. He grabbed the packet then slammed the compartment door closed. His breath came in rapid pants and his thigh muscles quivered as he wrenched a wipe from the pack. The damned tick in his face didn't let up.

"Come."

"Aagh!" Kai screamed as his release tore through him. He grabbed his dick and thumbed the head, the tiny amount of stimulation enough to have him shooting hard. He moaned in relief, levered his hand out from behind his back and applied the wipe to his dick. It was so sensitive that cleaning up actually hurt.

He dabbed at the triangle of leather seat between his legs. "I came on the leather, Sir."

Harry chuckled. "That's the advantage of having seats like these. They polish up nicely. Perhaps when we get home, I'll have you give them a rub over — in the nude."

"Buffing in the buff, Sir? I think that may be one of my hard limits." Kai laughed, as much from relief as at his own pun.

"Do you feel a bit less anxious about seeing your uncle now?" Harry asked.

"I'm not worried," Kai lied.

"I've told you before about lying to me, Kai."

"Is it still lying when I know that you know it's not the truth?" Kai nibbled at his lower lip.

Harry shook his head. "I don't want to be working out the real meaning of everything you say, Kai. One day I might get it wrong. Honesty is vitally important in the BDSM lifestyle. I can read your body language, analyze your responses but only you can control where we go together."

"So what we just did. What you did to me. That was all because you knew I needed a distraction?" Kai tried hard not to be disappointed.

"Partly, but more because I love making you squirm. The simplest acts of denial can be incredibly effective. I think there's a little bit of exhibitionist in you as well. The danger that someone might see what you were doing added to the experience, didn't it?"

"Yes, Sir." Kai pouted. Harry could see straight through him and they had only known each other for a few weeks. "I must be transparent as crystal."

"You have a beautiful, expressive face. What you hide with words is painted in every expression."

Kai thought about that for a while. He'd never managed to hide anything from his uncle, however hard he'd tried — and he had tried. Uncle Francis had caught him every time. He shivered at the memories of punishment that came flooding back.

"Bad memories?"

Kai gave a wry laugh. "You *can* see inside my head, can't you?"

"I won't push you, Kai. The story is yours to tell, when you want to. But I *am* here to listen. Is there anything I should know before we get there?"

"I've been rude, haven't I?" Kai mused. "I owe you the story of how I ended up at that clinic, if nothing else."

"You owe me nothing. Like I said, Kai, the story is yours to tell and I won't demand it of you, but if there's anything that would be useful for me to know about your uncle, then now would be the time to tell me."

"I wish I could forget all about him, but that's not going to happen, is it?" Kai sighed.

"He was part of your life for a long time, but you're a grown man now. You get to choose what path to take from now on and you have me to help you. Joe and Carey too. I'm sure Alistair, Olly and Aiden are giving you the benefit of their collective wisdom as well."

Kai giggled. It was a good job Harry didn't know what the four of them talked about during their regular video calls — he'd throw a fit. "They are full of helpful information, Sir."

"I'll bet they are." Harry cleared his throat. "And I never *ever* want to know what you all talk about."

"Good decision, Sir." Kai paused — he couldn't avoid the subject any longer. He took a shaky breath. "After my parents died, I don't remember very much about coming back to England. It was a blur of travel, strange people and sympathetic looks. Uncle Francis was waiting at the airport when we landed. I was tired and scared. All I remember is an impression of a big, bearded man in a hat. I must have slept the entire journey back to Norfolk. I woke up in a strange room full of dark wooden furniture. The only color was a crocheted blanket on the bed."

"You must have been scared."

"Strangely enough, not really. I think I was numb. I had a photograph of my parents next to the bed but as time went on, they didn't seem real and my uncle never spoke about them. Life was a round of school, homework, chores, church and, once I was old enough, work. I had a paper round first, then a Saturday job at the village store stacking shelves. I had an old bike and I cycled everywhere. There was only one television in the house and Uncle Francis had strict rules about what I could watch." Kai chuckled. "If I never see another nature documentary or hear David Attenborough's voice, I won't have a problem with that."

"It all sounds quite normal, if a little dull," Harry said.

"It was. I had school friends. I played football and ran cross-country. Academically, I managed okay but my real love was always art. I used the money I earned to buy sketchpads and pencils. That's what got me into trouble the first time."

"How so? Seems harmless enough."

"My uncle flicked through one of my pads—I was sixteen. He discovered that I wasn't drawing landscapes in the park. Most of the pictures were of men. Shirtless men. Kicking a ball around, playing Frisbee, sunbathing."

"Ah." Harry drew up at a junction, signaled then pulled smoothly onto a new road. "And that didn't go down well." It was a statement, not a question.

"You could say that. He built a bonfire in the garden and then made me stand and watch as he burned all my artwork. He also threw on any of my clothes that he decided were too tight or too revealing. Have you ever seen a pair of Speedos go up in flames? Those things are not fire retardant."

"Can't say I have, Kai, but I wouldn't mind seeing you in a pair."

Kai's face heated. "From then on he changed. He went from being disinterested to controlling. He took my bike away and drove me to my weekend job. I had to catch the bus to school. He bought all my clothes and I swear he took his inspiration from old knitting patterns. You know—hideous sweaters teamed with polyester slacks. Ugh. I saved my money and bought a couple of things, which I kept at school, but I didn't earn very much." Kai closed his eyes, remembering.

"It just got worse from then on. Bible classes. Lectures on morality. I learned to hide my feelings. I knew without a doubt that I was gay and no matter how hard he tried to keep me away from the real world, a large comprehensive school full of adolescent boys is a great source of information. If he hadn't been so mean with money, he'd probably have found a nice monastery school to send me to. I managed to keep my mouth shut through two years of college. I know it's hard to understand—why wasn't I stronger? Why didn't I just leave? But he had years to brainwash me into believing that I owed him—that I should be grateful and obedient...and straight. Being here, with you, has opened my eyes to things I was blind to before." Kai realized that his voice had risen and he sounded a bit hysterical. He took a few deep breaths. "I just wanted to finish my college course, find a job and get out of there. Then he saw me." Kai twisted his fingers around the seatbelt as if it were a lifeline.

"What did he see?" Harry asked, his voice grim.

"He picked me up from college as usual, but I was careless. I'd made a friend. A gay friend. We weren't dating or anything. He wasn't my type at all, but it was good to have someone to talk to. I'd been pretty upset that afternoon. Sometimes the whole situation got a bit much and I dreaded going home. Alfie hugged me and my uncle saw us." Tears welled in Kai's eyes and he brushed at them roughly. "That night he beat me. I thought he was going to kill me. He strapped me with his belt, all the while muttering about how I was filthy and diseased, not right in the head. I just curled up on the floor and tried to protect myself as best I could. Then he locked me in my room. He wouldn't let me out—not even to use the bathroom. He gave me a bucket and brought bread and water." Kai sniffled and stared out of the window. "I think it was about a week before he let me out. He stood and watched while I had a bath and dressed, then someone turned up at the door. It was a driver sent from the clinic. He packed me off with a small bag, the clothes I stood up in and not much else. His parting words were, 'Don't come back until you're straightened out.'"

"I'm so sorry, Kai. If I'd known all this, I wouldn't be taking you back there," Harry said.

"I have to go back, Harry. It will be the last time, though. I never want to see that man again after today. You saved me—you, Joe and Olly. Whatever happens from now on, I know I can live the life I want to live."

"I hope you'll want to live it with me."

Kai shifted in his seat and turned to fix his gaze on Harry's handsome profile. "I want to be yours, Sir. No doubts, no uncertainty. I want to belong to you."

Harry felt the weight of huge responsibility settle on his shoulders. It was a burden he welcomed. Kai was everything he had ever dreamed of finding in a submissive. The canvas of Kai's life had been cleaned and primed for new colors. Harry couldn't wait to begin building a new picture for him. It was a good job that Carey had arranged for a solicitor to meet them at Uncle Francis' house — with a witness, Harry might be able to restrain himself from giving the man a taste of his own medicine. Fury at what Kai had been through ran like fire through Harry's veins. From that point on, Kai was Harry's to protect, nurture and cherish. He frowned. It was no wonder that Kai responded so eagerly to any tiny hint of praise. He'd been starved of affection, had had his self-confidence shattered, been bullied and abused for years. It was a miracle that he wasn't more damaged.

Harry checked the satnav and turned off the main road. After half a mile or so, the narrow lane widened and a large thatched pub appeared. He pulled into the car park and turned off the ignition.

"We'll stop here for a bite to eat. We only have another hour's drive to go but I could do with a break. I don't know about you?"

Kai smiled. "I'm starving. For some reason, I feel like I've expended a lot of energy today. Can't imagine why." His smile widened into a cheeky grin.

Harry cuffed him lightly. "Out of the car, brat. It said on the Internet that this place serves food all day, so we should be able to get soup or sandwiches."

"We have to have something in a basket. That's what country pubs are supposed to dish up, isn't it? Chicken and chips in a basket or maybe a ploughman's lunch?"

Harry chuckled. "I think most places have progressed slightly in the menu department, but you can have whatever you like. Come on. Let's get inside."

When Harry got out of the car and circled it to open Kai's door for him, Kai looked at him with such adoration that Harry's face heated. He never blushed. What the hell was happening to him?

"After you." Harry gestured for Kai to go first.

Kai led the way through the back door of the building and followed the signs for the lounge bar. If someone had written every cliché about a country pub down on a list, then this place would have fulfilled every one of them. An open fire burned in a huge grate. In front of it, spread across a threadbare rug, a black Labrador opened one eye as they came in but made no attempt to get up. Horse brasses were tacked along every beam and there were enough knick-knacks around the bar to stock a small antique shop. A couple of tables were occupied but it wasn't busy. Behind the bar, a large woman with her hair tied up in a messy bun gave them an appraising look. For a moment Harry wondered if they would be refused service. With Kai leaning into his side it was obvious that they were together and tolerance wasn't guaranteed.

"Well, me lovelies, what can I be gettin' you?"

Harry relaxed as he was treated to a wink and a beaming smile. "Sparkling water with ice and a dash of lime for me, please. Kai, what would you like?"

"Can I have one of those orange and mango thingies?" He pointed at a small glass-fronted fridge displaying soft drinks.

"Of course you can, lovey. Now how about something to eat? Take a look at the menu while I sort your drinks." The barmaid gestured at a blackboard on the wall.

Harry repressed a snigger as Kai read out the choices.

"Homemade vegetable soup, Stilton ploughman's, Cheddar ploughman's, scampi and chips or chicken and chips... In a basket!" He gave Harry a triumphant look. "Ham and eggs, lasagna, or sausage and mash."

Harry shook his head. "Nothing beats decent sausage and mash. I'll have that."

"Scampi and chips for me." Kai bounced on his toes. "This is so exciting! I wonder if they have those little sachets of tartar sauce too?"

Harry placed the order, then picked up their drinks and headed for a corner table near the fire. A young couple drinking coffee smiled at them, and an old chap sitting alone tipped his cap. There was enough space between them that if they kept their voices low, they wouldn't be overheard, but after a few minutes, the young couple got up and left anyway.

"This is great. The only pub I've been in is a student bar near college. The floor's sticky and the Gents is nearly always flooded," Kai said.

"Sounds delightful." Harry remembered exactly what most student pubs were like.

"Oh, and The Underground, of course, but that doesn't count because it's a private club."

Harry sipped his drink and mused on just how sheltered Kai's upbringing had been. He was an innocent in so many ways, and Harry looked forward to corrupting him. Thoroughly.

Their food arrived, along with a dish of sauce sachets. Kai tucked in with relish.

"These sausages are fantastic," Harry admitted and he swished a piece into thick onion gravy. "How's your scampi?"

"Yummy. Tastes of lemon."

They ate steadily until their plates were clear. Harry
sat back in his chair with a contented sigh and watched
as Kai licked the salt from his fingers, one by one. The
act was intensely erotic and Harry's cock responded
accordingly. He shifted, trying to get comfortable. Kai
looked at him from beneath long lashes, eyes shining.
He took an extra-long moment cleaning the final finger,
letting it slide slowly between his lips.

"You already have a punishment lined up, young
man. The way you're going, you won't be able to sit
comfortably for a week."

"Who, me? What did I do?" Kai was all big-eyed
innocence. He ran his tongue along his plump lower
lip.

Harry scowled. "We need to talk."

Kai's lip jutted into an almost-pout.

"You're going to be trouble, aren't you?" Harry tried
his best stern stare.

Kai shook his head. "No, Sir. I'll be good. Promise."

Harry grunted. "We'll see. There's something I want
to ask you." He paused, trying to think of the best way
to put his words together. "I want to remove the 'no
sex' clause in our contract." He went for the simple,
straightforward approach.

Kai gasped. He went white. Then red. He grabbed a
part-melted ice cube from his glass, shoved it in his
mouth and crunched it.

"So, does it get replaced with some sex, lots of sex or
unlimited sex?" Kai asked, sounding expectant.

"Definitely the latter, but with one restriction," Harry
said, trying not to laugh.

"What's that?"

"Nobody touches you but me. Non-negotiable."

"I'm a virgin."

"I know." Harry wondered where Kai was heading.

"Okay then."

"Okay? That's it?"

Kai grinned. "That's it. I can't believe it's taken you this long. I was beginning to worry that my cute little arse wasn't tempting enough." He batted his lashes. "Sir."

Chapter Six

"We could turn around and go home. You could tie me up and fuck me through the mattress." Kai sounded hopeful.

"Appealing as that sounds, no we can't. You need to get this over with and besides, we're almost there." Harry gunned the Porsche down a deserted road. "Quiet, isn't it?"

"It's always like this. A runaway sheep is a big story on the local news."

For the last hour of the journey, Kai had become progressively quieter. Harry let him be. The ordeal would soon be over and there was plenty to look forward to after the journey home. They made one more brief stop to refuel and shortly after that, Harry pulled up outside a bleak, gray stone house surrounded by a low wall. He climbed out of the car and took a look around. The stone was clad with a dark carpet of moss and the gate that granted access to a short front path flaked with rust. Though not obvious from a distance, up close it became clear that the house and garden were in need of maintenance. Weeds threaded the concrete path in green seams. Yellowing paint peeled from windowsills and the front door frame. An air of neglect permeated every stone.

Kai remained in the car, so Harry opened the door and squatted down next to him. "Come on, sweetheart. I'm right here with you. He can't hurt you again."

Kai shivered. "Okay." He climbed out of the car and pressed close to Harry's side.

Harry put an arm around him, half expecting Kai to pull away, but he didn't. As they approached the gate, another car pulled up and parked behind the Porsche.

A smiling, sandy-haired young man got out of the car, dragging a briefcase with him. He waved.

"Hi, you must be Kai Smithson...and Harry Croft? I'm Blair Anderson. Carey Hoffman arranged for me to be here."

Harry shook Blair's hand when he'd walked across to them and Kai did the same.

"You've been briefed on the background to the situation?" Harry asked.

Blair nodded. "Yes. I have a pre-prepared letter with me stating that we have sought sight of Kai's parents' wills and access to all documents relating to their estate. Fortunately there aren't that many solicitors in this area and it wasn't too difficult to track down Mr. Smithson's. It will take a few days but as we are acting for Kai here, it should be straightforward, especially as he is an adult."

"Good. Shall we go in then? This place has bad memories for Kai and I don't want us to be here too long."

"Of course."

Blair strolled up the path and gave the door a firm knock. It opened immediately, as if someone had been waiting right behind it, and Harry got his first glimpse of Francis Smithson. The man bore no resemblance to Kai whatsoever. He was big and bulky, standing well over six feet tall. Harry guessed that he must be about fifty years old or more, though it was hard to tell. His face was concealed by a heavy beard and thick mustache. Bushy black eyebrows sat over dull brown eyes that peered past Harry to Kai.

"You're not welcome here, boy. You nor your...friends."

Kai edged behind Harry. Blair's friendly expression disappeared, exchanged for a stiff, formal look.

"Kai is here to collect his personal belongings, Mr. Smithson. We will take up no more of your time than is absolutely necessary."

With obvious reluctance, Kai's uncle took a step back. Blair stepped across the threshold, and Harry followed with Kai in tow. They crowded into the gloomy hallway, Harry placing himself between Kai and his uncle.

"I suggest Kai goes upstairs and collects his belongings. There are a few things that Mr. Smithson and I need to discuss. Perhaps there's somewhere we can go and sit down?" Blair asked.

Smithson grunted but pushed open a door into what looked like a small lounge from what Harry could see.

"After you," Blair invited.

Once he and Kai's uncle had moved into the other room, Harry gave Kai a hug.

"Not the most welcoming chap, is he?" Harry tried to keep things light because he could feel Kai's slender form trembling.

Kai shook his head and burrowed against him.

"It's strange, but this house hardly feels lived in at all," Harry observed. "Let's go and check out your room, shall we? The quicker we get this done, the quicker I can take you home."

"It's up here." Kai grabbed Harry's hand and pulled him up the stairs. Four doors opened off the landing. One already stood open and Harry could see that it gave access to a bathroom.

"My uncle's room is that one." Kai pointed at the last door. "This is mine. *Was* mine rather." He pushed open the door, and Harry looked inside, curious to see if the room reflected Kai's personality in any way.

The walls were covered with a faded, floral paper and there was a plain, threadbare carpet on the floor. A crocheted blanket covered the single bed—the multicolored squares the only bright things in the room. There was a desk, a small bookcase and a built-in wardrobe. There wasn't a single picture or poster anywhere.

"I wasn't allowed to put things on the walls."

Harry looked curiously at Kai when he spoke.

"I could see what you were thinking," Kai added.

"It is rather...austere. Is the blanket the one you mentioned earlier?"

Kai chuckled. "Yes. God, this place is a dump. It's depressing and I can't wait to get out of here." He pulled open the wardrobe and tugged out a holdall. He dumped it on his bed and began filling it with a few books. "My art supplies should be in the desk. Could you get them, Sir?"

"Sure." Harry emptied the drawers and added pads, pencils and paints to the holdall. Kai threw in a pair of worn boots and some underwear.

"There's nothing else I want to take."

Harry glanced around. "What about the bed cover?"

Kai shook his head. "It came from a charity shop. It can go back to one!"

They had barely filled half the bag. Kai zipped it shut. His hands were shaking.

"Come here." Harry held out his arms, and Kai ran into them. Harry wrapped him up in a tight hug. "You've been so brave, love. It's nearly over."

"Can we go now? I want to go home."

Harry loved that Kai thought of home as where they lived together.

"Of course. Let's go and see if Blair has finished talking to your uncle."

Instead of standing in the narrow, musty hall, Kai and Harry went out to the front garden. Harry stowed Kai's bag into the boot of the Porsche then rejoined him on the crumbling path. Kai grabbed his hand and held on tight. Harry rubbed Kai's palm with his thumb. After a couple of minutes, Blair came and joined them.

"Do you have everything you want to take, Kai? Your uncle has informed me that he intends to put this property on the market shortly, so this will probably be your only chance."

Kai frowned. "There's a tin in the kitchen drawer that might have some documents of mine in it. I'd better check."

"You do that. There are a few things I need to discuss with Harry."

Harry held tight to Kai's hand. "Wait— Do you want me to come with you?"

"No, I can do this. I won't be long."

The moment Kai let go of Harry's hand, he regretted his bravado. It would have been far better to admit his fear and let Harry accompany him back into the house, but that would have been ridiculous. He was a grown man, not a baby.

I can do this. I'm not a scared boy anymore. Kai walked through to the kitchen and tugged at the drawer that housed the tin he remembered. It was stuck and he had to yank hard to open it. It gave way suddenly, came free of its housing and landed with a crash on the scuffed linoleum, spilling the contents everywhere.

"Damn, damn, damn." Kai quickly scooped everything up and dumped the assorted rubbish back in the drawer. He lifted it onto the kitchen counter and rummaged through bits of string, loose batteries and bundles of coupons. The battered tin was still there. It had once contained shortbread or something similar and his frugal Uncle had long ago declared it to be the perfect size for paperwork.

Kai lifted the tin out of the drawer and prized open the lid. He started to sift through the contents, picking out his birth certificate and a couple of old school photos. He registered a creak behind him, started to turn but was brought to an abrupt halt by a stranglehold around his neck. His uncle was a big man, too strong to fight. Kai gasped as he was shoved against the kitchen cabinets and bent forward. A drawer handle dug into his abdomen.

"What the fuck are you doing in here, you little shit?" His uncle's voice was full of hate. Kai choked and tried to draw a breath. His vision was starting to fade as his air supply was cut off. He tried to shove back against his uncle's bulk.

"Listen to me and listen good. I don't want to hear another peep from that smarmy lawyer you've got babysitting you. If you know what's good for you, you'll get out of here and disappear, you fucking deviant. I thought I'd beaten some sense into you, but no. You had to come back. Digging up the past will get you killed, boy. Make trouble for me and I *will* find you. That's a promise."

With a desperate surge of strength, Kai ripped himself free and took a rasping breath.

"What did I ever do to you?" He turned around and looked his uncle in the eye.

Francis Smithson's face was crimson, his lips twisted into a snarl. He grabbed Kai's upper arm and dug his fingers in hard. He shook Kai until his teeth rattled in his head.

"You lived, you useless fuck."

"Kai?"

Kai took a shuddering breath. "Harry, I'm in here."

His uncle shoved him away, turned and stomped out of the door, pushing past Harry as he came in.

"Hey, are you okay? We can go if you're ready."

Kai grabbed the small sheaf of papers he'd collected. "Sure. I'm done." He didn't meet Harry's eyes. If he did, he'd blurt everything out — the threats, the assault — he couldn't do that. The less Harry knew, the better. He didn't want his lover becoming a target for his uncle. The man was deranged. Who knew what he might do. It took a huge effort to walk steadily outside when his body ached so badly. He locked down the tears that threatened to spill from his eyes and shut out his emotions. Moving on automatic pilot, he shook Blair Anderson's hand, gave him a false smile then went to stand by the car. As soon as a quiet beep announced that Harry had disengaged the locks, Kai opened the door and climbed inside. Even though Harry was still outside, chatting to Blair, Kai did up his seatbelt. It made him feel safer somehow to be strapped to the seat, cushioned by padded leather.

He pulled down the sun visor and angled it to get a look at his neck. His throat was sore and it hurt to swallow. The skin looked a little red but he couldn't see any bruises. He shuddered. For a few painful, gasping seconds without air, he'd thought his uncle might actually kill him. His only blood relative wanted him dead. Kai choked back a sob and when Harry joined him in the car, he gave him a weak smile and turned toward the window.

"I'm really tired. Do you mind if I nap a little?" There was no way he was going to be able to sleep. He wondered if he would ever rest again, but he couldn't face Harry's kindness for a while. He wanted to be alone with his thoughts.

"Go ahead," Harry said softly. "I think I'm going to do the journey in one go. I want you home, safely tucked up in my bed. We'll get back, order pizza and watch bad movies from under the duvet."

"Sounds perfect," Kai murmured. "No pineapple, though. Fruit does not belong on pizza."

Harry chuckled, the sound low and soothing. "I promise. No pineapple."

For once Kai felt grateful that he was small. He kicked off his shoes and tucked his knees up, curling into the seat as best he could. The curved back supported his head and if he didn't fidget, it was quite comfortable. He let the throaty roar of the car's powerful engine lull him in to a semi-doze. At some point, Harry turned on the radio to a new station, which played something classical. Kai couldn't name the tune but he liked it. It sounded like water, rippling and flowing.

As Harry drove through the lengthening shadows of early evening, Kai tried to focus on his future instead of the past. He didn't want anything from his uncle other than the few possessions he'd retrieved from the house. He couldn't understand why Francis wanted him dead. Even homophobic arseholes didn't usually spout death threats. Surely it was enough that Kai was out of his uncle's life for good. After trying to think about anything and everything that might distract him from imagining what his uncle might do to him, Kai finally realized that the only effective topic was Harry. He allowed himself a small smile. Today was a milestone day. Not only had Harry extended their contract, but he'd also removed the no sex clause from it.

Kai wondered how it would feel to lose his virginity. It was going to hurt. He knew that and the thought made his arse clench. He trusted Harry to look after him, though. Harry would make sure that his first time was memorable in the right way. Kai hummed to himself and wondered if he would be brave enough to ask for what he wanted. *I want to be tied down – or at the very least held down. I want his weight on me, pinning me. I want to be kissed and touched. I want to be ordered to submit.* His cock was getting hard. He moaned. *Oh God, did I do that out loud?*

"Kai? Are you okay?"

Fuck. I did. "I'm good, thanks."

"I didn't wake you, did I?"

"No, I wasn't asleep, just daydreaming." Kai didn't want Harry to worry about him.

"Sounded like a good dream. Was I in this one too?"

Kai twisted in his seat and stretched his legs out. He was surprised to see the outer suburbs of London flashing past.

"How can we be back already? What time is it?"

"You must have slept a little. We've been driving for over two hours. We'll be home in forty-five minutes or so. Why don't you tell me what you were dreaming about?"

Kai's face heated. "It's kind of embarrassing, Sir."

"Really? Now I'm even more intrigued. Those sweet little moans and whimpers you made were very entertaining."

"I was just thinking about the change in our contract." Kai didn't dare look in Harry's direction.

"If four weeks is too much for you, we can revert to one."

"I'm not... Oh, you're teasing me! You know that's not what I'm talking about."

Harry chuckled. "Sorry, couldn't resist. So, it's the sex thing?"

"Yes, it's the sex thing." Kai knew he sounded indignant, but he couldn't help it. This was a big deal.

"We are not going to do anything that you aren't ready for, Kai. You don't have to worry."

"Oh, I'm not worried. Well, not about doing it for the first time." He paused. "Okay, maybe I am a little anxious, but, you see, I've had plenty of time to imagine how it will be..."

"And you want it to be perfect?"

How the hell does he always know what I'm thinking? "Yes!"

"Well, that's only natural. You only get to lose your virginity once." Harry patted Kai's knee. "But I can't make it perfect if you don't tell me what's in your head, so spill it. Let me hear all these fantasies you've been cooking up."

Kai pulled his knees up and hugged them. He stared out through the windscreen but didn't see any of the passing streets.

"I know you'll never hurt me or force me to do something I don't want to, Harry, but I want... I want you to... Oh, this is difficult!"

Harry tapped his fingers on the steering wheel. "You want me to compel you? Hold you down? Restrain you?"

"Yes!" Kai exclaimed. "Yes. Is that bad? And how did you know?"

"Dom's intuition. No, it's not bad. Nothing consensual between us is bad. What we do together is our business. You have a safe word, Kai, and if you use it, everything stops. No debate. No question. I will never be angry with you for using it. Do you understand?"

"I do. I just feel guilty for wanting this. It can't be normal."

"Tell me this, Kai. Do you think it's wrong that I want to put you in bondage and spank you?"

"No, Sir," Kai shivered. Just talking about it made him hard.

"Desire is natural, Kai. How it manifests has no rulebook. Providing we are comfortable with each other, what anybody else thinks is utterly irrelevant. Don't try to categorize things into normal and abnormal. You'll just tie yourself in knots. Let yourself feel. You'll know what's right for you."

Kai closed his eyes. His mind hopped and jumped from thought to thought and it was exhausting. He'd spent half the day in the car but tiredness seeped through his bones. The last few miles of the journey slipped away as Harry left him alone with his thoughts. Soon the car was safely stowed in the garage and Kai stood in the warmth of Harry's front hall. Harry dumped his keys on the side table and gave him an expectant look. "Remember what we talked about, Kai?"

"Sir?" Kai's head felt woolly, like a cushion with the stuffing bursting out.

"I told you that I wanted you naked in the house from now on. Remove your clothes."

"Oh! You really meant it?" Kai stared at his Dom.

"I really meant it."

A smile tweaked at the corner of Harry's lips but didn't quite arrive. Kai undressed, folded his clothes and stacked them in a neat pile with his shoes resting on the top.

"Leave them on the floor for now. Let me look at you."

Kai took a position with his feet shoulder-width apart and his hands loosely clasped behind his back.

"What the fuck?"

Kai winced at Harry's angry exclamation.

"I'm sorry, Sir. Did I do something wrong?" He shifted from foot to foot, not sure what to do.

Then Harry cupped his face. "I apologize. I didn't mean to frighten you. I'm not angry with you, Kai, but you have bruises on your body and I didn't put them there."

Kai hung his head. He hadn't even thought about the possibility that his uncle's rough handling might have left marks. Nothing had been visible earlier on.

"There are bruises on your arm, your middle and your neck. Where did they come from?" Harry's voice was tight with fury. He didn't wait for an answer. "Your uncle. In the kitchen. That was the only time I left you alone."

Kai flinched as Harry brushed each bruise with his fingers.

"Yes, Sir."

"And yet you said nothing." Harry sighed. "I should call the police."

"Please don't. It's over. I'm not badly hurt and if you report it, I'll have to see him again." Kai waited for Harry's decision.

"Very well. Go and take a shower, then wait for me in your bedroom. You've already earned a punishment today but I also want you to think about why you should have told me about this. Concealing things from me will get you a sore arse, young man."

Kai scampered up the stairs. With just a few words, Harry had made him feel thoroughly ashamed of himself. He showered quickly and toweled dry. A quick blast with the dryer dealt with his hair, then he cleaned his teeth and scraped a razor over the fluff on his chin. He glared at his reflection in the mirror. "He'll forgive you, idiot. If you had half a brain, you would have realized that he'd find out. You're supposed to trust him, confide in him… No wonder he's pissed off." Skin tingling, he went quickly to the spare bedroom he was using and knelt next to the bed, facing the door. Despite his anxiety about taking punishment, his cock perked into hardness. Any lingering doubt as to whether he was a submissive disappeared. "You're on your knees, naked, waiting patiently for another man to tan your hide and you're looking forward to it. I think that makes you a sub." Kai addressed his comments to his cock.

"Oh, there's no doubt you're submissive, sweetheart. It remains to be seen whether you are also a true masochist."

Oh God, did he see me talking to my dick?

Harry stood smirking in the doorway. Kai needed to learn to pay more attention to his surroundings — and stop talking to himself out loud.

"Of course, if you do enjoy pain I'll have to get more creative with your discipline."

Kai tracked Harry as he walked across the room to the window. The Dom seemed calm and composed. There was no sign of the anger from earlier.

"How did you get the bruise across your abdomen?" Harry didn't turn, just kept gazing at the view.

"He shoved me up against the kitchen cabinets, Sir. He had his arm around my neck, choking me."

"Does your throat hurt?"

"Yes, Sir. It's a little sore," Kai admitted.

"When we're done here, I'll make up some warm honey and lemon for you." Harry came and stood directly in front of Kai.

Kai looked at Harry's feet, which were bare, slim and sexy. He could think of worse things to fix his gaze on. He didn't dare meet Harry's disapproving expression. Kai knew that Harry must look that way— disappointed and stern. He hated that he'd let his Master down. A light touch under his chin had him tilting his head regardless.

"Head up, Kai."

There was no way that Kai was going to disobey. Harry smiled at him, his eyes warm and twinkly. It was so confusing.

Kai twisted round as Harry sat on the bed and rested against the headboard.

"Come up here with me, Kai." Harry patted the space next to him.

Kai scrambled up and crawled along the bed until he reached the pillows. He turned to sit next to Harry, but instead Harry pulled Kai into his lap and held him close. Kai leaned against him, absorbing the warmth and comfort.

"I'll bet you're wondering what's going on, aren't you?" Harry asked.

Kai nodded, but didn't speak.

"Tell me what you were expecting me to do."

Kai made the effort to think before he opened his mouth. He wanted to be honest. "I thought you would beat me. Hard. With a cane or belt. You were angry…"

"And do you think you deserve that kind of punishment?"

"I…don't know. Isn't that for you to decide?"

Harry stroked his hair, and Kai pushed into the gentle touch.

"Your instincts are good. How you are to be disciplined is my decision, but I will never punish you in anger. If I'm angry then I'm not fully in control. I might hurt you, and I don't mean the hurt that comes from a sore arse. I might miss your safe word, not notice something about your posture. Anger isn't safe. I can't promise that I won't ever lose my temper or get mad with you because I'm human and so are you."

"I make a lot of mistakes, Sir."

"Mistakes are fine. Refusing to learn from them is not. I said you would be punished and, as you'll learn, I always keep my word. Tell my why you need correction, Kai. I'll give you a clue—it has absolutely nothing to do with the bruises."

Kai nibbled on his lower lip. He took a deep breath. "I kept something from you that you needed to know. Earlier, I lost control. I made demands. I thought of myself before you. I tried to cover myself... There are so many things..."

Harry chuckled, and Kai felt the vibrations through his body.

"Oh, Kai, you're learning. Don't put so much pressure on yourself. You've earned two strokes—one for trying to cover yourself, and one for hiding the fact that your uncle assaulted you. All the other things you mentioned are as much my fault as they are yours. I've been pushing you hard."

"You've been making me hard," Kai muttered under his breath.

Harry grabbed a spare pillow and placed it across his lap. "This will cushion your middle, as you're bruised. Lie across my thighs."

Kai got into position. The pillow made his arse stick up in the air and he felt very exposed. He jerked when Harry touched his bare skin.

"You have a perfect backside."

Harry stroked him and Kai whimpered. The gentle touches turned him on, sending fire to his cock. When Harry spread his cheeks and grazed the edge of Kai's hole, he nearly came. Utterly distracted, when the first blow struck his cheek, Kai yelped. Heat blossomed across his skin, and he pushed back, craving more. Harry spanked him again and this time Kai came. He couldn't stop it any more than he could stop breathing. The orgasm rushed through him like a freight train. Cum soaked the pillow beneath him. Harry rested his hand on Kai's backside.

"So, it seems spanking is out as a punishment."

Kai laughed, a little hysterically.

"Please…"

Harry spanked him rhythmically, never striking the same spot twice. Kai writhed beneath his hand, heat and pain flooding his system. It felt amazing, so good. Gradually the ache disappeared, replaced by warmth and a sensation of floating. His body spasmed and he came again. He lost awareness of where he was. Any self-consciousness dissipated and he floated in a semi-dream state.

A voice prodded at his consciousness, encouraging him to focus. He resisted for a while, wanting to hide in the calm, quiet place he'd discovered, but deep down he knew that hiding wasn't right. He opened his eyes.

"Welcome back."

Kai worked out that he was curled up in bed, his head resting on Harry's chest. His mouth was dry.

"Wha… What happened?"

"Don't you remember?" Harry asked.

"I... You spanked me... It was... Oh! I came, didn't I?"

"You did. You enjoyed your punishment so much, I felt obliged to carry on. You came twice. Then you drifted off to subspace."

Kai coughed, clearing his throat. "I feel... Wow, I ache." He shifted, and his arse gave him a reminder of what the aftermath of a spanking felt like. He grinned. "I like it."

Chapter Seven

"I swear, Carey, he's a brat in training, not a sub. He's getting more confident every day." Harry leaned on the bar.

Carey grinned at him. "And you love it, don't you? He's the perfect mixture of sweet and shy, mischievous and spirited. Too much subservience would grind on your nerves after a while, Harry." Carey surveyed the club. "It's busy for Thursday night. Membership is up."

"As are your profits," Harry commented.

"You've made some very shrewd investments for me, Harry, and I appreciate it. I have some plans I'd like to discuss with you soon."

Harry nodded. "Sure. Any time. What are you up to, Carey?"

"All in good time. We were discussing Kai, I believe. Have you taken the next step with him?"

"He's a virgin, Carey. I need to pick my moment. Not that he isn't enthusiastic about the idea — he is. But he also has some fantasies that I'd like to fulfill and that takes a bit of preparation." Harry grinned. He had plenty of kinky plans for his sweet submissive but there was no rush. The pleasure would be all the greater for a bit of restraint beforehand.

"You realize he's probably upstairs right now discussing those fantasies with Alistair and Christian?"

"I thought they were having a film night?"

Carey chuckled. "They are. I believe they're watching *Frozen*, which doesn't bode well for the songs we will be listening to over the coming weeks. They also have obscene amounts of processed sugar in all its forms and an unnatural propensity for gossip."

"But Alistair's so calm and centered. Christian seems pretty serene too — unless he's just come out of one of the private playrooms with Becket."

"Three subs on a sofa equals mayhem. Just be glad Olly's not here visiting. Add him to the mix and we'd be looking at chaos on a global scale." Carey tweaked an immaculate cuff and adjusted the gold link at his wrist.

"Are those new?" Harry asked.

"Present from Alistair. He found them on a stall at Covent Garden market of all places."

Carey held out an arm. The cufflinks were fashioned into the shape of little handcuffs.

"Very appropriate." He served a couple of customers with fruit cocktails, casting an eye in Goran's direction. The big man was busy but not overwhelmed, so Harry didn't feel too guilty about chatting with Carey.

"I was thinking about booking a course at The Edge. Joe and Heath have some weekends they run for new couples aimed specifically at inexperienced subs," Harry mentioned.

"That's a great idea. I've sent plenty of members up to Yorkshire for courses and I've only heard good things about them. Most people I know end up going back several times. I've often thought about going with

Alistair. I'd love to learn a bit more about rope work and I know Heath's been training to become a Shibari master."

Harry snorted. "He needs to know his knots to keep Aiden under control. Do you think you'd be able to spare me for a weekend? They don't run the courses in the week."

"Of course. As long as you can give me a bit of notice. Goran can step up to manager and you can make sure that the rest of the bar staff are available."

"It will probably be at least a couple of weeks. I need to check the schedule at The Edge and then call Heath. For all I know, they may be fully booked into the next century."

The muted sounds of Carey's ring tone came from inside his jacket. He rolled his eyes. "Alistair's idea of a joke." He pulled the phone out and moved a few paces away to a quieter spot to take the call.

"Why am I hearing *Kinky Boots*?" Goran shouted from the other end of the bar. "Surely that wasn't Carey's ring tone?"

"It was. That man is sadly under Alistair's thumb. He's a poor excuse for a Dom."

Goran guffawed. "And if Kai chose a tune for you? You wouldn't delete it, would you?"

Harry's face heated. "Okay. You've got me there, but I think he's got better taste in music."

"I hope you two aren't making fun of the man who pays your very generous salaries?" Carey took a seat on a bar stool.

Goran whistled tunelessly and turned away.

"Not us, boss. Never. Wouldn't do that." Harry grinned.

Carey shook his head. "This is the problem with employing Doms. I have none of these issues with the servers."

Harry raised an eyebrow. "I really can't see Goran in one of those leather kilts, Carey. He'd frighten all your customers away."

"Maybe I *should* look at redesigning the bar staff uniform. I've always thought it was a bit conservative."

Harry laughed at Carey's wicked grin. "Good luck with that."

Carey's expression became more serious. "That was Blair Anderson on the phone. He finally managed to get his hands on a copy of Kai's parents' will. Apparently it was a close thing. Francis Smithson visited his solicitor shortly after you went to the house and removed all the paperwork he had filed there. He gave them some excuse about relocating and wanting to use a new firm closer to his new property. When they offered to mail everything to the new office, he refused and got quite angry."

Harry clenched a fist. "I knew there was something not right about the situation."

Carey nodded. "Well, we're lucky that Blair has a lot of friends in the local law community. Smithson's solicitor gave him a call because Blair's firm had already lodged a legal request for a copy of the will. They'd scanned the hard copy and made a digital file. It made for interesting reading."

Harry kept his temper at bay by grabbing a bottle of water from the fridge and taking a long swig. He held the cold glass against the side of his face and let the little droplets of water run down his neck.

"Let's go to the office," Carey said firmly.

Harry nodded. "Should we ask Kai to join us? This concerns him, after all."

"There's time enough for that. I want to give you the details first—then we decide how to proceed. Kai's happy where he is. Leave him be for a while."

Harry took a moment to check that Goran was happy to cope on his own then followed Carey to his tiny office at the back of the club. Carey took a seat behind his desk and gestured for Harry to take the other available chair. Harry wanted to pace, but there really wasn't enough room in the cramped space so he sat, perched on the edge of the seat.

Carey frowned. "You understand that the only reason I'm being given this information is because Kai has provided written consent that you and I can be told on his behalf?"

Harry nodded. "Kai was absolutely clear that he wanted things filtered through us. The whole situation stresses him out and he trusts us."

"The will is very specific. All the money that Kai's parents left—and there is a substantial amount involved—is held in a trust. Francis Smithson is the sole trustee and he has control of Kai's financial affairs to a certain extent. A portion of the estate was set aside for Kai's education. The rest is to be released to Kai on his twenty-first birthday."

"That's next week." Harry scowled. "From what Kai tells me, very little has been spent on his education. He went to the local comprehensive school and then on to a local college."

"Unfortunately, the trust was set up in a way that meant his uncle could do what he wanted with the education fund. There was enough money there to pay for the best private education available."

"So what the hell has he been spending the money on? His house was a dump and Kai had hardly any things of his own."

Carey sighed. "I've no idea and that will be a matter for the police to investigate now. Blair has instigated proceedings with them and passed on the information. As Smithson is not his client, there's no confidentiality issue, though we could have just arranged a warrant if necessary. The more worrying thing is the rest of the trust. The will states that if Kai pre-deceases his uncle before his twenty-first birthday, then the entire estate goes to charity. Once he inherits, that clause is removed and it becomes Kai's decision as to who will inherit from him. That will stand until Kai makes his own will and, as he isn't even aware of these conditions…"

"My God." Harry felt chilled to the core. "Once Kai inherits, his closest relative is his uncle. His only relative, as far as I know. If he dies after that, his uncle would inherit automatically. Kai's uncle assaulted him while we were at the house. He has the bruises to prove it. I think if Kai had gone there alone, he might not have come back. Smithson could have hidden him away until after his birthday, then I dread to think what might have happened. He made it quite clear that he'd like nothing more than for Kai to be dead. Kai inherits in a week. As soon as that happens, he'll be a moving target."

Carey twirled a pen in his fingers. "You need to decide whether to tell Kai before his birthday or wait until he's of age. Whatever you decide, you'll need to keep him on a short leash for a while."

Harry shoved his chair back and stood up. He couldn't be still. "I can't keep this from him, Carey. This is *his* life and he deserves to know what's going on. He might be a little anxious but that should make him careful."

Carey nodded. "I agree. Why don't you go on up to the flat and talk to him now?"

Harry strolled across the club, giving only vague acknowledgments to those members who greeted him. He stabbed at the lift button and tapped a booted foot impatiently as he waited for it to descend. The ride up to the second floor took forever. The urge to get Kai into his arms and keep him there for as long as possible was overwhelming. The lift opened out onto a small landing and Carey's flat was the only door. Harry knew it would be unlocked but he rang the bell to give some warning of his arrival before opening it. Alistair appeared at the lounge door as Harry walked down the hall.

"Alistair, can you get Kai for me? I need to talk to him." His tone was brusque, and Alistair's eyes widened.

"He's not here, Harry."

A fist squeezed Harry's heart and he fought to stay calm. "What do you mean, he's not here?"

Christian appeared next to Alistair, looking sleepy. Alistair came out into the hall.

"He had a message on his mobile a few minutes ago. He said he had to go outside for a few minutes. We paused the film... Why? What's wrong?"

"What mobile?" Harry snapped.

"A package came from the clinic today, posted to Carey. It had Kai's mobile and his wallet in it. Carey gave them to him earlier, before we came up here. He borrowed my charger and then checked his messages when we were having a snack break." Alistair had gone pale.

Harry felt bad for scaring him but he didn't have time for niceties. "Did he say anything? Anything at all about the message?"

"No. Just that he had to pop out and that he'd be back. What's going on, Harry?"

Harry turned and ran for the lift. Maybe, just maybe, he'd catch Kai outside. As soon as the doors opened again, he ran past reception and took the staff staircase to the street. Frantically he looked both ways along the road but saw no one. He rounded the corner to the members' entrance and skidded to a halt in front of the bouncer. "Have you seen Kai? Did he come past you?"

"He did. About five minutes ago. I asked him if he should be out here alone but he just shrugged and walked to the corner." The bouncer gestured down the street. A light rain obscured the view but Harry could see no sign of a figure in the distance.

"Fuck!" He sprinted to the end of the street and took the corner without slowing. Fifty yards away, a sleek black limousine pulled up to the curb. Kai was walking in the direction of the car.

"Kai! Stop!" Harry yelled and began to run.

Kai turned and looked at him, then back to the car where a rear window slid smoothly down.

"Get away from the car!" Harry sprinted toward Kai. As he neared, there were a couple of soft popping sounds, then the car sped away with a squeal of rubber on tarmac.

Harry reached Kai just in time to prevent Kai's head from hitting the wet pavement. He knelt, holding him, trying to work out where the blood on Kai's face was coming from. There was a graze on his cheek but the source of the blood was a wound on his ear.

"Ow." Kai wriggled in Harry's arms and sat up. "My face hurts."

Harry laughed with a mixture of relief and mild hysteria. He hugged Kai close, petting his damp hair.

"Harry, is he okay?"

Harry looked up and discovered a circle of men surrounding him and Kai. Carey was there, Alistair pressed close to his side. Christian hovered next to them. Goran, the bouncer and what appeared to be half the club's patrons milled around.

"Yes. He's fine." He addressed Carey, who looked the least ruffled by the situation. "Perhaps everyone should get back inside?"

Goran began herding people back to The Underground.

"The police are on their way. Can you get up?" Carey asked.

Harry gathered Kai into his arms and stood up. Kai clutched at Harry's shirt. His face was bone white and his hair glistened with a layer of drizzle.

"There was a gun, Harry. They pointed a gun at me."

"They didn't just point it. They fucking fired it!" Harry regretted his words the moment Kai sagged in his hold.

"He's fainted." Harry cradled Kai against his chest. "I should get him inside. Carey, will you wait for the police?"

"Of course. See to Kai. Take him up to the flat and use the guest room. He can lie down in there. Alistair, go with Harry. Make sure he has everything he needs."

"Yes, Sir." Alistair led the way with Christian in tow.

Harry followed, carrying Kai, even when he regained consciousness.

Harry laid Kai on Carey's guest bed and stroked damp hair away from his face. One smooth cheek was marred with a diagonal graze that oozed blood in a messy trickle. A tiny nick in the top of Kai's ear showed just how close the bullet had come to hitting him.

"Why would anyone want to shoot me, Harry? I don't understand." Kai struggled to sit up. "I had a text from Blair. He said he had a packet of papers for me and it would be easier if he just met me on the street rather than coming into The Underground."

"We'll show the police the message. If you get any more texts like that, I want you to show them to me before you do anything." Harry gave Kai a careful cuddle. "Just relax for a few minutes. The police will be here soon and I think I know why this happened, love. I'll explain when the police get here."

"Okay."

Kai's eyes looked huge in his pale face. Harry took his hand and squeezed. "Don't worry, sweetheart. I'm not going to let anything happen to you."

"Oh my God, Harry! I could have died a virgin!"

Kai's exclamation was loud enough that anyone within fifty yards would have heard it. The tension of the moment broke and Harry couldn't stop laughing.

"Don't laugh at me, Sir. This is serious." Despite his words, Kai grinned.

Before Harry could take the conversation any further, Carey arrived in the company of a couple of uniformed policemen. By the way his eyes were twinkling, Harry guessed that he had heard Kai's outburst.

"Harry, do you remember PC Seddon? His little brother is Toby, one of our servers."

"Of course. You came after the fire a while back, didn't you?"

The young policeman nodded. "That's right. I'm sorry to be back under such circumstances. Can you tell me what happened?"

His colleague took notes as Kai recounted the story of receiving the text.

"We were having film night and I checked my phone during a break. I only got it back today. There was a message from Blair Anderson, my solicitor, asking me to meet him outside at ten so that he could give me some paperwork. I didn't think anything of it. I left the others at five to ten and went outside. I waited on the main road and right on time, a limousine drew up. I walked toward it and the window opened. I saw the barrel of a gun... Then I was on the floor."

"And do you have any idea why someone might want to hurt you?" PC Seddon asked.

"I may be able to help there," Harry interjected. He cupped Kai's face with his hand. "I'm sorry you have to hear about it like this, love, but we've recently discovered that you stand to inherit a substantial amount of money from your parents' estate on your twenty-first birthday next week." He pulled Kai into his arms and turned to the policemen. "His uncle, who's already threatened Kai once, is the beneficiary should Kai pre-decease him once he has inherited. The money is held in trust and Kai won't be able to alter the route of inheritance until after his birthday."

Kai gaped. "I didn't even know there was any money to inherit. Uncle Francis never mentioned anything about the will, only that my parents had barely left enough to feed and clothe me."

"We believe that Kai's uncle has been defrauding the trust since Kai was a child. The amount set aside for his education wasn't spent on schooling." Harry didn't let go of Kai's hand. "We only found this out earlier today when Kai's solicitor called. He's already informed the Norfolk police."

The two constables looked at each other. "We're going to have to call in CID on this. It's a lot more complex a case than we can deal with."

"That's fine," Harry said. "But can we continue this tomorrow? It's late and Kai's had a shock. I'd like to get him home."

"That's not a problem. We'll take statements from the other witnesses but if there's nothing more you can tell us, you're free to go. I'll take your address and CID will be round for a visit in the morning. We'll get an unmarked car to sit outside your house tonight. I hope the immediate danger has passed, but please take sensible precautions at home."

"Don't worry, Officer. I'll make sure he's locked up nice and tight." Harry smirked, and Kai's cheeks pinked.

PC Seddon chuckled. "No doubt. I'm glad you're all okay. Mr. Hoffman, perhaps you could help us out with organizing witness statements?"

The room emptied, leaving Harry and Kai alone. Kai hugged his knees and rocked a little.

"I'm frightened, Harry. Does that make me a coward?"

"No, love. It makes you human. It's my job to take your mind off of all this, so if you're feeling okay, I think we should go home."

Kai touched his face. "A quick clean-up and I'll be ready."

* * * *

The ride home with Kai pressed close to his back had Harry's cock aching and hard. Knowing how close he'd come to losing Kai made every sensation sharper somehow. He stowed the bike in the garage and lost no time in getting Kai into the house. The moment they got through the door, he maneuvered Kai against the wall and gave him an aggressive kiss.

"No more wasting time. I could have lost you today."

Kai let out a breathless gasp. "Sir... Please."

Harry kissed him again, demanding entrance. Kai yielded immediately, and Harry explored the warmth of his mouth, nipping at his plump lower lip. He pulled back and gave Kai an intense look. "Do you trust me?" His heart pounded as he waited for Kai's response.

Kai nodded, looking up from beneath his lashes.

"Good." Harry stroked Kai's injured face. "If you want this to stop, use your safe word. If you say 'stop' or 'no' it will make no difference. Do you understand?"

"Yes, Sir."

"Tell me the word."

"Scampi."

"You've changed it?"

"Yes, Sir. I wanted something more interesting than 'red'."

Kai's eyes looked a little glazed, and Harry could feel the rapid rise and fall of his chest. "Are you afraid?"

"A little," Kai admitted. "And excited... And really, really hard!"

He struggled a little, which sent a surge of desire to Harry's groin. He caught Kai's wrists in a firm grip and held them above his head. "You can fight me all you want, but there's no escape. You're at my mercy now."

Harry kept his hold gentle but firm. Kai's shoulders dropped and he relaxed enough to push forward and attempt to rub his erection against Harry's thigh.

"No you don't, brat. Time to play and I make the rules of this game."

"What are you going to do to me, Sir?" Kai's voice quavered.

Harry grinned. His sweet sub was going to play along. His voice cold, he growled, "You'll find out soon enough." He narrowed his eyes and examined Kai from head to toe, stripping him with his gaze.

Kai shivered. He was a convincing actor, though Harry suspected that his reactions were not entirely made up. Kai started to squirm and fight.

"Let go of me. Please... You're hurting me." Kai yanked his wrists from Harry's grip but Harry immediately caught them up again.

He stilled for a moment, waiting, giving Kai time to use his safe word. Kai's lips parted slightly, but he said nothing.

"You're mine and I'll do what the hell I like with you, but fight if you wish. I like it." He shoved a knee between Kai's thighs.

Kai groaned at the touch.

"We're in the house and you're still dressed. That's against the rules." He relaxed his grip and freed Kai's wrists.

Kai immediately twisted under his arm and ran for the stairs. Grinning, Harry sauntered after him, taking his time over the hunt. Kai headed for the master bedroom but failed to shut the door.

"I think my prey really wants to be caught," Harry mused, as he walked into the dark room. A sharp intake of breath gave away Kai's hiding place behind the door. Harry grabbed him, threw him over his shoulder and carried him across to the bed. He dropped him in a sprawling heap on the covers.

"You're going to pay for trying to get away from me, Kai."

Kai stared up at him, eyes bright. "Please don't hurt me, Sir. I promise I'll be good."

"Too late for that. Save your begging. Soon, you'll be so desperate to come you'll need all your breath to plead for release."

"No! You can't..." Kai squirmed his way up the bed until he could go no farther.

Harry grabbed his ankles and pulled him back. "Yes, I can." Harry unbuckled his belt and slid it from its loops. He rounded the bed and looped the leather around one of Kai's wrists.

Kai struggled a little but not enough to stop Harry threading the belt through the slats of the headboard. He brought the other end of the belt through and bound Kai's other wrist. Now Kai truly was at Harry's mercy. Kai tugged at his bonds a few times, testing their strength.

"You'll bruise yourself if you keep doing that." Harry liked the idea of marks on Kai's body. Apparently so did Kai, because he tugged even harder.

"You can't do this to me! Let me go."

"I don't think so. I can do anything I want to you now and you won't be able to stop me." Of course Kai could, if he wanted to. His safe word would bring everything to a halt and Harry would make sure to give Kai every opportunity to use it.

Harry stared down at Kai. "You look hot, tied there for my pleasure, but I think the picture can be improved." He shrugged off his jacket and threw it onto a chair. "Let's see what you're trying so hard to keep from me." Harry undid the stud fastening on Kai's waistband and lowered the zip. He left it hanging open and moved to the end of the bed where he pulled off Kai's boots and socks. Grasping the end of each trouser leg, he gave a sharp tug, pulling the garment down. "No underwear, you little whore? You really are asking for it, aren't you?"

Kai's engorged cock jutted up from his body, the plump head gleaming with pre-cum.

"I'm going to take your arse so hard, you won't walk straight for a week."

Kai whimpered. "No!"

"Oh yes." Harry trailed his fingertips the full length of Kai's body, allowing his nails to scrape Kai's skin. He pushed up Kai's T-shirt until his nipples were exposed, then spent a little time pinching them into hardened peaks. "Your body betrays you. You want this, however much you protest."

"No! I don't... Please let me go." Despite his words, Kai arched his body, seeking more contact.

Harry denied him and moved away, enjoying the look of desperation that shadowed Kai's pretty features. Harry went to the dresser drawer and retrieved the set of plugs he'd bought online. His fingers hovered over the biggest of the three, but he settled on the middle sized one, which had a nicely tapered end. He pumped some lube into his hand and gave the plug a good coating. Returning to the bed, he shoved Kai's knees apart. Before his surprised sub had time to react, Harry pressed the end of the plug against his rosy pucker. There was a little resistance before the toy slid smoothly home. It wasn't so big that Kai needed to be stretched first and Kai's channel grabbed it greedily, pulling it inside his body.

Kai squeaked. "Oh! No... Take it out. Take it out!" But he wriggled and pushed his arse against the mattress, driving the plug deeper.

"I want you ready for me. Think yourself lucky I'm taking the time to prepare you at all."

Harry undressed, leaving just his leather trousers on. He climbed onto the bed and straddled Kai's body before lowering his short zipper. His rigid cock slipped free and he made sure that Kai had a good view.

"You have a pretty mouth. It's time those lips were wrapped around my cock."

"No." Kai shook his head then turned it to the side, pressing his cheek against the pillow.

"Yes." Harry grabbed Kai's chin and turned his head. He gripped Kai's hair. Holding him firmly in place.

"Open your mouth, you little cocksucker, or I may lose patience with you. Even a hint of teeth and I'll whip you raw."

Kai blinked rapidly. Harry pushed his cock against Kai's lips, and Kai opened for him. Harry pushed forward, filling Kai's mouth until he touched the back of his throat. Kai gagged and choked, so Harry withdrew and gave him a moment to recover before pushing forwards again. This time Kai coped better. He even lapped a little, bathing Harry's dick with warmth.

"God, that's fantastic." Harry fucked Kai's mouth as hard as he dared. With his hands bound, Kai could do nothing but acquiesce, and Harry was careful not to overwhelm him. He was close to the edge anyway and would have to stop or come down Kai's throat. He wanted to save that pleasure for when he was buried deep in Kai's arse.

Harry retreated, leaving a shocked-looking Kai staring up at him. He stripped off his trousers and fetched condoms and lube from the dresser before resuming his position, straddling Kai's hips. Harry gave his aching cock a couple of strokes before smoothing on the latex and slicking himself up. He raised Kai's arse until it rested on his thighs. Kai's legs spread to either side of Harry's hips.

"I'm going to fuck you, now," Harry said starkly, as he found the end of the plug and twisted the toy.

Kai gasped and his eyes rolled back.

"But I want you to beg. Beg me to take you, Kai."

Harry manipulated the plug. Pulling it in and out of Kai's channel, angling it so that the rubber pressed against Kai's prostate. Kai screamed and thrashed.

"No! Never, you bastard."

"Beg me." Harry's grasped Kai's cock and tugged a couple of times. He stroked his thumb over the leaking tip and pressed his nail into Kai's slit.

"Fuck, fuck, fuck... Please!"

"Say, 'Please fuck me, Sir.'"

Harry withdrew the plug, leaving Kai empty. The black of Kai's pupils had expanded to cover almost all the color in his irises. He panted hard.

"Please. Fuck me, Sir. Do anything you want... Just fuck me. Fill me. Please!"

Harry turned Kai over onto his stomach. He struggled a bit more and the leather belt dug into his wrists. Harry shoved a couple of pillows beneath Kai's hips, raising his arse in the air. He gave the smooth, creamy flesh a couple of hard spanks.

"You want this. You need it." He gripped Kai's hips and probed his hole with a lube-slicked finger. The plug had loosened his muscles a little but he was still very tight. Harry pushed in a second finger and slapped Kai's arse simultaneously.

"Fuck me, you monster. If you're going to do it, then do it!" Kai yelled.

Harry positioned his cock at Kai's entrance and pushed in slowly. Despite their role-playing, there was no way he would risk damaging Kai's virgin hole by being too aggressive.

"You asked for it!" Harry pushed the rest of the way in. *Oh God, he's so fucking tight. Feels so good.*

"Oh, it hurts! Let me go... Please stop!"

Harry paused. Kai's cries were so plaintive that he almost believed them, but Kai pushed back, drawing him in deeper.

"Not gonna happen." Harry pulled back until his shaft was almost free of Kai's body, then drove forward hard.

Kai cried out. "Oh, God!"

"Beg me for more." Harry canted his hips and thrust again and again.

"Yes, so good! Please..." Kai slipped out of character and babbled continuously, begging for more.

"Mine!" Harry pounded into Kai's wonderfully receptive arse.

Kai screamed, the sound raw and primitive as he came. Harry knew from the arch of Kai's body and the scent filling the air. He thrust into Kai's arse, heart pounding, stars floating before his eyes. The hot rush of orgasm flooded his body and he came with a triumphant yell. He collapsed on top of Kai, pressing him down before realizing that he must be crushing his young lover. He rolled away and fumbled with the belt holding Kai's wrists until it fell free. He just had time to strip off the condom and dispose of it before he found himself with an armful of ecstatic sub.

"So good, Sir. So perfect." Kai snuggled against Harry's chest and planted little kisses on his skin. "When can we do that again?"

"Well, I hate to tell you this, love, but you can only lose your virginity once."

Kai giggled. "That's not what I meant and you know it. The role-play... It was so hot. I can't believe what a great actor you are. I have dreams of so many scenes we can play at. You'd make a great pirate or a highwayman or..."

"So you predict a certain amount of ravishment in your future?" Harry could definitely go along with those plans, especially if it left Kai as sated and blissed out as he seemed to be at that moment.

"Ravished. That's a great word." Kai hummed and scattered more kisses along Harry's collarbone. It tickled.

"I didn't hurt you?"

"No. Well, it burned a little at first—actually a lot—but then the pain disappeared and all my senses exploded. I never imagined in a million years that it would feel so good."

"You're great for my ego, Kai." Harry stroked smooth skin and allowed his fingers to roam toward the swell of Kai's arse. His cock was making a stubborn attempt to get hard again. "But I'll show some restraint until you've had a chance to recover. You'll be sore for a while."

Kai lifted his head and his eyes sparkled. "My mouth's not sore, Sir." He disappeared beneath the covers and it was Harry's turn to gasp.

Chapter Eight

Kai chopped vegetables into even pieces as fast as he could without getting careless. The knife he was using was very sharp and he had no desire to lose a finger. The movements were automatic enough that he could let his mind drift a little as he worked but he kept half an eye on the chef. The man had a temper and wasn't averse to dishing out a clip round the ear every now and again. The tip of Kai's ear was still sore from where the bullet had taken a little nick. His face itched as well, along the groove channeled by the same bullet. The wound had healed fine and wasn't deep enough to scar, but the temptation to scratch was driving him mad. He grabbed a carrot that was rolling across the chopping board in an effort to escape the knife. "Oh no you don't!" Kai hummed as he massacred the innocent root and tossed the pieces into a waiting pan of water. He shifted his weight and smiled as his arse reminded him of the previous night's activities. Harry had fulfilled every fantasy Kai had ever had about losing his virginity and now he had a pleasant ache, deep inside, as a memento.

Several other people were working at their stations. Kai knew some of them well enough to say hello to, but not well. The kitchen was busy, and Chef didn't encourage idle chatter during prep time, so Kai worked diligently and answered the occasional question thrown his way. An unexpected tap on the shoulder startled him so much that the paring knife flew from his hand. He whirled around, half expecting to see the knife sticking out of Chef's back but it was embedded in a cupboard door behind him. Alistair's gasp overlapped his own frantic apology.

"Oh my God, oh my God! I'm sorry!"

Alistair pulled the knife from its resting place and put it carefully on the counter. "I'm really not into knife play, Kai. Maybe this is something you should talk about with Harry?"

"I'm not… I mean, I don't think… What's knife play?" Kai's face heated.

"I'll have to tell you about it later." Alistair grinned. "Carey wants to talk to you and he's waiting in his office."

"Oh." Kai's stomach lurched. "I haven't done anything wrong, have I? I mean apart from trying to decapitate you. You're not going to tell Carey about that, are you? I don't think he'd be very happy about it." He slipped off his kitchen coat and hung it on a peg. Underneath he wore a thin white T-shirt and chinos. He smoothed the shirt and looked nervously at Alistair.

"Don't panic. It's nothing bad and if you had done something naughty, then it would be Harry's job to deal with you, not Carey's."

"I wouldn't mind another spanking," Kai murmured. "I should misbehave more."

"And as soon as you play up because you crave punishment, Harry will think up something you really don't enjoy."

"Doms are like that, aren't they? Does Carey seem to know what you're thinking all the time? I swear Harry's a mind reader. He seems to know what I need even before I know myself." Kai followed Alistair out of the kitchen and into the club.

With an hour or so to go before opening time, the place was unnaturally quiet. Somewhere, one of the cleaning crew was running a vacuum around, but the sound was distant and faint.

"A good Dom like Harry can read people. He needs to understand you and in time you'll learn to understand him too. You'll anticipate his desires just as much as he seems to know yours."

Kai sighed. "He must get sick of how green I am."

"Oh I doubt that!"

Alistair knocked on Carey's office door then pushed it open.

"Hello, Sir, I found him. Had to drag him out of the kitchen, kicking and screaming."

Carey sat behind his desk. Harry occupied the guest chair in front of it and he gave Kai a quizzical look.

"There may have been an incident with a knife, Sir, but I promise I wasn't resisting."

Alistair dissolved into giggles.

"I think it's probably best if Harry and I don't know the details of whatever the two of you have been up to," Carey said with a sigh.

Harry patted his lap and Kai immediately scurried across and clambered into his embrace. Alistair turned to go.

"Oh, please stay," Kai cried out.

"Yes, of course you must stay. Come here, darling." Carey moved his chair back so that Alistair could mirror Kai's position. Alistair gave a shy smile and went to Carey.

"Now we're all settled, I have some news for you, Kai. I've just been on the phone with PC Seddon. He said that they've just heard back from forensics and the bullets fired at you yesterday were plastic."

Kai blinked. "Oh wow, really? So my uncle wasn't trying to kill me after all?"

Harry stroked his hair. "Think about it, Kai. There's no value to your uncle in your death until after your twenty-first birthday. The gun was probably a scare tactic, an effective way of getting you on the ground so you couldn't run, but then I appeared and kidnappers do not want witnesses. The shots were badly aimed, though, if you'd been hit in the head or face rather than just grazed I dread to think what might have happened. Plastic bullets are still dangerous but I think it's more likely that he wanted you taken somewhere, held until after your birthday and then…"

"Oh my God!" Kai buried his head against Harry's solid chest. "He wouldn't really kill me, would he? Surely too many people know about him. He'd be a very obvious suspect."

"I doubt he was anywhere near that car yesterday. He could have hired people, set up alibis for himself… Who knows?" Harry's words were little comfort, and fear must have shown on Kai's face. "I'm sorry, Kai. We don't want to scare you, but I won't hide any of this from you either. You are not to leave the club alone under any circumstances, understand?"

"Yes, Sir." Kai had absolutely no intention of going anywhere without Harry to look after him. Every street corner and alley suddenly held unseen horrors.

Carey frowned. "I don't want to insult anyone or imply that you can't look after yourselves, but that means you don't go out without the company of a Dom. Venturing out with Alistair or Christian is not an option. If Harry or I aren't available and you have to go outside, then ask Goran or one of the security staff to go with you."

Kai nodded. "I won't. I promise. Fake bullets or not, I really don't want to get shot at again." He touched the graze on his cheek. "I've also been thinking... And I don't know if it's even possible... But do you think I could get a will prepared now? One that will become legal the minute I reach twenty-one? Is that too morbid...?" He leaned back a little so that he could judge Harry's reaction.

"It's a very sensible idea." Harry looked across to Carey. "Do you think your firm would sort that out, Carey?"

"Of course. I'll give them a call and set up an appointment. It won't take long and you shouldn't worry, Kai. Everyone should have a will. You're going to be a very wealthy young man and you should take all legal and financial matters seriously."

Kai chewed his lip nervously. "I want Harry to help me. You will, won't you, Sir? You know all about investments and things and I don't know anything at all. I've never even had a credit card... It's all a bit scary."

"Of course I will, but you need to be involved, Kai. No hiding." Harry held him tight, and Kai's fears drifted away.

Alistair slipped from Carey's lap. "If you're done in the kitchen, Kai, do you want to come upstairs and change? I feel like dancing tonight." Alistair's grin was disarming.

"Can I, Sir?"

Harry chuckled. "You certainly can. I'm working the bar until midnight so I'll be able to keep an eye on you."

Kai turned his face toward his Dom, hoping for a kiss. Harry grabbed his hair and pulled him close, crushing his lips and forcing them apart. Kai opened willingly, giving up all control. By the time Harry let him go, he was breathless and his cock had swollen into hardness.

"Don't worry, Kai… You have a while to recover before we start shaking our butts on the dance floor," Alistair teased.

"Oh no… No shaking of anything!"

"Sedate, conservative movements only."

Kai and Alistair dissolved into giggles as Harry and Carey spoke at the same time. Alistair pulled Kai toward the door. "Quick, let's get out of here before they go all Dommy and decide we need chaperones."

They escaped as quickly as they could, but not fast enough to avoid hearing Carey's parting comment— "Expect a warm arse tonight for that cheek, Alistair."

"Of course, Sir!"

Kai retrieved the bag of clothes he'd brought from home and the two of them went upstairs to the flat. Safely in the bedroom, Kai collapsed onto the bed, feeling a little breathless.

"What a day! Will Carey punish you much, Alistair?"

"God, I hope so." Alistair grinned. "And I think we should do our very best to make sure that Harry makes similar plans for you as well."

"But I haven't been bad!"

"Sometimes it's good to be bad!" Alistair laughed. "Now I sound like Olly. He's made an art form out of deliberate misbehavior. I'm sure we can come up with something that will make you less of an angel in Harry's eyes."

"Oh, I don't think he sees me that way, Alistair. I'm always getting things wrong. He's very patient with me."

"And so he should be! That's his job. He's training you and you're allowed to make mistakes. Me... Not so much." Alistair's eyes twinkled in the lamplight. Alistair stripped off his clothes. "I'm going to take a quick shower. There will be plenty of hot water left if you want one?"

"Sounds good. I smell of the kitchen." Kai found himself taking a good look at Alistair's body and comparing it with his own. Alistair was a little taller and his muscles were more defined, but he was still slender and there was no sign of washboard abs. Kai lifted his shirt and looked at his own flat stomach.

Not too bad. Still a bit skinny, though. Too pale as well. Alistair's skin had a hint of gold whereas Kai's was creamy, with the odd stray freckle. *And I am not going to think about dick comparisons. So uncool.* Alistair had a cute arse too. Kai giggled. Alistair was a good-looking man but there was no spark of attraction, just an appreciation of a fine body. Kai far preferred Harry's strong, muscular frame and handsome features.

After they'd both taken quick showers, Kai emptied his bag of clothes onto the bed.

"Still wearing Olly's clothes?" Alistair asked.

"Yes, I brought some of my own clothes back from Norfolk, but I didn't have any club wear. Harry keeps buying me things but we haven't had an opportunity for a proper shopping trip yet. I don't think Harry is much of a browser. He thinks shopping means going to one shop, buying the first thing he tries on and going home again."

"Carey has his clothes made by a tailor on Savile Row. He tried to make me go with him once, but I rebelled.

There's no way I'm having my in-seam groped by a stranger and besides — I'd end up dressed like Carey." Alistair shuddered dramatically.

"Carey always looks immaculate," Kai observed.

"I know! Wouldn't that be awful?"

"Olly has an amazing wardrobe. Everything's such good quality. I'd never be able to afford anything like he has... Oh, I suppose I will be able to soon." The thought upset Kai and he wondered why.

"Hey, don't think about it. It's a lot to take in and you have plenty of time to get used to it. I'm sure Harry will look after your money and make you loads more."

"Perhaps I could just ask him to give me an allowance. Do you think that's silly?"

"Not at all." Alistair wriggled into a pair of tight, burgundy leather trousers. "Carey gives me pocket money. He looks after the money I earn, even though that's not much at the moment. I far prefer him having the responsibility. It's just another way he takes care of me." Alistair rooted through the wardrobe and pulled out a black silk shirt. "This will do. I can leave it undone — that will really annoy Carey. Now what have you brought for tonight?"

"Black leather. Not very original I'm afraid, but Harry likes it." Kai shook out the trousers. "These are so tight, underwear is out of the question." He giggled. "I have to lie down to get them on. I brought talcum powder too."

Alistair nodded. "Essential. Let's see how you look."

Kai did a good impression of a contortionist and finally stood up.

"Oh my God! You can see everything! Perfect. I think you should just go with the club collar and some leather wristbands. No shirt. Harry will freak!"

Kai thought about it for all of one second. "Okay. I don't have any cuffs, though."

Alistair rummaged in the chest of drawers and pulled out a pair. "Here you go." He buckled the leather around Kai's wrists then helped him with the collar.

"You need some makeup. Eye liner and lip gloss at the very least."

Kai grinned. "Those I have." He went into the bathroom and outlined his eyes. He slicked his lips with clear gloss and gave his reflection a critical look. "I think I'm going to be in big trouble." He grinned. "Let's go, Alistair, before I lose my nerve." Kai marched from the bathroom, then pulled on his boots, leaving the tongues loose and knotting the laces so that he wouldn't trip over them.

"Wow! You look scorching hot. I reckon we'll get about two minutes on the dance floor before Harry drags you off to a playroom for punishment."

* * * *

By the time they got down to the club, the place was teeming. A heavy beat pounded from the dance floor, which was already packed with a seething mass of bodies. Kai grabbed Alistair's hand and shimmied through the crowd. As they passed the bar, he took a sideways look. Harry was just visible behind a three-deep crowd of customers waiting to be served. Kai thought there was little chance that he'd been spotted. He and Alistair joined a group of subs and started to bump and grind like their lives depended on it. Kai bounced and let the beat sink into his bones—the vibration seemed to come up from the floor and crawl the length of his body. Heat put a shine on his skin and dampened his hair. It felt good to lose himself in the music and forget about his worries for a while.

Behind the bar, Harry served drink after drink as fast as he could. He couldn't remember a night when the club had been so busy and though it was great for business, it was also exhausting. He, Goran and the two other bar staff could barely keep up. The customers were patient and good-humored, so he didn't get too much grief. When the relief staff arrived at ten, he heaved a sigh of relief. He took advantage of the respite to grab a couple of bottles of water from the fridge.

"Can you see Kai?" Harry asked Goran who could see over the heads of the crowd much more easily than he could.

Goran grinned. "Uh-huh. He and Alistair have been making quite the impression on the dance floor for the last fifteen minutes."

Harry scowled. He pushed up the bar hatch and elbowed his way through the press of people. There was quite a crowd standing around the edge of the dance floor gawping and commenting. He stood and listened, trying to work out what was going on.

"I could come just watching them. Fuck, the little guy can move."

"If he shakes his arse any harder, those trousers are gonna fall down and I really want to be here to see that."

"Isn't that Harry's boy? I'm surprised he hasn't got him chained to the bar where he can keep an eye on him."

"Fuck," Harry muttered as he overheard comments from various observers. He made it to the edge of the dance floor and his jaw dropped. He clamped his mouth shut and fought back the urge to rub his rapidly hardening cock. Kai was dancing like he was the only person in the room. His eyes were closed and his lips slightly parted. With his arms raised, his lean torso was nicely defined and glistening in the light. The obscenely tight leathers he wore rode so low that the top of his treasure trail was clearly visible. Harry growled. He thrust the water bottles at the nearest spectator. "Hold these." The crowd of dancers parted to let him through, but Kai was completely oblivious to his approach. Harry moved in behind his sub and pressed close to his back. He grabbed his hips and pulled him back so that he could grind his erection into Kai's arse.

"No! I'm taken..." Kai whirled around to face Harry. His eyes widened when he saw who it was holding him.

"You certainly are. Time to go somewhere a little more private, don't you think?" Harry wasn't asking and he could see from the way that Kai lowered his eyes that he knew it. Kai followed meekly, as Harry turned and marched toward the back of the club and the door leading to the private playrooms. Harry measured his pace—just long enough that his shorter sub had to trot to keep up but not so quick that he appeared to be in a hurry. He made a mental note to give Kai some training on walking to heel as they almost collided at the playroom door. Harry extracted the key from his pocket and opened it.

"In." He shut the door and observed as Kai took in his surroundings. His eyes grew huge at the sight of the steel cross, positioned in the center of the room. It was an intimidating piece of equipment and deliberately so. Unlike the other crosses at the club, which were fashioned from wood and heavily padded, this one was bare metal, held together by thick rivets and drilled with holes to allow chains to be positioned at various heights. One wall held a range of equipment suspended on hooks but other than that, the room was bare. Harry didn't speak. He simply waited for Kai to decide what to do.

Kai turned to face him, dropped to his knees and clasped his hands behind his back. He looked up at Harry through his lashes.

"Did I do something wrong, Sir?"

He sounded coy. Far too fucking coy. *Little brat's playing me!* Several responses played through Harry's mind. "Who do you belong to, Kai?"

"You, Sir. Always!"

Harry resisted the smile that threatened. "It's good that you remember. For a moment, I wondered…"

"Sir! I'm yours." Kai's lower lip trembled.

"Half the men watching you dance wanted to fuck you — the other half wanted to *be* you. But you're *mine*, Kai, and I want my marks on your body to show it." Harry paused and let the silence stretch out between them. "Strip."

Kai moved with gratifying speed. He kicked off his boots and peeled his trousers off.

"How the fuck did you get those on in the first place?" Harry wondered out loud.

"Talcum powder and a lot of wiggling, Sir."

"No underwear. Again."

"No room, Sir."

Harry shook his head. "You may as well have been dancing bare-arsed naked — cuffs off, and the collar."

Kai gave him a quizzical look.

"It's not mine and you don't need it in here with me. Now, I want you to be quiet. No talking unless it's to give me your safe word. Feel free to make those sweet little whimpering noises, though… I like those."

Kai's eyes widened and a little moan escaped his lips. Harry couldn't resist. He grabbed a handful of Kai's hair and pulled him to his feet then kissed him hard. Those pretty lips needed to be kiss-swollen, the smooth pale cheeks reddened by stubble friction.

"Face the cross." Harry turned Kai around and left him to get into position while he selected some thick leather straps. He used them to attach Kai to the cross by wrists and ankles, tight enough that the bare metal touched his skin. Harry smirked as Kai tried to keep his body away from the center of the cross — the metal must have been cold. It didn't seem to be affecting his sub's excitement, however. Kai's erection was enduring very nicely. Harry admired the curve of Kai's smooth arse and the pristine skin of his back. He stroked his hand the length of Kai's body, ending the touch at the swell of his buttocks.

"So perfect. I can't wait to make you glow."

Kai squeaked and Harry smiled even more. He pulled off his shirt and let the cool air caress his heated skin. "Now, what to use... Whip, flogger..." he hummed to himself as he went through the selection of implements available to him, before settling on a bootlace flogger. He walked across to Kai and dragged the stiff strands across his shoulder. "This is a great toy," he said in a conversational tone. "Delivers a nice thud, or a sting if I just use the tips. I think you'll like it." He took up a firm stance and flicked the flogger through the air. Kai's arse muscles tensed, and a tiny pang of guilt flashed through Harry's mind. It didn't last. Kai was well overdue a flogging and from the way he was quivering and making needy little sounds, he didn't disagree.

Harry began slowly, laying light strokes across Kai's shoulders. He worked the flogger with a loose wrist action, enjoying the heft of a well-made instrument.

Keeping a consistent rhythm, he worked Kai's back, thighs and arse until his skin pinked. He paused and rolled his shoulders then walked to the front of the cross so that he could see Kai's expression. He looked blissed out, lips parted and eyes bright. His erection jerked and gleamed with pre-cum. Harry gave him a soft kiss, and Kai raised his head.

"How are you doing, love?"

"Too good, Sir." Kai's smile lit his face. "Want more."

"Oh, do you now? And who gets to decide what you do and don't receive?" Harry fought to keep a straight face. Kai was adorable and there was no way that Harry would be able to deny him.

"You, Sir. Please?"

Harry took hold of Kai's rigid shaft and stroked it. Kai gasped and tried to thrust into Harry's fist.

"I'll allow you to come, but it has to be without me touching you. Let's see if the flogger is enough." Harry returned to his place and raised the flogger. He brought it down harder, focusing on Kai's arse, allowing the tips to sting. Only two strokes later, Kai came with a scream, back arching, muscles flexing.

Harry grabbed a condom and lube. He ripped open his fly and gloved his aching cock, smearing it with a thick layer of slick. Much as he wanted to stake his claim, he took a few moments to loosen Kai's channel, using two fingers with haste that was still a little rough. Kai still shuddered with the after-effects of his release when Harry drove home, sinking his cock into Kai's tight heat with a shout. Protective, possessive feelings flooded Harry as he pounded Kai's arse, unable to show restraint.

Kai pushed back. His channel gripped Harry's cock with tenacity. *Just as possessive as me.* The thought pushed Harry over the edge and he came hard, the orgasm ripping through him, unstoppable and perfect. He grabbed Kai's hip with one hand and his cock with the other. Kai screamed and came for a second time, thick cream coating Harry's hand. Harry was glad that Kai was bound in place. His knees were shaking so much he didn't think he could support his sub's weight. He took a few deep breaths and reluctantly slipped free of Kai's clenching muscles. He grabbed some wipes then cleaned himself up quickly before tucking his cock away with some care. Kai was slumped against the cross, making sweet whimpering noises. The playroom wasn't equipped for the best aftercare and Harry wanted to get Kai home as quickly as possible so that he could pamper him appropriately. He unstrapped Kai's wrists first, then his ankles. He checked his skin, which was reddened but not broken. He drew Kai into a hug, careful not to squeeze too tightly and hurt him.

"Time to go home, sweetheart. You did so well. I'm proud of you."

Kai clung to him like a limpet.

"Let's get you dressed."

Kai was floppy and uncoordinated. He didn't really seem aware of his surroundings as Harry helped him dress. He followed instructions in silence, a dreamy expression on his face. Harry couldn't help but smile. It pleased him no end to know that he had put Kai into such a state. He closed up the room and guided Kai through the club, responding to Carey's knowing nod with a brief wave. He found a quiet corner where they could sit for a while and an attentive server brought bottled water, which Harry made sure that Kai drank. Once Kai became a little more alert, Harry decided it was time to go home.

"Let's go, love. Time to go home and cuddle."

"Yes, please, Sir."

They made their way upstairs, Harry with his arm around Kai's shoulders. Kai managed a wave for the bouncers as they left.

In the parking garage, the night air was chilly. Harry zipped Kai into his padded leather jacket and tucked a scarf around his neck.

"Don't want you getting cold, love. Are you going to be okay to hold onto me on the bike?"

"Mmm." Kai giggled. "Like holding onto you."

"Once we get home, I'm going to put you in a bubble bath then soothe your back with warm oil. Who knows where some of that oil might get to…" Harry laughed as Kai flung himself into his arms.

"You're too good to me, Sir."

"Yes, I'd say that was true."

Four men appeared from behind the van parked in the corner of the garage. Harry didn't recognize any of them. Their expressions, however, he had seen before — cold, calculating and utterly ruthless — faces with grim mouths and narrow eyes. He'd seen men like these in boardrooms and on the trading floors. Men who would stop at nothing to get what they wanted. Men who didn't care who got hurt in the process. He pushed Kai behind him, shielding the smaller man.

"I suppose Francis Smithson sent you?" Harry spoke calmly, casting around for an escape route.

"Hardly." The four men formed a rough circle around Harry and Kai, cutting off the exit. "In fact, dearest Frankie was last seen swinging from a tree, and not by his hands, if you know what I mean. Tragic how debt can drive a man to such a desperate act." The spokesman's grin went nowhere near his eyes.

"You killed him?" Kai whispered, trembling against Harry's side.

He got a shrug in response. "Maybe. Maybe not. The police will find a note. Very poetically written too, even if I do say so myself."

Harry growled. "What do you want? If you think I'm letting you take Kai then you're very much mistaken."

"No need to get aggressive. I have no intention of laying a finger on the pretty little rich boy. You're a different story, however. It's open season on you."

The slightest gesture from their leader, and the other three thugs went for Harry, shoving Kai out of the way. Harry felt a good deal of satisfaction as his fist connected with flesh and bone. The first man who came at him had a nose big enough to make a good target and it crunched nicely as it broke. Blood splattered in an arc as the man twisted away with a shout of pain. His companions stepped up and attacked. Harry countered the first two punches and swept the legs out from under one of them with a well-timed kick. He grunted as a blow struck him from behind and two more punches to his kidneys had him wheezing in pain. As he straightened from his bent position, an elbow struck his jaw and his vision darkened momentarily. All three of his attackers were back on their feet and he had to fight more defensively. He kneed one of them in the groin and stabbed at another's eyes with his fingers, but his wrist was caught mid-swing and he lost his balance. His body was left open to a couple more hard punches and he was beginning to tire, taking more and more hits. When one of his attackers drew a knife, he backed up against the van and didn't struggle as his hands were cuffed behind him. His stomach flipped over as the gang's leader grabbed Kai and twisted his arm up behind his back.

"Leave him alone, you bastard!"

Kai struggled gamely but a vicious slap across the face subdued him. Tears rolled down Kai's face, mixing with the trickle of blood oozing from his nose. With a knife to his throat, Harry could do nothing. Inside he seethed with fury and frustration.

"Tell us what you want!" he shouted, ignored the sting of the blade on his skin.

"I want to find out just how much pretty boy here is prepared to pay to get you back."

"No!" Kai screamed, and Harry struggled as two men attempted to bundle him into the van.

"Before he shrugged off his mortal coil, Frankie let slip about your inheritance, boy. I'll be in touch in a few days to let you know how much and where. If you want your boyfriend back in one piece, then you'll do as you're told. Enjoy your birthday — blow out a candle and make a wish. It might even come true."

Harry scrabbled on the metal floor of the van, desperately trying to get a grip, but it was slippery, his hands were cuffed behind him, and three against one were not good odds. He swore and kicked out. Kai's terrified screams rang in his ears. He could not, would not leave Kai alone.

From behind him came a crash then angry shouts. The men pinning him down jumped from the van, and Harry managed to roll himself out onto the floor, landing heavily on his hip. He used the side of the van to inch into a sitting position. To his delight, Goran, the club bouncers and three or four Doms crowded into the garage.

A no-holds-barred fist fight got underway. Harry wished he could get back into the action but he was stuck in cuffs and could only watch as Goran floored his opponent with a single punch then polished his fingernails on his shirt before throwing himself into a seething mass of bodies.

"Watch out for knives!" Harry managed to shout out as Goran ducked a swinging blade.

"Got it, boss!"

Harry laughed as Goran grabbed a thug by his belt and hoisted him into the air before giving him a flying lesson. The airborne body crashed into the back of the van, leaving a sizable dent.

Harry looked for Kai between struggling bodies and saw him peeking out from beneath a car, eyes wide. They locked gazes and Kai started to move.

"Stay where you are!" Harry screamed. Blood splashed across his face and he prayed that it had not come from one of his friends. Sirens cut through the noise and the dim light strobed blue. Half a dozen uniformed police stormed down the parking ramp and the outcome of the fight was determined.

Once the bad guys had been separated from the cavalry, someone released Harry's arms, and he shot across the garage to where Kai was shivering next to Goran. Harry held his arms open, and Kai rushed into them with a cry.

"I thought they hurt you!" Kai sobbed. "Your face…"

"Hey, hey… Calm down. I'm fine. A bit rough around the edges. That's all. Just the way you like me."

Kai shuddered and melted against him. "I was so scared…"

"You're safe. Nothing can hurt you now, love."

"My uncle…"

"Gone, by the sounds of it. I'm sorry…" Harry petted Kai's hair. "He was an evil man but he didn't deserve to die."

One of the policemen tapped Harry's arm. "If you wouldn't mind going back into the club, sir. We need to take statements from everyone and find out just what the hell is going on around here."

Harry scooped Kai up in his arms and carried him up the ramp. Kai clung to him all the way, burrowing against his chest. Carey was waiting at the door, phone in hand.

"I think those concealed security cameras were worth the money, don't you?" He commented with a grin.

Harry laughed. "Every penny."

* * * *

Hours later, Harry nudged Kai awake. Kai stirred in his lap and snuffled.

"The police need to talk to you, Kai. Then we can go home." Harry coaxed him into an upright position on his lap. Kai blinked and moaned.

"It wasn't a dream, was it?"

"No, love, it wasn't."

He and Kai occupied one chair in a small circle next to the bar. Carey was there, holding a sleeping Alistair. Most of the club members had gone, slipping away after their stories had been recorded. Goran puttered behind the bar, one arm heavily bandaged, refusing to leave before Harry and Kai. A bleary-eyed policeman came and joined them.

"Mr. Smithson, I'm sorry to confirm that we have found what we believe to be your uncle's body in woods near his home. His wife will be taken to identify him."

"Wife? But he wasn't married…"

"It seems he was. He has a second address, which he is registered as sharing with her."

"My God..." Harry muttered. "That's where the money went. No wonder the house was so neglected. He had another, secret life."

"The men who attacked you are well known for providing muscle for a loan shark. It's likely that your uncle owed him money. According to his wife, he was addicted to gambling. Without jumping to conclusions, you were probably a way of getting the debt repaid. The first attempt to take you failed, Kai, so they tried a different tack and went after Harry instead."

"But how the hell did they find us?" Harry asked. "Kai didn't give his uncle an address or any contact details."

"Fuck!" Carey exclaimed. "The phone. It must be the phone... And I gave it back to him. I didn't even think..."

"Tracking device," the policeman confirmed. "We had one of our tech boys check your phone, Kai. They're common enough on kids' phones these days."

"It must have been your uncle that arranged to have your things returned from the clinic, Kai. I'm so sorry."

"You couldn't have known, Carey. It's not your fault," Kai said. "The only people to blame here are my uncle and the men he was in debt to. Can we go home, Harry? I really want to go home."

Harry's heart melted at the pain in Kai's voice. He wished he could take away everything that had happened, but he couldn't. He *would* make it his mission to ensure that Kai was never hurt again, though.

Chapter Nine

Harry took Kai's hand and led him into the seminar room, giving his fingers a reassuring squeeze as they walked. Kai was nervous about the whole trip to The Edge, though it was an excited kind of nervous. He'd been bouncing off the walls for days, constantly asking questions about the timetable and what they were going to be doing. In the end Harry had tied him up, gagged him and given him a thorough fucking. The blissfully quiet after-effect had lasted for all of fifteen minutes before the chatter had recommenced. Still, it had been a very enjoyable interlude. Harry smiled to himself. Every day brought Kai further out of his shell and though he was still shy, he was also full of mischief. He'd also confirmed Harry's assessment that he was one of the most natural submissives Harry had ever come across. He loved to please. He responded to praise with the biggest beaming smile and he was eager to try anything and everything. Harry's challenge was to keep the progress of their relationship to a pace slightly shy of whirlwind.

He glanced around the room where three small couches were set in a circle around a sling that hung from the ceiling. They were the first couple to arrive, but Joe had let Harry know that two other couples would be attending the course he had signed up for, which was for new couples where at least one of the pair was new to the lifestyle. The course was just a couple of days long but the agenda was packed and Harry was really looking forward to some of the sessions. This first one was about trust and Joe would be leading it. Harry picked a couch and sat down, pulling Kai onto his lap.

"Feeling good, love?"

Kai nodded, his eyes bright. "I am. Do you think Joe will use the sling? We haven't tried one of those yet. I'd love to have a go in one."

Harry had a vision of Kai, naked and suspended, his arse exposed. His cock sprang to life. *Fuck, now I'm going to have to sit through this entire session with a hard-on.*

Kai wriggled in his lap and made the situation worse.

"Sir…" Kai whispered. "Are you…? I mean, you have a…"

Harry clamped his hand over Kai's mouth. Kai's eyes widened, and Harry could feel him giggling against his palm. He was still having a mild fit of hysteria when the other two couples walked in. The first pair just nodded and took the opposite couch. The second pair consisted of a huge bear of a guy and a dapper, older man who gave Harry a knowing look and stuck out a hand.

"Nice to meet you."

Harry shook with his free hand. "You too."

"Looks like you have your hands full there."

Harry grinned and glanced at the man's enormous sub. "Uh-huh."

"I know… I suppose I do too." The man wrapped his arm around his boyfriend. "This is Alan and I'm Jerome."

"Harry. The misbehaving brat in my lap is Kai."

The other couple took a seat. Harry laid a hand over Kai's crotch and applied pressure. "Behave yourself." He took a chance and removed his hand from Kai's mouth. "If we weren't in company, I'd put you over my lap and give you a good spanking."

"Sorry, Sir." Kai did not sound sorry at all. He batted his lashes and looked cute.

Harry sighed. He was saved by Joe's arrival at the door looking, as always, like a highly paid model. He was dressed in the uniform that all the staff at The Edge wore—black cargo trousers and a fleece with the company name written across the back—but still managed to look immaculate. Olly stood a couple of paces behind Joe, looking demure and well behaved, though Harry spotted the wink that he sent Kai's way.

"Good morning, everyone, and welcome to The Edge." Joe came and stood at a point where all three couples could see him clearly. He then walked around the room introducing himself to the other couples first. Harry lifted Kai from his lap and stood to shake Joe's hand but got a hug instead.

"It's great to see you, Harry, and you, Kai. Welcome. May I?" Joe asked Harry's permission before he gave Kai a welcoming hug too.

They all resumed their seats except Joe, who remained standing. Olly knelt at his side and kept his gaze firmly on the floor. Harry marveled at how well trained Olly was. His posture and demeanor were perfect. He was certainly doing a spectacular job of promoting his Master's abilities. Kai crawled back into Harry's lap and stilled, as if he didn't want to risk missing a word.

"I hope you all had a comfortable night and that your rooms are satisfactory," Joe said.

There were nods and murmurs of assent. Harry suspected that he and Kai had been given a special room because it had been quite luxurious, with a two-person-sized sunken bath and an enormous half-tester bed.

"Good. It's important that you are comfortable while you are here with us. The course can get quite intense at times, so if you need quiet time alone or together, feel free to escape for a while. We want you to talk about the things you are learning and hearing. There will be opportunities for the subs to get together without their Doms and vice versa. Everyone will have different perspectives on the sessions and we acknowledge that what feels right for one couple might not suit another. There are no tests here and no right or wrong answers. There are also no stupid questions. Ask what you need to ask as we go along. If there's something that you are wondering about, then the chances are that someone else would also like to know the answer to that question."

He paused and made eye contact with each of them in turn. "Now, I'd like to introduce you to my submissive, Oliver Glenn. Olly and I have been together for more than two years and he already had some experience of the lifestyle when we met. I have been a Dom all my adult life. I don't pretend to be an expert on the lifestyle, but Olly and I live it twenty-four hours a day. I understand that all of you are already in that situation but that some of you are quite new to the scene. I hope we can give you some insights into the way things work for us. What you take away from this weekend is up to you. At the very least, you will get to spend some time as a couple in a supportive environment." Joe rested a hand on Olly's head, and Olly rose gracefully to his feet.

He undressed, stripping down to a pair of fitted black shorts, then stood quietly with his hands clasped behind his back.

"This session has a dual purpose," Joe continued. "Trust is the foundation of any D/s relationship and we are going to use the sling to demonstrate how that trust has to be both psychological and physical. A sub places his well-being in the hands of his Dom. He has to be able to trust that his needs will be considered and met at all times. Doms must have faith in their own ability to recognize a sub's limits and respond accordingly."

All Joe had to do was nod and Olly moved to stand in front of the sling. He appeared more serene than Harry could ever remember seeing him. He watched with interest as Joe began to fix straps in place, checking their security as he went. He touched Olly constantly, stroking his shoulder, brushing his cheek, and murmuring compliments about how well he was doing. Never having seen Joe work with his sub outside of The Underground, Harry was impressed. It was clear how Joe had gained his reputation as a brilliant Dom. Harry aspired to meet his standards as closely as he could. Kai deserved that and nothing less.

"Lean back, love." Keeping a steadying hand on Olly as he allowed the leather sling to take his weight, Joe turned back to the audience. "A sling is a good way to establish trust. It's a contradiction in a way. The sub is bound and yet can feel weightless and free. It can be difficult the first time because there are only a few strips of leather to hold up the sub's body. Olly was afraid he was going to fall the first time we did this and I wouldn't be surprised if you do too. Over the weekend the Doms will get the opportunity to be tied into the sling—you should always endeavor to understand how your sub is feeling and this is a practical way to achieve that."

Harry looked on with interest. He loved the idea of suspending Kai in bondage. He wasn't quite so keen on trying it out himself, but for Kai he would, and he trusted Joe's opinions.

"Will you try it, Sir?" Kai whispered in his ear.

"I think I will. If I understand how it feels, I can make sure you're safe and comfortable when we try this ourselves."

Kai cuddled closer.

"Are you purring?" Harry chuckled.

"I can't help it, Sir. It means a lot that you would do something like that for me. I love you so much."

A fist squeezed Harry's heart. His vocal chords were paralyzed. If he spoke, it would be in an unmanly squeak, so he just held Kai tight and watched Joe trussing Olly up in more straps. Harry's eyes burned and he had to blink away tears. Kai loved him. He was tempted to sling Kai over his shoulder and carry him off.

"You can see that Olly is perfectly safe and secure," Joe announced. "His back and neck are properly supported. There are multiple ways of using a sling, but you must always be careful to avoid muscle strain. If used properly, there's no reason I couldn't keep Olly in the sling for hours. Now, we'll move on to sensory deprivation. This can be a hard limit for many subs, so you need to make sure that you are both completely comfortable with what you're doing. It would be wise to begin with just one sense. Perhaps use a blindfold alone, for example. Keep talking for as long as your sub can hear you." Joe tied a blindfold around Olly's eyes.

"Olly looks so relaxed," Kai said. "I think I'd be scared. I don't like the dark very much."

"We've used a blindfold before," Harry replied. "You seemed to like it."

"Oh, I did. But it's a bit different being tied to the bed than suspended in a contraption like that."

"Well, we don't have to do anything you don't want to. You know that. It's good to be nervous... Excited.... But I would never want you to be scared. What we do is for pleasure and that has to be for both of us. I wouldn't enjoy doing something unless you were into it too."

Joe fixed a ball gag around Olly's head.

"If your sub is unable to speak, you must have another method of safe wording. If he can still move enough, then a gesture may be appropriate. I like to use a bell ball." He pressed a small ball into Olly's hand. "Once you take away all sound, your sub will feel very isolated. Touch is important." Joe pushed a foam earplug into each of Olly's ears. "Make sure you check regularly that none of the straps are pinching or rubbing. Your sub can no longer communicate with you, which means you have to be doubly aware of everything that's affecting him. If you intend to use pain, you must agree to this beforehand. If you're going to fuck him in bondage, the same thing applies. Do something unexpected and trust is lost." Joe stroked Olly's thigh. "Please come closer and take a look at the way the sling works — but don't touch."

Harry stood and took Kai's hand. "What do you think, sweetheart? Does this look like something you'd enjoy?"

"I think Olly's enjoying it, Sir." Kai gave a pointed look in the direction of Olly's shorts. His erection was clearly visible, as was the damp patch.

"Hmm, I guess he is. I have to say, just the idea of you in that position instead of Olly is keeping me hard as a rock."

Kai giggled. "I'd love you to fuck me like that. You could swing me back and forwards onto your cock. That would be soooo much fun!"

Harry took a couple of steps back and collapsed onto the couch, his mind creating all kinds of delicious scenarios. "I think I may need to gag you now. Any more comments like that and I'm going to embarrass myself."

Kai curled up next to him and snuggled close. "I could suck you, Sir. I don't think anyone would mind."

"Oh God." Harry tried to think of something, anything that might help deflate his raging erection, but came up blank.

Joe came and sat on the arm of the sofa next to him. "You two look...inspired," he said with a completely straight face before adjusting his position to address the wider group. "You can see that I haven't touched Olly for a couple of minutes now. He's used to these sessions and happy for me to leave him for a little while but I wouldn't recommend that for any of you. Try to stay in constant contact. I'm going to release Olly now, and then there will be an opportunity to ask questions. Please feel free to ask us anything you want."

Joe got up and began to reverse all his actions, removing the earplugs, the gag and the blindfold before methodically undoing all the straps. When Olly's feet hit the floor, he wrapped him in a hug and petted his hair.

"Well done, love. Beautiful as always. Harry, could you fetch me a bottle of water from the fridge over there?"

Harry collected a bottle and handed it over. Joe gave Olly a drink and waited until he was settled and calm. Olly knelt at his feet and smiled at everyone.

"Okay. Who has a question?"

Joe and Olly answered questions for the next half an hour, then Joe split the group so that the subs could have some time with Olly and the Doms with Joe. Harry listened with interest to the other two Doms, neither of whom had used a sling before. He had made use of one at The Underground several times with willing subs and was more interested in Joe's observations than the more practical aspects of its use. Gradually they drifted back to their own partners and Joe declared the session complete. Harry was surprised to see that over two hours had passed since they'd started. If things kept going the same way, the weekend would be over in a flash.

"Everyone should have an individual schedule, which has been designed according to the requirements you set out on the booking forms," Joe said. "There should also be a map in your folder. I suggest you take a coffee break, get your bearings and work out where you're supposed to be next."

Olly scrambled into his clothes, then pulled Kai to one side, bouncing on his toes.

"If he had a tail, I swear it would wag right off," Joe said as he came and stood next to Harry. "Did you find the session interesting? I feel like I'm preaching to the converted when it comes to you."

"Not at all. It was really useful to see how Kai reacted to it all. The trust between us has built quickly, but it's only been a few weeks and I haven't pushed him hard yet. It's good for him to be around an experienced sub like Olly. They're alike in a lot of ways, though Kai is still very shy."

"You look very comfortable together. After everything he's been through, Kai needs stability and an experienced Dom. He knows you won't let him down."

"I love him, Joe. It kind of crept up on me and bit me in the arse. I've never fallen for a sub before but he's different. He's so innocent and untried. I love being the first to take him through these experiences."

"True love. Every Dom's downfall. Well, come and join Heath and me for dinner this evening and we can commiserate with each other over the fact that we are all hopelessly manipulated by a bunch of adorable brats. Olly has insisted that he, Kai and Aiden have their own meal together. In fact I think his words were, 'I need quality sub-time, Sir. I need to bubble with people who won't pop me.' They can use our place. Heath has offered to host the three of us at his, and don't worry. I know you'll want to spend time with Kai so we won't keep you late."

Harry smiled. "It sounds perfect. Kai will love to spend some time with Aiden and Olly. It's good for him to see them in context. I think he sometimes finds it hard to understand how we can live the lifestyle twenty-four/seven and still have a measure of independence. He's a very wealthy young man now with a whole host of opportunities open to him. I want him to see that he can have a career and be his own person whilst still fulfilling his need to submit."

"This is as good a place as any to show him how amazing healthy D/s relationships can be. Let's go and caffeinate. I think you have a class with Heath next, don't you?"

Harry nodded. "Yes. I've wanted to learn about rope work for a while. Kai responds so well to bondage that I thought it might be something he'd enjoy, and I know Heath's been training for a while."

"It's just the three of you. The other two couples are less experienced, so I'm taking them through the basics of D/s psychology. They have some very interesting dynamics. I saw you speaking to Alan and Jerome — all kinds of issues there with a big, strong guy doubting his place and why he wants to submit at all. He doesn't fit the perceived stereotype and is having a hard time getting it into his head that there is no one size fits all in BDSM. Then the other couple — Charlie and Piers — that's really interesting. They work together — both surgeons, would you believe? — and they've been a couple for a while but just recently realized that they wanted something more. I think they're both finding it a challenge to accept that kinks are okay, especially the guy that likes to be dominated."

Harry chuckled. "You love this, don't you?"

Joe grinned sheepishly. "It's fascinating. When I went into psychology as a profession, I never guessed that this is how I'd end up using it. I'll catch up with you later — don't let Heath get you too tangled up in knots!"

* * * *

After coffee and the most amazing, crumbly cherry Danish pastries, Harry consulted the map he'd been given and got up to go to the next class. He started off in one direction and Kai grabbed his hand.

"I think you're going the wrong way, Sir."

"Are you sure?" Harry looked at the map again.

Kai took it from his hands and turned it up the other way. "Try it now, Sir."

"Ah. I was just testing you, obviously."

"Of course, Sir." Kai spoke like he would to a toddler trying to get plastic shapes through their holes for the first time.

"I think I'm going to need to spank you soon, Kai."

Kai bounced. "Yes, Sir! But can I get all tied up first? Can I?"

With the map the correct way up, Harry managed to navigate the building and find their designated room. It turned out to be a library and Heath was already there, waiting for them. He wore an identical outfit to Joe but looked twice as intimidating. Harry grinned as Kai edged behind him a little.

"Heath, great to see you. We've been looking forward to this for weeks."

Heath's smile was warm and welcoming. "That goes for me too. Hello, Kai… You can stop hiding back there. I won't bite. I promise. That treatment is reserved for Aiden."

Harry tucked Kai into his side. "Where is Aiden?"

"Working, I'm afraid. Sometimes I think he has two Doms. If Becket didn't have Christian to keep him busy, he'd probably be even more demanding. Still, he'll be free for dinner with you and Olly later, Kai."

"That's good. I like Aiden," Kai whispered.

"Well, come and get settled. I've got the fire going, so it's nice and warm in here. I'm going to demonstrate a relatively simple technique, but it looks spectacular. I wasn't sure if you'd want me to bind Kai, so I've brought a dummy along."

"What do you think, Kai? Would you be comfortable with Heath tying you up? I'll be here every second."

"Harry will be assisting, in fact," Heath said. "But no pressure. It will be just as good if you watch."

Kai nibbled on his lip and scuffed one foot into the carpet. "I'd like to do it, Sir, so long as it's okay with you?"

Harry gave him a hug. "I can't wait to see the ropes against your skin."

Heath walked across to the area in front of the fire. "Come over here and take your clothes off, Kai. You're going to have to stand still for a while and I don't want you to get chilled. I could do this over your clothes but the effect just isn't the same."

Harry gave Kai a gentle pat on the arse. "Go on, love."

Heath moved the dummy to one side and gestured to the coils of red rope lying on a chair. "I like to use red because it shows up so well against pale skin. This is a very soft rope, made from natural fibers, and though it leaves nice marks on the skin, it's not abrasive. The marks will disappear in an hour or two."

Harry picked up a length of rope and tested its weight. "It's very light."

Heath nodded. "By the time we're done, there will be a lot of rope around Kai's body. If it were heavier, it would be quite uncomfortable. Kai, I'd like you to start by kneeling on the rug."

Harry nodded when Kai glanced at him for confirmation. Seeing Kai naked in front of another man, Harry wondered if his sub would be uncomfortable, but Kai seemed quite content and his cock was half hard. Harry resolved to stop worrying and enjoy the lesson. He looked on in admiration as Heath wrapped Kai's torso in rope and tied a series of intricate knots that held Kai's arms firmly behind his back.

"How are you doing, Kai? Is anything pinching or chafing?" Heath asked.

"No, Sir. The rope is soft. It's quite comfortable."

"Good. I need you to stand now."

Once Kai was on his feet, Heath continued the criss-cross pattern down his body.

"Now, stand with your legs a little farther apart, Kai," Heath instructed. "Harry, I'll let you do the next part."

The two free ends of rope dangled from just above the small of Kai's back.

"I'll tie a knot, bringing the ropes together. The idea is that the knot will press against Kai's taint, so the position has to be as accurate as possible. You don't want to be redoing it over and over. Now you take the ends and pass them between Kai's legs. Pull it quite tight."

Harry did as he'd been told. The knot in the rope sat perfectly, pressing into the sensitive skin just behind Kai's balls. It then split into two, and Heath explained to Harry how to loop it, then create a figure of eight which had the effect of separating Kai's sac and lifting his now erect cock away from his body.

"That's it. Very good. You're doing exceptionally well, Kai. Cross the ropes down the length of Kai's shaft and then repeat the pattern back again. You should have just enough rope left to pass it back between his legs and tie the ends off to the loop around his waist."

Harry finished off and took a step back to admire the result. Kai seemed a little dreamy but he was still steady on his feet.

"You are spectacular, love." Harry's cock jerked happily. "How does it feel?"

"So good, Sir. Restrictive but not painful, and the ropes are rubbing in very interesting places. I want to come, but there's no way…"

"If you have him kneel again, Harry, he's in a perfect position to take you in his mouth. The lesson is over now, so feel free to release Kai when you're ready. I'll give the two of you a few minutes."

Heath left the room and shut the door quietly behind him. Harry knew he was not going to be able to resist Heath's suggestion. Kai whimpered as Harry pushed him to his knees. His lips parted expectantly, and Harry couldn't stop the growl that rumbled from his throat. He yanked open his fly and released his aching dick.

"Did you enjoy Heath seeing you naked, Kai? You're hard in front of another man. I'm not sure I approve." Harry kept his tone light and teasing.

"Hard for you, Sir." Kai ducked his head, trying to catch Harry's dick between his lips.

"Perhaps there's some exhibitionist in you, love. How do you like the idea of being tied up on the stage at The Underground?"

"Oh! I…"

Harry stopped Kai's words by filling his mouth with cock. He grabbed Kai's hair and held him in place while he jerked his hips in a slow rhythm.

"I don't think so. You're far too fucking hot tied up like this. I don't need the competition." He pushed his dick into Kai's throat and held it there for a couple of seconds before withdrawing. "Shake your head if you want me to stop, sweetheart. You can't use your safe word with my cock down your throat." He thrust forward again and grinned as Kai scraped his length with his teeth.

"Feisty brat." He fucked Kai's mouth harder. His balls drew up, hot and tight. The fire of orgasm streaked the length of his spine as he shot hard.

Kai hummed, sucked and licked him clean, making happy little noises. Harry glanced down and was pleased to see Kai's bound cock bobbing. It would be fun to keep him wanting for a while.

"If you behave for the rest of the day, I may let you come later."

Kai wriggled, trying to gain some friction against his shaft, but the ropes didn't budge.

"Come without permission and I'll lock you in chastity for the rest of the weekend," Harry said quietly as he zipped up his trousers.

Kai stilled instantly and looked up at him with sad eyes.

"Oh don't try the whole puppy-dog thing." Harry chuckled. "It won't get you anywhere."

Kai stuck out his lower lip.

"And neither will that!"

Harry released the ends of the ropes and gradually reversed the knotting process. It took a while and when he was done Kai limbs were dented and marked. He pulled him into a hug and rubbed his arms.

"Okay? Not too sore?"

"No, Sir. It was really hot. Do you think you'll take more lessons?"

"Would you like that?"

"If you practice on me, Sir." Kai gave him a cheeky grin.

* * * *

That night Kai lay in bed, warm and happy. He looked up at the partial canopy above him and admired the rich embroidery. The room he and Harry had been allocated was gorgeous.

"This bed is sooo comfortable, Sir, and the pillows are all...poofy."

"Poofy?" Harry prodded a pillow. "They are soft."

"Like baby clouds, Sir."

Harry came and sat on the edge of the bed. He was shirtless, and Kai couldn't tear his gaze away from the hard, muscled plains of Harry's chest. He whimpered.

"Are you all right, Kai? You look a little pale." Harry dragged the covers down, revealing Kai's naked body. "Could it be something to do with this?"

"Sir! Please!" Kai squirmed as Harry lifted his cock, which was imprisoned in a clear acrylic tube, fastened with a tiny padlock.

"It was fortuitous that I packed this, considering the session we had with Heath this afternoon."

Kai spread his legs, hoping to tempt Harry into releasing him. "Yes, Sir. Very good planning on your part," he said dryly. "I feel sorry for Aiden, though. If Heath tests all those chastity devices he showed us on Aiden, then he probably only gets to come once a month."

Harry chuckled. "Some of them were rather extreme, weren't they? Did you see the cock ring with the spikes on the inside?"

Kai shivered. "That was one of the scariest things I've ever seen. You don't have one of those in your bag, do you?"

"Not today."

Kai sucked in his breath. 'Not today' meant that maybe Harry had one of those evil things at home somewhere. Having his cock locked away was not fun at all. Heath's session on edging and chastity play had been intriguing, but to Kai's mind, Harry had been a little bit too interested in some of Heath's suggestions.

"Your dick looks pretty, all nice and secure. Perhaps in a week or so, I'll remember where I put the key." Harry's wicked smile sent shivers down Kai's spine.

"The key is on the same ring as your car keys, Sir. You told me that earlier." Kai pouted. "I had this thing on all through dinner with Olly and Aiden. They both guessed I was wearing it too! They teased me. A lot."

Harry bent down and kissed him. Kai opened for his master and enjoyed the hard press of Harry's lips against his own.

"Hands and knees," Harry ordered.

Kai flipped over and stuck his arse in the air.

"Did they guess you had this in as well?" Harry jiggled the bulbous plug that filled Kai's channel.

He moaned. The plug hit his gland continually but he couldn't get hard. It was torture. He clawed at the sheets, then screamed when Harry spanked him a couple of times, driving the plug deeper.

"It's good to know you're eager and ready for me."

The sound of a condom packet ripping and the squirt of lube reached Kai's ears. Harry twisted the plug free and pressed the blunt end of his cock against Kai's hole. "Shall I fuck you like this? Keep you frustrated and needy?"

Kai wanted to beg and plead but he didn't. He took a deep breath. "Whatever pleases you, Sir." It felt so good to put Harry's desires first. He settled and pushed back a little. If Harry wanted to fuck him all night and not let him come, then so be it. He'd get his pleasure from knowing that his submission made Harry happy.

"You've come a long way, Kai. I'm proud of you."

Kai almost complained when Harry climbed off the bed but a couple of minutes later Harry used his tiny key and released Kai's dick from its confinement. Kai thought he had set the world record for getting hard, though he was quite glad that no one from the *Guinness Book of Records* was leaning over him with a stopwatch.

"You still don't get to come until I say so."

Harry returned to the bed. Kai ached for him. Ached to be filled by his Master's cock. Harry petted his arse.

"Sir! I'm so close, Sir..." Kai tensed all the muscles he could think of, and a few that he hadn't, in his effort not to spurt across the sheets. A tiny part of him wished he was still safely in chastity then there would be no risk of disappointing Harry. All Kai's ability to reason, to worry, to doubt himself disappeared as Harry thrust into him. Stretched by the plug, there was still a slight burn. Harry was bigger than the toy and he wasn't being gentle. Kai loved it. He loved every single second of the arse-pounding, hip-bruising fucking that Harry rewarded him with. His pulse pounded in his ears, stars flashed before his eyes but some clever part of his awareness registered Harry's order to "Come!"

The wave of his orgasm crashed over him. Swept along by the force of it, Kai let himself ride the sensation of ecstasy. A hint of copper in his mouth told him he'd bitten his tongue. He giggled, then gasped as Harry's final thrust shoved him down the bed. Harry's shout of release gave Kai a second rush of pleasure and his cock jerked in a brave effort to join in.

"Holy fuck!" Harry withdrew carefully and flopped onto his back.

Kai waited for him to get rid of the condom then snuggled up as close as he could get.

"That was…"

"Yes it was, Sir." Kai smiled into Harry's chest.

"Denial makes the orgasm even better, doesn't it?"

"If I say yes, will you lock me back in that…thing, Sir?"

Harry stroked his hair. "Not tonight, sweetheart."

"Then, yes. I came so hard my eyes watered. Bits of me are still tingly." He tried to get even closer to Harry's warmth, and his Dom pulled him into a firm embrace.

"Normally I'd suggest a shower," Harry murmured into his ear. "But I fully intend to fuck you again. In fact, I don't see much sleep in your immediate future."

"Sounds perfect, Sir."

Harry pinched his nipple, sending spikes of desire straight to Kai's cock.

"Are you looking forward to tomorrow's classes?" Harry rolled the tender nub between his thumb and forefinger. Kai tried to concentrate enough to pull some thoughts together.

"Tomorrow and every day after that, Sir."

"I love you, Kai. There are so many things I want to do to you. With you."

Kai gasped. "You… You love me?" Warmth flooded his body. He trembled and his eyes filled with tears.

Harry stroked his back, his arse, then slipped two fingers between his cheeks and sought out Kai's hole.

"Why? Don't you believe me?"

Kai gasped as Harry penetrated his channel.

"I do… I do, and it's wonderful. I love you so much… I just never thought…"

"You think too much," Harry said and started to do things with his fingers that meant Kai could no longer think at all.

SCORCHED
EDGES

Dedication

To keeping the flame alive.

Prologue

"Flicker fast, red fury… I think this is a poetic moment, deserving of a verse.

Who falls into the fire shall burn with heat;
While those remote scorn from it to retreat.
Yea, while those in it, cry out, O! I burn,
Some farther off those cries to laughter turn.

Yes, yes…very good. He'll see me now. See *my* heat. See *my* flame. Watch *me* dance."

The man who called himself Spark lit a match. The familiar scrape of the tip against the rough strip on the side of the box sent a shiver of expectation down his spine. He gave his cock a quick rub through paint-stained denim, but the flame creeping down the flimsy wood of the match was more important. Just as the heat was about to reach his fingers, Spark touched the flame to carefully prepared kindling. A lazy swirl of wispy white curled upward from the conical pile of wood shavings and petrol-soaked cotton wool. Spark was, as always, fascinated by the way the tiny wooden curls glowed red then blackened and crumbled to ash. Just a touch was enough to ignite the next bit and the next until the whole pile glowed and hissed with life.

"That's it...speak to me, baby." Spark pushed the flaming pile carefully back into a hole in the skirting board. He had painted the edge of the hole with fuel and stuffed it with torn-up newspaper. He had no doubt that his baby would take hold and spread. The entire building was a fire waiting to happen, he was just giving it a helping hand. Bare, cracked floorboards, peeling paper, trash in every corner. "Not long now." Spark loved the thought of his baby climbing and growing inside the wall cavities. Hidden death primed to explode.

"Unstoppable now." Spark grinned with satisfaction. His cock grew fat and eager. He slipped his grimy hand down the front of his trousers and got a grip on his erection. He sighed in pleasure at the heat that soaked into his fingers. Around him smoke seeped from every crack and crevice in the wall. Glints of amber flickered from bigger spaces. He jerked himself quickly, tasting the acrid fumes on his tongue. He held his breath. *Come, come...come!* His strangled gasp as viscous fluid filled his hand was part triumph, part result of the smoke ferreting its way down his throat. "Time to go." Spark wiped his hand down his jeans and zipped up. He scuttled through the ramshackle lean-to at the back of the building and through the crawl space he'd kicked through the crumbling brick. The backyard, full of junk and the rusting shell of an ancient Morris Minor, was so overgrown he had no fear of being seen. Brambles grasped at his legs, trying to hold him back. He paused briefly and grinned. The property oozed gray mist and spoke in crackles and spiteful murmurs. A dull glow seeped through the walls.

"That's it, my love…embrace it, wrap the dump in your arms and squeeze the life from it." As he watched, flames shot through what remained of the roof. "Soon. Soon, he'll come." Spark moved away. He pushed through the rampant undergrowth to a rusting gate and shoved it open. He had time. He pulled the can of blood red spray paint from his pocket and scarred the wall with his message. He checked the back alley, then sauntered along it to the road, humming softly. In the distance, the wail of sirens split the night air. Blue light pulsed as two fire engines roared along the street. Curtains opened and people in their nightclothes came out to their gardens to gawk and gossip with their neighbors. Spark pulled up the hood on his sweatshirt and circled the block. He tossed his paint can into a random wheelie bin—no one took any notice of him amid all the excitement. He mingled with the growing crowd held back by a cordon and watched as his baby showed her temper.

The fire crews ran hoses and had gushing jets of water on the flames in moments but Spark knew they were too late. By the time water drowned the fire, there would be nothing left but a charred ruin. Despite the intensity of the blaze, two firemen in masks with oxygen tanks on their backs kicked through the front door and entered the building. Spark held his breath. *It's him, I know it's him. He sees me now. Sees me dance.* Satisfied, Spark walked away.

Chapter One

"We have ourselves a firebug, Beau, and he or she seems intent on destroying every derelict building south of the fucking river." Commander Norm Archer kicked the leg of his battered desk as he passed. A new dent joined several already present, creating a pattern on the abused wood. Steel toe capped boots came in handy at times of stress. Archer threw himself into his chair and slumped forward to stick his elbows on the desk and rest his head in his hands.

Salter Beauman took an 'at ease' stance automatically. Eight years in the marines had fixed the position into his body's memory and he couldn't help himself. He stood, legs shoulder-width apart, hands clasped loosely behind his back, and maintained eye contact with his boss. His cranky, soot-streaked, exhausted boss.

"He picks his targets well," Beau said. "This one isn't stupid or careless, he only torches places where he can prepare thoroughly without much risk of anyone seeing him." Beau had little doubt that the arsonist was a man — the vast majority were. He'd eat his boots if the bug turned out to be a woman. "So what's his motivation?"

"Who the fuck knows?" Archer scrubbed his hands through what remained of his filthy hair. Normally silver, it was currently ash gray. "Could be your average fruit loop with too much time on his hands or he could be trying to get someone's attention. It might be the fires are the only things that get a rise out of his dick. Fuck. Should have taken early fucking retirement when it was offered."

Beau chuckled. "They'll take you out of here in a box, boss, we all know that. Sooner or later this guy is going to make a mistake, they all do eventually, you know that. He'll get complacent, then he'll get careless."

"No doubt," Archer agreed. "The only question is how much this idiot is going to escalate before the boys in blue are able to arrest his ass and toss it into a nice, fireproof cell."

Beau grunted. That had them all worried. Every fire put the entire crew in danger, but those started by a criminal who delighted in making things burn were far more risky. "He's already getting more ambitious. Allotment sheds first then that derelict fish-packing place, this time a house. The property might have been boarded up and empty but it was in a terrace and there were plenty of people around. A residential area. Jesus, if we hadn't arrived as quickly as we did, it could have been much worse. As it is, two families are going to be living in temporary accommodation for a while, until their homes are cleaned up. You know how long smoke damage takes to deal with."

"I do. Fucking carbon sticks like glue to every available surface. You're second in command. You're closer to the men than I am. How are they dealing with this?" Archer asked.

"Well, we've assumed that we had a serial bug on our hands for a while now. The old hands are angry but professional. The newbies are scared and trying not to show it. Every shout that comes in they half expect to be another nasty one and that puts them on edge. Being off for the next forty-eight hours will help. Fatigue makes everything seem worse than it is." Beau rolled his neck and listened to the cracking joints.

"You're a little haggard yourself, Beau. Are you worrying about the same thing I am?"

Beau frowned at the cryptic comment but nodded. "All the shouts that can be attributed to the firebug have been during our watch."

"Could be a coincidence," Archer said, tapping his pen on the desk.

"And I might meet a nice girl, settle down, produce a couple of kids and adopt a mutt from Battersea."

Archer snorted. "Pigs might levitate. Maybe the next forty-eight hours will prove us wrong. If the next watch find spray-painted messages on the walls, we're off the hook. If not, we have a serious problem. In the meantime go get cleaned up, find yourself a nice young man and get laid. It'll do you good."

"I might just do that, though I can't guarantee he'll be 'nice'." Beau checked his watch. "Nine o'clock. Shit. I don't suppose I'm getting paid overtime for this, am I?"

Archer had a bout of mild hysteria, and Beau took that as his cue to leave the room. As he walked down the corridor toward the showers he could hear laughter and chatter coming from the recreation room. The night shift were settling in and a tempting aroma of cooking food permeated the air.

"Beef stew and dumplings." Beau identified the meal under preparation. His stomach rumbled. "Dinner at the club, I think." The smell made up his mind and he changed his plan for a quiet night in. In the locker room he stripped off his grimy kit and dumped it in the laundry crate. The big plastic bin was almost full, testifying to the fact that his watch had already passed through and the rest of the team were on their way home. Naked, Beau padded to his locker and grabbed his washbag. He stank of smoke and sweat and couldn't wait to get the acrid stench out of his nostrils.

One of the things the fire service managed to get right was the shower facilities. Endless hot water and powerful water pressure were essential at the end of a long, dirty shift. Beau scrubbed away some of the stress of the day along with the grime. He shampooed his hair twice and let his head hang as mucky water sluiced down the drain. Jet-black strands hung in front of his face, a little longer than regulations strictly allowed. Tiredness washed over him and he pushed it away. His two days off couldn't come soon enough.

Beau dressed quickly. He hadn't planned to go to the club that night so didn't have his leathers or even a dressy pair of trousers, but his jeans were clean and the pale blue button-down shirt he wore was smart enough. Carey Hoffman, the owner of The Underground, didn't enforce a dress code, but very few members showed up in casual clothes. Beau only intended to go there to eat, so he wasn't too concerned about fitting in. He pulled on his jacket, slammed his locker door decisively and left.

From the fire station it was a thirty-minute walk across Westminster Bridge, around the Houses of Parliament to The Underground. Beau took his time, enjoying the cool night air. He loved the relative calm of London by night as opposed to the noisy bustle of the day. There were still plenty of tourists around snapping pictures of the Thames and Westminster

Abbey. Big Ben told him it was nine-thirty as he made his way into quieter streets and eventually to The Underground's discreet entrance. The only indication that the building housed a club was the presence of a couple of impressively muscled men loitering on the pavement. Beau nodded to the bouncers, flashed his membership card and went inside.

Beau smiled at the pretty, slender redhead manning reception. "Hi, Christian. I haven't seen you for a while. How are you doing?"

"Very well thank you, Mr. Beauman. I only work a couple of evenings now that I have a decent day job."

"Becket told me about your gig at the Natural History Museum. It sounds great. You must be over the moon that he's made a full recovery since the Temple Church bomb. He's a lucky man."

"Thanks to you." Christian had a pretty flush on his delicate cheekbones. "He wasn't the best patient in the world while he was injured. I think sheer bloody-minded determination got him well. He's here tonight, waiting downstairs for me to finish my shift. I know he'd love to see you."

"I won't be staying long, I'm just here to eat," Beau said.

"I'll call him if you want some company?" Christian picked up a slim phone from the desk and paused, waiting for instruction. He was so eager to please, Beau gave in.

"Okay, but only if he's not busy. I don't want to drag him away from friends or anything."

Christian gestured to the lift doors. "You go on down. I'll let Becket know that you're going to the restaurant."

Beau took the lift down a level and walked out into the warmth of the club lounge. He waved to a couple of people he knew but didn't stop. As he strolled through to the restaurant he relaxed. The familiar atmosphere, low background music and chatter of the club always had the same effect. Beau felt at home, and all the remaining tension of the day melted away. A smile crept up on him.

It wasn't that late and the restaurant was three-quarters full. Beau waited less than five seconds before a leather-kilted server scurried toward him clutching a menu.

"Sorry to keep you waiting, Sir." The young blond blinked up at Beau anxiously. Beau gave him a reassuring smile.

"I just got here, Benjy, and I'm not in a hurry. I'd like a table for two if you have one, please." Beau always made a point of being polite and attentive to the service staff at the club. He tried to remember all their names, and the beaming smile he got from Benjy made the effort worth it.

"Please follow me, Sir."

Beau fancied that there was an extra swing in Benjy's hips as he made his away across the room to a quiet corner table. Wearing just the club uniform of a short leather kilt and collar, Benjy had a trim body and a sweet face. Beau could appreciate the appeal, but Benjy wasn't his type, too confident. Beau preferred less certainty. He enjoyed coaxing responses from a sub. He sat down and took the menu that Benjy offered him.

"What's good tonight, Benjy?"

The server's brow crinkled in concentration. "Well, Mr. Zachary said that the seafood risotto was 'orgasmic'. Mr. Edwards ordered a second portion of the steak and kidney pudding so that must be good. Oh, and Mr. Colton's sub seemed very happy when his Master fed him the chicken paprika." He cocked his head to one side. "But I love everything on the menu. I'm not helping, am I, Sir?"

"I'll take the risotto." Beau winked at Benjy, and the server blushed to the roots of his hair. "And a bottle of sparkling water, a glass of ice and a slice of lime."

Benjy nodded.

"Oh, could you bring a second glass? Mr. Becket may be joining me."

"Yes, Sir. I won't be long."

Beau watched as Benjy shimmied through the tables toward the kitchen.

"Cute, isn't he?" Dave Becket approached Beau and extended his hand.

Beau shook it warmly. "Nice to see you, Dave, and yes, he is, if you like that kind of thing."

"And you don't?" Becket pulled out a chair and took a seat.

"You know my taste runs more to cute little spy-geeks."

Becket rolled his eyes. "It's been four months since the fire and you haven't so much as taken Marty for coffee. If you don't take the plunge soon he'll be snapped up by someone else."

"Is he seeing anyone?" Beau snapped, a surge of jealousy rushing through him.

"Not that I know of, so relax. He's shy and, as far as I know, is not in the habit of frequenting bars or clubs."

Beau's knee bounced in agitation. He held it still. Benjy returned with their drinks, placed them on the table and waited.

"Do you want anything to eat, Dave?" Beau asked.

"I had something earlier, but you could bring a bowl of nachos and a dish of sour cream, Benjy." He didn't speak again until Benjy moved away. "So why haven't you asked young Marty out? *You're* not the shy type."

"No, I'm not, but he is. I've been thinking about it a lot. I'm a Dom through and through, Dave, and you told me that Marty has no experience of the scene. I don't want to scare him off. I suppose I've been waiting for the right time, but after the day I've had, I've realized that waiting is stupid. I need to grasp the nettle and hope it doesn't sting too badly."

Becket sipped his drink. "Just take it slow. Marty may not know it, but he's just as submissive as you are Dominant. There's a spark in him, though, and he's very bright...he'll overanalyze everything you say just because that's what he does. I asked him last week why he preferred tea to coffee and ended up getting a lecture on the health benefits of different levels of caffeine, the use of plantation slave labor in India and South America and the entire history of the East India Company."

Beau swirled his water and listened to the clink of ice against the glass. "I have a really nice new gag that I haven't used yet."

Becket laughed. "Well it could come in handy."

Their food arrived and Beau remembered just how hungry he was. Conversation took second place for a while as he appeased his neglected stomach.

"Bad incident today then?" Becket asked, dipping a nacho in his bowl of thick cream.

Beau glanced around to check that no one else was close enough to overhear their conversation. He knew what Becket did for a living and had no qualms about talking to him about the fire, but it was confidential information as far as anyone else was concerned.

"No fatalities or anything like that, but we have a serial firebug on our hands and he's only striking when my watch is on duty. He's escalating and I've got a bad feeling about this one. Sooner or later someone's going to get hurt...or worse." He pushed his plate to one side. "This one's clever...calculating. He's playing a game, and at the moment, he has the upper hand. The police have nothing concrete." Beau massaged his neck, digging his fingers in deep. "He's leaving messages at the scenes as well. At the earlier locations, we've only found paint traces but more recently we've had the words 'see me dance' in red paint sprayed where we can't miss them."

Becket's eyes darkened. "The world's full of fucking psychos. You need anything, you let me know. It's not my jurisdiction, but I can always pull in a few favors for a friend."

"Thanks, Becket, I appreciate that." Beau paused. "How about Marty's phone number for starters? Or I suppose I could just stalk him outside your not-so-secret offices."

Becket rolled his eyes. "I can't hand out his number as you well know, but I'll give him yours and make sure he rings you, how does that sound?"

"Sounds great. Thanks, Dave, you've got my contact details, haven't you?"

Becket nodded.

"I'm not working for the next forty-eight hours," Beau added. "First weekend I've had off for weeks, the rota has not been playing in my favor, which is why I'm going home to crash. It's been a fucking long week." Beau smiled as Christian came toward the table. "You're a lucky man, Dave."

Christian moved like a dancer. He still wore his club uniform, the leather trousers and snug T-shirt accentuating his slender form perfectly.

Becket spotted his lover and his face lit up with pleasure. Christian knelt at his side, head demurely bowed.

"Hello, love. All done for the night?" Becket stroked Christian's dark red locks.

"Yes, Sir." Christian peeked up from beneath his lashes.

Beau watched the exchange of heated glances between his friends and rose from the table.

"Enjoy the rest of the night, you two. Will I see you here tomorrow?"

Becket nodded. "Christian's working the evening shift again, so I'll be camping out until he finishes, national security allowing." He pulled Christian into his lap. "I'll get in touch with Marty now and make sure he calls you in the morning. We're not working the weekend either."

"That'll be great, and thanks for your company this evening." Beau shook Becket's hand and gave Christian a brief pat on the shoulder. He left the club with a pleasant feeling of anticipation warming his gut.

* * * *

In Beau's opinion, blackout blinds were one of the best inventions ever. Whoever thought them up deserved a Nobel Prize. He'd gotten a quizzical reaction from the shop assistant on the day he'd ordered them as she was more used to expectant mothers buying them for nursery installation. Beau was male, not pregnant, and therefore a curiosity. When he'd explained that he worked odd shifts as a firefighter and needed to sleep during the day sometimes she not only gave him a hefty discount but slipped him her phone number as well.

Beau's home was a loft-style apartment in a converted grain warehouse. The landlord, an ex-cop lottery winner, rented the spacious units out to service personnel at peppercorn rents. Beau's neighbors consisted of policemen, other firemen, nurses, a couple of paramedics… There was even a guy who worked river rescue on the Thames. Beau was incredibly fortunate to have such a luxurious place to live so close to the center of the city and an easy walk from work. His unit was in a prime position on the top floor. The windows were huge and in the morning the sunlight poured through them. The blinds had been his first purchase after he'd moved in and a lot of his friends had followed suit, taking their business to the kind young lady who'd treated Beau well. He'd heard that she was now dating a police sergeant who lived on the first floor.

Beau lay on his second major purchase — a supremely comfortable king-sized bed — and tried to decide whether or not he could be bothered to drag his lazy ass out of it to make coffee. The whole getting-up dilemma was solved for him when his phone rang. Instead of putting it on the bedside table, within easy reach, Beau had left it on the dresser along with his wallet and loose change and keys.

"Fuck." He kicked back the duvet then rolled out of bed and reached the phone before the third ring. He didn't recognize the number. "Beauman," he answered the call.

"Um, hello?"

Beau's morning grumpiness instantly disappeared when he recognized the hesitant voice. "Marty, why are you asking me a question? Didn't Becket give you this number?"

"He did, and he told me I had to call you…ordered me actually. But I wasn't sure if you really wanted me to…"

Beau could just imagine Becket issuing instructions. "I'm very glad he did and delighted that you called. I've been meaning to get in touch for a while. What are you doing this evening, Marty?"

"I... um... Well, I was planning on reading a new book I've got on Fermat's Last Theorem and ordering takeout... Why do you want to know?" He sounded adorably confused.

"How about trading that for a date with me?" Beau asked. "I don't know who this bloke Fermat is, but I'd hope to be more stimulating company." The silence that followed was long enough that Beau began to wonder if he'd been cut off.

"Fermat was a French mathematician who's given credit for early developments that led to infinitesimal calculus, including the technique of adequality. He researched number theory, analytic geometry, probability and optics. But you don't care about that... Sorry. You *really* want to go out with me?"

"Why do you sound so surprised?" Beau grinned at the receiver.

"But you're so... And I'm just... And I don't, I mean..."

"Marty... I'll pick you up at seven. What's your address?" Beau let a little of his inner Dom filter into his voice. Marty immediately reeled off the details. *He responds so well to orders. One hundred percent sub... definitely.* Beau listened to Marty's short, fast breaths.

"I have your number now, so if I'm delayed for any reason, I'll give you a call. I'll look forward to our evening very much, Marty... See you later."

"Yes... This evening. Thank you!" There was a thump and the line went dead. Beau guessed that Marty had dropped his phone.

Beau made himself a coffee and crawled back into bed with his laptop. He did a quick scan of the news and read an article about the previous day's fire. Thankfully the journalist had stuck to the facts and there was no mention of the painted message. Beau had no doubt that should even a hint of suspicion that a serial firebug was on the loose get out, the Internet would be full of speculative stories. The early fires had been too minor to even make the local gossip sheets, let alone the nationals, but the guy was escalating and the latest burn had gained some coverage, albeit just a column or two.

"He's not after publicity," Beau mused. "He's trying to attract attention, but from an individual...someone on my watch. We need to start talking to each other, to hunt for clues." He ought to start with himself. Beau couldn't think of anyone he'd annoyed enough to cause such obsessive behavior. He hadn't dumped anyone in years. At the club he was careful only to play with willing house subs and Carey would soon let him know if he'd upset anyone. The Underground took care of its staff and Carey didn't stand for ungentlemanly behavior.

"So if not me, who could it be?" Beau ran what he knew about his colleagues through his head. Most were happily married, both to the job and their respective partners. In his regular watch there were two other guys who were out, neither of whom was into the scene. Of the younger, single guys, Beau wasn't aware of any issues. The station house had a few women on staff but none were on his watch. Even the station cat was a pampered ex-stray. The plump ginger moggy had probably befriended every mouse within a mile radius and made some kind of mutually beneficial 'nochasing' agreement to allow him more time to snooze in the equipment locker.

"This is getting me nowhere," he muttered. He brought up a list of local restaurants and focused on where to take Marty for dinner. Serial arsonists could wait until his weekend was over.

Chapter Two

"He's going to be here any second." Marty folded his arms and gave himself a hug that did nothing to calm his nerves. "Why the heck did I give him my address? We could have met at the restaurant." He did yet another circuit of his tiny flat and plumped a cushion. Everything was tidy and in its place. The space was too small for him to have the luxury of being a slob. Marty added another log to the wood burner, then took the half a dozen paces to his bedroom to check for the third time that the bed covers were straight. He'd already changed out of his comfy old jeans and varsity sweatshirt into dark wool trousers and a soft sweater of deep burgundy. His hair flopped into his eyes and he pushed it away with a shaky hand. The intercom buzzed and he almost jumped out of his skin.

"Oh God, oh God, oh God!" Marty ran to the panel and stabbed at the button. "Yes?"

"Marty, it's Beau."

"Yes, yes…of course. Please come up." He pressed the release button for the street level entrance then took a few deep breaths.

When the knock at his front door came, Marty was tempted to run away and hide in the bedroom. "He'll just chop his way in with an axe — firemen are good at that kind of thing." He plucked up his courage and opened the door. Six feet five inches of ebony haired gorgeousness walked in like he owned the place.

"You're beautiful, Marty." Beau smiled.

You have to be kidding me, I am not a girl! Marty lifted an eyebrow and forgot his nerves but then Beau handed him a bunch of stunning sunflowers and Marty melted. His knees threatened to give way.

"You brought me flowers?" *Oh, that's smooth, you idiot. Talk about stating the obvious.* The tiny lines at the corner of Beau's eyes crinkled with amusement. *He has eyes like thunderclouds. Wow.*

"I did." Beau walked to him and encircled Marty's waist with his arms. His lips parted as he dipped his head toward Marty.

"Hello."

Marty froze. He had no idea what to do, but it didn't matter because Beau took charge. The kiss was gentle, chaste and utterly perfect. Marty parted his lips, but then he remembered himself and stepped back. He had to break it off or he'd end up letting Beau do whatever the hell he wanted, and Marty had no intention of coming across as a needy slut.

"I... I should put the flowers in water." Marty went to the kitchen and dug out his only vase. His hands shook a little as he filled it then arranged the flowers. He left them on the draining board and went back to join Beau.

"Can I get you a drink or anything before we leave?"

"No thank you." Amusement flickered in Beau's eyes but he made no attempt to take hold of Marty again. Marty felt a little disappointed. He'd half hoped that

Beau might decide to ravish him right there on the rug in front of the fire. His face heated at the thought.

"Do we need to leave straight away?" Marty asked.

"We have a few minutes." Beau crossed to the couch and made himself at home, stretching his legs out then crossing them at the ankles.

"You're really tall," Marty blurted out. "Oh God."

"Hey, relax, sweetheart. No need to be nervous. Come and sit here with me." Beau patted the seat next to him. "When did you last go out on a date?"

"Um…never," Marty admitted. He took a sneaky peak at Beau's face, expecting to see an expression of scorn or maybe pity, but Beau appeared to be delighted. "I've never had a boyfriend. At university I had a few hook-ups but students aren't interested in commitment… Damn, why am I even telling you this? You don't need details of my semi-sordid past." He was making an idiot of himself. It wouldn't surprise him if Beau decided to get up and leave. "How about you tell me a bit about you instead?"

"Only if you sit here next to me." There was a tone of command in Beau's voice, and Marty found himself obeying immediately. He perched on the edge of the seat as far as possible from his date. A smile twitched the corner of Beau's lips.

"Well, let's see. I've been with the fire service for just over five years. Before that I was in the Royal Marines. Signed up out of school at eighteen. Spent some time in Belize, Afghanistan and Germany. My parents live in Devon. They were both teachers but they retired early. Now they run a B&B on a farm and keep assorted livestock including a bunch of rabid chickens that I loathe. I have a younger sister, Imogen. She lives in New Zealand with her sheep farmer husband and two kids. That's it. Not very exciting."

Marty pushed his specs up his nose. "It sounds a lot more interesting than six years at university followed by a job as an analyst."

"You realize I know that you're not just any old analyst, don't you? Don't worry...I know you can't talk about it."

"I work in an office, chained to a desk, Beau. Apart from the day we met, when Becket tried to get me killed, they don't really let me out."

"Chains huh? Sounds like my kind of employer." Beau smirked.

"I don't— I mean that's not what... Oh, you're teasing me." Deciphering codes came a lot easier to Marty than working out the nuances of other people's conversation. "I'm sorry, I've never been properly socialized."

Beau fell about laughing. "You are so fucking adorable. I think we should go out now before I'm tempted to throw you down and fuck you unconscious."

Marty gasped.

"I've shocked you." Beau stated the obvious. He didn't seem at all bothered by that possibility.

"No, well yes. Maybe a little." Marty was so flustered he didn't know what to do with himself. It didn't help that his cock was tenting his trousers, practically begging that Beau live up to his words. Marty resorted to a change of subject. "Where are we going to eat?"

"Well, I wasn't sure what kind of food you liked, so I went for Thai. Plenty of different options and lots of vegetarian if you're not a carnivore."

"I'm a meat eater, I particularly enjoy chicken."

"Then we are going to get along very well indeed."

"So, we're not going to your club?" Just thinking about what The Underground might be like sent shivers of delight down Marty's spine.

Beau gave him a questioning eyebrow raise. "Would you like to go there? The food's fantastic, but I thought it might be a step too far for a first date."

Marty considered his answer carefully before he spoke. "I know you're a Dominant, Beau. If that didn't intrigue me I wouldn't have agreed to see you. I don't want you to think that you need to be anything other than yourself when you're with me."

Beau tapped his fingers on a black denim-clad knee. "I can cancel the Thai Orchid. It's Saturday night so they'll have no trouble filling the table." He paused, and Marty held his breath. *Please don't ask me, tell me what to do. I don't want to make any decisions.*

"Fine. The Underground it is." Beau pulled out his phone and canceled the table reservation.

Marty took a couple of secret deep breaths and pushed down the urge to hyperventilate.

"Time to go then." Beau stood and offered Marty his hand.

Marty took it and was surprised by how gentle such a strong man could be. Beau didn't yank him to his feet or attempt to crush his fingers, he just lent support while Marty rose from the squishy sofa.

"Thank you." A 'Sir' hovered on the tip of Marty's tongue. He bit the inside of his cheek to stop it spilling out. While Marty went through his routine for going out, Beau kept a hand on the small of his back, never losing contact. The reassurance of that touch prevented Marty from bolting.

Beau hailed a cab on the street outside Marty's building, and needless to say, one pulled up immediately. Marty rolled his eyes. If he'd tried to flag a taxi down a new ice age could have started while they waited for one to stop. On the short drive, Marty was grateful that Beau didn't attempt to make small talk. Marty's mouth was dry, his heart pounded to the beat of mild panic. *What the hell am I doing? I love Thai food and instead I'm on my way to a BDSM club. Fuck.* Marty chewed on his lip. He didn't feel comfortable swearing, even in his head. He could almost hear his mother scolding him. *'Martyn Jonathan Standish, wash your mouth out. Cursing is just a sign of a lack of intelligence. If you can't think of a more erudite phrase, keep quiet.'* He hadn't realized that his knee was bouncing until Beau put a hand on his thigh.

"Sorry."

"I know someone else who has the exact same habit, so don't worry. We can still go somewhere else, Marty."

"No. I want to go. How can I know what it's like unless I experience it first-hand? Otherwise I'm just making uninformed assumptions based on…"

"Marty…we're having dinner. That's all." Beau put his arm around Marty's shoulders and pulled him close. "I'll take care of you, so stop worrying. The Underground has a great restaurant and a talented chef. If it helps, you can imagine you're at any old restaurant." He paused. "Of course you may have to focus on me and not check out your surroundings…"

The warmth and strength of Beau's hold were exactly what Marty needed. He calmed instantly. "Sorry, I have a tendency to overanalyze things. I like to have all possible information, do my research before trying something new."

Beau chuckled. "All the research in the world won't help you when it comes to the lifestyle. You can scour the Internet, talk to dozens of people, read books…but you'll never get the same answers twice. BDSM is unique to every individual involved. It's what you want it to be."

When they arrived outside the club, Marty was impressed by the immaculate building and the polite security staff. At the reception desk, Beau introduced him to the very pretty attendant.

"Marty, I'd like you to meet Christian."

Marty stared. "Christian? As in Becket's Christian?"

"That's right." Christian smiled. "It's lovely to finally meet you. Becket talks about you all the time. I'm glad Mr. Beauman finally got up the nerve to ask you out."

"Cheeky brat," Beau said with a grin. "I just wanted to pick my moment, that's all."

"Of course." Christian winked at Marty.

Marty couldn't take his eyes from the slim strip of leather around Christian's neck. *Oh my God. My boss's boyfriend is wearing a collar. That's...that's...so hot! I wonder what it feels like.* Marty touched his neck then jerked his hand away. Christian didn't bat an eyelid.

"So, I can sign Marty in as your guest, Mr. Beauman. Have you explained that he'll need to wear this?" Christian produced a strip of black leather from his desk drawer.

Marty stared at Beau in shock, then back at Christian. "I... He... Oh."

"I may have neglected to mention it, Christian. Marty, you need to wear a club collar so that other members know that you are not to be approached. If you have it on, no Dominant will speak to you without my permission. I'm going to put it on you now."

"Everyone wears one?" Marty felt proud that his voice didn't tremble.

"All submissives who aren't available to play," Christian explained.

Beau didn't ask permission, he just slipped the collar around Marty's neck and fastened the buckle.

"Okay?"

"Um...yes?"

"You need to tell me if it's too tight."

"No, it's fine. Comfortable." *Why the hell aren't I freaking out about this? He put me in a collar!*

Beau cupped the nape of Marty's neck. "It suits you perfectly. Now, I don't know about you, but I'm starving. Let's go and eat."

Glad that he didn't have time to overthink the situation any more, Marty followed Beau to a lift that took them down a floor, then out into a very plush lounge, which they crossed to reach the restaurant. The deep pile carpets and polished wood oozed quality. Classical music played in the background but wasn't obtrusive. Each table had a delicate floral centerpiece and a chunky cream candle.

"Wow, this is lovely," Marty said.

Beau beamed at him. "Isn't it? You don't get candles and flowers at lunchtime. They make an extra effort with the romantic atmosphere in the evenings. The food is fantastic — not too fancy, just really tasty. I'm glad you like it, this is a home from home for me."

A server, wearing not very much at all, greeted them with a big smile and took them to a free table. Beau held Marty's chair for him and invited him to sit. As Marty took everything in, he realized that not everyone used the furniture. Some men knelt on the floor while others sat in their partner's lap. The outfits he observed were equally diverse, though there was a preponderance of leather. Some of the diners wore even less than the waitstaff. Marty stopped ogling everything and admired his dinner companion instead. Beau was very handsome in dark jeans and a crisp white shirt. Even though his hair wasn't quite tamed, it suited him and there was just a touch of curl in the ends.

"Mr. Beauman." A slight, white-blond server stopped by the table. "Good evening."

"Good evening. It's Ellis, isn't it?"

The server nodded and bounced on his bare toes.

"I'll have iced water please. Marty, what would you like to drink?"

Marty was tempted to ask for something that would act as a sedative because he felt like he was sitting on hot coals, but checking around he saw that there was no alcohol on any of the tables.

"Could I have apple juice please?"

"Of course." Beau nodded to the server, who scurried away.

Marty picked up his menu, not because he wanted to examine the meal choices but because it gave him something to do with his hands. "What's good here?"

"Everything. The chef is brilliant. I generally prefer the pasta. What are your favorites?"

Marty frowned a bit as he studied his menu. He didn't want to say anything without thinking about it first, in case he made a fool of himself. "There's not much I don't like. Nothing too hot, though. I'm a complete wuss when it comes to chili or curry. Did you know that the hottest chili in the world is the Carolina Reaper? It's like a lumpy red golf ball. It comes in at two point two million SHUs. That's Scoville heat units. The Scoville scale is the measurement of the spicy heat of chili peppers or other spicy foods. It's also known as the Scoville Organoleptic Test."

"I didn't know that." Beau grinned.

Marty couldn't stop himself. Nerves kept him talking. "It's fascinating. In Scoville's method, an exact weight of dried pepper is dissolved in alcohol to extract the capsinoids then diluted in a solution of sugar water. Increasing concentrations of the extracted capsinoids are given to a panel of five trained tasters, until a majority can detect the heat in a dilution. It's imprecise due to human subjectivity, depending on the taster's palate and their number of mouth heat receptors, which varies greatly among people. Another weakness is sensory fatigue because as you can probably imagine, the palate is quickly desensitized to capsaicins after tasting a few samples within a short time period." Marty paused and met Beau's eyes. "Oh my God, I'm so sorry..." He slapped the menu down and hung his head. He was mortified that he'd let his enthusiasm for facts get away from him yet again.

"Don't apologize." Beau reached across the table and took Marty's hand.

Marty tried to pull away, but Beau held him firmly. "Don't ever be ashamed of how intelligent you are. I find it incredibly sexy and you just taught me something new. I wouldn't want to be one of those tasters, though."

"I like to learn things too," Marty whispered. "I want you to teach me..."

"About what?" Beau squeezed his fingers.

"You're going to make me say it, aren't you?"

"Yes, I am. Nothing happens without your permission."

"I want you to show me all this—" Marty waved his free hand. "I want to find out what it's like to be with a Dominant and I don't want you to dilute anything, I want the real you."

"It will be my pleasure, Marty. In fact, it will be a pleasure for both of us."

Beau's eyes had such a sexy twinkle. He exuded energy and mischief. Those eyes held Marty in a trance.

"Thanks, Ellis. We'll both take the smoked chicken pasta please with a side salad to share."

Marty hadn't even noticed the server return with their drinks.

Ellis bobbed his head then skipped away toward the kitchen. Marty had never had anyone order for him before. Strangely, he liked it, but it also made him feel shy and nervous. *It's no different from work. Becket orders me around all the time. I'm not crazy for enjoying this, I'm not.* His mental foot stamp gave him courage.

"You made the perfect choice. I adore smoked chicken and not many places serve it."

"And I'll bet you could tell me all about the smoking process, couldn't you?" Beau teased.

Marty wrinkled his nose. "I could, but I'm not going to. It's not that interesting."

Beau stroked the back of Marty's hand. "Tell me about yourself instead, Marty, your family I mean. I know you can't really talk about your job."

Oh God, it's so hard to concentrate when he touches me. "Okay, well…I'm an only child and I haven't spoken to my parents since I graduated. They don't like the choices I've made."

"Because you're gay?" Beau didn't sound judgmental, just a little disappointed. Marty prayed that he'd never be the cause of that tone.

"Oh no, I think my mother knew that before I did." Marty chuckled. "A teenage obsession with any sport involving Lycra was a bit of a giveaway. I always insisted on watching the swimming and diving events at the Olympics. Gymnastics too."

"I can sympathize, though for me rugby players were the ones to drool over."

Marty giggled, picturing a younger Beau leering at his TV screen. "No, the reason I'm such a disappointment is because of my job. My dad is a neurosurgeon, my mother is Head of Research at University College Hospital for Tropical Diseases. I was supposed to study medicine…but I elected to read mathematics. Then, an even worse sin, I became a civil servant."

"They don't know what you really do?"

"Nope. As far as they are concerned I have some low level analyst's job in the Department for Work and Pensions. I am truly the black sheep of the family."

"Oh, so you're a rebel? I can see I'm going to have my hands full with you."

"No! I'm no trouble at all, I promise," Marty protested. "I hate arguments and confrontation." He realized too late that Beau was teasing him again. "Sorry, I have a tendency to talk too much when I'm nervous."

Beau kept petting the back of Marty's hand. "Does it make you uneasy when I touch you?"

"No... I— Yes, a little." Marty was thrown by the sudden change of subject but understood that Beau was trying to distract him from thoughts and memories that made him sad.

"Good." Beau smirked, but had to release Marty's hand when their food arrived so that Ellis could set the plates down. "I'd hate for our evening to be boring."

Ellis served with quiet efficiency. The meal proved to be delicious, and Marty relaxed enough to enjoy it. Beau chose a simple dessert of vanilla ice cream with brandy snap curls, which came in a single bowl with only one spoon. Marty soon discovered that being fed by his date was a major turn-on and he was a little sad when the sweet treat was gone. Beau ordered coffee to round off the meal. It came served with handmade chocolates and the combined bittersweet flavors had Marty's taste buds doing a dance of pleasure.

"I'm surprised you're not the size of a house if you eat here all the time," Marty said. He leaned back in his chair with a contented sigh. "That's the best meal I've had in an age."

Beau patted his flat stomach. "The benefits of a physically demanding job and a local swim tank."

"Swim tank, what's that?"

"It's a small pool that generates a current for you to swim against. It's harder work than swimming in an ordinary pool and you don't have to fight a crowd. I book a twenty-minute session four times a week. It's a surprisingly good workout and much cheaper than a private leisure-club membership. The place I use is open twenty-four hours a day so I can go after my shifts, no matter what time it is. I find it a great way to wind down."

Marty really wanted to see the results of Beau's regime in the flesh. He could visualize washboard abs and hard pectoral muscles. He realized far too late that the tip of his tongue was poking from between his lips. He gave Beau an anxious glance and caught his grin.

"Sorry, I was just…" Marty didn't quite know how to finish his explanation.

Beau laughed. "Thinking about my gorgeous, ripped body?" He gave Marty a cheeky grin.

Marty decided that honesty was the best policy and nodded.

"Well, play your cards right and I might just let you catch a glimpse later." Beau stood up, rounded the table then pulled Marty's chair back for him to stand as well.

Beau really enjoyed playing the gentleman. He hadn't often had the opportunity. Marty had an air of vulnerability that kept Beau on his best behavior. He didn't want to do anything that might stop Marty accepting a second date. Other than a few wide-eyed stares, Marty was dealing well with the unique surroundings of The Underground. Beau was proud of him. Marty's curiosity was evident but he hadn't freaked out or run away. That gave Beau hope that the cute young man would be happy to take the next step.

He had no doubt that Marty felt physical attraction toward him. He doubted that Marty could hide a single emotion he felt. His expression, his eyes, gave away everything he was thinking. Beau already felt ridiculously protective and, he had to admit, possessive. Covetous glances from other Doms in the restaurant hadn't escaped his notice. Beneath his wire-framed specs, Marty was gorgeous, but seemed completely unaware of the stir he was causing. An aura of innocence surrounded him and it was like a siren call to half the club members. Beau wanted to attach a heavy chain to Marty's club collar and stamp the word 'taken' on his forehead.

"Maybe not on a first date," he muttered.

"Pardon me?" Marty asked.

"Nothing." Beau covered his embarrassment at being caught talking to himself. "I was just wondering what you'd like to do next. If you're up for it, we can go downstairs to the club proper and I'll show you around. There will probably be a demonstration on as it's Saturday night and I'm sure there will be a few people around who would love to meet you. But if you'd rather, we can catch a movie, go for a walk along the river...anything you like."

Beau watched Marty's face carefully. It was patently obvious that Marty got insecure when it came to making decisions. He fidgeted, sucked on a knuckle or let his glance flick anywhere but on Beau. This time he went for the knuckle. Beau was quite happy to take control and decide for him but he wanted to tread carefully. He still couldn't be sure how Marty would react to more obvious dominance on Beau's part, though all the signs indicated that submission would be a very comfortable state for him. Sure enough, Marty was true to type.

"I don't mind, whatever you'd like to do is good with me."

The light flush on Marty's cheekbones told Beau which option Marty really preferred, even if he wasn't prepared to say it out loud.

"Then we'll stay." Beau made sure his tone was decisive. He held out a hand to Marty who grasped it like a lifeline.

"There's air conditioning downstairs, but it still gets quite warm. You might want to take off your sweater," Beau suggested.

Marty immediately pulled it off as if he'd been ordered to do so, revealing a plain white T-shirt that clung to his lean form like a second skin. The V-neckline also served to make the club collar he wore appear more prominent. Beau wanted to devour Marty like the delicious morsel he was.

"Maybe that wasn't such a good idea."

"Why?" Marty pulled at his T-shirt. "Is it too scruffy?"

"No, not at all. It's just that all the big bad moths downstairs are going to be attracted to your pretty flame and I don't like that idea one bit."

"Oh…sorry?"

Beau chuckled. "It's hardly your fault that you have a beautiful body. Don't worry—I'm a big boy. I'll cope. Just don't be scared if I come across as a bit possessive."

"Are you going to go all caveman on me, Mr. Beauman?" The twinkle in Marty's eyes betrayed his amusement.

"I just might." *Anything to make the point that no one else gets to lay a hand on you.*

Chapter Three

As they headed down to the lower ground level of the club, Beau made sure that Marty was tucked close to his side. He didn't want the young man to feel nervous or intimidated, he wanted him to love the club atmosphere as much as he did. To Beau's delight, as they wound their way through the occupied tables searching for a free place to sit, Marty kept his hand in Beau's. Doms and subs alike turned curious gazes on Marty as they would any newcomer. Beau acknowledged the appreciative leers and spoke briefly to a few people he knew, but he wanted to get Marty settled. The dance floor was crowded and all the tables around its border seemed to be taken, but then Beau caught a wave and a shout.

"Beau, come and join us!"

He hunted for the source of the voice and found it belonged to Carey Hoffman, who occupied a prime table near the edge of the dance floor. He gave Marty a gentle tug and guided him over. Carey stood to greet them.

"Good to see you, Beau. Christian said you might be along tonight. He and Becket will be here for the show in a little while."

Beau shook Carey's hand. "We'd love to join you. This is Marty… Marty, this is Carey Hoffman, owner of The Underground."

Carey nodded at Marty. "It's a pleasure to meet you, Marty. My partner, Alistair, will be back soon, he's at the bar getting drinks."

"Hi," Marty said, his voice soft.

Carey smiled and retook his seat. Beau slid in next to Carey and pulled Marty onto his lap.

"Is this okay?" Beau whispered in Marty's ear.

Marty nodded, leaned against him and looked around at everything, wide-eyed and a little flushed. Every now and again, he touched the collar around his neck as if to check it was still there.

"We had a delicious meal in the restaurant, Carey. Your chef is worth his weight in gold," Beau said.

Carey grinned. "He is. You'd never guess he was a sub by the way he orders everyone around in the kitchen, but once he's out of that environment he undergoes a personality transplant and becomes the sweetest man. Mind you, he can wind his Dom round his little finger. All he has to do is threaten to withhold home-baked treats. Ah, here's Alistair."

A slender blond wearing skintight black leather trousers and a diaphanous silver shirt approached the table, balancing a tray of drinks, which he slid onto the table. Carey pulled him down for a kiss.

"Thank you, love. You know Mr. Beauman, and his companion is Marty," Carey said by way of introduction.

"Hello," Alistair said with a dimpled smile. "I saw you at the table so I brought some extra glasses and bottles of water over. It was busy at the bar!"

"Harry, the bar manager, is away for a while," Carey explained. "He and his sub, Kai, are up at The Edge, taking a course. Goran, the deputy manager, is doing his best, but it's a little frantic."

"What's The Edge?" Marty asked but then cast his eyes down as if realizing that he'd spoken out of turn.

Beau tucked a knuckle beneath Marty's chin and lifted his head. "Ask all the questions you like, sweetheart. If I want you to be silent, I'll tell you."

Marty's smile was so sweet that Beau knew he'd said exactly the right thing.

It was Alistair, after a quick check for permission from Carey, who answered Marty's question. "The Edge is an amazing place. It's a company that provides specialist training courses, mainly for the security services, but two Doms own it. Heath and Joe run BDSM courses as well. Everything from a beginner's introductory workshop to advanced knife play and bondage. They cover things you might not expect as well, like psychology, human anatomy, diet and nutrition... All kinds of subjects that can be useful for people who are heavily into the lifestyle."

Carey nodded. "We recommend courses at The Edge to all our members and the vast majority have been up to Yorkshire more than once."

"Their place is on this cool island just off the coast with its own causeway to the mainland," Alistair added.

"It sounds amazing." Marty conjured up his best pleading expression. "Maybe we could go one day?"

Beau almost melted into his seat. Marty's words meant that he could see a future for them, and Beau really liked the warm feeling that gave him.

"Of course if you do go you'll get to meet Joe's sub, Olly, and Aiden, he's Heath's sub. The two of them couldn't be more different but if you're after a variety of perspectives on the lifestyle from a submissive's point of view they'll tell you anything you want to know. And I do mean anything!" Alistair giggled.

"He doesn't mind sharing personal stuff?" Marty asked.

Beau gave him a gentle squeeze. "If you'd met Olly, you'd understand. He resembles an angel but he's part demon. Fortunately Joe is a very strict Dom with a well-deserved reputation for discipline. Exactly what that brat needs."

"Olly has a heart of gold," Alistair said. "He's an amazing friend, but he does have a tendency to get up to mischief."

Beau nodded. "Can't disagree with that. Aiden is much more stable — in fact, you'd probably get along really well with him, he's something of a genius when it comes to computers. You could discuss interesting equations or something."

"I already know Aiden... Well, know of him," Marty said. "Becket sings his praises all the time, and it was Aiden who worked out the Templar connection to the bombing I got caught up in."

"Of course... I didn't make the connection," Beau said. "It sure is a small world. You and Aiden have the same boss. Talk of the devil... Dave!"

Beau waved to attract Dave Becket's attention and soon their little group had grown to six as Becket and Christian joined them. Beau wondered how Marty might react to his boss seeing him with leather around his neck.

"Good evening, Marty, enjoying yourself?" Becket asked as he took a seat.

"Yes, Sir, very much, thank you."

Marty had a light flush on his cheekbones but Beau didn't think it had anything to do with embarrassment.

"I keep telling you to call me Becket, Marty. Beau might take exception to you calling another man 'Sir'."

Marty tensed. Beau had no doubt that Marty had applied the honorific to Becket out of habit and a natural subservience to a more Dominant man, but he didn't want him to worry. He carded his fingers through Marty's hair, settling him. "We haven't discussed appropriate forms of address yet, Becket. I'm happy with Beau. For now."

The stress disappeared from Marty's frame and he relaxed against Beau. It felt good and right for Beau to have Marty in his lap, holding him, taking care of him. Beau had never felt so much at ease with a man he'd only met a couple of times. As his friends chatted and caught up on the latest news, Beau pulled Marty close. "The show will be starting soon. It's a whipping demonstration. Are you going to be okay with that?"

"Yes...Sir."

Beau met Marty's questioning gaze. Marty had let the 'Sir' roll off his tongue in a way that made Beau think he was experimenting, testing Beau's reaction. Beau's cock certainly had no problem responding and Beau had little doubt that Marty would be able to feel the physical reaction. He could... A pleased smile played around the corners of Marty's lips. Beau's smile was a little more rueful. Marty read expression and body language as he might a demanding textbook. They were puzzles to be solved. Beau was going to have to practice his poker face.

Beau swiveled Marty around in his lap. He positioned Marty's limbs so that his legs were spread and his hands resting on his thighs.

"Comfortable?"

"Mmm." Marty's back pressed against Beau's chest. His head rested in the crook of Beau's shoulder and his ass was in the perfect place to feel every jerk of Beau's cock. It was a shame Marty had clothes on. Watching the show with Marty naked in his lap, preferably impaled on Beau's cock, would have added to the ambience. Beau grinned, glad that Marty could not observe the lascivious expression that Beau knew must be on his face.

The club lights dimmed and the volume of the background music reduced. A single spotlight illuminated the center of the stage where a St. Andrew's Cross had been erected. Marty stiffened. He stared toward the stage, transfixed. Beau rested a hand lightly on Marty's shoulder and gave it a reassuring squeeze.

"Okay?"

Marty nodded but didn't turn around.

"The bullwhip isn't a toy. These guys know what they're doing," Beau said quietly in Marty's ear.

The Dom that strolled confidently onto the stage had ebony skin and the muscles of a professional wrestler. His bald head gleamed almost as brightly as the gold rings in his nipples. Bare-chested, he wore black leather trousers with a red stripe down the outside seams. They were tucked into highly polished combat boots. In one hand he held a coiled whip, in the other he gripped the wrist of his tiny, Japanese sub.

"Oh my God, he's huge!" Marty said to no one in particular.

The group around the table all laughed. Marty twisted around and stared at Beau. "Are you sure this is safe? The little guy...he's so...well, little!"

"Kato is an experienced sub, Marty. He's been with Lash for years and they do these demonstrations regularly. Lash is the best I've ever seen with a whip."

"Appropriate name." Marty paid attention to the stage, where Lash was positioning Kato against the cross. He bound Kato's wrists and ankles in place, whispering to him constantly. Other than a tiny yellow thong, Kato was completely bare. His slight body was lightly muscled and firm.

"I can't see any scars," Marty whispered.

"Of course not. I told you, Lash is an expert," Beau replied.

Lash faced the audience. "It's not the toys that are dangerous, it's the men that wield them." He uncoiled the whip and let it trail across the stage. "Lesson one — clearance. Use a four-foot whip and you need a minimum eight feet of clearance." He flicked his wrist and the whip rippled. "I've been throwing single tails for more than ten years. I still practice about four times a week." He glared sternly around the room. "Lesson two — if you intend to start using a single tail, buy a quality whip, even at first. The better whips are accurate and can last a lifetime. If anyone's interested, come and examine mine after the demo." He walked over to the cross and stroked Kato's back. "Safe, sane and consensual applies to all whip play. I would never recommend trying this without expert guidance and a hell of a lot of practice on items that don't bleed. Soft toys make great target practice. Lesson three — never ever crack a whip toward anyone's face." Lash stroked Kato's hair. "And finally, there's no place for ego when you have a whip in your hand. Your actions should only be directed by this head" — he tapped his skull — "not this one." He grabbed his crotch. "Use your brain, fully engaged and under the influence of nothing but common sense."

Lash stroked the firm curve of his sub's ass. Marty fidgeted in Beau's lap.

"Anticipation is the best part of BDSM play. I'd bet you a week's salary that Kato's hard as a rock by now," Beau said quietly.

"Did you know that the crack of a whip is a miniature sonic boom?" Marty said. "The cracker at the end of the lash breaks the sound barrier. The whip acts like a magnifying glass, taking the motion, momentum and energy you place into the whip's handle and focusing that energy into the whip's tip."

Beau grinned then planted a soft kiss on Marty's neck. "I'll bear that in mind when he starts to make some noise with it."

Marty fidgeted. "Oh God, I'm so sorry. I see science and maths in everything and it just kind of spills out."

Beau hugged him close and took a calculated gamble. "I have a few, very effective, gags to use on you when I want you quiet, don't worry."

Marty's little gasp was followed by a low, sexy moan. He turned his head away, and Beau guessed that Marty was blushing to the roots of his hair. The fact that he didn't leap from Beau's lap and make a run for the exit was very promising.

Still with his hand palming Kato's ass cheek, Lash addressed them again.

"One interesting thing about the bullwhip is that the wielder does not need to be a big guy like me. Some of the best whip crackers I've seen have been small women. A gentle stroke made with grace carries more power than an uncontrolled, strong swing." Lash held his whip for them all to see, and Marty sat straighter, clearly fascinated by what he was hearing.

"The bullwhip has a short, rigid handle and a flexible thong which can come in various lengths. The longer the whip, the less accurate it will be. Until you are an expert, protect your eyes. You only get one set, so it's better to cover up than lose one of them. Goggles or even a hat with a brim can work. Before you start swinging, make sure there is no one behind you and nothing loose on the ground because if you strike just right, you can send an object flying like a bullet."

Rotating his wrist, Lash began to spin the whip in a circle around himself like a propeller. He created a disc of movement above his head, keeping his body at the center. "If you need to release the whip's energy, crack it into the ground." He snapped the whip down and a sharp sound split the air, bringing a gasp from the crowd.

"I'm going to demonstrate three basic shots — the overhand throw, the circus crack and the reverse snap."

Lash proceeded to do just that. His commentary gave a detailed description of each movement and position. On every stroke his accuracy was astounding. The tip of the whip grazed Kato's flesh, raising a reddened line, nothing more. The audience remained respectfully silent as they watched a master at work.

Once the show was over, the lights on the stage dimmed to give Lash some privacy with his sub. The volume of the music increased and a steady flow of men hit the dance floor. Beau stroked Marty's bare arm and rotated him until Marty straddled his thighs, facing him.

"You're trembling. How are you doing?"

Marty frowned. "I'm...good. I think. I'm not sure why I enjoyed that so much..." His voice trailed off.

Beau slipped his hand beneath Marty's T-shirt and rubbed small circles over his back. His skin was smooth and very warm.

"Do you… Do you whip your subs, Beau?"

That's what's worrying him. He thinks I'll want to take a bullwhip to his back. "Does that bother you?"

"I think it does." Marty's nose wrinkled for a moment, lifting his spectacles. "I mean, I understand the dynamic that was going on up on stage. The sub was just as into it as the man with the whip. He enjoyed the pain… He was turned on by it. I know all about endorphins and the rush that pain can bring, but I don't think I'd want that. For me, I mean."

"It's not something that appeals to me either, Marty. I'm a totally different kind of sadist. I fully admit that I would enjoy making you suffer, but not in that way." Beau kept rubbing.

Marty leaned back into his touch, inviting more. "In what way then?" Marty spoke so quietly Beau could hardly hear him over the thudding beat of the music.

"How do you think it feels to be held on the edge of orgasm for hours? Or to be denied the option to come completely?"

Marty's eyes widened but he didn't reply.

"Do you know what predicament bondage is?" Beau asked.

"I could make an educated guess," Marty replied, blushing.

"Well, I enjoy all those things. I'd like to see your skin pink under my flogger or paddle, spank you with my bare hand, keep you in chastity and control your pleasure…put you in chains and fuck you until you scream." Beau's cock hardened. The thought of all the delicious things he would like to do to the young man in his lap was intoxicating. "But not tonight."

"No?"

Beau was fairly certain that he detected disappointment in Marty's voice.

"No. Tonight I'm going to take you home, walk you to your door and, if you allow it, kiss you goodnight."

Marty gifted him with a shy smile.

"Tomorrow, when we have our second date, we'll see."

"We're having a second date? You want to see me again?" Marty sounded astonished and delighted at the same time.

"We are and I do. I'm keeping you out late, so I'll let you lie in tomorrow then I'm going to pick you up for brunch. If the weather holds, we'll take a walk along the river and you can ask me all the questions I know that brain of yours will conjure up while you're dreaming about me tonight. I'll take you back to my place and prove that I can cook by making you dinner. After that, well…that will be up to you."

Marty squirmed in Beau's lap.

"I don't know what to say."

"'Yes, Sir' will do nicely," Beau said. He picked Marty up and set him on his feet.

Marty scuffed his foot into the carpet before glancing up.

"Yes, Sir. That sounds perfect."

"Then it's time we were going."

Beau said his goodbyes to Carey and Becket. Marty got hugs from Alistair and Christian and indulgent smiles from the two Doms. Beau escorted Marty toward the exit, walking tall and proud. He'd spent plenty of evenings watching other Doms show off their subs, now it was his turn.

Chapter Four

Unusually uncaring about tidiness, Marty let his clothes drop where they would as he undressed. He pulled on a pair of cotton pajama bottoms and climbed into bed. He plumped his pillows and lay back with no intention of sleeping. It was late, or rather early at two in the morning, but his mind buzzed with the events of the evening. After the cab ride home, Beau had insisted on walking him to his front door, then left him with the parting gift of a searing kiss that had all but melted Marty's limbs and taken away his ability to stand. Beau had had to take the key from his shaking hand and open the door for him, then he'd left with a smile full of promises.

Marty just wanted to close his eyes and remember the sights and sounds of The Underground. He needed to give himself a chance to consider why he felt the way he did — so many unexpected things turned him on. His ordered mind needed to compartmentalize his experiences and analyze them objectively. Just as he did in his job, Marty collected information then came to rational conclusions. There was no reason why he couldn't do the same when considering why the thought of Beau taking a flogger to his back made his cock stand to attention.

Beau, of course, needed a compartment all of his own.

"Sex on a stick." Marty moaned. "Did I just say that out loud?" He created a mental checklist of all the things he liked about Beau. Dark hair, dark eyes... That whole tall, handsome, brooding thing he has going. That body...even though I haven't seen it properly yet. The way he kisses, the way he takes control, the way he makes me feel safe. Marty sighed. He was getting hard...yet again. He slipped his hand beneath the waistband of his pajamas and gripped his aching dick. And he's a gentleman. Kind and attentive. He doesn't make me feel like I'm invisible. I should have invited him in and let him screw me through the mattress. He pulled on his shaft, too gently to bring on an orgasm but enough to keep him teetering on the edge. It would be so much better if Beau was the one holding me back, denying me. "Oh God!" Marty's body had its way and he came with a hot spurt into his hand.

Sated for a while at least, Marty wiped his sticky fingers clean and got back to his dreams. He put himself in the position of the subs he'd seen, kneeling next to their Dominants, being led around, controlled, spanked... Marty could still feel where the collar had gripped his neck and he missed it.

"Why do I want this? It's not logical to crave punishment. How can a caring relationship involve pain?" He mulled that over for a while and came to the conclusion that he needed to do some research into pain receptors in the brain and the psychological impulses that drove submissive behavior. If he could just identify the science behind it all, it might be easier to accept his feelings.

"Or I could just go with the flow for once, follow Beau's lead, because that man can certainly lead." He grabbed the spare pillow next to him and hugged it. "God, I feel like a schoolboy with a crush." Marty glanced at the luminous dial of the clock on his bedside cabinet. The hands crept toward three a.m. "Only eight hours until I see him again." Marty sighed happily and let himself drift slowly into sleep.

* * * *

Beau arrived at Marty's place promptly at eleven the following morning. He buzzed the intercom but elected to wait outside for Marty to join him rather than going up to Marty's apartment. There was too much temptation up there. Marty's bed. The soft rug in front of the fire. A sofa back at the perfect height to bend Marty over. Several other assorted flat surfaces. Beau shook his head and managed a wry grin. Marty had no idea how attractive he was. His geeky charm and aura of permanent bewilderment with the real world pushed all Beau's protective buttons. He wanted Marty for himself. It was inconceivable that any other man would ever lay a hand on him.

Beau leaned against a convenient lamp post and waited for Marty to come down. The lobby door opened and Marty was there, giving him a shy smile. He was also falling...

"Fuck!" Beau dashed forward and caught Marty as he tumbled over his front step and took a dive toward the pavement. He caught him and pulled him upright before giving him a quick check over. "You need a bodyguard."

"Sorry." Marty straightened his clothes—a baggy green sweater over faded jeans. "I've always been a bit clumsy. My dad says it's because my head is always too busy analyzing things to take enough notice of where my feet need to be. I got a bit distracted when I saw you."

Beau took a tight grip of Marty's hand.

"When you're with me, I'd prefer that you focused enough to at least remain in one piece," he said firmly. He squeezed Marty's hand. "Does this bother you? Me holding your hand in public?"

Marty shook his head. "I've been out a long time. I firmly believe that unless more gay couples are open about their relationships, the general public will take a hell of a lot longer to get used to it. In my experience, most Londoners couldn't give a toss about public displays of affection."

"Good, because I have no intention of letting go."

"Where are we going?" Marty asked as they set off toward the river.

"I know a place...a twenty-four-hour diner set up just like something you might find in the States. The owner's an American import—moved here and married an English girl twenty years ago. He's been running this place ever since. You haven't lived until you've tried one of his pancake stacks."

"Do they have bacon? Oh...and coffee, I need coffee."

Beau laughed. "Yes to both. I'm sure they'll be able to accommodate your every desire."

Little spots of color appeared on Marty's cheekbones, making Beau wonder what he was thinking about. He stroked the back of his hand down Marty's face. "If breakfast gets you this excited, we'll have to do it as often as possible."

"Oh! I wasn't thinking about food..."

"You have other desires, huh?"

"Maybe."

Beau chuckled. "Well, we're here...so hold those thoughts. You can give me some details later." He pushed open the door of Dilly's Diner and towed Marty into the welcoming warmth. Beau picked a booth toward the back of the diner and settled Marty onto the red leatherette seat.

Marty examined the place with a grin. "They've really gone all out for an authentic style, haven't they? Everything's all polished chrome. Wow, there's even an old-fashioned jukebox. I haven't seen one of those in a while."

"I'm not sure whether places like this do actually exist in real life or whether I'm just making assumptions based on old episodes of *Happy Days*."

"Oh, they do. Lots of small towns have them, and in the cities diners are often open twenty-four hours."

"Have you been to the US then?"

"Yes, a couple of times. My parents took me to see a space shuttle launch one year and I spent a summer at space camp with NASA when I was sixteen."

"Of course you did." Beau chuckled. "Well, authentic or not, I love this place and the food is fantastic."

A waitress, neatly dressed in a pink and white striped dress, came over to take their order. "Hey, Beau, weekend off, huh? Who's this sweetie you've brought to see me?"

"Beryl, this is Marty. Marty, meet Beryl—best waitress in the south of England." Beau made his introduction, and Beryl beamed.

"Such a charmer. Now what can I get you boys?"

They hadn't even picked up a menu but Beau didn't need it. "The works please, Beryl, times two. Extra bacon on the side for Marty and two mugs of coffee."

"Coming right up." She sauntered off with a sway in her hips.

"I think I have competition," Marty said.

"Her husband works the grill, so I don't think you have anything to worry about. He's the Dilly of Dilly's Diner." Beau loved that Marty wanted to stake a claim on him.

"That's all right then, we can stay." The twinkle in Marty's eyes betrayed his teasing.

"So you want to be in control of our day, do you?" Beau raised one eyebrow a fraction and waited with interest to see how Marty would react.

"Would you let me?"

"It might make a nice change," Beau said without committing to anything.

"That didn't answer the question," Marty said, his brow drawing into a frown. "I think you'd let me if I asked, but you'd hate every minute of it. You need to be in control. It's in your blood."

"Does that put you off? Scare you?"

Beau could visualize the cogs whirring in Marty's brain as he contemplated his answer.

"What scares me more is how much I like the idea of you ordering me around." He fixed his gaze on the tabletop and began to tear a napkin into tiny shreds.

Beau reached across the table and covered both of Marty's hands with one of his own. "That shouldn't frighten you, Marty. How you feel is perfectly natural for a submissive."

Marty gave a short laugh. "I'm only just coming to realize that's what I am. Something in me thinks I should fight it. Years of conditioning, I suppose."

Their food arrived. Reluctantly, Beau released Marty's hands so that Beryl could unload her heavily laden tray. He missed the sensation of skin on skin instantly. Marty was made to be held, touched and kept safe. Beau experienced a moment of regret that he'd sat opposite Marty rather than right next to him. He craved closer contact.

"What's the matter?" Marty was too intuitive for his own good.

"Just thinking about how much I enjoy touching you and how far away you seem right now." Beau opted for honesty.

"I'm not nearly as far away as you might imagine. My heart knows what it wants, my mind's just taking a while to get with the program." Marty forked up a chunk of syrupy pancake and shoved it into his mouth. Orgasmic noises followed, making Beau laugh.

"If I can get you to sound like that, then I'm doing something right."

Marty smiled around another huge bite of pancake. He chewed and swallowed before he spoke. "There's not much to beat a good mouthful of something sticky." His eyes glinted. Beau had no idea how Marty managed to keep a straight face.

"You are so overdue a good spanking," he said, munching on a rasher of perfectly crisp bacon.

Marty giggled. He actually giggled. The sound was carefree and joyful. It sent a shiver of desire through Beau's frame. Watching Marty eat was almost voyeuristic. He managed to convert the entire meal into a sexual display. He licked his lips slowly, dipped a finger in the syrup and sucked it clean, leaned back as he swallowed his coffee, baring his throat so that Beau could watch his Adam's apple bob. Beau shifted in his seat and decided there and then that the walk he'd planned could wait. The river wasn't going anywhere and he had a brat to deal with.

"Tell me what being a Dom means to you," Marty said.

"Where did that come from?" Beau asked, buying himself some time before he had to answer.

"You're sitting there, just eating breakfast, yet you have this aura of complete certainty about your place in the world. You want to punish me. I think you want to fuck me. Maybe both at the same time, but why? What makes you tick, Mr. Beauman?" Marty cocked his head to one side and waited for a response.

"Your need to know how things, and people, work is insatiable isn't it?" Beau shook his head. "I'm not sure I can give you a straight answer, but I'll try." He sipped his coffee. "I only feel comfortable when I'm in control of a situation. That applies in my job and in my private life. I understand the need for discipline and hierarchy from the military and from the fire service. I believe it works on an emotional level too."

Marty listened intently, his body language open.

"I want to be worthy of a man's trust. Submission is the ultimate expression of that trust. As a Dom I want to give my submissive what he needs on every level — protection, fulfilment, even pain if that's what he desires. Physical control of his body is part of that, through bondage, chastity, denial, torture."

Marty's eyes grew round but he didn't speak.

"CBT, that's cock and ball torture, can bring great pleasure," Beau explained. "Nipple play can be seen as torture as can the use of hot wax, breath control, even spiked gloves or cock rings. Pain can be pleasurable in the extreme, Marty. I'm not talking about waterboarding a la Guantanamo here."

"I know." Marty batted his lashes. "You need to command. I, apparently, enjoy taking orders. It seems we are very compatible."

"You also know exactly how to get a rise out of me, don't you?"

Marty sniggered.

Beau sighed. "That's not the kind of rise I was referring to, though it does seem to go along with it. That little exhibition you just put on with your food. You knew exactly what you were doing, didn't you?"

"It was an experiment," Marty admitted. "I wanted to get an idea of your tolerance levels. They aren't very high, by the way."

"You can be a brat all you like," Beau said. "Just be prepared to take the consequences. If I think you're playing me because you want to be punished, I can guarantee you won't always enjoys what comes next. There's a big difference between a spanking for punishment and one for sexual enjoyment."

Marty nibbled on his lower lip. "I like proof. I like statistical evidence. I think you'll have to give me a demonstration to convince me."

Beau smirked. "Then you should put some thought into how many times my palm will need to make contact with your bare ass before you come."

Marty's breath hissed from between his lips. "Velocity will be a key factor in deciding that." His voice cracked as he spoke.

"It will, and if I get my timing right you won't be thinking about anything but when, where and how hard the next strike will be." Beau waved to Beryl and indicated that he wanted the bill. She brought it over straight away.

"Hope you enjoyed the food, boys. Will we be seeing you again soon?" she asked.

"No doubt, Beryl, though I'll need to get some exercise in first. You won't love me any more if I get fat and flabby, will you?" He patted his stomach and ignored Marty's snort of amusement.

Beryl flipped her hair and stuck her hip out in an exaggerated pose. "If I was twenty years younger, you wouldn't stand a chance, even if you do prefer men."

"True, Beryl, very true." Beau chuckled and slid out from the booth. He grabbed Marty's hand and tugged him out too.

"Enjoy the rest of the day," Beryl called as they escaped out of the diner onto the street.

Beau kept hold of Marty's hand as they strolled along in the early afternoon sunshine, occasionally bumping together.

"Exercise, huh?" Marty said.

"Absolutely. We'll walk off some calories on the way back to my place."

"No romantic stroll along the river?"

"No. I have other plans for you that I don't think should wait."

Marty was quiet for a bit as they walked, and Beau worried that he was pushing him too fast. "Nothing happens that you don't agree to, Marty."

"Oh, I know... It's just...well, my dick is so hard and you're walking fast... It's chafing. I don't want to come before we even get started." He finished the sentence in a whisper.

That made Beau want to get home even sooner. Perhaps they could jog? "How can I distract you, then?" He settled for a less energetic option.

"Well, Becket mentioned that you might have a serial arsonist on your hands. Why don't you tell me about firebugs — how do you know when you're dealing with someone like that? Apart from the fires themselves of course."

That was something Beau could talk about. He slowed his pace out of consideration for Marty's dick.

"I don't pretend to be an expert, you'd need to talk to one of the fire-investigation teams for real insight, or someone like Joe Dexter — he's a criminal psychologist, a profession that comes in handy when he's dealing with his sub, Olly."

"I can't wait to meet this Olly, he sounds like a lot of fun," Marty said.

"He'll do nothing but teach you bad habits and lure you into mischief." Beau grunted. "Fire is a far safer topic than that menace. Where was I? I suppose most people know the term 'pyromaniac' and associate that with fire starters, but that's not accurate at all. Apparently, pyromania is a recognized clinical disorder and quite rare. Pyros act because of an incontrollable impulse. They can't help themselves even though they know exactly what they're doing, they don't have any motivation other than a fascination with fire. Arsonists are a whole different ball game."

Marty skipped a little to keep up with Beau. "So, that must mean that they do have motive then?"

"Yes, but unfortunately not one single motive. Arsonists start fires for lots of reasons, though personally I'd say they have one thing in common — they take enjoyment out of seeing things destroyed by burning. There's malicious intent. Fire is their weapon of choice and just as lethal as any gun or knife."

Beau felt familiar anger at the thought of how reckless and disrespectful of human life these people were.

"So, I imagine their motivations are no different from any other criminal. Greed, jealousy, revenge. Attention-seeking, covering up another crime…"

"Absolutely, but there are also the pseudo hero types, those who start fires so that they can rush to the rescue, and fire groupies, who just want to watch firefighters at work."

"You have groupies?"

"Who doesn't love a man in uniform?"

Marty went quiet. Beau waited for a while, expecting him to speak, but he didn't. Beau came to a halt, circled his hand around the back of Marty's neck and pulled him close. "What's wrong?"

Marty's expression was one of bewilderment, betrayed by the little furrow between his brows. "I...I don't like the idea that other people get to drool over you. How can I be jealous? I've known you all of two days and I don't want anyone else pawing you but me."

Beau chuckled. "Feeling possessive? I thought that was my thing."

Marty ducked his head. "Don't make fun of me."

"I would never... Marty, you've known me for a lot longer than two days. More like six months... I hope I've had a little place in that pretty head of yours since the explosion. You've certainly been in my mind since then. You were mine from the moment you fought your way out of the debris to get help for Becket. You just didn't know it."

"You thought of me all this time?"

"I did. I even checked with Becket, in his hospital bed, that he had no claim on you. But I'm a patient man, Marty, as you will discover. It wasn't the right time with Becket so badly injured and you busy clearing up the aftermath of the operation. I don't play around, Marty. All my attention will be focused on you. You can be my groupie from now on."

Marty buried his face in Beau's chest. "The uniform is kind of hot," he mumbled. "I thought about you too, you know... I just never thought that someone like you would be interested in a boring geek like me."

"Geek, I can't argue with. Boring, never, and I don't want you to put yourself down like that. Do it again and I'll assume you're fishing for compliments, and that's just another reason to punish you."

Marty moaned and tugged on Beau's hand. "Can we keep walking now?"

Beau's building wasn't much further. Within five minutes or so Marty stood before the imposing façade of a huge warehouse, right on the river.

"Wow!" Marty exclaimed. "This place is amazing. How on earth can you afford to live here? Oh...sorry, that's none of my business. Ignore me. My brain and my mouth are not connected very well."

"Think nothing of it. Sometimes I can't believe I live here either. The landlord is something of a philanthropist. He rents these places out to underpaid, overworked public servants like me for much less than the usual rate for a place like this." Beau squeezed Marty's shoulder. "All my neighbors wear uniforms. Don't let me catch you admiring any of them."

"I promise not to ogle. The government owns my building... I get a subsidized rate too, but all my neighbors are boring civil servants. Well, most of them are probably spies, come to think about it, but they don't wear uniforms."

Beau laughed. "I love the way you talk so nonchalantly about espionage."

"Only because you already know what Becket and I do for a living. As far as the rest of the world is concerned I'm a boring desk-jockey spending my days buried in tedious calculations." He sighed. "Even if they knew the truth, I doubt it would make much difference. I'd still be a disgrace to the family name engaging in such a sordid profession." He shrugged and smiled at Beau. "Are you going to invite me in?"

Beau pushed open the heavy double doors and led the way into an imposing lobby. A set of mailboxes was fixed to one wall, and opposite, a notice board overflowed with all manner of flyers and posters.

"The lift is a bit temperamental. I prefer to use the stairs, it's a fireman thing," Beau said, pushing open the door to the stairwell. "My place is on the top floor." He set off at a jog, Marty close at his heels. Access to the top floor apartments was from a single corridor that ran the length of the building. "All the units are identical inside in terms of layout. Arnie, that's the landlord, lets everyone decorate however they want. I quite like the industrial design, so I haven't done a great deal." Beau found his heart was thumping a little and it had nothing to do with the run up the stairs. He wanted Marty to like his home, to feel comfortable there. It seemed important. He unlocked the door then indicated to Marty that he should go in first. Beau pulled the door closed behind them. The latch engaged with a gentle snick.

Marty took a few paces forward and gazed around. "I love it!" He did a pirouette, taking everything in. "You were right to leave it in its original state. The exposed pipework is a distinctive feature and the brick is a lovely warm shade of red."

"Thanks. There's this living, dining, study space. One bedroom and a decent-sized bathroom. Not exactly palatial, but it suits me."

"You could fit my place in here three times over," Marty said. "I love the sense of space and those huge windows are fantastic." He ran across to them. "You have a view of the river too."

Beau wandered across to join him. "I've got the best side of the building. The flats on the back have a view of a meat-packing plant. Whenever someone moves out from the riverside, there's a draw for the other tenants and someone gets to move across. New people in always get the back view first. I lucked out and got the river from the start—I was one of the first to move in. Had to put up with the racket of ongoing building work for a while, but this was worth it." He stood at Marty's shoulder, stroked his arms and gradually pulled them behind Marty's back until he could restrain him with one hand.

Marty stilled. Keeping hold of his wrists, Beau slipped his arm around Marty's slender waist and spread his fingers over Marty's stomach. He kissed his neck.

"How does this make you feel?" Beau squeezed Marty's wrists tighter. He moved his hand lower, sliding just the tips of his fingers beneath Marty's waistband. The heat from Marty's skin was intense.

"I...don't know."

"Yes you do. Tell me."

"Vulnerable. Safe. Turned on... Confused. That makes no sense..."

"It makes perfect sense to me."

"When you touch me, I can't think."

Beau took a step back and let Marty go. The foot of clear space between them might as well have been a mile. Marty swung around.

"Did I do something wrong?"

"Not at all. I just want you to have a clear mind when you decide whether or not to obey my next order." Beau wanted to grin as Marty's pretty eyes widened, but he kept his expression emotion free. "Strip."

Chapter Five

Marty froze. Every limb locked in place, arms at his sides, legs shoulder-width apart. It was decision time. *Walk away or give up control?* The decision was far easier than he'd thought it would be. Marty toed off his shoes then bent to remove his socks. He at least had the presence of mind to realize that there needed to be an order to undressing if he didn't want to come across as a complete idiot. He pulled his sweater over his head, folded it neatly and laid it on top of his boots.

"Good. Face me." Beau's voice was low and rough. It sent shivers down Marty's spine. He did as he'd been told and found himself pinned by Beau's stormy gaze. "Now you can carry on."

Marty swallowed, his throat dry. He pulled off his T-shirt next and added it to the pile of clothes. His nipples ached as if they were clamped. At least Marty guessed that's how they might feel. He wanted to pinch one, but didn't. Instead he unbuckled his belt and slid it free of its loops. His jeans dropped an inch or so onto his hips even before he undid them. He took a deep breath and let them fall to the floor, stepped out of them carefully then rolled them up and set them aside. He straightened up, painfully aware of how his erection tented his underwear.

"I don't recall telling you to stop," Beau said.

Pathetic sub I make. Can't even follow a simple order. Forget modesty. Get the feeling there's no place for shyness in a relationship with Beau. Marty rolled his clingy briefs down his thighs then kicked them off. He pushed them toward the clothing pile with his toe then stood still.

"Put your hands behind your head and lock your fingers together."

Oh God. As he got in to the required position, Marty wondered if he gave off a terrified vibe. His fear had nothing to do with submitting to the gorgeous man in front of him — that came all too easily. But what if his body didn't pass muster? Beau had muscles that Marty could only dream about. His own small, slim frame was toned, but muscles were a work in progress. As Beau raked him with a critical gaze, Marty's erection drooped.

"Stunning. Absolutely beautiful." Beau gave his verdict, and Marty's cock perked right back up.

My penis has an ego. Who knew?

Standing still became a huge challenge as Beau circled Marty. Marty had to admit defeat when Beau cupped his ass and dragged a finger down his crack. He took half a pace forward and immediately regretted the action as Beau's palm renewed its contact with a stinging slap.

"I didn't tell you to move."

"Sorry...Sir."

Beau proceeded to touch and stroke every inch of Marty's quivering body. *Well, almost every inch. Why the hell isn't he touching the bits I want him to touch?* Marty's dick and balls ached for contact, though he suspected that if Beau kept up his gentle torment then Marty might well come regardless. He squeezed his eyes shut. Thoughts and images flooded his mind, uncontrollable, unstoppable. He gasped and snapped his lids open again.

"Clear you mind. Focus on my touch, nothing else."

Somehow Beau's instructions penetrated Marty's brain. His fingers, locked behind his head, cramped. His arms ached. His body burned with a desperate need for release.

"You may lower your arms. Clasp your hands behind your back." From his pocket, Beau extracted a short, narrow strip of leather. When he wrapped it around the base of Marty's cock and balls then cinched it tight, it was all Marty could do not to scream.

"You don't get to come unless I allow it," Beau said, with far too much pleasure.

There was something incredibly erotic about being naked in the presence of a fully dressed Dominant. Never especially confident in his body, Marty found it difficult to understand why he wasn't making a dive for his clothes or at the very least covering himself with his hands. Instead he allowed Beau to touch him at will and to cut off his chance of orgasm. Surely there had to be some trade off for his submission. *He has to let me come, for Christ's sake, this is so unfair!*

Beau stepped toward him, cupped his face in both hands and kissed him. The kiss wasn't rough but it was forceful. Marty parted his lips and granted Beau entry. He tasted of coffee. All instructions forgotten, Marty wrapped his arms around Beau's body and pulled him closer. Beau grew more aggressive, ravaging Marty's mouth, nipping at his lips, then suddenly pulled away.

"Oh dear." Beau shook his head. "Such disobedience can't go unpunished, Marty."

Hot tears sprang into Marty's eyes. He clasped his hands behind his back again, nails of one hand digging into the palm of the other. Apologies were pointless. He'd ruined everything. He dropped his head only to have it lifted as Beau's knuckles pushed at his chin.

"None of that. Mistakes are expected. Correction is part of the process. You'll take your punishment and we will move on." Beau stroked Marty's hair. The logic of his words slipped into a neat little slot in Marty's brain and he smiled then nodded.

Beau glanced around the room. "Over the back of the couch, I think." He guided Marty to the sturdy piece of leather-covered furniture and pushed him down, nudging his legs apart with a booted foot. "Three strikes feels appropriate. Count them."

Marty didn't even have time to tense or breathe in before Beau's hand landed on his bare ass. The initial sharp sting faded to a dull aching burn. Marty's breath sped up. "Ow! One."

Beau spanked him again and pain bloomed across Marty's other cheek.

"Two!" The word came out as a gasping squeak.

"You're doing beautifully, sweetheart. Such lovely, rosy skin."

Marty felt the rush of displaced air and pushed his ass back toward Beau's hand. The third strike landed centrally, Beau's fingertips curling between Marty's legs to catch his balls. This time Marty did scream.

"Three!" He sobbed and a tear rolled down his face, landing with a splash on the back of the couch.

Beau reached around him and unsnapped the cock ring. The release of pressure was all it took. Marty's orgasm didn't so much take him unawares as crash over him with sudden ferocity. Splatters of cum hit the back of the sofa. He struggled to take in enough air and his chest heaved. Then Beau was there, holding him, supporting him.

"I've got you." Beau's voice was firm and steady.

Marty sagged against him, his contentment tempered by the knowledge that he'd not only come without permission, he'd done it all over the furniture. His cheeks burned.

"One of the benefits of a leather couch is that it can be easily wiped down," Beau said.

"Did you just read my mind?"

"Of course." Beau didn't deny it. "It's a Dom thing."

Marty giggled. Beau scooped him up and carried him around to the other side of the couch where he sat down, settling Marty in his lap. Beau's jeans were soft but still felt like sandpaper to Marty's sore ass. He shifted, trying to get comfortable.

"Why am I the only one with no clothes on?" Marty asked, pouting a little.

"Because that's the way I want you. You have no idea how perfect you are. Bare, debauched...with my handprints on your ass. If I had my way, you'd be kept like this all the time." Beau pinched one of Marty's nipples between his thumb and forefinger. Marty squirmed but didn't pull away.

"These need to be pierced," Beau said.

"They do?" Marty attempted to imagine how that might look if he had gold hoops through his flesh, or how it would feel if Beau tugged on them. The whole idea short circuited his brain. It was enough to make his limp dick swell a little.

"They do. I want to thread a chain between the rings then run another one down to a cock ring. Then you'll have no chance of forgetting who owns you." Beau fondled Marty's balls as he spoke.

"I don't think it's likely to slip my mind, Sir." Marty nuzzled back against Beau. Warmth and a sense of security enveloped him. *I'm naked, sitting in the lap of a man who just spanked my ass and wants to do Lord knows what to my body, and there's nowhere else I'd rather be. I've lost it. Completely.*

"I can practically hear the cogs in your brain whirring, Marty. You need to learn to relax. Accept that this is okay."

Beau didn't sound cross or impatient. Anything but.

"Acceptance is going to take me a while. This is all so new…and I'm a little scared of how powerful my feelings are. You make the world brighter, sharper…more alive."

"Submission is in your bones, Marty. It's not wrong, it's certainly not a weakness. Embrace it and I guarantee that you'll be happier and more settled than you've ever been."

"It's not just about me, though, is it? I don't want to let you down, Beau. What if I'm not the kind of submissive you need?" A tiny thread of doubt threatened to make a hole in the solidity of Marty's peace.

"I wouldn't have taken you this far if I wasn't already sure about you, sweetheart."

"Oh… That's… I don't really know what to say."

"Then don't say anything."

The shrill ring of the telephone interrupted the comfortable silence that followed. Beau groaned. "I'm sorry, I have to get that in case it's work." He lifted Marty and placed him back on the couch, pulling a soft fleece throw over him. He marched across the room to the phone.

Marty was glad he wasn't the target of the glare that Beau was giving the innocent instrument. Beau snatched up the handset. "Beauman," he snapped into the mouthpiece.

Marty couldn't hear the other end of the conversation, but Beau's brows drew together in a frown. "And you're sure there's no one else?" He listened for a while longer, scrubbing an agitated hand through his hair. "Fine. Give me forty minutes and I'll be there." He replaced the receiver with a click.

"You have to go?" Marty asked, already knowing the answer.

Beau nodded. "I'm so sorry. The shift captain for the next watch called in sick. I have to go in to work."

Though Marty was disappointed, he understood the demands of Beau's job.

"Of course. I understand. When do you next have time off?"

Beau massaged his temples. "In a couple of weeks' time I'll get a four-day break. Do you think you'll be able to take leave at the same time?"

"I can ask. I have a lot of holiday time owed to me, so unless something comes up it should be fine." The idea of spending four full days with Beau revived Marty's cock. He made sure it was fully covered by the blanket.

"You're welcome to stay here as long as you want. Take a bath, have a nap...whatever you like." Beau walked across the room and leaned down for a long, passionate kiss that left Marty breathless. "Once I know what shifts I'll be working I'll give you a call... I'd still like to make you dinner if we can make it work between our schedules."

"I'd love that," Marty said.

"I'm going to leave before it gets too difficult. My uniform's at the station and I need to get there for a handover briefing. Keep an eye on your phone, I'll be texting you some instructions." Beau smirked.

"Instructions? Wait...what do you mean?" Marty called after Beau's retreating form.

"You'll see." Beau waved and closed the door behind him.

Marty slumped back on the couch and stared at the ceiling. He had no idea what Beau meant by instructions but he had a feeling that finding out was going to be an adventure.

* * * *

Closing his apartment door on Marty counted amongst the hardest things Beau had ever done. Firefights in Afghanistan were up there, finding his first corpse in a fire was pretty high on the list too. Knowing that Marty, naked, with a glowing pink ass begging to be fucked, sat on his couch when Beau could do nothing about it was worse.

"Definitely tops the chart of shitty experiences," Beau muttered. "Still, I'm a glass half full kind of guy and there are ways and means of making the most of a situation." He pulled out his phone, brought up Marty's mobile number then tapped in a text. As he finished, he couldn't help the grin that curved his lips. He held the phone up to check what he'd typed before pressing send.

Shave everything from the neck down.

He added a smiley face emoticon and pressed send. Once he knew which evenings he'd be free he would ring The Underground and book a private playroom. Marty had responded so well, submitted with such grace, Beau was confident he would enjoy a more demanding session. Beau wanted to test Marty on some equipment that he didn't keep at home, then he would take him back to his bed and fuck him into unconsciousness. He might even let him come.

Reaching the fire station, Beau found the engine shed doors open so he walked in through the vehicle bay. He got waves from several of the crew coming to the end of their shift but didn't stop to chat. He hit the locker room and changed into uniform before moving onto the watch commander's office. He knocked and waited.

"Come in."

Beau took up an 'at ease' stance in front of the desk, which was manned by the station's second watch commander, Alvin Morley. Beau grinned. He got on well with the big Jamaican, who was highly professional behind a wicked sense of humor.

"Thanks for coming in on such short notice, Beau. Atkin's wife called in to say he's praying to the porcelain god and much as she would have liked to ship his, and I quote, 'useless male ass' down here, she didn't think he'd be a great deal of help in the event of any kind of emergency. In fact she said he probably couldn't even rescue a kitten from a tree at the moment, let alone put out a fire."

"Miriam's one tough woman," Beau said with a laugh. "Four teenage boys and Atkin to deal with, she needs to be."

"Atty hasn't had a sick day in years, so he must be feeling rough. Anyway, I appreciate you giving up your day off. The previous watch dealt with one chip-pan fire and an RTA that needed cutting equipment. All closed down and nothing else to handover. We'll be on standby. Run some equipment drills—you're a complete bastard compared to Atkin, it'll do the watch good to get their asses in gear for once."

"Thank you for that ringing endorsement, boss. It will be my pleasure to give the boys and girls a workout."

Beau left the commander to an unenviable pile of paperwork and went to check that the rest of the watch had booked in for their shift. As he approached the rec area a collection of groans rose from the gathered group of eight men and two women.

"Ladies, and the rest of you...it's my pleasure to be here too." Beau glanced around. He knew all the people present. Most were experienced — just two probationers to keep an eye on and both of them were working out fine as far as he knew. "Atkin is...indisposed and I was offered the opportunity to give up my day off just for you. Apparently you've all gone soft since I last covered this watch."

"Fuck...I couldn't feel my arms by the time we'd finished your last set of drills, Captain."

"I know you were in the marines but that doesn't mean we have to polish the damn tender to the same shine as your boots."

"I climbed up and down that fucking ladder so many times I could have been training for an ascent of K2."

The general griping and lighthearted banter continued as mugs of tea were passed around and Beau outlined his plan for the watch. He was just about to send everyone out to their various tasks when the alarms sounded.

"Brings new meaning to 'saved by the bell' doesn't it, boss?" one of the youngsters quipped as he bounced past. Beau grunted and jogged after him to get suited up.

* * * *

Less than two hours after he'd left Marty, Beau and five other members of his watch walked into a blazing building, oxygen tanks on their backs, breathing apparatus covering their faces. Their information suggested that three, possibly four people were trapped by the fire. The premises housed a self-storage company. The low brick structure was single story with a basement. Each floor consisted of fifty plus small rooms, all of which had to be searched and cleared. There were two main corridors with rooms off to either side. Beau and his team took one route while men from another attending crew took the other. They worked in pairs, Beau and his partner taking the lead, breaking in doors and clearing debris whilst the others took a side each and checked for people.

It was a systematic and thorough process. Beau wanted to be absolutely sure they didn't miss anyone. Many of the rooms were crammed with furniture, boxes and assorted junk, making searching difficult. As they reached the point farthest from their place of entry, Beau's radio crackled into life.

"All crews withdraw. All crews withdraw. We've been told there are gas canisters in the basement. Clear the building now!"

Immediately Beau shoved his partner forward.

"Run for the exit. Don't stop for anything. Go!" He pulled one pair of men from the room they were searching and sent them after his partner.

The second pair was concealed from view and it took him a few precious moments to get them into the corridor. Beau sent them on their way, did a three-sixty degree visual check of his position then started after them. All six men hurtled along the corridor as fast as their heavy equipment would allow. An evacuation order would only have been given if the danger were imminent. Beau had no doubt that all their lives depended on how fast they could run.

The world exploded into a fractured cascade of red and orange. Clouds of thick black smoke blocked all light. Beau stumbled then threw himself to the floor as the roof came down around him. A crushing weight slammed into his shoulder just as he hit the ground. Dark spots scattered in front of Beau's eyes, dimming the bright glare, then everything went black.

Chapter Six

"Beauman here." Beau finally managed to respond to the nagging voice shouting at him through the helmet mike. Someone had sandpapered his throat and he sounded like one of those depressed country and western singers after a few too many fingers of Jack.

"Thank fuck. This is Control. What the hell were you doing in there? Sleeping?"

"Something like that." Beau twisted and shoved a heavy wooden beam away from his body. He gasped as pain shot through his shoulder.

"Can you move, Beauman? What's your situation?"

Beau managed to roll to his knees. The weight of his oxygen tank pulled on his injured shoulder, forcing another groan from his lips. His mask and helmet were still in place and apart from general aches and pains, he couldn't detect any other obvious injuries.

"It's darker than Hades in here, Control, and hotter than a fucking blast furnace. I can't see much. Did the others get out?"

"Yes, though I'm gonna have to chain their asses down to stop them coming back in there after you. The building's not stable, Beauman, you're on your own."

"Fantastic." Beau peered through the gloom. "You tell those idiots I'll kick all their asses if they so much as set one toe in here against orders."

"Understood. Now, from what we can see, the building has collapsed on the southeast corner. When the ceiling came down, you became separated from the rest of the team by debris. If you head northwest, you should find a way out."

Beau thumped the torch on the front of his jacket. "Yes!" A feeble beam flickered into life. Thick black smoke drifted in the air. Beau could hear his own breath, an asthmatic rasping, as he sucked life-sustaining oxygen from his tank. He struggled to his feet, the weight of his equipment three times heavier than usual. Everything seemed different as he tried to get a sense of direction. He tried to identify any recognizable feature but the tangle of debris created an alien landscape. In his peripheral vision, flickers of amber told him the fire had a good hold. His options were limited, so he took the only route clear enough to get through and hoped that he was moving toward safety rather than into the jaws of the fire.

The torchlight was so weak that he still had to feel his way along. His instincts kicked in and he reached a wall he could lean on and follow. He found a door and eased through it. Sweat slicked his face beneath the mask. Every step took an increasing amount of effort.

"I'm through to the next room, there's some kind of blockage. Hold on."

"Copy that."

The only way through that Beau could make out was at floor level. He dropped to his stomach, located the low, narrow gap and wriggled under what appeared to be a section of suspended ceiling. He forced his way through then froze as debris rained down on his back and head. Nothing heavy came down on him so Beau pushed on until he was once again able to stand.

"Is there anyone trapped in here?"

"Everyone's out, Beauman. Concentrate on yourself."

He felt his way along another wall then was forced to squeeze through a tight gap. His tank caught and he had to rip himself free, wrenching his injured shoulder in the process. Momentum spun him around and he had to pause to orient himself again before he lost his bearings completely.

Slow, steady and you might just survive this. Get through, get out. But there was nothing but darkness, acrid fumes and cloying heat.

"Fuck a duck." Beau hit an impenetrable barrier and had to retrace his steps.

"Talk to me, Beauman. What's going on?"

"Hit a dead end. I'm going back but it's getting fucking hot in here. If I wanted a tan I'd go to Spain."

"We're training every hose we've got on your possible exit points. Keep calm and keep going."

"Do you have that printed on a mug, Control?"

"Fucking comedian."

Beau grunted then yelled as he stepped forward and plummeted downward. His fall was broken by split planks and debris but it wasn't a comfortable landing and he cursed up a storm.

"Beauman? Beauman!"

"Keep your hair on, Control. I was on the ground floor, now I'm in the fucking basement. I'll have to climb out again."

"Are you hurt?"

"Of course I'm fucking hurt. I just fell twelve feet strapped to twenty pounds of metal." Beau ignored the pain and started to climb.

Sweat poured down his face and if it hadn't been for the dense black smoke he would have ripped off the mask. "No fucking way I'm going to be buried alive in this hellhole," Beau muttered as he hauled himself upward. Splinters pierced his gloves. His limbs took a battering from projecting metal and wood.

"Control your breathing, Beauman, conserve oxygen."

"No shit, Control."

Muscles on fire from the effort, Beau heaved himself out of the grave and began to crawl. Above him everything was on fire. Showers of sparks rained around him. The heat built and built. In the distance a square of gray appeared. Frantically, Beau crawled then staggered toward it. He reached the window opening with flames licking at his boots. The glass had long since blown out and he climbed through. Every muscle screamed at him to stop but he kept crawling, unable to see.

Hands grabbed him and dragged him forward. Beau registered the light and ripped off his helmet and mask. He was burning up. He struggled to unfasten his jacket, clawing at it desperately.

"Need to get you clear, Beauman."

Beau didn't hear the blast but he felt its force as he, and his helpers, were thrown forward onto unyielding concrete.

"Well done."

Beau managed to lift his head enough to see who was speaking. Alvin loomed over him.

"Thanks, boss." He dragged himself to a sitting position, and Alvin helped him to his feet.

"That was a close one."

"Close enough." Beau discarded his tank and pulled off his jacket. His navy T-shirt was sodden and every inch of exposed skin was streaked with sweat and soot.

"There's someone here who seems to be concerned about your survival." Alvin waved.

A slight figure hurtled toward them and skidded to a halt in front of Beau.

"Marty! What are you doing here?" Beau struggled to his feet.

Marty looked on edge from his head to his toes. "I want to hug you..." He glanced around anxiously.

"Then what are you waiting for?" Beau held out his arms.

"I wasn't sure..."

Beau folded Marty's trembling form into a firm embrace. "Thank you for your caution, but I have nothing to hide. I've always been out at work and I am very proud to have you in my arms." Beau held Marty back a little. "Though I *am* making you all dirty."

Marty had a satchel slung over his shoulder. He pulled a bottle of water from it and handed it over.

"I love the husky thing you have going on, but this might help."

Beau grabbed the bottle and took a long swallow. The icy cold liquid was better than champagne to his parched throat but he wanted Marty back in his arms. He put the bottle down and drew him close.

"I had the TV on at your place while I was getting ready to go home. I knew you'd be here. I couldn't just sit around and wait, so I followed the smoke. I managed to get Commander Morley's attention, told him I was your friend and he was kind enough to let me wait at the Control point. I think he guessed we were more than friends."

"I'll just bet he did." Beau grinned, and breathed in Marty's fresh, clean scent.

"I was terrified that you weren't going to come out of there, Beau. I thought I'd lost you before we even got started and I couldn't bear it."

"Hey, I'm just fine. Tough as an ox." Beau's throat tightened with emotion.

"Put that man down, Beauman," Alvin said gruffly.

"Don't want to." Beau pouted, making Marty giggle.

"Would you rather spend the night in hospital?"

Beau peered over his shoulder at his very annoying boss. "No way. There's nothing wrong with me."

"The paramedics will be the judge of that and if you don't present yourself at that ambulance over there" — he gestured behind him — "then I will not only recommend you be admitted, I'll write you up for insubordination at the same time."

"I like him, Beau. Now do as you're told." Marty slapped at Beau's arm.

Beau gaped. "Who's the injured party here? You two stop ganging up on me!"

They both ignored him. Alvin lifted the tanks from where Beau had discarded them. Marty grabbed his hand and towed him toward the ambulance.

"Get yourself checked out, right now. I swear...stubborn alpha males, you're all the same. You could have a limb hanging off and say it was nothing more than a paper cut. You're bleeding, damn it."

Bemused by the new, feisty Marty, Beau followed him meekly, clutching his jacket. He sat on the back step of the ambulance, where two female paramedics gave him equally impatient glares. Before he could protest one of them took a pair of scissors to his T-shirt and cut it efficiently from his body.

Marty pressed his lips together but a snort of laughter escaped. Beau narrowed his eyes at him and fidgeted as he was poked and prodded.

"Keep still, you big baby," one of the paramedics scolded. "You have extensive bruising and several penetrating wounds from large splinters. How do your ribs feel, are you having any difficulty breathing?"

Beau shook his head. "No. Had oxygen on the whole time. A beam crashed into my shoulder and I fell through the floor, but there was plenty of debris to slow me down."

"We'll need to examine your bottom half as well. Drop 'em, sunshine."

"Better get in to the back of the wagon so we can close the doors. Don't want to give the onlookers a show."

"You two are quite the double act," Beau snarked, but he climbed into the ambulance. "He comes too." He offered Marty a hand and pulled him up the steps.

"Well, this is cozy. I'm Serena and this is Caroline. Let's take a squiz at you."

Beau bent to pull off his boots and didn't quite conceal a wince. He managed to get them off, then pushed both his protective overtrousers and his uniform blues down in one go.

"Did you hit your head at all, lose consciousness?" Caroline asked, making some notes on a clipboard.

"Briefly I think, when the ceiling came down." Beau touched the side of his head. "There's a bit of a lump here."

"Any headache or nausea?"

"Head hurts a bit from all these fucking questions. I don't feel sick."

Caroline tapped her pen on the clipboard. "Attitude...normal."

"Sorry." Beau decided that being rude was not going to help keep him out of the hospital.

"Wow. That's quite the rainbow you have going on there." Serena crouched down in front of him. "You are going to be black and blue. Your right thigh and hip are especially bad." She probed gently with purple-gloved hands.

Beau remained stoic and silent but the examination hurt. He shot a glance at his body and swallowed hard. Blood and grime streaked his skin over dark reddish-purple patches.

"Nothing that needs stitching," Serena said.

"No need to sound so disappointed."

"We can take you in to the General to get those splinters in your shoulder removed, or I can take them out here."

Beau pulled his uniform trousers up but stepped out of his protective outer layer. "Do it now. I hate hospitals."

"You and every other fireman in London," Caroline said. "I'll leave you to it, Serena. I'll go and see if anyone else needs help." She left the vehicle and pushed the doors closed behind her.

"This will be easiest if you lie face down on the gurney," Serena suggested.

Beau got into position without causing himself too much pain.

"I'll just sit here." Marty pulled down the folding seat opposite and gave him an encouraging smile.

"I'm swabbing your back with alcohol wipes," Serena explained. She switched on a bright overhead light then used a pair of tweezers to extract a number of splinters, dropping each one into a metal dish as she went.

"Your shoulder is a pincushion. Once I've got all the pieces out I'll flush the deeper wounds then put some sterile gauze on. You can take a shower or bath but you'll need to reapply antiseptic spray and keep the area covered overnight. If there is any sign of redness or inflammation in the morning, check in at the hospital. Is there someone who can examine the wounds for you? You won't be able to see them yourself."

"I'll do it," Marty said.

"Good." Serena switched her attention to Marty. "He's going to need to take it easy for a few days. You can use arnica on the bruises, and ordinary over-the-counter painkillers should be adequate. Gentle exercise only to stop the muscles stiffening."

"Hey! Still here, remember," Beau butted in.

Serena rounded on him and narrowed her eyes in a way that seemed to be unique to the female of the species, her expression saying 'don't fuck with me or you'll regret it'.

"You" — she pointed at him — "keep quiet. I know full well that you'll pretend to listen to me then ignore every instruction I give you. Marty here will keep you under control and make sure you do as you're told."

If only you knew the irony of that statement. Beau wisely kept his thoughts to himself. The determined set of Marty's shoulders told Beau that his sweet sub would be no pushover when it came to his care.

Serena scowled at Beau then gave Marty the smile of an accomplice. "You'll need to keep an eye out for any signs of concussion but the bruising is probably from the edge of his helmet pushing into his skull rather than a direct hit. The pain and shock of the ceiling beam hitting him could have caused a momentary loss of consciousness. Frankly, I'm amazed he got out of there without more damage."

"I'll mind him, Serena. Thanks for patching him up." Marty went to the back of the ambulance and pushed open the doors. "We need to find you something to wear, Beau."

Grateful to escape, Beau followed him. "We keep spare T-shirts in the rig. I thought you'd like me wandering around without a shirt." He smirked.

"Oh, I do." Marty gave him a shy smile. "Doesn't mean I want everyone else getting a free peek, though."

"Hey, don't forget these!"

Beau caught the rolled-up bundle that Serena tossed at him.

"Your jacket and overtrousers."

"Thanks." He waved, and Serena gave him a brief smile.

The storage facility was a ruin. Several crews had hoses trained on the smoldering wreckage but the flames had been put out. The ground in front of the building glittered with a carpet of broken glass. "Looks like the whole place will have to be demolished," Beau murmured, half to himself.

"You'd have thought a place like that would have had a sprinkler system, smoke detectors, the works, considering the range of stuff stored there," Marty said.

"Yes, you would." Beau knew full well that the business wouldn't have been able to get insurance without the appropriate fire-safety certificates in place. He didn't voice his suspicions to Marty because he didn't want to worry him without proof, but Beau thought the chances of the fire being caused by arson were high. If any evidence was found that the firebug who had been plaguing his watch was to blame it was a worrying development because it made Beau the only common link amongst the fire crews. Only a few people would have known about his shift change, and they were people Beau trusted with his life. That only left one logical possibility — that he was being watched. His gut clenched at the thought. If he were under observation then the watcher would know about Marty and that put him in danger too. That was unacceptable.

They reached the command post, and Beau dumped his filthy gear on the floor while he hunted for a spare shirt. The one he found was a little on the small side but it was better than walking around half naked. Marty looked him up and down then licked his lips.

"Wow."

Beau chuckled and walked across to his boss. "Hey, Alvin, I've been let out for good behavior. No hospital. What can I do?"

Alvin scowled. "You can get your ass home and rest up for the next five days, that's what you can do. You are officially signed off from duty."

"But—"

"But nothing," Alvin cut him off. "You were lucky to get out of there alive. Caroline came by and warned me that you need to rest. I don't want to hear any arguments."

Beau knew when he was beaten. "Fine I'll catch a lift back to the station to collect my street clothes then head off. Is it all right if Marty comes along for the ride? He's going to babysit me tonight."

"Sure. It was nice to meet you, Marty. I only wish it could have been under better circumstances."

Marty bounced on the balls of his feet.

"What's got you so excited?" Beau asked.

"What do you think?" Marty said, as if it were the most stupid question in the world. "I get to ride in a fire engine!"

* * * *

Marty's excitement was infectious, and by the time they got back to the station he had charmed the entire crew with his eager questions. He wanted to know how every piece of equipment worked and was fascinated by fire-related statistics. Beau sat back and let Marty chatter away. It was good to see his normal shyness overcome by his quest for information, which Marty sucked up like a sponge. Once the engines were parked, everyone trooped inside. The watch still had a couple of hours left of their shift, so they sorted a rota for showers and someone set about pulling together a meal.

Beau and one other member of the crew had been signed off. Annie had twisted an ankle, and when her husband arrived with their car to take her home he offered Beau and Marty a lift. Beau took up the offer, opting to get cleaned up at home. Darkness had descended when they finally reached Beau's building. For once, Beau agreed to use the lift rather than haul his exhausted, aching ass up the stairs.

As soon as they were inside, Marty ran Beau a bath. Beau took a quick shower first to rinse off the grime then sank into the warm, scented water with a happy sigh.

"You could join me," he suggested to Marty, who lounged in the bathroom doorway watching him.

Marty shook his head. "You're hurt and you need to rest."

"I want you to stay here tonight."

Marty scuffed at the floor with his foot. "I'll stay because there's a possibility you might have concussion and someone has to keep an eye on you."

Beau sighed as the hot water soothed his aching muscles. "This isn't how I pictured our first night together."

"How did you see it going then?" Marty asked, mischief in his eyes.

"You gagged and bound to my bed, laid out for me to play with. A nice fat plug stuffing your ass, ball splitter, cock ring...nipple clamps." Beau palmed his cock beneath the water.

Marty drew a sharp intake of breath.

"You all smooth and shaved for me. Did you get my text?" Beau raised an eyebrow.

"Y-y-yes."

Marty's stammering reply was too adorable.

"Are you hard, Marty?" Beau teased.

Marty nodded frantically.

"Drop your trousers and jack yourself off. I want to watch you come apart for me."

Marty fumbled with his belt buckle and zip. He shoved his jeans down, exposing an impressive erection, the gleam of pre-cum evident. He was cute as hell with his clothing round his knees, his T-shirt riding up to expose a nice strip of smooth skin. He sank his teeth into his lower lip and closed his eyes as he wrapped a fist around his shaft.

"Eyes open," Beau ordered.

Marty moaned. His lashes flickered up. The flush on his cheeks darkened.

"That's it—rub your thumb over the head. Not too fast..." Beau yanked on his own hard dick. He'd much rather have it compressed by Marty's ass than his own fist, but that pleasure would have to wait.

Marty's lips parted, his tongue ran across his plump lower lip. His hand blurred into faster motion.

"Come for me, baby," Beau commanded.

Marty wailed. He came in jerky spurts, back arching.

"Such a beautiful sight." Beau fisted himself hard. He raised his hips so that his dick emerged from the water and he came with a triumphant shout. The twinges of pain from his bruises were cheap payment for the release. He shuddered and sank back into the water's embrace. Marty bent to raise his trousers.

"No. You'll stay like that until I'm done. Then I'll clean you up."

Marty straightened, his face an even darker shade of pink.

"Hands behind your back." Beau admired the view.

Marty's flaccid cock rested against his thigh.

"I can't wait to see you shaved. You have a pretty cock… It needs to be displayed properly for me."

Marty fidgeted. "Those bruises haven't affected your evil mind, have they?"

"The pain just enhances my sadistic thought processes." Beau grinned. "Amazing how a close brush with death brings such clarity. You're mine, Marty, and nothing will change that. Nothing."

Chapter Seven

Marty sat at his desk and stared at the clock on the wall. It was one of those big round ones, almost two feet in diameter, similar to the kind found in schools and factories everywhere. The office was quiet, many of his colleagues having taken advantage of the good weather to leave early and extend their weekend. Marty didn't dare leave before five o'clock. He'd pushed his luck with his hours over the last two weeks, distracted by caring for Beau and making sure that he didn't do too much too soon. Becket had been tolerant but his patience could only be stretched so far and Marty respected him too much to take advantage. He fixed his gaze on his computer screen and went back to searching for patterns in the rows of code in front of him. The numbers soothed him and he became absorbed in his task. Becket cleared his throat.

Marty lifted his head, blinking in confusion. It took a while for his vision to refocus on Becket's face.

"Oh, hello, sir, I wasn't expecting you back today."

"And yet here you are, working away when everyone else has scarpered." Becket pushed a paper cup of coffee across the table to Marty's side of their shared space.

"Are you checking up on me, sir?"

"No. I have a conference call booked in with Aiden this evening. I'll be working late."

"So you won't be at the Club tonight?" Marty sipped his low-fat vanilla latte and gave a contented sigh.

"Christian's working. I should be done by the time his shift finishes, then we're having date night at home for a change. Late night horror movies, unhealthy snacks and a long lie in tomorrow morning. But I hear on the grapevine that you have a big night tonight." Becket's eyes twinkled.

Marty's face heated. "Beau's booked a private room. He goes back to work next week so this is a bit of a celebration. Alistair helped me shop for a new outfit. How did you know?"

"Alistair told Christian. Those two gossip like old women. They're happy for you and so am I. Beau is a good man and a fine Dom. He'll take excellent care of you."

Marty smiled. A few weeks earlier he would have been astounded that anyone thought he needed 'taking care of' and would likely have protested any such suggestion. Now he accepted the statement without a problem. Beau did take care of him. That didn't mean Marty wasn't an intelligent, independent man in his own right. He had gradually come to understand the nuances of a D/s relationship. It made Beau feel good to be his protector, it gave Marty deep satisfaction to please Beau. They complemented each other perfectly.

"The last week has been tough. Beau is not a good patient. He's desperate to get back in to the action."

"I'll bet that's an understatement," Becket chuckled. "Forced inactivity would not sit well with a man like

Beau. Has there been any progress with the arson investigation?"

Marty's good mood dissipated instantly. "The storage unit fire was confirmed as arson. The investigators believe the preparations were made well in advance. Two units were hired under a false name, using cash. There were two seats of the fire, in those units. An industrial solvent was used as the accelerant, ethyl ether based. It has a sweetish odor and wouldn't have been noticeable. The fire spread through the roof, which was the building's weak point. The fire protection systems had been disabled."

"Calculated and efficiently executed. This guy knows what he's doing." Becket steepled his fingers.

"What's worse is that it is now fairly certain that Beau is this idiot's target. All the fires have been on Beau's watch. That wasn't enough of a link until last week's incident. Beau was the only firefighter that changed shift that day. It's not categorical proof, but I don't believe in coincidence. There was another message as well, found on the back wall of the building in red spray paint. 'See me dance'."

"That's been found at all but one of the fire sites, is that right?" Becket asked.

"Yes. The very first suspicious fire was an allotment shed. It was completely destroyed—nothing left but ash, so if there was a message there it went up in flames."

"I'm going to get Aiden to do some digging into backgrounds of The Underground's members. If anyone holds a grudge against Beau, there might be a likely candidate there."

"He can't come up with any ideas. He's thought long and hard, but he's never dumped anyone and he can't think of any particularly persistent subs or jealous

Doms. Won't you get into trouble using our resources on this?"

Becket shook his head. "I have clearance. This concerns your safety, Marty. Aiden can dig in places other investigators won't be able to reach."

Marty finished his coffee and glanced at the clock. To his surprise an hour had passed. "Thank Aiden for me. I hope I get to meet him in person one day. I really appreciate your help. You'll let me know if you find anything, won't you?"

"Of course. Now go and enjoy your evening. Forget about all of this for a few hours and have some fun."

Marty grabbed his jacket and made his escape. Just knowing that Becket and Aiden were on the case made the weight on his shoulders a little lighter.

* * * *

Marty made it home in record time. He'd been anticipating the night ever since Beau had told him he'd booked the playroom. Since then, Marty had received regular texts from Beau adding to his list of instructions. "In no particular order," Beau had said. He sent the messages when they popped into his head. Marty was determined to follow them all to the letter. Beau was picking him up at nine — that meant he had a little less than three hours to get ready. They wouldn't be eating at the Club so he had to fit a meal into that time as well. Beau had said to eat light but Marty wasn't sure there was any room in his stomach for food, it was already full of hyperactive butterflies.

The peace and quiet familiarity of his flat calmed him. Marty stripped to his boxers and put his clothes away neatly. The first two tasks on his list were the ones he dreaded. He wanted to get them over with. Beau's first instruction simply read *Clean Inside*. An enema kit in a sealed package sat waiting in Marty's bathroom cabinet. After that came shaving, most of which could be accomplished in the shower. Alistair had recommended some depilatory cream for the harder to reach bits, much to Marty's relief. It seemed a much safer option than putting a razor anywhere near his balls.

Ninety minutes later the worst was over. Marty was buffed, polished and fuzz free from the neck down. He cleaned his teeth and dried his hair, using some product to make it more tousled than usual. Alistair had taken him to a shop in Soho called The Fetish Forum to find an outfit that fulfilled Beau's next text, *Leather and Lace*. That trip had been a real eye-opener for Marty. He had no idea that kinky clubwear was so readily available. The assistant, a flamboyant goth going by the name of Arcan, had taken charge and persuaded Marty into a variety of outfits consisting of scraps of fabric.

"You have a perfect body under those baggy clothes, you need to show it off," Arcan had stated confidently.

Marty didn't want to show off, he wanted to run away and hide, but Alistair had made all the right soothing noises and Marty had walked away with a pair of low-rise, form-fitting leather trousers with a zip that started in the front and finished in the rear, allowing the trouser legs to be separated 'for easy access'. He'd also invested in a pair of ankle boots with chunky soles and a series of buckles. Choosing underwear had been an exercise in humiliation for Marty as Alistair had held up item after item for him to consider. With Alistair's smiling encouragement, Marty had eventually given in and purchased stretchy black lace shorts.

With a towel slung around his hips, Marty laid the new garments on his bed. He intended to go shirtless at the club so a plain black T-shirt, which he'd take off later, finished his ensemble. He had found a sheet of skin transfers featuring hearts surrounded by flames. One of those went on his chest, above his left nipple.

Now for the next instruction. *Plugged.* Next day delivery from an online supplier had brought him a bulbous black rubber butt plug. The smooth version had seemed a bit of a cop out so Marty had purchased the one covered in interesting bumps. In real life it appeared a hell of a lot more daunting that it had on his computer screen. It took several attempts and a liberal coating of Astroglide to get the thing inserted. Marty stood still for a while, getting used to the sensation of a foreign object filling his ass. The moment he moved, the damn thing nudged his prostate. Marty moaned. "Oh God! I'm never going to fit an erection into those trousers, my dick's going to stick out over the waistband it's so low." He considered jacking off to relieve the pressure, but Beau's final text had said, *No touching.* That message had arrived the previous evening and was the cruelest one of all.

"The man is wicked. Evil. He's twisting me up into spirals." Marty's mind clicked into maths mode. "That's it, spirals…reciting mathematical facts should put my dick to sleep." Marty picked up the packet containing his new underwear. Just catching sight of the picture on the front made him harder. "Oh God. The logarithmic spiral is a spiral whose polar equation is given by r equals ae to the power of b8 where r is the distance from the origin. The logarithmic spiral is also known as the growth spiral, equiangular spiral and spira mirabilis. It's related to Fibonacci numbers, the golden ratio and the golden rectangle, and is sometimes called the golden spiral. It can be constructed from equally spaced rays by starting at a point along one ray and drawing the perpendicular to a neighboring ray. As the number of rays approaches infinity, the sequence of segments approaches the smooth logarithmic spiral." He peeked beneath his towel. "Yes!" His cock was no longer iron hard. Quickly, with equations still swirling through his head, Marty dropped the towel, ripped open the package, removed the scrap of lace then pulled on the shorts.

"What the hell am I doing?" Marty stood in front of the mirror and stared at his reflection. The shorts barely covered his ass. The stretchy fabric molded to his body and though it wasn't quite see-through it might as well have been, because his package was on full, lace-clad display. Marty grabbed his new trousers from the bed and shoved his feet into the legs. It took some wiggling and cursing to pull them up, but he managed it. The fine leather clung almost as tenaciously as the underwear, but moved with his body. "Surprisingly comfortable," Marty murmured. "But I look like a slut." He gave a wry smile. "Beau will love them."

Marty thought it was adventurous to shop in Hollister. Never in a million years would he have pictured himself wrapped in leather like an offering to the bondage gods. "But that's exactly what I'm doing...offering myself on a platter to Beau." Marty's heart beat a little faster. He pressed a hand to his bare chest and took some deep breaths. "I can do this."

His phone buzzed, making him jump. He picked it up to find a new text from Beau.

Pick a safe word.

Marty collapsed onto the edge of the bed. "Fuck. That's it. Sorry, Mother, but I'm taking up swearing." The phone buzzed again.

Don't panic.

Marty snorted. "Too late!" He wandered barefoot to the kitchen and had a drink of water. He fixed a plate of cheese and crackers and ate them leaning against the kitchen counter. To sit down meant pressing the plug deeper into his ass and it was already driving him insane. Eating settled his stomach but not his nerves. He cleared up then went back to the bedroom to finish dressing. He cleaned his teeth again then applied a smudge of charcoal eyeliner. He barely recognized his own reflection.

At half past eight the intercom buzzed.

"It's Beau. I couldn't wait any longer. Are you ready or should I come up?"

Marty swallowed. "I'm ready," he lied. "I'll be right down." He shrugged into his jacket, checked that his wallet and keys were in the pocket and headed for the stairs.

* * * *

Beau on any day was, to Marty's eyes, a stunning specimen of manhood. Beau in leather was a walking wet dream. Marty's confined dick twitched and his ass clenched around the plug. He stood on the pavement, shifting his weight from foot to foot, not sure what to do.

"Stand still. Hands behind your back. Let me admire you." Confidence and control reflected in Beau's voice, his posture, even his expression, which was part amusement, part understanding.

With instructions to follow, Marty relaxed.

Beau made a circuit around him. "You are stunning."

Beau kissed him. No gentle caress of lips, this was a demanding, possessive assault on Marty's mouth. Marty's knees buckled, but Beau was there to support him. When Beau finally pulled away, Marty's head was spinning.

"Perfect. Stubble burn and kiss-swollen lips. Everyone will know you're taken."

Marty opened his mouth but no words came out. Beau pressed a finger to his lips.

"Hush. I've got you." He started to walk down the street, gripping Marty's wrist. "I have a cab waiting. The company has a contract with The Underground — owner's a member."

"That's a relief," Marty mumbled. "Walking with a hard-on is uncomfortable. Oh, did I say that out loud?"

"Yes, you did." Beau chuckled and guided him into the back seat of the car. "Have you followed all my instructions?"

Marty nodded and leaned against Beau's shoulder. "Yes, Sir."

"What's your safe word?"

"Fibonacci, Sir."

"Good. From this point on, consider yourself in a scene. Use that word at any time. Everything stops, instantly. Do you understand?"

"Yes, Sir."

The car rumbled through the back streets, avoiding the traffic pinch points that never got better, even during the evening.

"Using your safe word is not weakness, it's what I demand. You're very new to all this, Marty, and I don't want to scare you. We haven't had a chance to discuss your hard limits yet—I doubt you even know what they are. If anything I do makes you uncomfortable, use your word. We will discuss how you feel and agree your limits before we continue."

"You sound so serious, Sir."

"I *am* serious. I want you to get as much pleasure out of our relationship as me and that means consent, at all times. It's not like we're going to the park to feed the ducks."

"We're not? Damn." Marty giggled.

"Brat." Beau pulled him close and sucked on his neck. "The more of my marks on you, the better."

Minutes later the cab pulled up outside The Underground. Beau escorted Marty inside with an arm around his shoulders. They went through the rituals required to get inside, and Beau fitted the club collar around Marty's neck. Christian gave Marty a knowing smile but didn't attempt to talk to him directly. Marty appreciated his consideration. He didn't feel much like talking to anyone. All his attention was fixed on Beau.

They went first to the members' locker room and stowed their jackets. Marty pulled off his T-shirt, revealing the temporary tattoo on his chest. Beau traced it with a fingertip. "This is beautiful. A permanent one would be even better." He flicked a nipple. "When we get these pierced, we can add some ink to the appointment."

"Yes, Sir." Marty found he liked that idea. A lot.

"*You* are temptation walking, Marty. Those trousers are...sinful." Beau ran his finger down the zip. "This is a nice touch."

Marty moaned. "Sir...please. You'll make me come."

"I should have included a cock ring in your instructions, shouldn't I?" Beau pressed the heel of his hand to Marty's groin. "But you won't come. Not without my permission."

Marty's response came out as a strangled gasp.

"We'll go straight to our room. I can't wait to torment you some more." Beau's grin was feral. He pulled a lead from his pocket and attached it to Marty's collar. "Keep your hands behind your back. Don't make eye contact with, or speak to, anyone. If I stop to greet another Dom, go to your knees."

"Yes, Sir." Marty could deal with clear instructions — less chance of him fucking things up.

He wanted to make Beau proud to be with him. If that meant crawling naked behind him, then he would do it. He locked his fingers together and pressed them in to the small of his back. When Beau moved and the lead went taut, Marty was ready. He stayed a consistent distance behind Beau, who took even paces, helping him. Beau stopped twice, and each time Marty sank to the floor as gracefully as he could and bowed his head. They reached the corridor leading to the private playrooms without incident and Marty counted it as his first success.

"I'm proud of you, Marty. I've seen seasoned subs perform far worse than you just did." Beau entered the access code for the room into a keypad next to the door.

A warm glow enveloped Marty from head to toe. Beau's praise made him shiver with delight. Such a simple thing and yet so significant. His worries slipped away.

"In you go." Beau ushered him into the room. "Carey has all the playrooms kitted out in different themes. This one's just been redone and I wanted to try it out. I think it suits you." He waited, allowing Marty to take everything in.

"I didn't know what to expect, Sir, but it wasn't this."

"Nothing like a dungeon, is it?"

"No." Marty hardly knew where to look first.

The room was lined with brushed steel panels. Flexible neon tube lights snaked around the walls, glowing iridescent blue and lilac. The flooring was black rubber, not smooth but covered in a pattern of raised circles. At intervals, pieces of equipment stood gleaming, the lights shimmering on polished metal. Restraints of all descriptions hung from pegs along one wall. Marty's balls tightened as he counted the whips, floggers, paddles and canes. A chiller cabinet held bottles of water. Silver bowls full of lube, condoms and smaller restraints sat on a shelf. A metal tray next to them had rows of implements in neat lines. Marty had no idea what most of them were for.

"It's like being inside a spaceship…"

"Well, let's see if we can get you into subspace. You remember your safe word?"

Marty nodded.

"I want you barefoot, in display position in the center of the floor."

Marty sat down to remove his boots and socks. He didn't trust himself to stay balanced on one leg. He set them in a corner and took up a position with his legs spread shoulder-width apart, fingers locked behind his neck. He kept his head up and his eyes down.

Beau prowled around the room. Marty decided that was an apt description. Beau was a predator, top of the food chain, and Marty had no doubt he was prey. Beau selected some items from the bowls and palmed them. Marty couldn't see what Beau held and he really wanted to know. Beau rubbed the backs of his knuckles over Marty's belly.

"You have beautiful skin. Silky. It marks well." He lowered Marty's zipper a couple of inches, just enough for Marty's lace underwear to be exposed. To Marty's horror, his cock poked from the top, slick with pre-cum. He whimpered.

"Very nice," Beau said. He lowered Marty's zipper farther so that it was half between the front and back of his trousers. He pulled the stretchy lace down and lodged it beneath Marty's balls, causing them, and his cock, to jut out lewdly. "Better. Now I can fit this."

Beau soon had a thick metal ring snugly locked in place. Marty was relieved. He teetered on the edge of orgasm and didn't want to come by accident.

"Clamps next."

Marty fidgeted and received a sharp slap to his ass as reward. His cock jerked.

"These are screw clamps. Good for a beginner because they are adjustable. Better than tweezer style because they don't come off easily." Beau flicked at a nipple until it peaked then he attached the clamp, screwing it down until Marty hissed at the sharp pain. The second one went on, and Beau linked them with a chain. Then he tugged it.

"Ow! Sir…please."

"Please what? Pull it again? I don't think you want me to stop do you, Marty?"

The pain seemed to have a direct connection to Marty's cock. Each twinge increased his need to come. There had to be some kind of equation to describe the effect. Beau ran a second chain from the cock ring to the center of the one joining Marty's nipples. Every time his dick so much as twitched, there was a tug on his tits.

"Effective, isn't it?"

Beau didn't seem to expect an answer so Marty concentrated on not groaning. Beau played with the clamps and chain for what seemed like hours but was probably minutes. Marty's balls ached as much as his nipples but he managed to stay in position. Finally, when Marty was ready to beg and scream for release, Beau led him to a metal frame that curved back in an arch. Beau positioned Marty with his spine to the metal. It was cold against his bare skin but soon warmed.

"I'm going to bind you in position. Just relax. I'll put you where I want you."

"Yes, Sir." It helped to acknowledge the statement, though Marty was under no illusion that he had any choice in the matter.

Beau used leather straps to bind Marty's ankles to upright poles. They were spaced far enough apart that Marty felt the stretch in his thigh muscles. Next was his waist with the buckle behind the pole at his back so that it didn't dig in.

"I'm going to make a star shape. Reach up and out with your arms."

Beau climbed the frame to secure Marty's wrists and elbows in place. Further straps went around his chest and neck. The curvature of the contraption meant that he was bent backward, with an excellent view of the ceiling unless he strained his head forward. It also served to thrust his groin out and tighten the chain between his cock ring and the nipple clamps.

"Stay in position. Don't fight it or you'll choke yourself." Beau checked all the bindings. "Does anything pinch?"

"No, Sir." Marty's head was a whirl of sensation. Pain, arousal and restraint combined to fog his mind. He'd never felt so vulnerable. So exposed. His purpose was to pleasure Beau but Marty had no control over how that might happen. He had handed all the power to Beau and it made him giddy with exhilaration.

Beau finished the job of unfastening Marty's zip, separating his trousers into two pieces. He shoved the leather down Marty's thighs.

"I like your choice of underwear, sweetheart. Much more interesting than black cotton." Beau ripped the scrap of lace away. "I'll buy you some more. You should wear them all the time."

"Is that an order, Sir?" Marty whispered.

Beau cocked his head to one side, considering. "Yes. It is. You'll wear microscopic underwear from now on—the kinkier the better. We can have an online shopping session and I'll choose my favorites. How are you doing with that plug?" Beau moved behind the frame and gave Marty's ass a sharp slap, driving the plug deep. He got a hold of the end, pulled it out slowly then plunged it back in.

Marty gasped and babbled a series of pleas that were mostly nonsense. Beau fucked him with the plug, twisting and manipulating the toy to hit Marty's sweet spot. Marty screamed and thrust his groin out as far as his bonds would allow. The nipple chain pulled taut, sending a bolt of pleasure pain to his balls.

"No! Sir...stop, please stop!"

"I don't hear your safe word, Marty."

Marty wailed. If Beau stopped he would never get to come. The pain was not severe. The exquisite agony came from being denied when tremors of need rolled through his body, one after the other. Using his safe word was unthinkable.

Beau removed the plug completely, leaving Marty even more desperate.

"Empty, Sir, please..."

"All in good time."

Beau moved in front of him. Marty tried to see his face but the strap around his neck was too tight to move far.

The next thing he felt was Beau's mouth on his cock. Marty howled. It was too much. Doms didn't do that, did they? This one did and fuck was he good at it. Beau focused only on the head of Marty's dick. He sucked and licked until Marty thought he would go out of his mind. Then it stopped. Marty couldn't decide which was worse — to be touched or to be left wanting.

"This is torture!"

Beau licked his way up Marty's stomach.

"I did warn you that sexual torture is my specialty," Beau said, his tone mild. "Let's see if your cock can handle pain as well as pleasure."

Marty listened to his steps as he crossed the room and selected an implement from the wall. He tried not to panic. Part of him was detached, floating. The other part fought his bondage but the straps were immoveable. Something slapped across his dick. Soft strands that tickled.

"It's a flogger, a short one designed especially for the more sensitive parts of your body."

Marty could tell that Beau was smiling. Helpless to do anything but take whatever punishment Beau dished out, Marty closed his eyes. Beau began with soft, regular strokes that tormented rather than hurt. Ever touch to his hypersensitive skin increased Marty's desperate need to come. Beau used a little more force and the blows began to sting. He covered Marty's thigh, his cock and balls, with repeated strokes that raised a heated glow. Beau whipped the flogger across Marty's chest, catching both clamps. He screamed. His safe word hovered on the tip of his tongue but, as if sensing how close to breaking Marty was, Beau didn't strike again.

"You really want to come now, don't you, love?" Beau teased.

"You're an evil, sadistic, wicked man...Sir." Marty panted. Sweat trickled down his back.

"Indeed I am. Time to move you, I think."

Beau undid the straps around Marty's neck and chest first, then his wrists, taking care to lower each arm slowly. He rubbed the muscles until the burning sensation faded, then unfastened the rest of the bonds. Marty kept his weight against the frame. He didn't dare take a step in case he fell over.

"The clamps are coming off now. It's going to hurt. A lot." Beau removed them both, detaching the chain to the cock ring but leaving the ring in place.

"I'm on fire!" Marty gasped. Unstoppable tears streamed down his face as Beau massaged the pain away. He fell into Beau's arms, desperate for some sign of affection.

Beau held him close, stroked his hair and whispered calming words in his ear. "You are doing so well, Marty. With more training, you are going to make a stunning submissive for me."

"For you?" Marty could hardly dare to hope that Beau might want to keep him.

"Nobody else is ever going to touch you again. I'm not letting you go."

Beau steered him across to a padded leather and steel construction. "You can lie down and take a rest now." He patted the top section. "Your chest goes here, leaving your lower body free for me to play with. The four lower sections will support your arms and legs."

"Very relaxing, Sir," Marty snarked as he crawled into position.

Soon Beau had him firmly strapped in place. Beau patted his ass. "I won't forget that little hint of attitude, brat."

Marty wiggled his ass, trying to draw Beau's attention away from his misdemeanor and back to letting him come.

"And there was me thinking you'd be on your best behavior. Perhaps you don't want to come after all?"

"I do! I really do, Sir. I'm sorry... I'll do anything. Pleeease!" Marty wasn't above begging. He'd try puppy eyes if only he wasn't staring at the floor between chin and forehead rests.

"I do love it when you beg." Beau stroked Marty's ass. "But I think you can take some more denial."

"No!" Marty pleaded. He'd been hard forever. His balls ached. The promise of orgasm tickled and nudged at his gut.

Beau just laughed. Marty gave up trying to interpret Beau's movements. However much he listened he couldn't tell what new torment he prepared. He tugged on his bonds, testing their strength. They were immovable.

A hard, cold object pressed against Marty's hole. He squeaked and tried to relax as Beau pushed it inside him.

"What is it, Sir?" he managed to ask.

"Wait and see."

Christ, he is the most annoying, frustrating... "Oh!" A slow vibration started up in Marty's channel. Tremors shot through his balls. Before he could adjust to the new intrusion and the sensations it brought, sharp prickles ran across his scrotum.

"It's called a pinwheel. A ring of rotating spikes that I can run across your skin. The more pressure I apply, the more it will hurt."

"Oh God! Sir... I need... I have to..." Marty couldn't breathe. There were too many sensations to deal with all at once. The vibrator buzzed faster. The pinwheel dug deeper, along his cock, around his tender balls. He loved and hated every second. "Please, please, please…" The litany spilled from his mouth.

"Open your pretty eyes, Marty."

Marty hadn't even realized that Beau was no longer using the wheel. Instead he stood directly in front of Marty's head. A foot pedal tilted the bench to an angle where Marty's mouth was at a perfect level to receive Beau's cock, and as Beau unzipped his leathers Marty could almost ignore the insistent buzzing in his ass. Almost.

Beau's cock was long and thick, the bulbous head gleamed. Marty opened his mouth, hoping that Beau wouldn't deny him this pleasure too.

"Keep absolutely still," Beau ordered. "Your mouth is mine, just as much as your ass." He thrust forward, and Marty reveled in the sensation of being filled at both ends. His ass throbbed. He stretched his jaw wide to accommodate Beau's girth but made no attempt to do anything else. Beau fucked his mouth, pushing back to his throat and withdrawing before Marty could gag. Marty couldn't wait to taste Beau's cum. He craved it, but Beau moved slowly, holding back. When he withdrew, Marty almost cried. Beau fisted his cock right in front of Marty's eyes.

"You are perfect, spread and exposed to me. Helpless. Available to serve my every whim. I want to paint you with my cum. Mark you with my scent." Beau's hand blurred and the spatter of warm cum hit Marty's cheek, his lips.

He slid his tongue out to catch the drops and tasted Beau's bittersweet essence. Beau must have switched the vibrator to a new setting because the whirring accelerated. Marty screamed his frustration then Beau touched Marty's dick. The pressure of the cock ring disappeared.

"Come, sweetheart."

Marty shot instantly. The orgasm tore through him like wildfire. Every inch of his flesh burned. He screamed and his vision blurred. Muscles spasmed and contracted. He came again. Exhausted, he sagged, boneless, grateful for the bench holding him in place. He was vaguely aware of Beau releasing him, scooping him up and cradling him. His head swam.

"I've got you, love."

Instinctively, Marty pressed against Beau, snuggling close. Beau sat with his back to the wall and rocked Marty gently.

"You were beautiful. So responsive."

Beau continued to murmur in Marty's ear but he didn't really hear the words. He felt safe, secure and…loved. A warm glow enveloped him.

Marty had no idea how long they just sat, but eventually Beau helped him dress. Made him drink a full bottle of water, then walked him from the Club. The journey home to Beau's apartment went by in a blur and Marty didn't really emerge from his daze until he lay snuggled in Beau's bed. He scratched at his cheek.

"I have your cum on my face, Sir. You missed it when you cleaned me up."

"I didn't miss it." Beau slapped Marty's hand away. He climbed beneath the covers and fondled Marty's dick. "Turn over."

Marty rolled lazily. The snick of a plastic cap gave him some warning but he still jerked when Beau's lubed fingers pressed into his ass.

"Are you sore at all? From the plug and vibrator?"

"No, Sir. Feels good." Marty raised his hips, trying to encourage Beau's fingers to probe deeper. He got his knees under him and tilted his ass in the air.

"I've waited more than six months to fuck you. I wanted to do it here rather than at the club." Foil tore, then the blunt head of Beau's ample cock pushed at Marty's hole. "No bondage, no playing...just this." Beau pushed forward, and Marty gasped at the fullness and the slight burn.

"You're big, Sir... Burns."

"You're good for my ego, Marty." Beau held still, but when Marty relaxed he set up a punishing rhythm. Marty stretched out his arms and got a grip of the headboard. Holding his body stiff meant Beau went deeper, harder.

"So good. So full."

Beau pounded his ass then withdrew, flipped Marty onto his back and pulled his calves up to his shoulders. "Want to see your face when you come."

Marty writhed as he was skewered over and over. He reached for his cock but Beau pushed him away. "Hands off. That's mine." Beau gripped him and tugged.

As he came, Marty screamed Beau's name and let the aftershocks roll through him. Beau didn't let up and seconds later thrust hard then froze, his expression a picture of ecstasy. Marty would remember the sight for as long as he lived. *I did that. I put that expression on his face.* He sighed happily as Beau's weight pressed him into the mattress, holding him down. The night couldn't have been any more perfect.

Chapter Eight

Marty waited outside The Marmalade Factory, scanning the street for Alistair and Christian. He checked his watch. "Ten to six, I'm early." He hopped up onto the low wall that fronted the building behind him. The South Bank buzzed with activity. For once the weather was mild and tourists and Londoners alike had taken advantage of the opportunity to get some fresh air. Street sellers had their wares laid out on brightly colored blankets and a caricaturist made lightning fast, uncannily accurate sketches for his customers. On the river, several pleasure boats and tugs chugged up and down.

Marty swung his feet, not caring that he was acting like a big kid. Beau was working the night shift so when Alistair had called inviting Marty along to a 'sub social' as he called it, he'd jumped at the offer. Christian was joining them along with Kai and a couple of the waitstaff, Ellis and Benjy. Marty remembered Ellis from his first date with Beau at the Club but he didn't know Benjy. Kai was the bar manager's sub. Marty was keen to get to know a few more Club members because he guessed that he'd be spending quite a lot of time there with Beau. It would be good to have some friends of his own to meet with.

Alistair had given Marty directions to the venue they were meeting at and he'd searched for it online. The Marmalade Factory was just that, an old factory owned in Victorian times by a company manufacturing jams and spreads. It had recently been converted to a social center and housed a range of small craft shops, artisan businesses, a restaurant, coffee shop and an art house cinema. The coffee shop was in the basement and that was where the 'sub social' would take place. Marty chuckled. "Strange kind of gathering, but more interesting than meeting up to discuss trainspotting or stamp collecting."

Beau's attention was drawn to the sound of laughter and he grinned at the colorful group strolling along the riverbank toward him. Christian spotted him first and waved. Soon Marty found himself surrounded by a gaggle of chattering young men, all trying to introduce themselves at once.

"Hush, you lot, you'll scare Marty away," Alistair scolded. He lined everyone up. "Marty, let me introduce you in a civilized manner. You already know Christian." Christian gave Marty a hug. "I think you've met Ellis?"

Ellis shook Marty's hand. "He has, though I wasn't wearing very much at the time so I probably don't seem very familiar." He giggled.

"Ellis served Beau and I in the restaurant at The Underground," Marty explained to the others, his face heating.

"Of course. Well, Benjy here is another server, so you can expect to see him semi-naked as well." Alistair chuckled. "And last but not least, meet Kai. Kai managed to snare the gorgeous Harry, our bar manager at The Underground."

Kai gave Marty a shy smile. "And you've bewitched Salter Beauman, haven't you? What's it like to be with a hunky fireman Dom? I'll bet he's got muscles on his muscles, hasn't he? You will tell us won't you? We share everything."

"I apologize, Marty," Alistair said. "Kai's mouth to brain functionality needs a little attention. He's been up at The Edge and I think Olly has rubbed off on him. You only need to share what you want to."

Marty laughed, appreciating the warm welcome to the group. "I have lots of questions for you all... I'm new to the scene."

"Oh goody!" Kai clapped his hands. "Me too... Well, I was. Harry has been training me." He peered down at his groin and pouted. "He's trying out a new chastity device. He's really mean."

Christian patted Kai's back. "He adores you and you know it."

Kai beamed. "I do. I'm a very lucky sub." He bounced on his toes. "I wish Olly and Aiden were here. They helped me a lot, Marty, especially Olly."

"I've heard a lot about Olly." Marty grinned. "He has quite the reputation. I'll meet him soon, though, because Beau's taking me to a party at The Edge in a few weeks' time."

"The masked ball? That's fabulous! We're all going too."

Alistair nodded. "Carey's closing the Club that weekend so that everyone can go. Most of the members have taken courses at The Edge at one time or another so the Club would be empty anyway. He's organized a coach for anyone who doesn't want to make their own way, but hey...we're stood here gossiping on the pavement when we could be doing it in comfort. With coffee."

They trooped inside and down the stairs to the lower level.

The café proved to be warm and inviting. Comfortable chairs and couches surrounded low tables. Bookcases lined the walls and eclectic knick-knacks were strewn everywhere. On the counter, glass domes covered a dozen or more huge cakes, all with slices cut ready. A blackboard listed an enormous variety of hot drinks.

Marty and his new friends commandeered a seating area. Ellis took their orders.

"Aren't you going to write them down, Ellis?" Christian asked.

"Nope. I'm used to taking orders..."

"Aren't we all!" Benjy fell about laughing.

"Not those orders, dummy... I mean in the restaurant. I can remember. Two cappuccinos, one low-fat vanilla latte, one disgusting double espresso, one peppermint tea and a hot chocolate with whipped cream, chocolate curls and marshmallows for Kai." He rolled his eyes at Kai's whoop of joy. "Three slices of chocolate cake, one lemon drizzle and two Victoria sponge."

"Make sure you get the biggest slices."

"You need a hand?" Alistair asked.

"Nah—the guy at the counter will help me out, though I might have to pay him with Benjy's phone number from the way he's been slobbering in his direction ever since we walked in."

Benjy immediately stood up and stared. "Oh, very nice. Just see if you can gauge how Dommy he is."

Ellis shook his head. "There is no hope for you." He went off to fetch their drinks.

* * * *

Two lattes and a huge amount of hilarity later, Marty decided that the call of nature couldn't wait a minute longer. He stood up.

"I'm going to find the men's room...be back in a bit."

"Follow the corridor and take a right, it's down there somewhere," Ellis said.

The bathrooms were at the back of the building, a fair way to go, but Marty was grateful to stretch his legs. He hummed as he walked, stopping now and then to peer into little shops. *They are such a nice bunch, I can't remember the last time I had such a good evening. And they really like to share! I've learned more about D/s relationships in the last two hours than I'd ever get from the Internet. They all seem so happy and relaxed too. I suppose that's what accepting yourself brings. I need to stop stressing about what's right and wrong in the eyes of other people and concentrate on what I need.*

He pushed open the door to the bathroom and moved to one side as another man left. For a second their eyes met. Marty shivered and a cold trickle of fear slid down his spine. "What the hell?"

Mr. Evil Glare had gone.

"Anyone would think I just murdered his puppy. Must have been having a bad day." Marty shook off the feeling of foreboding that tensed his shoulders. He made use of the facilities then gave his hands a scrub. He raised an eyebrow at his reflection in the mirror. "Time to get back to the fun."

Marty pushed at the bathroom door but it seemed to be stuck. He shoved harder but it wouldn't budge. He rattled the handle and tried again, shoving with his shoulder, but there was no movement at all. "Some idiot's locked me in!"

There was no glass in the door and when Marty ducked down to peer through the keyhole he found it blocked up. He sniffed. A strange scent filtered into the room. Marty caught movement at his feet. Wispy curls of smoke drifted beneath the door. His stomach knotted.

"Oh my God!" He stepped back as more and more smoke seeped through the gap. He patted his pocket, hunting for his phone. "Damn! Left it on the table." Searching around frantically, Marty could find no escape. He retreated into the room. There were no other exits and no windows. He jumped as a fire alarm started screaming.

"Don't panic...someone will be here soon. The others know where I am." He went back to the door and began to bang on it, shouting for help. Someone would hear him. They had to.

* * * *

Beau sat in the station rec room and pretended to read a book. In his head he replayed the previous evening's scene with Marty over and over. He had years of experience of playing with willing subs but nothing could compare with the perfection of that simple scene with Marty.

"What the hell you grinning about, Beau? Did you win the lottery or something?"

Beau looked up into the smirking face of his friend and colleague, Griff Jones. "Something like that."

"Well it's either that or you got laid last night and don't give me any details." Griff held his hands up. "My poor straight mind can't handle it."

Beau smirked. "That's got nothing to do with being straight, you idiot, it's because you've got mashed leeks for brains."

"Hey! That's my national plant you're insulting. Gotta love a country that picks a phallic vegetable as its emblem."

Beau snorted and tossed his book down on the seat next to him. "Now you're making me hungry. Who's on the cooking rota?"

"I am." Griff grinned. "My infamous pot roast has been simmering for a while now. It'll be ready in half an hour or so." He threw himself down next to Beau. "Hey, you're vibrating... Man, you need to leave those toys at home."

Beau rolled his eyes. "It's my phone you idiot." He pulled his mobile from his pocket. "Text message... Oh shit."

"See me dance, betrayer." Griff read the words when Beau held up the screen.

"Spurned lover?" He frowned. "Fuck, that's our firebug isn't it?"

"Who else would know that reference?"

"If he's got your number, it's personal. Who have you pissed off recently?"

Beau shrugged. "Damned if I know." He checked for a number but it had been withheld. He saved the message anyway. "Better go and tell Archer." He got up and headed for the boss's office, Griff right on his heels. Before they got there, the klaxon announcing a shout began to wail. Beau and Griff switched direction and jogged toward the engine bays. They stopped to pull on their boots and gear alongside their colleagues. Archer pulled a sheet from the printer and read it out as they prepared.

"We've got one in progress. All units required. The Marmalade Factory on Egerton Road, South Bank."

Beau checked his watch as he climbed aboard his assigned vehicle. "Eight o'clock, broad fucking daylight." Then his entire body went cold. Marty had told him that he was going to meet up with a group of subs from The Underground after work. He hadn't said exactly where, just that it was a café on the South Bank. Beau prayed that it was too early and that Marty was still firmly chained to his desk under Becket's tender supervision. Archer and Griff were both in the other engine. Beau kept his worries to himself. He and his crew needed to focus on the job ahead. Distraction in firefighting cost lives.

The two fire engines screamed toward Egerton Road, sirens wailing and lights blazing. Cars scattered to the sides of the roads like multicolored marbles. Pedestrians stopped to stare. A few little kids waved and jumped up and down in excitement. Beau tried to call Marty's mobile but it went to voicemail. Becket's number did the same. He had no time to make more calls.

As they approached their destination, the lead truck slowed. Two other fire trucks from another station and several police cars were already on the scene. Beau's heart skipped a beat as caught sight of The Marmalade Factory from the side window. Black smoke billowed from the roof.

"Seems like this one's fully engaged, boys. Stay alert and listen for orders. We're second on scene so we'll take our lead from Station Fifteen." The crew dismounted and joined their colleagues. Archer walked toward the commanding officer, easily identified by his white helmet. Beau ordered his team to start preparing and they went into action like a well-oiled machine.

After a while, Archer crossed the road and joined them again.

"Are there people in there?" Beau asked.

"Yes. The building manager believes up to six people may be trapped in the basement. There are shops, a cafeteria and bathrooms down there. It's all a bit vague because they don't have a sign-in system so we're relying on witnesses and people with missing friends. In the confusion it's possible that people left by different exits, have wandered off or are just stuck in the crowd. The upper floors of the building were successfully evacuated via the outside fire escapes. Fire wardens checked the spaces up there before leaving themselves. It's unlikely that anyone would have headed up toward the roof."

Beau extracted his phone from the depths of a pocket and showed the test message to his boss. "This arrived just before the shout came in."

Archer read it. "Fuck. I can't let you go in there, Beau. That's playing right into this lunatic's hands."

"Are we going in or just providing support?"

"As soon as Fifteen's crews come out for relief, we're next up."

"Then you need me. There aren't enough of us for me to sit out here fucking knitting, and besides, I don't think he wants to kill me. What would the point of that be? He wants attention."

Archer didn't seem convinced but he had little choice and Beau knew it.

"Two teams. You and Jones, Francombe and Woods. Go suit up."

Beau desperately wanted to try Marty's phone again but he knew it wasn't a good idea. It didn't matter who was in the building, he had to do his job regardless. That didn't stop him praying that Marty was safe and well. He helped Griff get his tank on, then did an about-face so that Griff could return the favor. Beau took the opportunity to scan the onlookers. Quite a crowd had gathered beyond the police barriers.

"Is he watching?" He knew from his training that arsonists often liked to observe the results of their work. To his astonishment, he spotted Alistair and Christian from The Underground along with three other young men he recognized. Alistair spotted him and waved frantically.

Carrying his mask, Beau strolled across to the barrier.

"You guys shouldn't be here."

"We can't leave, Mr. Beauman... Marty's in there. He went to use the bathroom. We were all in the cafeteria having coffee and cake. He hadn't been gone long, then the alarms went off. There was smoke everywhere. It got bad really quickly and no one would let us back in the building."

Beau's heart felt like a lump of ice in his chest.

"You're sure he didn't get out another way?"

"As much as we can be. He would have come to find us. He doesn't have his phone with him either. We found it on the table in the coffee shop." Alistair acted as spokesman.

Beau noticed that Alistair's face was bone-white and streaked with soot. Kai and Benjy were sobbing. Ellis seemed frozen with fear and Christian's pale skin was tinged with green.

"Take everyone back to the club. As soon as I know anything I'll get word to you, but you mustn't stay here. This blaze is on the news." He pointed at the TV cameras. "If Becket or Carey sees any of you here at the scene they'll be frantic with worry."

Alistair nodded. "We'll do that... Please be careful in there."

"Don't worry about me." Beau patted Alistair's shoulder and headed back toward the building. He walked without seeing where he was going and only Griff's voice knocked him from his trance.

"It's our turn, buddy." Griff gestured toward the four firemen staggering from the building.

"My boyfriend's in there, Griff. Bastard set a trap. He knows me. He could be here watching this all go to hell."

"There are cameras everywhere. Investigators will pull all the footage and make requests for witnesses to send in their cell phone pictures. If he's here, you'll get your chance to spot him. Now let's go get your boy."

Beau pulled his mask down and let his eyes adjust to the slight distortion in his vision. There was so much color and movement everywhere it was a relief to have slightly muted hearing. More fire trucks rolled up. Several jets of water were aimed at the building and ladders extended into the smoke-filled sky. Hoses like thick yellow pythons slithered up the ladders, hauled by men facing smoke and heat and the distinct possibility of injury.

He and Griff walked into a nightmare, followed by a second team. The entrance hall ran with black water while above their heads flames boiled and rolled. Beau blanked his mind. He had to get his head in the game or he'd be putting his colleagues' lives at risk. Griff took the lead. He moved through the dense curtain of smoke, using hand signals to indicate which direction they should take. Beau and Griff went for the bathrooms while the other pair took the route toward the cafeteria.

Beau listened to the fire, which had a language all of its own. A background roar was interrupted by hisses, crackles and spitting. It was a language of violence, of defiance.

"Back off, bitch," Beau muttered. "He's using you. This place is no challenge."

Griff made it to the top of the basement stairs. He pointed downward and gave a thumbs up. Beau responded in kind. Fire had eaten away parts of the wooden handrail but the steps were stone and intact. The flames had followed the path of least resistance and gnawed through the ceiling to the floor above. Fire caressed the walls and danced overhead along the charred beams. Beau could admire the beauty and the horror of it. The colors and lights tempted him like a siren, seducing him with her display. He had to block out his instinct to run, focusing instead on Griff's back and the need to find Marty.

Beneath the bitter smell of smoke, the tang of petrol was evident. Huge quantities of accelerant must have been used. Beau didn't have the luxury of time to consider how the fire had been set. A section of the ceiling collapsed ahead of them, venting the fire, feeding it so that it reared up as a lethal wall.

Griff dropped to his knees, and Beau followed his lead as the furnace rolled overhead.

"Fuck that was close." The fire parted before them. Beau tapped Griff's shoulder and gestured forward. "Let's go." Beau's entire body vibrated with the need to move faster, and that was exactly why Griff took the lead. He would ensure that they were careful, methodical, that they didn't miss anything or anyone.

"Why the fuck did they put the bathrooms in such an inaccessible place?"

Every minute counted. Beau uttered a little prayer. If Marty got hurt it would be Beau's fault. He was the firebug's target. Marty was just in the way. Griff came to a halt. Beau peered through the dense smoke and saw they'd reached the bathroom door. Griff ripped off a glove and pressed his fingers to the wood. He signaled that they were good to go. Griff kicked at the door but it didn't budge. Beau removed the axe from his belt and pushed past him. He sank the blade into the wood over and over, splintering the panels. He stepped back and Griff charged the door. This time it gave way and the two of them pushed past the debris.

The smoke in the bathroom wasn't quite as dense, but it still rivalled London smog. Beau peered through the gloom, desperately searching for any sign of Marty. Griff grabbed his arm and pointed to the far corner of the room.

"There. Under the basins."

A body lay curled in the fetal position as far back in the corner as it was possible to get. Beau reached it in three strides.

"Marty! It's him, Griff." Beau pulled off his glove and felt for a pulse. It was there, strong and steady. "Let's go." Beau picked Marty up and slung him over one shoulder.

Griff gave him a thumbs up and they moved, one behind the other, back to the corridor. The stone steps to the ground floor were intact but the wooden handrail was still burning, the varnish providing an effective accelerant. Everything flammable was alight. Paint curled and blackened, ash like dirty snowflakes rained around them. The heat was intense, and Beau knew the firebug had done a thorough job. For such a large building to go up so fast, so violently, there had to have been several ignition points.

As he reached the ground floor, Beau hefted Marty's body and fixed his attention on the narrow rectangle of light that meant life-giving fresh air. He could not, would not, allow himself to contemplate that Marty might not survive. Despite the best efforts of his colleagues on the outside of the building, the fire had taken command. As he and Griff pushed toward the exit, behind them everything was being consumed. Beau knew better than to look back. His escape route grew narrower and narrower, the light swallowed by writhing amber and gold. He didn't hesitate, just ducked his head, protected Marty's body as best he could and dove through the flame. He hit the ground hard and rolled, keeping his weight from Marty. Griff landed half on top of him. Immediately they were doused with water as someone directed a hose on them.

"Must have been smoldering pretty good," Griff commented to no one in particular. Beau yanked off his headgear and gauntlets then scrambled to his knees. He leaned over Marty and whispered a short prayer.

"Wake up, damn it, this is no time for taking a nap. I swear I'm going to tan your hide for scaring me like this."

Marty's eyes flickered open and he coughed. "Sounds like fun..." He broke into another coughing fit. "Why am I wet? Is it raining?"

A pair of paramedics shoved Beau unceremoniously out of the way.

"Move it, fire boy, let the magicians do their work. Don't go far, though...you're next."

"Why does that sound like a threat?" Beau asked Griff, who lay on his back staring at the sky.

"Because it is. They can't wait to start poking and prodding. Committed sadists, the lot of them." He coughed up a laugh.

Beau decided on the least life-threatening option and got out of the way. As the paramedics worked on Marty, Beau scanned the crowd of onlookers. He focused on one face at a time, trying to spot anyone that seemed familiar. Crimson and gold shimmered on skin and glinted in hair. The spectacle of the fire had drawn all sorts, which was not surprising considering the pyrotechnics going on behind him. The building was fully ablaze and beyond saving. The shell might survive, but not much more. Fire shot out through the roof, visible in flashes through the dense clouds of black smoke. Beau's senses were assaulted on all fronts. He could taste the smoke, smell an acrid mix of scents. His eyes stung and he flicked flakes of ash from his skin. Teams of men directed forceful jets of water at the building, aiming to contain rather than control the conflagration.

One of the remaining windows exploded outward in a shower of jagged, glittering shards. A collective gasp came from the crowd. Even at a safe distance from the building, Beau could feel the intensity of the heat and muttered a quiet prayer of thanks that he, Griff and Marty were all safely out of the building.

Someone tossed bottles of water in his direction. He caught them and handed one to Griff. "Did the other team get out okay?"

Griff twisted the cap off his bottle. "They're over there." He pointed to a group of men standing by one of the fire engines. They're in better shape than we are." He took a long swallow of water then wiped his mouth with the back of his hand.

Shedding his kit, Beau heaved himself to his feet and went to stand as close as he could to Marty. He had an oxygen mask strapped to his face and the paramedics were about to load him onto a stretcher.

"He needs to go to the hospital to get checked out properly." One of the green-uniformed men addressed

Beau. "You can ride along and we'll check you out on the way."

"Is it bad?" Beau asked. Marty had his eyes closed and his skin was pale beneath the soot streaks.

"Hard to tell, but hopefully not. There was some blackening around the airways and that is a worry but he's not coughing as much as I would expect from a really bad case of smoke inhalation. I don't think there's burn damage. He does appear to have some bruising on his hands. He's definitely in shock, so we need to get moving."

The paramedics lifted the stretcher until the wheels beneath it locked in place. They rested the oxygen cylinder between Marty's blanket-wrapped legs and strapped him down. Beau walked alongside, keeping his eyes on Marty's face. He yelled to Griff that he was heading to the hospital, and Griff jogged over.

"How is he?" Griff asked.

"Don't know. Can you let the boss know where I'm going?"

"Sure thing. I've got you covered. Hope your boy pulls through, mate." Griff patted Beau's shoulder and let him go.

As they reached the back of the ambulance, Beau shivered at the sensation of déjà vu. "I fucking hate these meat wagons. Hate hospitals. Fuck."

"Well aren't you just a ray of sunshine." One of the paramedics nudged Beau out of the way so that they could load Marty's gurney.

Beau recognized his mood for what it was, a reaction to the helplessness that threatened to overwhelm him. The sight of Marty lying so still, the danger that he and his colleagues had been thrown into, the fear that the firebug would not be caught all combined to blacken Beau's disposition to match the soot on Marty's skin.

He climbed wearily into the vehicle and strapped in. Opposite him, Marty stirred so he leaned forward and grasped his hand. Marty held on tight but didn't open his eyes.

"I love you, Marty. This isn't the place I wanted to say it for the first time, but you need to know. Squeeze my hand if you heard me, sweetheart."

The pressure on his fingers increased. Marty's eyelids fluttered, then Beau was meeting his gaze.

"Love you back." The words were little more than a croak but the best Beau had ever heard.

Chapter Nine

Marty languished in Beau's enormous bed. Oh, he was warm and comfortable, but he was bored. Mind-numbingly bored. When he was home from work, Beau cosseted him like an invalid and only allowed him up to eat and use the bathroom. Even then he hovered like an overprotective mama bear. It had been more than a week since the fire at The Marmalade Factory and Marty had stopped coughing up his guts a while back. He felt fine.

The two days he had been forced to stay at the hospital had driven him round the bend. The doctor had proved to be almost as Dommy as Beau, but he had at least been clear in explaining the symptoms and effects of smoke inhalation and the need for caution. After his rescue, Marty couldn't even guess at how long he'd been unconscious. He had done everything he could to stay safe. Banging and shouting on the bathroom door had proved hopeless. He'd retreated to the back corner of the bathroom and soaked some paper towels in water. He'd wedged as many as he could under the door in an attempt to reduce the thickening smoke. He'd stayed low to the floor and curled up in a corner but couldn't remember blacking out, just that it had gotten harder and harder to breathe.

In the casualty department, Marty had displayed all the common symptoms of smoke inhalation, including shortness of breath, hoarseness and a pounding headache. Black particles had clogged his nose and colored his lips. His eyes had been so red he could have been out partying for three nights straight. He'd been subjected to several chest x-rays. A light probe had been attached to his finger to determine the amount of oxygen in his blood, tubes of which were extracted for dozens of tests. Marty was convinced that the doctors had been irritated that they couldn't find anything really wrong with him. He'd begged Beau to take him home, and Beau had agreed, but set conditions. One of those rules had Marty confined to bed.

"Enough is enough." Marty checked the bedside clock. He had an hour before Beau was due home. "Plenty of time." He threw back the covers and trotted to the bathroom. "This may get me in trouble but I'm beyond caring."

* * * *

With ten minutes to spare he finished his preparations and got back under the covers, pulling them up to his chin so that Beau wouldn't see what he was wearing. Marty chuckled. He couldn't wait to see Beau's reaction. "Thank God for online shopping." He wriggled and groped beneath the sheets in an attempt to adjust the position of his rapidly swelling cock. "With any luck, Beau will feel obliged to punish me." His lips curled into a smug smile.

When the scrape of Beau's key in the lock reached Marty's ears he had to fight back a giggle. He plumped a pillow and attempted to affect a just-woken-up appearance. Beau strode into the bedroom, gorgeous as always. He'd showered and changed at the fire station because the ends of his hair were still damp, and Marty smelled the familiar scent of Beau's favorite mint shower gel.

Beau stopped at the end of the bed and examined Marty with suspicion. "What have you been up to? You're acting like a little boy who's been caught scrumping."

Marty widened his eyes in an attempt at innocence.

"Who me?" His voice came out as a squeak.

"Yes. You." Beau frowned. He checked out the room as if searching for clues.

Marty snorted and hid his face in a pillow. Beau ripped back the covers and sucked in his breath.

"Holy fuck!"

Marty tossed the pillow away, spread his legs and rubbed the bulge stretching the front of his red latex shorts. Thick, red leather cuffs wrapped his wrists, matching the set around his ankles. Beau pounced.

"You have been a very, *very* bad sub." He straddled Marty's thighs and slapped his hand away from his cock.

"Uh-huh. I have, Sir."

"And why have you misbehaved? You're supposed to be resting."

Marty jerked as Beau pinched his nipples in turn. "It's a proven fact, Sir, that a lack of sex can induce psychotic episodes. I wasn't in my right mind when I shaved myself smooth and stuffed my ass with the biggest plug I could find."

"Does lack of sex lead to an unstoppable urge to shop for kinky underwear, as well?" Beau stroked the latex.

"Very perceptive, Sir." Marty bobbed his head. "It does."

"And this is your subtle way of telling me you feel better?"

"No, Sir. This is me begging you to fuck me before my balls change from blue to purple."

"You really are pushing your luck, aren't you? You'll get your wish. My cock is definitely overdue an appointment with your ass. Whether you deserve to come is open to debate."

Marty blinked. "That's just mean...Sir."

"I *am* mean."

Beau hooked a finger in each side of Marty's shorts and pulled. They turned inside out as they descended smoothly. "You used talcum powder."

"It's good to be prepared Sir. Sweaty latex is not attractive, and anyway, I hoped that I wouldn't be wearing them for very long."

"Seems we both have the gift of perception." Beau finished stripping Marty bare. "Love the cuffs." Beau yanked Marty's hands above his head. "Keep them there. Were you enough of a Boy Scout to bring supplies?"

"Under the pillow."

Beau groped around and pulled out a strip of condoms and a tube of slick. He held up the length of foil packages. "Feeling optimistic?" His eyes glittered with promise.

"Feeling horny, Sir."

Beau shook his head. "What happened to the sweet, shy little sub I knew?"

Marty pursed his lips. "A week ago I came very close to being fried to a crisp. It gave me new perspective, Sir. I only get one life. Time I start living it for me. For us."

"I like the new you." Beau grinned and hopped off the bed. For a moment Marty panicked, thinking that Beau was going to leave him hanging, but the feeling dissipated as Beau stripped off his clothes, tossing garments randomly around him. Seconds later, Marty began a rapid slide into a haze of lust as Beau began to lick and bite every inch of his body. When Beau took Marty's aching cock into his mouth, Marty teetered on the brink of orgasm. He fought it back.

Oh Christ. Should have worn a cock ring. Don't have permission. Did I miss him telling me I could come? Perhaps I did. Fuck, fuck, fuck. Can't hold it! Wild thoughts skittered through Marty's mind as Beau played with his body.

"No coming till I'm inside you," Beau ordered, his voice deep and growly.

Marty whimpered and squirmed, trying to get the message across that he needed that to happen. Immediately. The telepathy worked because Beau lifted one of Marty's legs and rested his calf on his shoulder. He slid the plug from Marty's body, gloved and slicked his cock and pressed the blunt head against Marty's eager hole.

"Yes! Finally!" Marty bucked his hips. "Oh...did I say that out loud?"

"You did." Beau pushed home, driving deep and hard.

A sharp burn preceded the bliss, but Marty welcomed it. Beau pistoned into him, and Marty grabbed for the bedrails to stop being thrown around by the force. Beau snapped his hips over and over, withdrawing almost completely before plunging forward. Marty snuck a hand down, reaching for his cock.

"Touch what's mine and you won't get to come for a month," Beau snapped. Marty put his hand back where it was supposed to be. A week's abstinence had been hard enough to put up with—a month was unthinkable. His muscles trembled. His balls drew up hot and tight.

"Pleeease!" The word came out as a wail.

"Come." Beau commanded, and Marty could do nothing but obey.

Cum fountained from his aching dick. He jerked like a puppet on a string with no control over his body's responses. Beau continued to pound into him, and as Beau shouted his own release, Marty's vision faded to black.

* * * *

Marty came round to warmth and the security of Beau's hard body curled around him.

Oh wow, it still feels like Beau's dick is in my ass. Marty shifted, and Beau's grip tightened. *Does he think I'm trying to escape?* Marty melted into Beau's embrace. *If only we could stay this way forever.*

"You're thinking too hard again. I thought I cured you of that last night." Beau's voice was rough from sleep.

"We slept all night?"

"*You* did. I've never fucked anyone into unconsciousness before." Beau sounded inordinately pleased with himself. "I cleaned you up and you didn't stir. I had a shower, made a snack…came to bed and you were still out cold. It just goes to show that you *are* still healing. Your body knows when it needs rest."

"I'm fine." Marty's stomach growled. "But hungry." He rolled onto his back and realized that the cuffs were still strapped around his wrists and ankles. "And I need the bathroom."

Beau let him go. Marty rolled out of bed and crossed the room, making sure to wiggle his butt a little as he went. Beau's groan made him laugh.

Marty freshened up, cleaned his teeth and ran his fingers through his hair. When he got back to the bedroom, Beau was gone and the enticing smell of brewing coffee drifted on the air. By the time Marty had pulled on clean underwear — cotton, not latex — the aroma of crisping bacon mingled with the coffee. He made a beeline for the kitchen area. Beau waved a spatula at him. "Bacon sandwiches. Quick and easy. I intend to spend the rest of the weekend fucking that tight little ass of yours, so you need sustenance. Why did you put underwear on? I don't recall telling you to do that."

Marty hesitated. Beau hadn't issued an order but it was implied. His face heated even before he moved. Once he'd lowered his shorts and stepped out of them, Marty was convinced that his entire body must be blushing.

"That's better. Why don't you get the OJ from the fridge and pour us a couple of glasses?"

When Marty bent to do as he'd been asked, Beau wolf whistled.

"I can't believe you did that!" Marty whirled to face him.

"Why not? You have a hot ass."

Marty sighed. "So why am I the only one naked? You have a delicious butt, but I'm stuck putting up with denim."

Beau shrugged and plated their breakfast. "Naked sub, dressed Dom. That's just the way it is."

"Why?" Marty asked, genuinely curious.

"Because that's the way I like it. Now sit and eat."

Marty ferried juice and coffee to Beau's small table while Beau carried the food. Once he'd deposited his cargo, Beau put a cushion on the leather-covered chair.

"Don't want to have to peel you off your seat." He smirked.

"Very thoughtful," Marty said as he sat. *I'm naked apart from a set of cuffs. What the hell am I doing?* He took one bite of his sandwich and forgot all about his lack of clothes. "Oh...my tongue is having an orgasm."

Beau chuckled. "I'm glad my food is appreciated." He ate a few bites himself. "I meant to tell you last night before you led me astray... I caught up with the fire-investigation team at work yesterday. The bug made it seem simple, but it was anything but. He must have visited The Marmalade Factory several times to get things prepared because he set the fire in such a way that it would progress behind the walls and through the voids between floors. He was helped by the age of the building. Plenty of fuel, timber beams, years of dust and debris. The landlord had an excellent sprinkler system and alarms installed but they'd been disabled. Our bug wanted the place to burn to the ground and he didn't care who was in there when it happened."

Marty shuddered. "But he did care, didn't he? He wanted me trapped in there. He wanted me dead. If he had to visit several times to get everything prepared, does he work there?"

"It's a possibility. The police are investigating the backgrounds of all the staff, but it's a big place with several businesses, cleaning staff, contractors and a lot of temporary labor. Loads of students who pick up a few hours here and there makes it even more difficult. Even a customer could easily slip into the staff areas. There is no security system, just 'staff only' signs. Who's going to notice a regular coffee drinker disappearing for a while between lattes? He could be shopping or just going to the bathroom. Those places are too busy and unless our firebug is walking around with handfuls of petrol-soaked fuel he might as well be invisible. If someone were to buy a ticket for a film, they'd easily have a couple of hours to move around. There are several exits from the screening room."

"Whoever it is has some gall."

"Working in plain sight. Attracts much less attention than sneaking around."

"But why does he want *me* dead?" Marty said, perplexed.

"Because of me, though I still have no idea why." Beau sipped his coffee slowly. "I've wracked my brains trying to think of who could possibly be this obsessed."

"Someone you gave the brush-off?" Marty asked. "We should go back to the date of the first incident and check out what was going on in your life at the time."

"Okay. Let's make this morning Operation Flame." Beau grinned. "Once we've cleared up breakfast, I'll get the calendar and my diary and we'll take a trip back in time. You can make notes and let that analytical brain get to work."

"That sounds great." Marty's excitement had him bouncing on his cushion. He couldn't wait to get started. "Can I get dressed, Sir?"

"Are you cold?" Beau lifted an eyebrow.

"No...it's lovely and warm in here." Marty's confusion must have showed on his face.

"You don't need clothes to use your laptop. You'll stay as you are," Beau said firmly.

"I..." Marty's cock hardened. "Yes, Sir."

Beau cleared the table, then stacked the crockery and cutlery in the dishwasher. He disappeared into the bedroom for a minute or two, and when he came back, he placed a bottle of lube, a large butt plug and a cock ring on the table in front of Marty.

"Bend over the table."

Marty stared at him. *Surely he can't be serious? Oh my God...he is!* He pushed his chair back and leaned over the polished wooden surface, grasping the far edge of the tabletop for stability. His legs shook. He couldn't see what Beau was up to but the snick of the cap on the lube was distinct. Slicked fingers pressed against his tender hole.

Two, that's two fingers, not one... Marty squirmed and pushed back. He yelped as Beau landed a firm smack on his ass.

"Be still."

The somewhat cursory preparation complete, Beau pushed the plug against Marty's entrance. Marty clenched his muscles, fighting the invasion. Not because he objected to his Dom's actions but because his body seemed to have a mind of its own.

"Relax. Let it in." Beau's words soothed Marty enough and the plug slipped into him.

"Oh! So big..." The plug filled him, stretched him. It nudged his prostate and he gasped.

Deftly, Beau fastened the restrictive ring around the base of his cock and balls. The urge to come didn't subside but a few panting breaths made things bearable.

"I wonder how long you'll stay hard," Beau mused, teasing. "You certainly respond well to being stuffed full." He gave Marty's ass another firm slap. "Once we both get tested, I'll enjoy pumping you full of my seed, then plugging you to keep it inside you all day."

"Oh God. How do you expect me to focus when you say things like that?" Marty's inner muscles contracted around the plug.

"If I can focus with you naked and tempting right next to me, then I'm sure you can manage too," Beau said sternly. "Get your laptop set up on the table and we'll make a start."

Marty dashed to the bedroom to fetch his machine and soon had it operational. He set up a spreadsheet and began to plug in the dates of all the fires suspected to be the work of the arsonist. Beau had notes of the dates stored in his phone. He used the wall calendar from the kitchen area to check his social engagements and Marty added those to the list. Next came nights Beau had spent at The Underground.

Marty squinted at his data. "From a quick analysis, I can see that the fires have all happened within a day or two of you spending time at the Club. There's normally a short gap. The exception is the fire that happened after the night we had the private playroom."

"The day my shift changed," Beau noted.

"Yes."

"I often go to the club the night before a day off. The bug only strikes when I'm back at work, so that makes sense. He knows my routine. There's a definite link to The Underground, so why can't I think of anyone that might be responsible?"

"This date here corresponds with something called The Nightlife Exhibition. What was that?"

"You know Alistair is a photographer?"

Marty nodded.

"Well, after Joe and Olly rescued him from the clinic his father sent him to, Carey celebrated by putting on a surprise showing of his work at the club. It was a huge success. He used it to expose Alistair's father. It was quite a night."

"But you weren't involved in the rescue or anything to do with Alistair's father, were you?"

"No, not at all." Beau scrubbed at his hair in frustration. "Why can't I see it...? Wait. Go back a bit." He peered at the screen then prodded a line with his finger. "That night there was an incident at the club. A small fire. I was there with another member who's also a fireman. We put the fire out before it really got started and checked the club for any other risks. Carey later got a text with a threat that worse would happen if he tried to get Alistair back."

"Did the person who set that fire ever get caught?" Marty asked, excited that they might finally be getting somewhere.

"Yes. I can't remember the guy's name but he was a club member that Alistair's father had bribed. He was the one who let the men in that took Alistair as well. Aiden was involved in identifying him. I think he was arrested. I didn't take much notice of what happened with him."

"So he wasn't someone you played with?" Marty fought back a surge of jealousy.

"No. I don't think I ever noticed him at all. Fuck." Beau clenched his fists.

"What?"

"See me dance. The message from the fire sites — that's what was written. Perhaps that's the whole point. I didn't *see* him at all. Not at the club anyway."

"But he wanted you to." Marty reached for Beau's hand and gave it a pat. "I'll call Becket. He and Aiden will be able to track this man down, whoever he is.

They can pass the information to the police and maybe this nightmare will be over."

Beau nodded. "There's something missing, though. From what I recall, Carey removed the guy's membership, so he can't have been tracking my movements at The Underground. Surely I would have noticed someone hanging around, following me? It doesn't make sense."

"It's a start. Let me get Becket on the case and we'll see where it goes."

Marty made his call and gave Becket a rapid explanation of what he and Beau had come up with. He rang off.

"All we can do now is wait and see what they come up with. However are we going to pass the time?" He batted his lashes at Beau.

Beau pounced, dragging him from his chair and throwing him over his shoulder. Marty yelped when Beau's hand connected with his ass, driving the plug deeper.

"How about some role play? Fireman rescues naughty sub caught playing with matches and teaches him a lesson."

Marty bounced on Beau's shoulder as he was carried toward the bedroom. His rock-hard cock rubbed against Beau's firm chest.

"What kind of lesson, Sir?"

"The kind that makes you forget your own name." A couple more smacks connected with Marty's behind. He squirmed happily.

"Sounds perfect."

Chapter Ten

Marty still found it a little odd to be socializing with his boss at The Underground. It wasn't like going round to a colleague's house of an evening for a barbecue or potluck supper. It was leather and chains, collars and cuffs. Becket in the office was a calm, efficient professional, albeit with a penchant for giving orders. At the club he was all Dom, radiating power and authority like a beacon. He only spoke to Marty if Beau allowed it. The whole situation was surreal. Marty tried to wrap his head around the psychology of it all but in the end gave it up. *Go with the flow. This is real. My boss is a Dom but not* my *Dom. Respect for Becket at work is not the same as the submission I give Beau.*

Marty wriggled closer to Beau and leaned against him in an attempt to absorb some of his strength and calm. They sat on one side of a booth in a quiet corner of The Underground. Becket and Christian sat opposite them. The table held four glasses of iced juice and bowls of Becket's favorite cheesy nachos. Beau picked out a savory treat and fed it to Marty.

"Oh yum, that's delicious, thank you, Sir." Marty smacked his lips together happily. "I'm quite hungry." He reached for the bowl.

Beau slapped his hand away. "Oh no you don't. You'll eat from my hand or not at all. Perhaps I should cuff you."

"Oh! Wait...you carry handcuffs on you?"

"Of course I do. You never know when they'll come in handy for restraining a misbehaving sub."

Across the table, Christian giggled. Becket gave him an indulgent hug.

"Now, sweetheart, Beau's not the only Dom who likes to be prepared." He patted his belt where a pair of black steel cuffs resided. "No making fun or I might have to use these."

"Please?" Christian made the soppiest puppy eyes Marty had ever witnessed.

"Later, love. I promise." Becket's hand disappeared down the front of Christian's trousers.

"Thanks for inviting us over tonight, Becket." Beau raised his glass in a toast. "But I get the feeling that this isn't just a get together and chat kind of night."

"No, it isn't. I didn't want to go into detail on the phone, you never know who's listening. I'm expecting a couple of other people who should be here any minute." He glanced across the room. "Heath and Aiden will be joining us soon."

"Has Aiden found something? Why didn't you tell me at work?" Marty blurted out. A slight increase in the pressure of Beau's hold on him was the only sign Beau gave to acknowledge Marty's lapse.

"Oh! I'm sorry, Sir. I spoke out of turn." Marty lowered his eyes.

"Understandable given the circumstances, love. You're forgiven."

"No punishment?" Marty secretly wished he might get one.

"I didn't say that." Beau stroked the bulge in Marty's leather trousers and gave him an enigmatic smile.

Marty swallowed nervously.

Becket cleared his throat. "To answer Marty's question, yes, Aiden has some information. I never got a chance to tell you at work, Marty, because I had to get a few facts checked out first. Heath had to come to London on business today and he doesn't like leaving Aiden behind so I decided it would be a good opportunity for him to come in to the office for some overdue staff training. That's tomorrow. They're staying at Joe's house tonight and Heath thought it would be easier if we all got together here."

There was a slight change in the noise level of the club as the general chatter reduced.

"Sounds like they've arrived." Becket rolled his eyes. "Heath does have a way of drawing peoples' attention."

Marty swiveled around. He gaped. The couple walking toward them would stop traffic. He knew instantly that Heath was the taller man of the pair. He dressed simply in black jeans and a plain shirt but moved with a confidence bordering on arrogance. Slightly behind him a young man in skintight leather scowled at the world. He went shirtless, and when Marty glanced down, he saw that he was also barefoot. Around his neck was a collar that could have been fashioned in a medieval dungeon. It didn't detract from his beauty. Aiden was stunning.

Beau and Becket both stood to greet Heath. Marty stole a glance at Christian. "Is that collar cast iron?" he mouthed.

Christian nodded, fingering the soft strip of leather around his own throat. Marty gulped. He didn't think he'd like to have something so obviously uncomfortable around his neck. The Doms took their seats, and Beau pulled Marty into his lap. Aiden sank to his knees at the side of Heath's chair, clasped his hands behind his back and bowed his head. He kept perfectly still.

"Marty, I'd like to introduce you to Heath Anders and his sub, Aiden," Becket said.

"You may speak, love," Beau added when Marty gave him a questioning glance.

"It's nice to meet you. Sir. I've heard a lot about you," Marty said, addressing Heath.

"None of it good, I imagine." Heath's eyes twinkled, and Marty realized that despite the intimidating appearance, Heath was not a threat. "It's a pleasure to meet you too, Marty. We were very relieved to hear you survived the Temple Church bomb." He pulled Aiden's head up by his hair. "Say hello, Aiden."

Aiden snarled and jerked his head free. "Fucking dictator." Aiden switched off the scowl he directed at Heath then smiled sweetly at Marty. "It's great to meet a colleague, Marty, and it will make a change to have an intelligent conversation for once. Becket speaks highly of you. I hope we'll get to spend some time together at the office tomorrow."

"That's ten you've earned so far this evening, love," Heath said mildly.

"Yes, Sir." Aiden sighed and resumed his examination of the carpet.

"Just ten strokes, Heath? You're getting soft," Becket teased.

"Not strokes. Days. Ten days of deep submission. In chastity." Heath stroked Aiden's hair, and to Marty's surprise, Aiden rested his cheek against Heath's thigh.

"Aiden has been a little high-strung recently and needs grounding."

Beau chuckled. "Man after my own heart."

"Sir!" Marty exclaimed in a panic. "You wouldn't?"

Beau just gave him a look that said, yes, he definitely would. Marty discovered his cock had hardened. He wriggled in Beau's lap, trying to find a comfortable position. *Stupid dick. Why the hell is it getting excited at the idea of being locked up? Completely irrational response.*

Becket put his arm around Christian's shoulders and pulled him close.

"So, tell us what you've found. No need to mention *how*, though."

Heath nodded. "Aiden, please explain."

Aiden raised his head. "I was getting precisely nowhere until Becket passed on what Marty and Beau worked out. It was the hook I needed to draw out other information. The club member that set the fire here called himself Jonah Salter. That should have been a clue in itself—he stole your name, Mr. Beauman. His club registration documents listed him as Jonah Salter-Smith. The club requires a National Insurance number for identification purposes and I was able to determine that his real name is just a simple Jonah Smith."

Marty wondered how Aiden had managed to hack the national database containing *that* information. A warrant to do it officially would have taken days to obtain.

"Wow. This obsession has been going on a long time," Beau said with a frown.

"It has. Once I knew his real name, the search got a little easier. I used some facial recognition algorithms on photographic records of fires where you were in attendance. Jonah Smith came up three times in photographs of onlookers. He's been following you for months."

Marty wanted to ask how the algorithms had worked but restrained himself. He and Aiden could talk about that another time.

"And all because I didn't notice him here?" Beau sounded perplexed. "It's not as if I deliberately ignored him. He just didn't make it onto my radar."

"No, that's part of the reason but not the whole story," Aiden said. "He joined the club *after* some of the fires. I think it's likely that this obsession started out as some kind of hero worship. I haven't found anything solid yet but I believe it's likely he would have been involved in an earlier incident, not as an arsonist but a victim. With a bit of perseverance it wouldn't have been hard for him to find out that Beau was a member here."

"That makes sense. The messages left at early fire scenes were not often legible, but at least one was definitely worded slightly differently. *See me burn* rather than *See me dance*. I'd lay money that the change occurred after he joined the club."

"We've passed all the information on to the police," Becket chimed in. "There was no sign of this guy at his listed address. His photograph has been circulated and a warrant issued for his arrest. If he surfaces, he'll be spotted sooner or later."

"What about work?" Marty asked.

"He had a job at The Marmalade Factory. He was deputy manager of the cinema there, appointed three months ago. They have some scheme where they take on offenders on probation. No surprise, he hasn't been seen since the fire."

"Wow. He would have had all the time in the world to set things up there. It's a miracle no one was killed." Marty shivered, and Beau drew him closer.

"He's caused millions of pounds worth of damage and put several people in the hospital. He's risked my colleagues' lives needlessly," Beau said. "But there's still one thing I don't understand. How has he managed to keep such close tabs on me? Carey threw him out of the club and even if he's been watching me he can't have managed that twenty-four hours a day."

"And how did he know that that the sub social would take place at The Marmalade Factory?" Marty blurted out. "He has to have a connection here at The Underground."

"I think we need to talk to Carey," Heath said. "Maybe he can help."

Becket slipped from his seat. "I'll go and find him. I'll order another round of drinks and snacks while I'm there."

"I'll help, Sir." Christian followed him, leaving Beau, Marty, Heath and Aiden together.

Marty snuggled as close as he could get to Beau. "This is a nightmare, Sir, but I can understand how someone could get obsessed with you."

"The only stalker I want on my tail is you." Beau stroked his hair.

A low chuckle drew Marty's gaze to Heath.

"You two are good together," Heath said. "Perhaps it's true what they say — that what doesn't kill you makes you stronger."

"I'd prefer not to test that premise too often," Beau said wryly. "On a more pleasant subject, I should thank you for your invitation to the party at The Edge. We're thrilled to be coming."

"It's going to be quite the weekend. It's hard to believe that Joe and I have been in business together for so long. So many of our friends have been through hard times in the last couple of years, it's a good opportunity for us all to let our hair down and celebrate."

"Whose idea was a masked ball?"

At Heath's side, Aiden snorted but kept his head bowed.

"As soon as we're done here, you're going to be strapped over the nearest spanking bench, my love," Heath growled.

Marty just caught the muttered "fuck you" that came from Aiden.

"Oh I will be. Fucking you, that is. You won't be coming, though, not for a very long time." The threat in Heath's tone was crystal clear.

Marty shuddered. Heath and Aiden had a strange relationship—they both seemed to get off on the conflict between them. As if sensing Marty's distress, Beau gave him a gentle kiss.

"Remember there are many kinds of submission, love. It's not a one-size-fits-all kind of thing."

Marty relaxed in his arms. "Of course. I should know better. It's just that Heath is a little scary," he whispered in Beau's ear.

Heath smirked.

"I think he heard you, love." Beau laughed.

"To answer your question, the ball is all Olly's work. It's going to be the event of the year, though I have a feeling he's not just planning a party. Devious urchin is definitely up to something."

Before Heath could expand, Becket and Christian came back followed by Carey and Alistair. Behind them, Goran, the assistant bar manager, had his huge arm around Benjy's shoulders. Benjy, dressed in his waitstaff uniform, was wide-eyed and shaky.

Heath pulled up a few more chairs and they all sat in a ragged circle. Goran pulled Benjy onto his lap, making him seem even smaller.

Carey cleared his throat. "I think you all know Benjy. You may not know that his surname is Smith."

There was silence as everyone absorbed Carey's words. Marty spoke first, "You're his brother. You're Jonah's brother. Oh, Benjy, what have you done?"

Benjy burst into tears. "I didn't know! I'm sorry!" He curled into Goran's arms.

Beau scowled. "Carey? Why aren't you calling the police?"

"Because Benjy had no idea what his brother was up to. He's an innocent pawn in all this."

Benjy took in some sobbing gulps of air. "I had no idea. Please believe me. Jonah did community service after the fire here and he said it was a stupid mistake, that he'd only done it for the money. Everyone deserves a second chance so I accepted what he said. He seemed to have changed. He asked about everyone here, took an interest in my job and my friends. Then he got a post at The Marmalade Factory cinema and I didn't see him very much. He always seemed to be working or out and about. He suggested that we go to the café for our social and I thought he was trying to make up for not being around." Benjy snuffled and wiped roughly at his wet cheeks.

Goran petted him and made soothing noises.

"After the fire, he disappeared. I tried calling him but he's not answering his phone. I worked out that he had to be involved but I didn't dare say anything. I knew you'd all hate me."

Marty's heart broke for his friend, who was clearly distressed. "We don't hate you Benjy. You didn't set the fires. None of this is your fault."

That made Benjy cry even harder. He buried his face in Goran's enormous chest. Benjy's entire body shook with sobs. "I should have said something straight away but I don't know where he is, I really don't. I'm not hiding him or covering up. He could have killed people. He could have killed me! He doesn't care about me or anyone else."

"Goran is going to take care of Benjy," Carey said. "He'll take him along to the police station to make a statement, then home."

"Am I...am I fired?" Benjy didn't face them and the words were muffled.

"No you're not fired. You owned up as soon as I asked you if you knew anything." Carey patted Benjy's bare back. "I'll expect you back at work tomorrow with a smile on that pretty face. Okay?"

"'Kay. Thank you, Mr. Hoffmann. I'm really sorry, Marty, everyone." Benjy wrapped his arms around Goran's body and did a fine impression of a limpet.

Goran nodded and carried Benjy away.

"So, Goran's finally found his sub?" Becket asked, not directing the question to anyone in particular.

"It seems so." Carey smiled. "I'll buy in a stock of tissues because half the house subs will be devastated he's off the market. I don't think there's much more we can accomplish tonight, we just have to hope that the police find Jonah before he does any more damage. So dinner is on the house if you'd all care to join me?"

Marty's stomach growled.

"Sounds like perfect timing," Beau said.

Heath got to his feet, tugging Aiden up by his collar.

"If someone could order us the house special, I believe I have time to warm Aiden's ass before we eat."

Aiden gave him a belligerent scowl but followed willingly enough.

"That's not a bad idea," Beau murmured.

"What? No! It's a very, *very* bad idea," Marty protested. "It's a proven fact that spankings cause indigestion."

"Really?" Beau's expression told Marty that he was digging himself deeper.

"Well, no, but...but... I got nothing." Marty sighed heavily, resigning himself to the inevitable. To his disgust, his cock hardened. "Unbelievable. My body has no logic whatsoever."

"My hand on your ass does not require analysis, Marty. However, we'll save it for dessert. It is a very sweet experience, after all."

Marty rolled his eyes. "I'm beginning to understand Aiden's attitude." He still let Beau tow him toward the restaurant.

Chapter Eleven

As Beau slipped his key into his front door lock, his innate sense of danger sent a cold shiver down his spine. He scanned the landing, half expecting an intruder to emerge from the stairwell.

"What's up?" Marty stepped closer to him.

"Not sure...just an itch." Beau shook his head. "It's nothing, I'm feeling a bit paranoid." He summoned up a reassuring smile and opened the door. "Ignore me."

"I'd rather you trusted your gut, it seems pretty reliable." Marty patted Beau's rock-solid abs.

Beau growled and picked Marty up, getting a firm hold of his ass cheeks. He carried him into the apartment and kicked the door shut behind them. Marty wrapped his legs around Beau and held on tight. He tilted his head back, waiting for a kiss.

"Demanding brat," Beau muttered. "Time to remind you who's the boss in this relationship."

"You did that earlier." Marty wiggled. "My ass is on fire."

"Good, I'll be able to feel the heat while I'm fucking you." Beau pushed Marty back against the wall and kissed him thoroughly. A slight noise from behind had him whirling around instantly.

"You two make me sick." A man stepped from the lounge doorway in front of them. He held a stubby black gun in both hands, his arms stiff and straight.

"Beau!" Marty gasped as Beau put him down carefully and moved to stand in front of him, protecting Marty with his body.

"Surprise." The intruder waggled the gun barrel. "Don't even think about making a move, Beauman. I'm a good shot and there's not much you can do with shattered kneecaps...except scream."

"Who the fuck are you?" Beau said, keeping his voice low and calm. He knew it had to be Jonah Smith but he wanted to hear it from the man's mouth. He seemed vaguely familiar, but Beau couldn't recall ever meeting him at the club or seeing him anywhere else. He had the kind of face that would blend into a crowd, not unpleasant, just...ordinary. Everything about him was average, his build, his clothing. His hands, holding the gun, were scarred, his nails lined with black.

"You're blind to anyone but that sniveling geek behind you, aren't you? I tried to get him out of the picture, tried to make you see me dance. I made beautiful flames just for you and you still didn't see me." The stranger's voice grew steadily more strident, the tone rising until he finished with a screech.

He's a fucking psycho. And that makes him dangerous. Beau searched surreptitiously for a potential weapon. "You have my attention now, so why don't you tell me your name?"

"Jonah. Jonah Salter." He grinned. "We even share a name... You see, we were meant to be together." He sounded gleeful.

"That's not your real name, though, is it Jonah?" Beau pushed.

Jonah twitched and the gun jerked.

"I know exactly who you are and so do a lot of other people, including the police. You're Jonah Smith. You were the one who set the fire at The Underground when Alistair was being held at that clinic. You were paid to let Eastman's goons into The Underground — it was your fault Alistair was taken in the first place. You evil son of a bitch. If that fire had taken hold, people could have been killed." Beau paused and drew Marty close to his side. "But you don't care about that do you? Just like you didn't care when you set all the other fires."

"You should have seen me at the club... I wouldn't have had to go to so much effort to get your attention. You're to blame for every fire I've set."

"Liar!" Marty blurted out. "People have been hurt and the only one to blame is you. Beau's completely innocent so don't try to transfer your guilt to him. You're sick and you're not going to get out of this. You're going to spend a very long time in prison."

"Oh, I think I will get away with it. But if I don't, Beau will always be mine and no one else's."

"Use that gun and a dozen policemen will be in here before I drop," Beau snapped. "All my neighbors are cops and firemen. That's not how you want this to end, is it? Give up now and you'll get the help that you need."

"I don't need anyone's fucking help." Jonah took a pace forward. "I have one last fire to set and while my baby dances, you and I will escape to our new life while he" — Jonah spat on the ground at Marty's feet — "goes up in flames."

"Why don't we just leave together? Marty's no threat…leave him out of this. It's me you want." Beau tried to buy some time. If he could convince Jonah that he was willing to go with him he might leave Marty alone.

"Fire purifies. He will be cleansed from your life and there will be nothing left to disrupt our future. Ashes to ashes. Take comfort in his return to the earth."

Horror struck Beau along with the realization that there would be no reasoning with this madman. Jonah meant to burn Marty to death. "We have no future if you get caught here. Isn't that more important? Stop wasting time. We need to get away."

"Maybe. But I'm smoke. I've disappeared after every fire so far, I can do it again."

Beau's ploy to be cooperative, to offer himself up, was not going to work. He decided to change tack.

"Fuck you, Jonah. You're going to burn in hell and I'm not leaving Marty. I love him. The only way you'll separate us is if you promise to leave him alone."

Jonah took another step forward, and Beau took a corresponding step back, pulling Marty with him.

"So fucking predictable. That hero complex you have is appealing but there are plenty more firemen in the station, as it were." Jonah shrugged. "Shame. We could have been so good together. Set the world alight." He giggled hysterically. "So what to do? I got everything set up for *him*." He waved the gun at Marty. "If you've been so taken in by him then you deserve to share the same fate."

Jonah edged around the room. Beau and Marty swiveled, following his path. He pointed the gun at the bedroom door and gestured. "In there. Both of you."

The stench of petrol assaulted Beau's nostrils as soon as they entered the room. *The entire place must be saturated in fuel.* Beau saw that the upper pane of the window was broken, creating a chimney to ensure the fire could grow. Jonah had done his research. Once the fire got going it would be impossible to put it out without extinguishers. The nearest one was in the hall. It might as well have been a mile away.

Thinking about extinguishers took Beau's attention away from Jonah for less than five seconds, but it was long enough for Jonah to grab Marty by the hair and shove him to his knees with the gun pressed to the base of his skull.

"One wrong move and I put a bullet in geek-boy's brain."

Beau froze. Marty blinked up at him with... Wait, Beau expected Marty to be terrified but his eyes sparked as if the fire had already been lit. *Oh, my boy is pissed off!* Beau suppressed a grin. Sometimes he forgot what Marty did for a living and the people he was around every day. Of course he would be good in a crisis. He might not be a field agent but he came from a world where danger was a fact of life.

"Get on the bed, *Salter*. On your knees. Hands behind your head."

He's not stupid, he knows it will be difficult for me to get up quickly from that position. Beau didn't move straight away.

"Why me, Jonah?" Beau asked, hoping to distract Jonah and stop him from hurting Marty. "It wasn't me that put out your fire at The Underground, it was Charlie. I just checked that things were safe afterward."

"You were mine long before then. You saved me."

Beau wracked his brains but came up blank. "When? I don't know what you're talking about."

"Three Acre shopping center. Ring any bells?"

"You have to be kidding me? That wasn't a fire, it was a false alarm caused by some idiot smoking in the toilets. We showed up, checked it out and were gone again in less than half an hour." Beau began to realize just how deluded Jonah was. "We didn't rescue anyone that day. The center was evacuated before we arrived."

"Get on the fucking bed!" Jonah screamed. He kicked Marty in the hip. "He'll get another bruise for every second you stand there."

Beau clenched a fist. Marty didn't make a sound, but Beau could see the pain reflected in his eyes. He clambered onto the bed.

"You don't get it, do you? Did you have any idea that I was a member of The Underground? Did you see me?"

"It's a big place, Jonah. Lots of people."

"I might as well have been invisible. Eastman offered me a lot of money to help save Alistair. Setting the fire was part of the deal. It was so easy to paint the lighting gels with accelerant. Nobody took a blind bit of notice of me. All the same as you. I thought if I made the place burn you'd see me, but you didn't. My baby didn't even get started, so you see I had to try again. I got booted out of The Underground, lost my job because of the court case. Doing community service gave me plenty of thinking time. Finding out your work schedule was easy. I followed you, watched you, and my stupid, naïve little brother told me the rest."

Keep him talking. Wait for a chance.

"So you set the fires knowing my watch would be called out?"

"It takes practice, you know. My first couple of attempts failed. I had to do my research, learn the trade. It's amazing what you can find on the Internet these days. Your boy here is not the only one with a brain."

Jonah slapped Marty across the face, snapping his head back. He pushed him down and stood over him.

"You're shaking." Jonah laughed. "Perhaps if I show your big, strong lover here what a slut you are, he'll want me instead of you. What do you think?"

Marty glared and spat blood, his lip puffy and torn. Jonah tore Marty's shirt open.

"Leave him alone," Beau yelled, but Jonah swung around and aimed the gun at him.

"Shut the fuck up. You get to watch."

Marty whimpered as Jonah threw him forward so that he was bent over the bed, his head near Beau's knees. Jonah stuck his free hand down the back of Marty's trousers and groped him.

"I'll kill you," Beau spat. He couldn't sit by and watch as his lover was raped. Just the sight of Jonah touching Marty made Beau's blood boil in his veins.

"Who's holding the gun, Salter?" Jonah traced the barrel down Marty's neck. "Who's in fucking *charge*?"

"You are." It was Marty who spoke. "You are, Jonah, and I like that."

What the hell? It took Beau a few seconds to realize what Marty was doing. *Christ, he has nerves of steel!* Marty was deliberately attempting to keep Jonah's attention even though the man was doing Christ knew what with his fingers and had a gun to him.

"I like it rough. Why don't you give it to me?" Marty whispered.

Jonah tore at Marty's trousers, pulling them down to his thighs, baring his ass. Marty twisted up. He swung out with his forearm, slapping away Jonah's gun hand, then punched out with his other fist toward Jonah's face. His knuckles connected and a bright arc of blood sprayed, splattering over the bedcovers. The gun flew from Jonah's grasp and landed with a thud before skittering under the dresser. Beau leaped from the bed and pulled Jonah away from Marty.

"Get the gun!" Marty yelled.

Beau and Jonah went for it at the same time, crashing to the floor in a tangle of limbs. Beau struck out, kicking and punching, desperate to keep Jonah away from his weapon. As they grappled, Marty reached beneath the furniture and grabbed the gun. He rolled to his feet and aimed it, yanking his trousers back into place with his free hand. Beau shoved Jonah away, scrambled up then stepped back to stand next to Marty. He touched Marty's bloody face. "You okay?"

"Oh God!" Marty gasped.

Beau stared in horror at Jonah, who held a lighter in his hand, the flame flickering.

"You'll both watch me dance now, won't you?" he screeched.

"Don't. For God's sake. It's not worth it," Beau yelled. "You'll go up like a torch."

"You, too." Jonah grinned as he held the flaming lighter in the air. "Try and ignore me now, you son of a bitch." He threw the lighter on to the petrol-soaked bedding.

The entire bed exploded instantly into flame. As the fire rolled toward them, Beau grabbed Marty around the waist and threw him out of the bedroom door. He dove after him, surged to his feet and slammed the door shut behind them.

The screams began. Animalistic, tortured cries. Beau could only imagine the inferno in his bedroom. He caught hold of Marty's hand and dragged him out of the apartment. In the corridor he smashed the glass on the fire alarm and a cacophony of bells sounded throughout the building. People began to appear, running for the exits.

"Get outside, Marty!" Beau grabbed a fire extinguisher and was joined by a couple of his neighbors. They ran back in to Beau's apartment, leaving Marty alone.

Marty collapsed against a wall. He couldn't seem to stop shaking. The man he loved had just run into danger yet again.

"Fuckfuckfuck, stop standing here like an idiot and get outside." Marty ran for the stairs, ignoring his aching hip. He hurtled down at breakneck speed, barely keeping his footing. He reached the outside just as two fire engines roared up. Marty ran across and was relieved to see Alvin jumping from the cab.

"It's Beau's place, apartment four on the top floor. Beau and two other men went back in there. There was petrol everywhere."

Alvin began to issue orders. Hoses were unwound and ladders extended. Two more engines rolled up and men streamed out. For Marty everything happened in slow motion. Detached from the action, he slumped to the ground and leaned against the wheel of one of the vehicles. He gave himself a shake. "Pull yourself together." It started to rain. Marty stared into the darkness and let the cool drops splatter his face. He pulled out his phone. It was after midnight but he guessed that nobody would care. He rang Becket first, then Carey, who promised to contact Heath and Goran. At a loss for anything else to do, Marty closed his eyes and prayed that Beau would be okay.

"Marty. Marty!" An annoying voice interrupted Marty's semi-conscious dreaming.

"What?" He dragged his eyes open and realization crashed over him. The fire. Beau.

"Beau!"

"Hey, calm down."

He was pulled to his feet and wrapped in a strong embrace.

"Beau's a big boy. He can take care of himself."

"Becket?" Marty tried desperately to understand what was going on.

"You take him, honey," Becket said.

Christian's face appeared in Marty's field of vision. "Let's get you out of the rain, sweetie, you're all wet. The café across the road has opened and is dishing out hot drinks. Let's go and sit in there."

Marty allowed Christian to lead him across the road. Installed at a table with a steaming mug of tea in his hands, Marty finally managed to focus.

"Christian, what's going on? Where's Beau? How long has he been gone?"

"We got here less than ten minutes after your call—we were already in the car. I'm sure he's fine. Becket is waiting for him and he knows where we are. He'll bring him here as soon as he can. We couldn't leave you sitting in the rain."

"Thanks for coming. You didn't need to." Marty wiped at a tear that tumbled down his face. "Jonah Smith was in Beau's apartment. He had a gun. He was going to burn—burn me." Nausea boiled in his guts. "We got away but he—he set everything alight. He screamed, Christian... I'll never forget that sound as long as I live." Marty sobbed into his tea, barely aware of Christian stroking his hands, trying to provide comfort.

"Marty."

The voice he longed to hear broke into his bleak thoughts.

"Beau!" In his haste to get to his lover, Marty's tea fell to the ground and his chair tipped over. He threw himself into Beau's waiting arms. Relief coursed through his body. Beau stank of smoke and petrol. His skin was streaked with sweat and grime. Marty didn't care. It was the best moment of his life. Beau held him close and safe, murmuring nonsense words in his ear and ruffling his hair.

"It's over, sweetheart. It's all over. Jonah is gone and he's not coming back."

Marty gazed into Beau's eyes and saw the regret there.

"I'm sorry it came to this. I wouldn't wish that end on anyone."

"Better him than you, love."

"But your home…"

"The advantage of living with a load of firemen as neighbors is that they know how to contain a blaze. The bedroom will need a remodel but the rest of the place will be fine after a good scrub. I'll take you bed shopping and we can choose something with a headboard that I can tie you to."

Marty groaned. "Now is not the time to get me hard, Sir. Not when we can't do anything about it."

"Becket has a car. He can drop us off at your place. Everything else can wait until the morning."

Marty gave a little whoop of joy. "What are we waiting for?"

Beau scooped him up and carried him out into the rain.

Epilogue

"Sir?" Marty tried not to plead.

"Yes, love." Beau adjusted a strap, tightening a buckle.

"You love me, don't you?"

"What kind of a question is that? You know I do." Beau's leather-clad groin came into view. Marty desperately wanted Beau's cock in his mouth. Covering up such a treat wasn't fair.

"Then please let me go." Marty tested his bonds. He couldn't move an inch.

"I don't hear your safe word, Marty. Until I do, you stay right where you are."

"But I can't come like this, Sir."

"Oh, I know you can't, love. That's the general idea."

Marty's world tilted as the padded board he was strapped to swung to a horizontal position. The mirrored ceiling provided him with a clear picture of his position. Each limb was strapped in place by several wide strips of leather. His neck and forehead were similarly restrained. The rest of his body, from thighs to chest, was wrapped in wide strips of translucent black latex that melded to his form, outlining every ridge of muscle. Beau had cut a tiny slit in the material at groin level and pulled his cock and balls through the hole so that they stood stark and proud. A weighty cock ring ensured Marty had no chance of coming. His nipples jutted through two more tiny slits, ready for Beau to play with.

Marty's ass dipped into a hole in the board beneath him, exposing him for Beau's pleasure. Beau had just finished positioning what he fondly referred to as 'my favorite fucking machine' beneath Marty's ass. His hole had been thoroughly stretched and lubed, a process that had had him screaming and begging for release.

"There, all set. I do love the set-up stage. The build of anticipation gets me nice and hard." Beau tore off his leather jock and proved his point. His stiff cock, framed by leather chaps, bobbed enticingly.

Marty whimpered. "When you said we were going to celebrate the completion of renovations at your apartment, Sir, this wasn't quite what I had in mind."

"No?" Beau flicked both Marty's nipples, sending a sharp jolt of need to Marty's cock. "I think it's the perfect way to mark the occasion. Having this equipment fitted was a stroke of genius on my part. It's ingenious — it collapses and slides under the bed."

He leaned beneath the bench and switched on his pet machine. It whirred into action. Marty held his breath. He'd seen the thing work when Beau had tested it and he knew what would happen next. Beneath him a rubber dildo on a pole would rise and fall at a speed controlled by Beau. Perfectly positioned, the lubed rubber pushed against his hole. Beau had prepped him well and there was only a slight burn as the toy thrust inside his channel. Just a couple of inches and nowhere near as wide as Beau's cock, it was still a significant intrusion and there was no stopping it. The machine rose and fell with inexorable regularity. Marty tried to relax his muscles. The stimulation was unbearable and his trapped cock ached. Beau turned up the speed.

"I think I'll just sit and watch for a couple of minutes." Smirking, he took a comfy chair and began to stroke himself. Held in place, Marty could do not but accept the repeated plundering of his channel.

"Sir, please!"

Beau levered himself up with an overly dramatic show of reluctance. "Let's see how well you can beg, love." He began to torture Marty's nipples, tweaking and pinching until Marty could take no more. Then he switched his attention to Marty's cock, flicking and squeezing the head over and over again. Marty's vision blurred. He floated on a sea of sensation that threatened to take away his sanity. Someone screamed. Marty guessed it had been him. His safe word hovered on the tip of his tongue but he couldn't bring himself to say it because despite the erotic agony Beau tortured him with, he didn't want it to end. He drifted, vaguely aware of the pounding in his ass and the pain of Beau's touch. The grip of the cock ring released, and Marty came with a cry that was part exaltation, part torment. He lay boneless as Beau released him from his bonds and bent him over the bench. Penetration was swift and brutal. Marty jerked against the side of the bench as Beau pounded into him. Heat flooded his channel as Beau came, his weight resting over Marty's back.

Marty regained consciousness snuggled beneath the duvet in Beau's brand-new bed. He didn't feel sticky, which meant Beau had already cleaned him up. Marty smiled. Beau always took great care of him after a scene. Since they had given up the condoms he had been even more attentive. Waking up with cum-stiff skin was not fun. The mattress dipped slightly as Beau joined him in the bed. Marty wriggled close and pressed himself against Beau's hard body. His ass ached delightfully.

Beau held him close and peppered his neck with kisses, making Marty giggle.

"Tickles."

Beau nuzzled and licked.

"You taste delicious."

Contented and lazy, Marty let Beau have his way.

"Will it always be like this, do you think? Warm and safe."

"Who knows?" Beau whispered. "We have each other. That's what matters. We may be a little scorched around the edges, but we survived. You know I'll always do my best to protect you, Marty."

"I know." Marty sighed. "I can't believe how much has changed in just a few short months."

"For the better, I hope."

"Of course." Marty laid across Beau's chest, a better position for kissing. "I have you. I have lots of new friends. I've discovered a kinky streak a mile wide." That brought on a fit of giggles.

"What? Why is that funny?"

"I did a bit of research into arousal. Sometime in the mid-80s, a Boston University scientist did a bit of experimenting. Apparently, men are more likely to get an erection under duress. He told men who had no problem achieving or maintaining an erection that if they didn't get in the mood, they would receive an electric shock. The tangible effect was that the threat of shock increased sexual arousal. That's why when you threaten me with all kinds of mean Dommy things, it turns me on."

"Good to know. We haven't tried electrostim. Yet. I think we should confirm his results, don't you?"

"Isn't it enough that you're making me hard just by talking about it?"

"You're the one who always wants categorical proof, Marty."

"Sir. I think you should gag me. Every time I open my mouth I come out with something really dumb."

Beau flipped Marty onto his back and straddled him. "How about I just stuff your mouth with my cock for now?"

"That should work, Sir." Marty smiled, then parted his lips.

About the Author

Lucinda lives in a small village in the English countryside, surrounded by rolling hills, cows and sheep. She started writing to fill time between jobs and is now firmly and unashamedly addicted.

She loves the English weather, especially the rain, and adores a thunderstorm. She loves good food, warm company and a crackling fire. She's fascinated by the psychology of relationships, especially between men, and her stories contain some subtle (and not so subtle) leanings towards BDSM.

L.M. Somerton loves to hear from readers. You can find her contact information, website details and author profile page at http://www.totallybound.com.